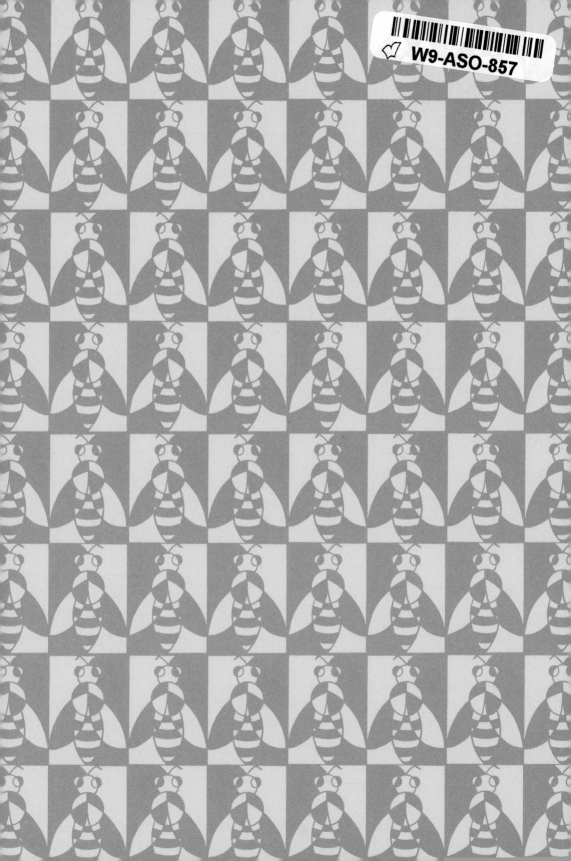

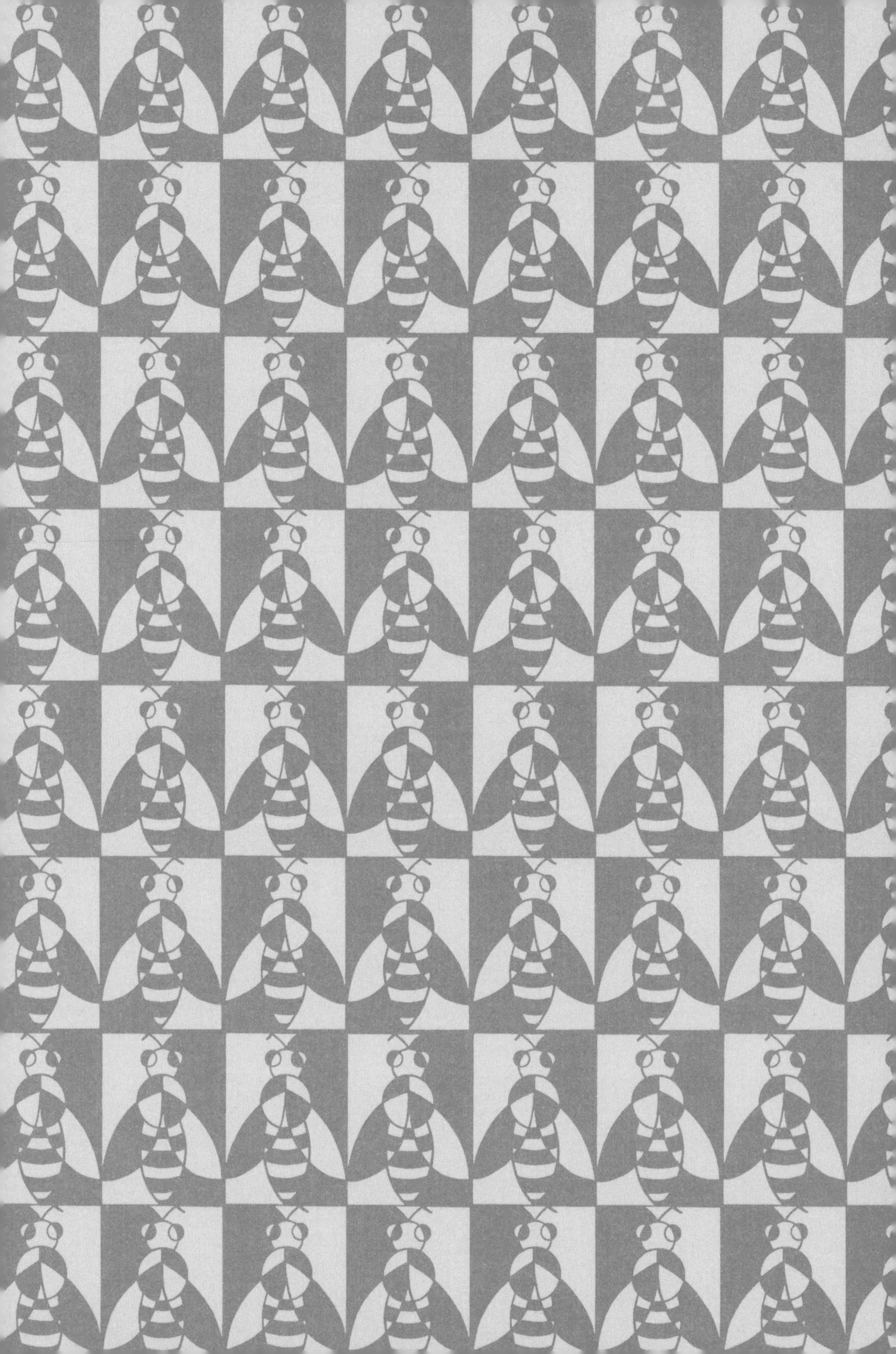

MARY FLEENER

fantagraphics

1

BILLIE the BEE LIVED IN A COASTAL LAGOON BY THE PACIFIC OCEAN.

SINCE PART OF IT WAS ALSO AN ESTUARY, THE COMBINATION OF BOTH FRESH AND SALTWATER CREATED A FERTILE ENVIRONMENT FOR BIRDS, FISH, MAMMALS, AMPHIBIANS, REPTILES, AND INSECTS.

BILLIE'S HIVE WAS IN A EUCALYPTUS GROVE.

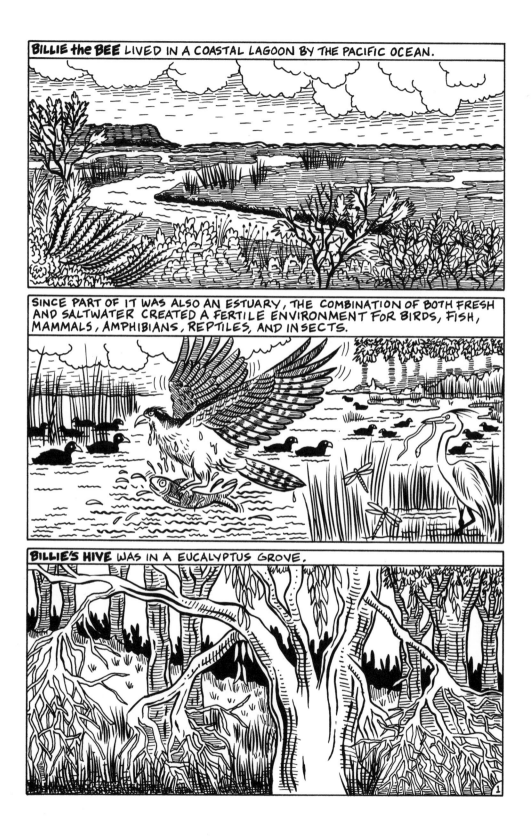

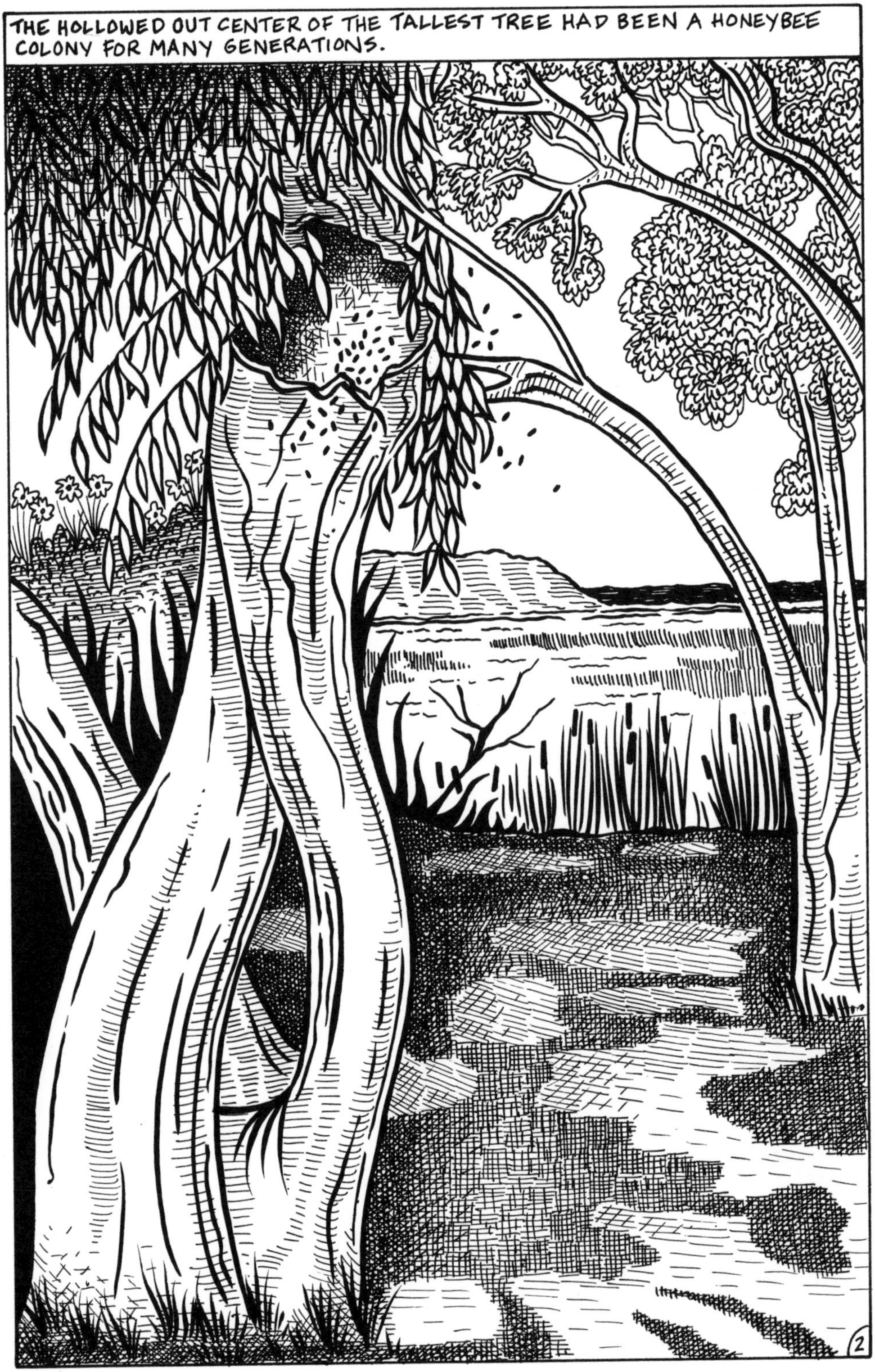
THE HOLLOWED OUT CENTER OF THE TALLEST TREE HAD BEEN A HONEYBEE COLONY FOR MANY GENERATIONS.

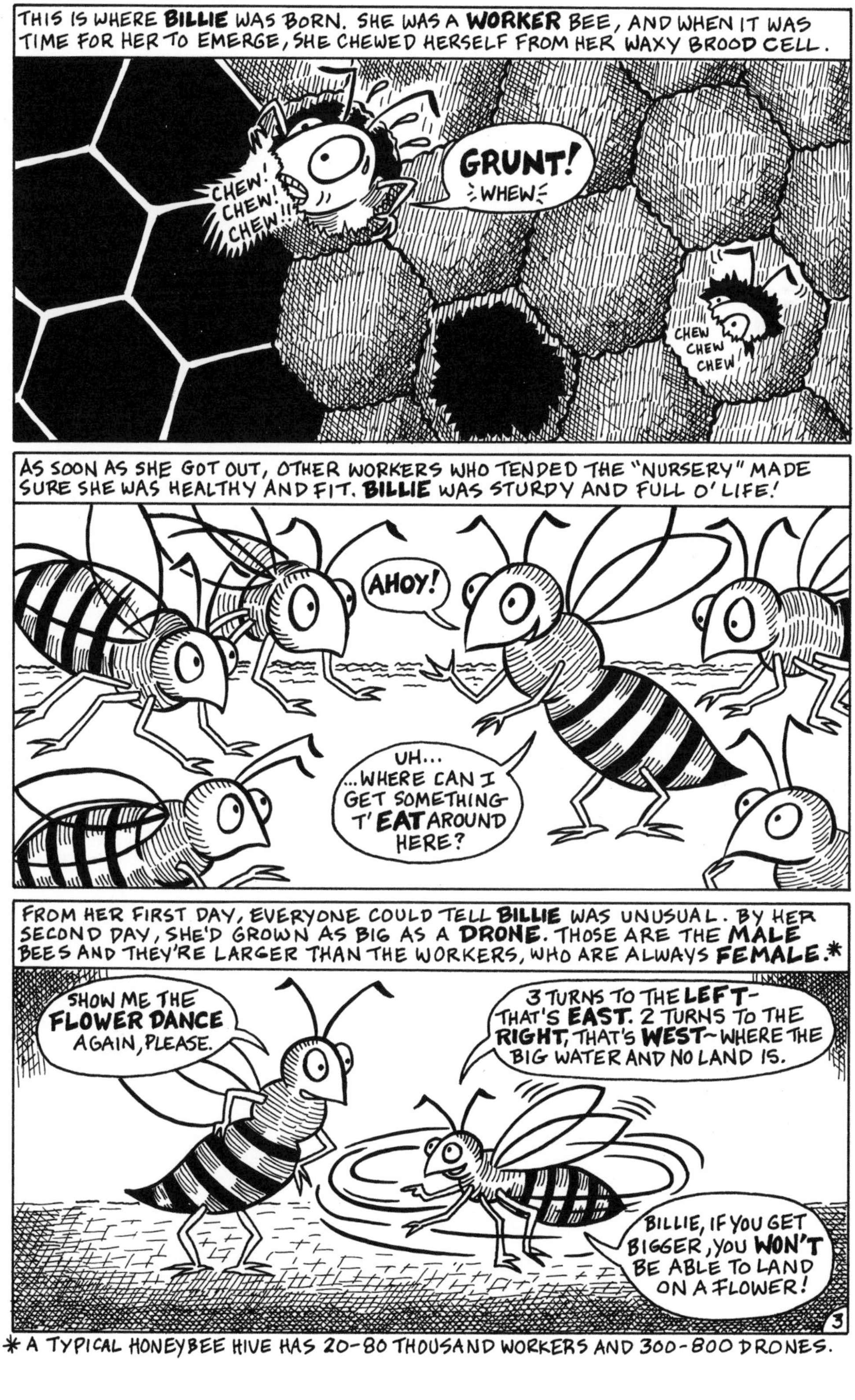
THIS IS WHERE BILLIE WAS BORN. SHE WAS A WORKER BEE, AND WHEN IT WAS TIME FOR HER TO EMERGE, SHE CHEWED HERSELF FROM HER WAXY BROOD CELL.
CHEW! CHEW! CHEW!!
GRUNT! WHEW
CHEW CHEW CHEW
AS SOON AS SHE GOT OUT, OTHER WORKERS WHO TENDED THE "NURSERY" MADE SURE SHE WAS HEALTHY AND FIT. BILLIE WAS STURDY AND FULL O' LIFE!
AHOY!
UH... ...WHERE CAN I GET SOMETHING T' EAT AROUND HERE?
FROM HER FIRST DAY, EVERYONE COULD TELL BILLIE WAS UNUSUAL. BY HER SECOND DAY, SHE'D GROWN AS BIG AS A DRONE. THOSE ARE THE MALE BEES AND THEY'RE LARGER THAN THE WORKERS, WHO ARE ALWAYS FEMALE.*
SHOW ME THE FLOWER DANCE AGAIN, PLEASE.
3 TURNS TO THE LEFT- THAT'S EAST. 2 TURNS TO THE RIGHT, THAT'S WEST~ WHERE THE BIG WATER AND NO LAND IS.
BILLIE, IF YOU GET BIGGER, YOU WON'T BE ABLE TO LAND ON A FLOWER!
3

* A TYPICAL HONEYBEE HIVE HAS 20-80 THOUSAND WORKERS AND 300-800 DRONES.

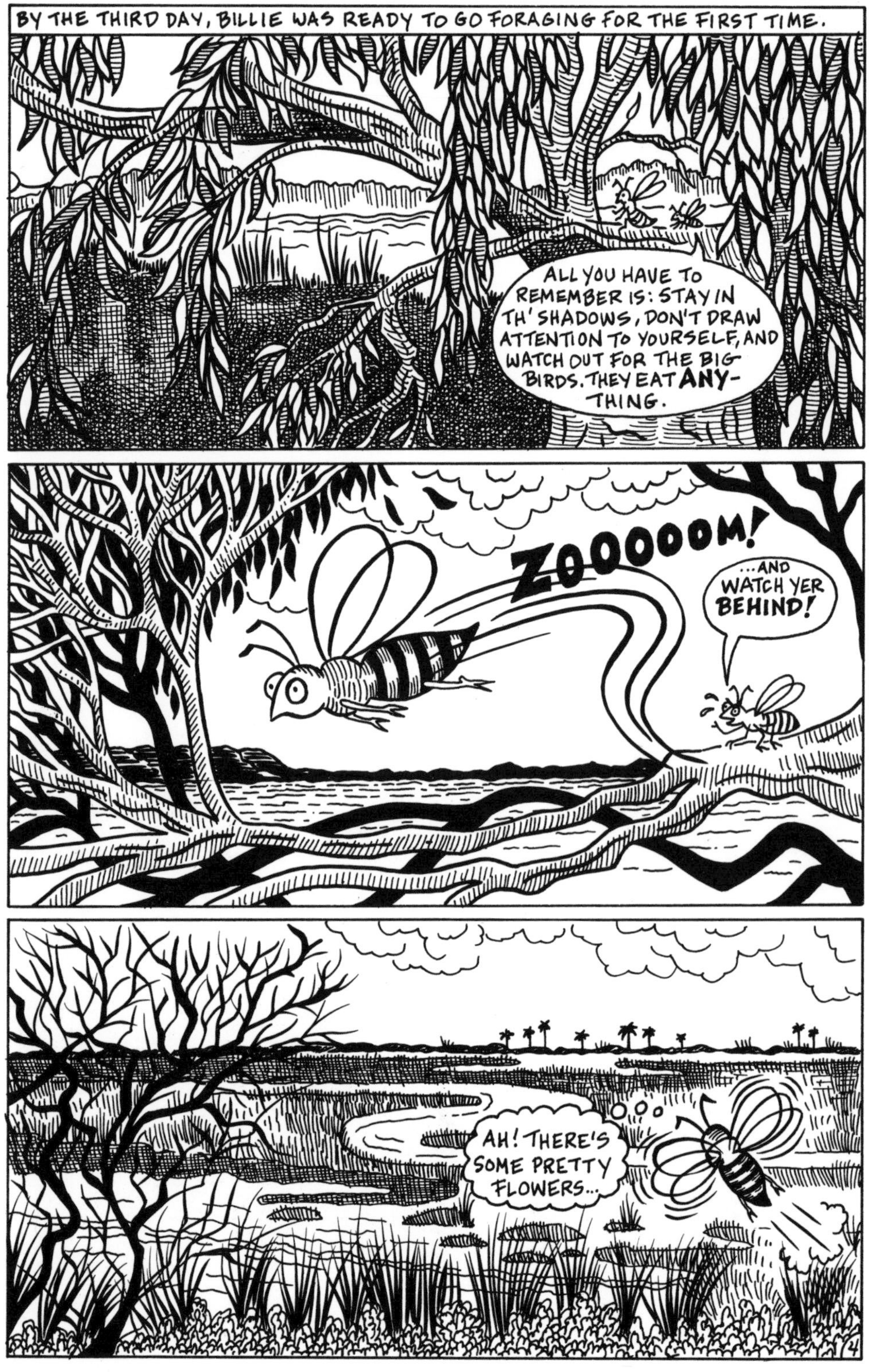
BY THE THIRD DAY, BILLIE WAS READY TO GO FORAGING FOR THE FIRST TIME.
ALL YOU HAVE TO REMEMBER IS: STAY IN TH' SHADOWS, DON'T DRAW ATTENTION TO YOURSELF, AND WATCH OUT FOR THE BIG BIRDS. THEY EAT ANY-THING.
ZOOOOOM!
...AND WATCH YER BEHIND!
AH! THERE'S SOME PRETTY FLOWERS...

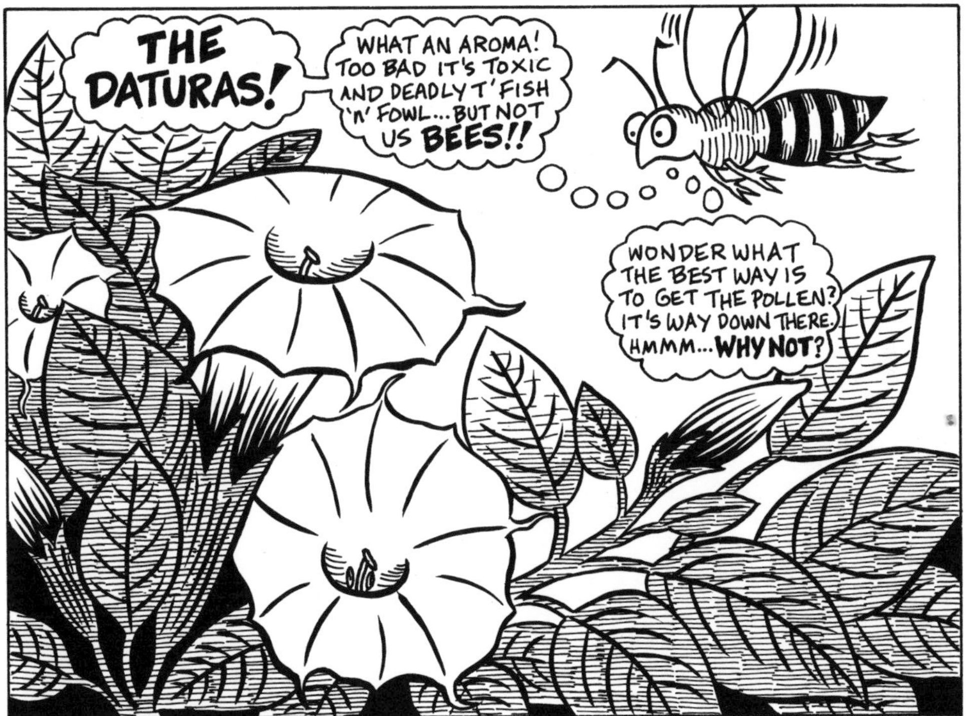
THE DATURAS!
WHAT AN AROMA! TOO BAD IT'S TOXIC AND DEADLY T' FISH 'N' FOWL... BUT NOT US BEES!!
WONDER WHAT THE BEST WAY IS TO GET THE POLLEN? IT'S WAY DOWN THERE. HMMM... WHY NOT?

*Datura wrightii (JIMSON WEED... A HALLUCINOGENIC AND POISONOUS PLANT.)

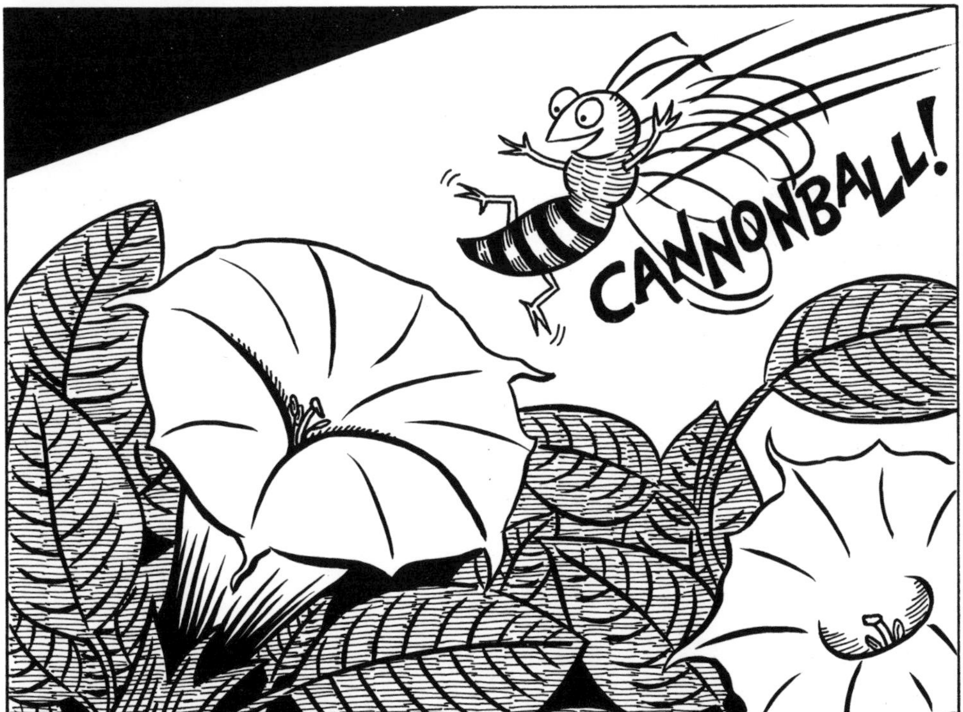
CANNONBALL!

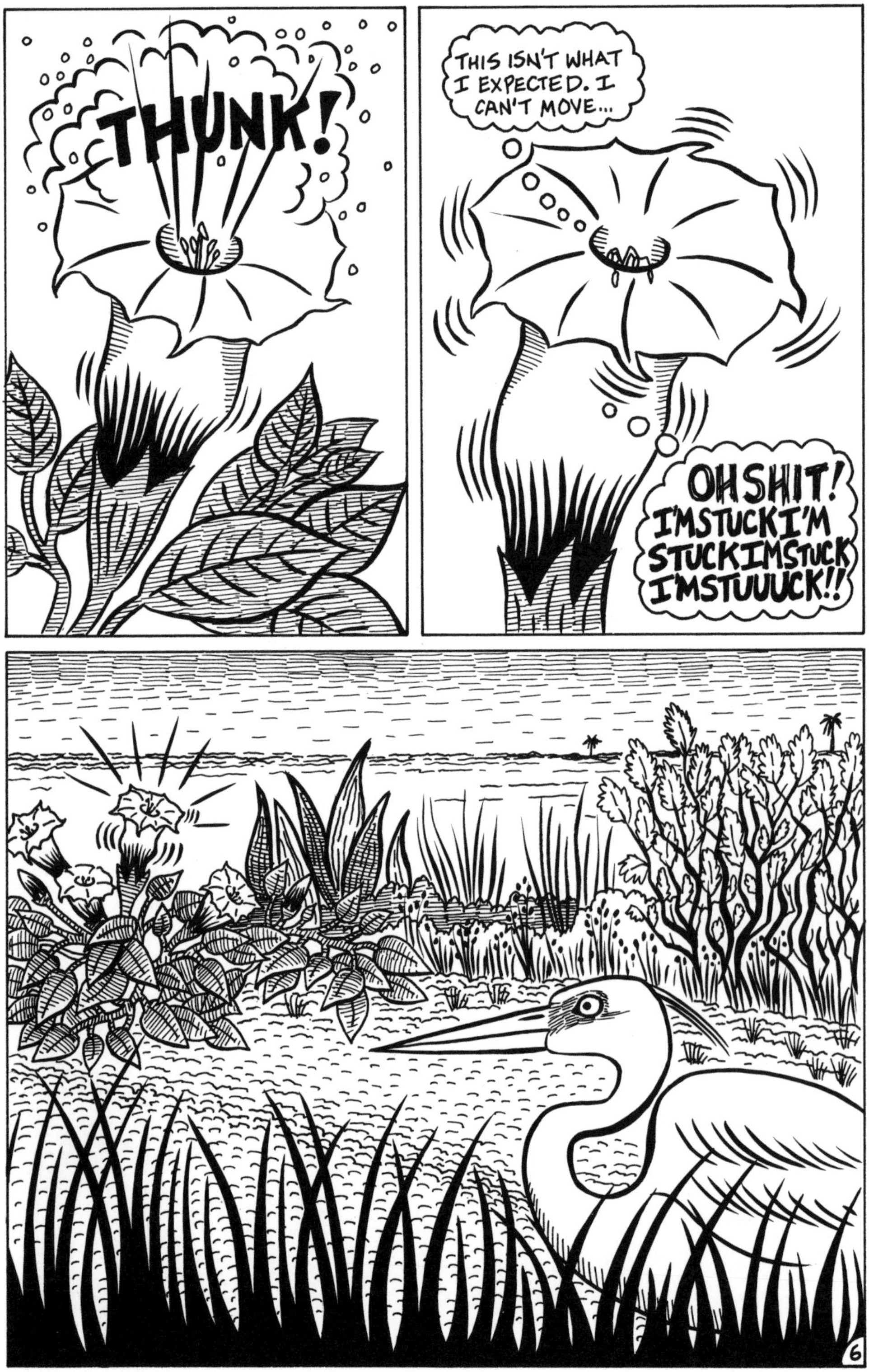
THUNK!
THIS ISN'T WHAT I EXPECTED. I CAN'T MOVE...
OHSHIT! I'MSTUCKI'M STUCKIMSTUCK I'MSTUUUCK!!
6

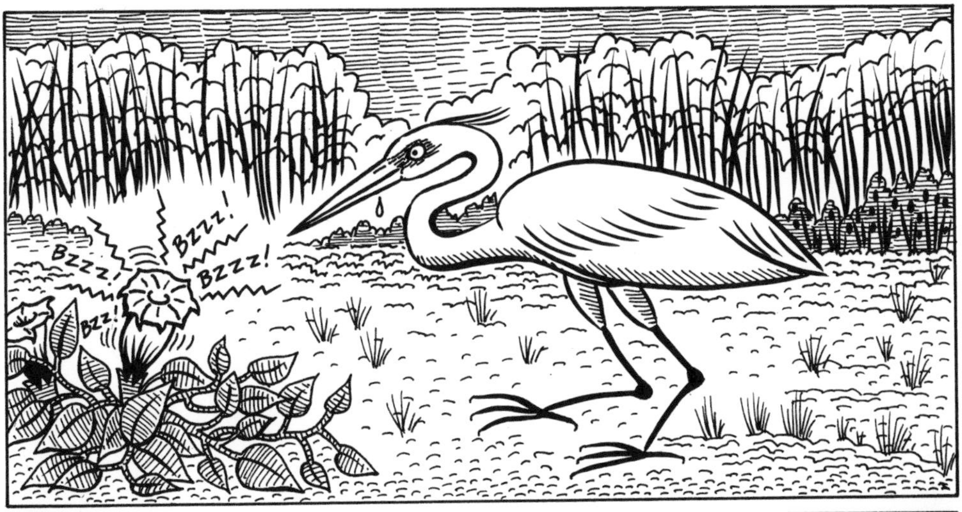
Bzzz!
Bzzz!
BZZZ!
Bzz!

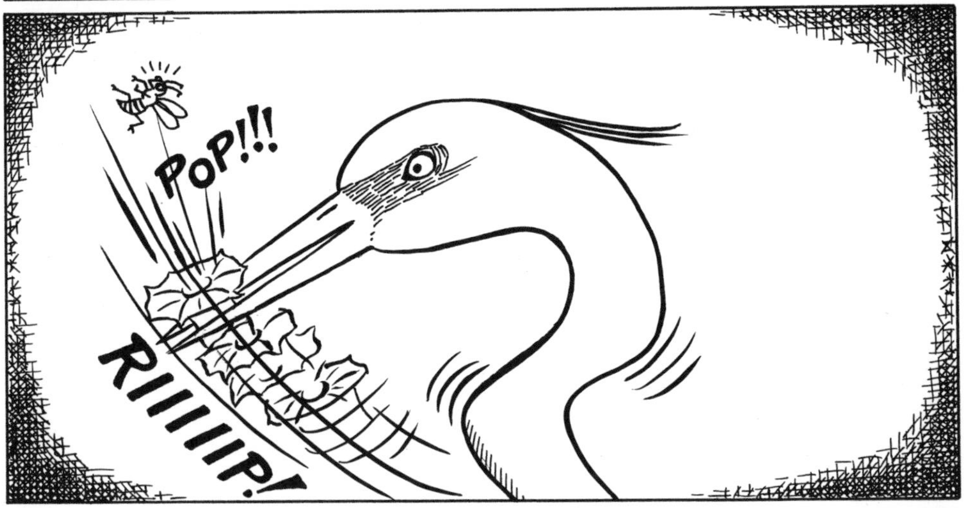
PoP!!!
RIIIIIP!

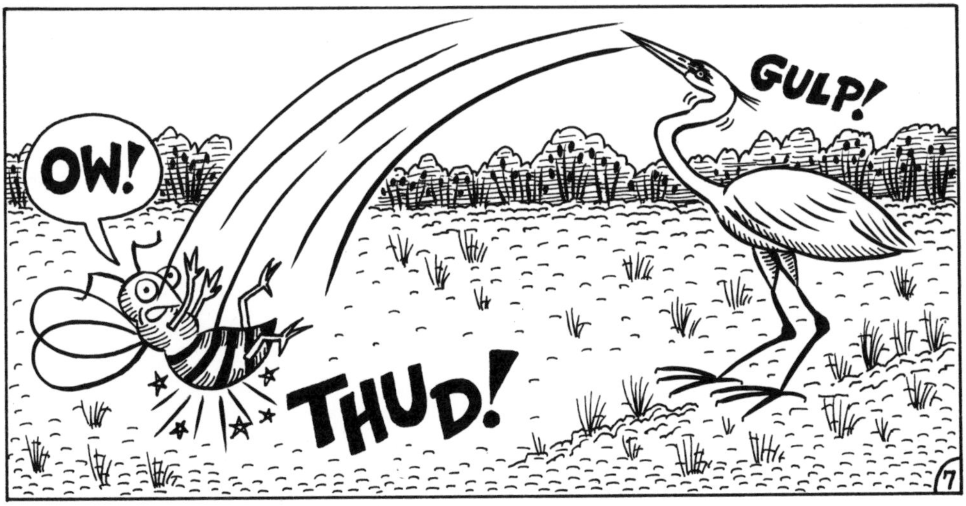
GULP!
OW!
THUD!

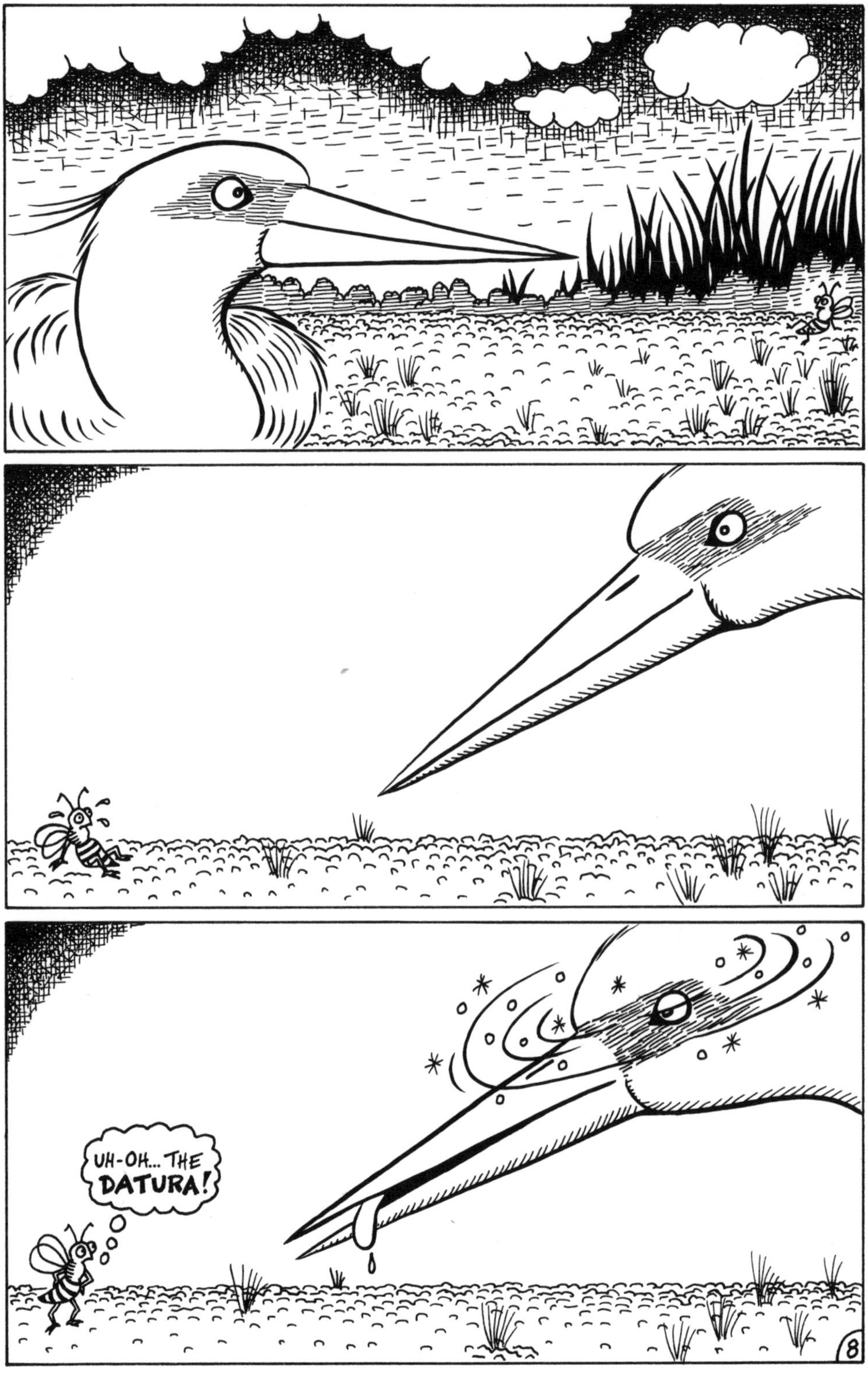
UH-OH... THE DATURA!
8

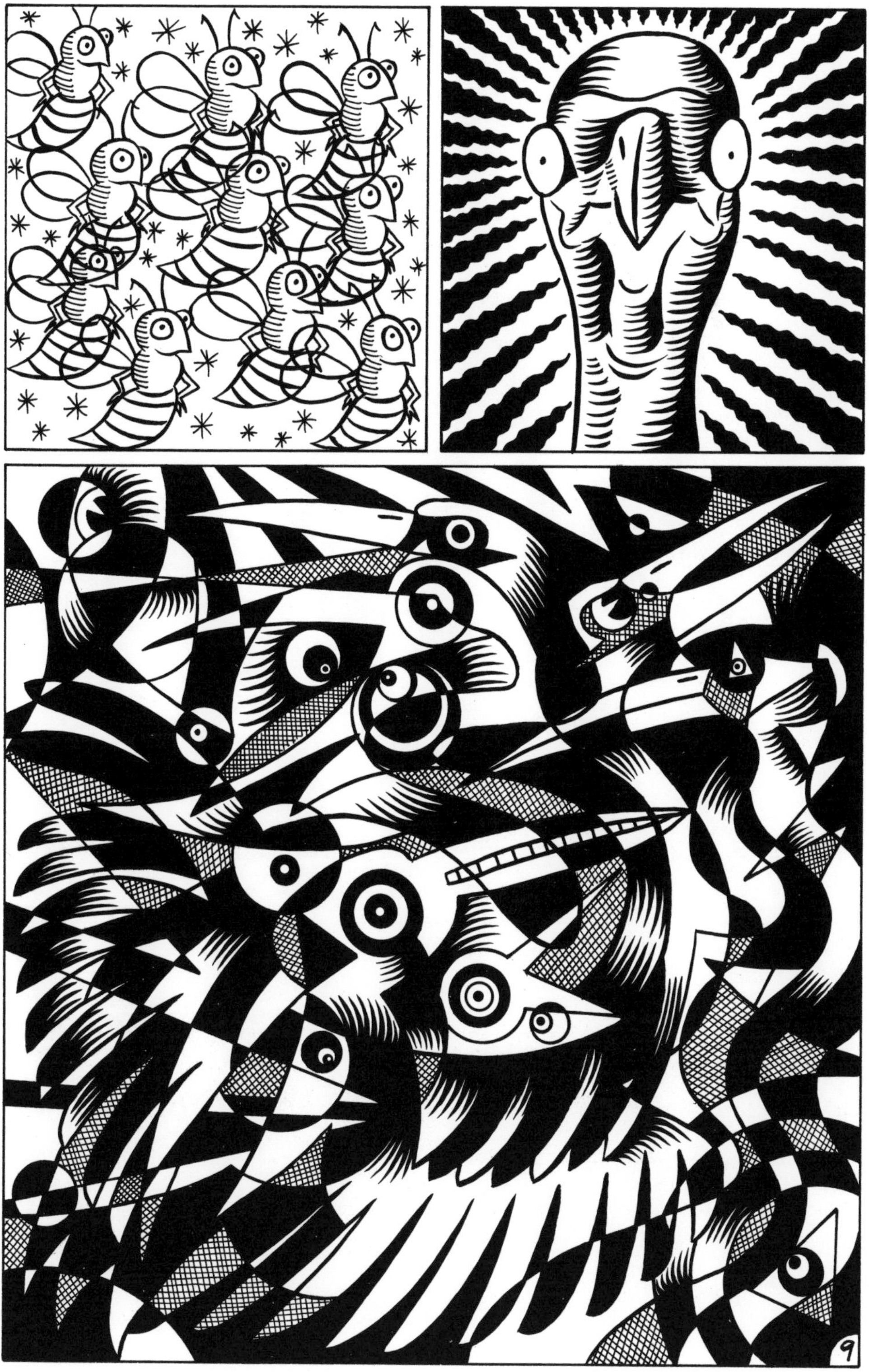

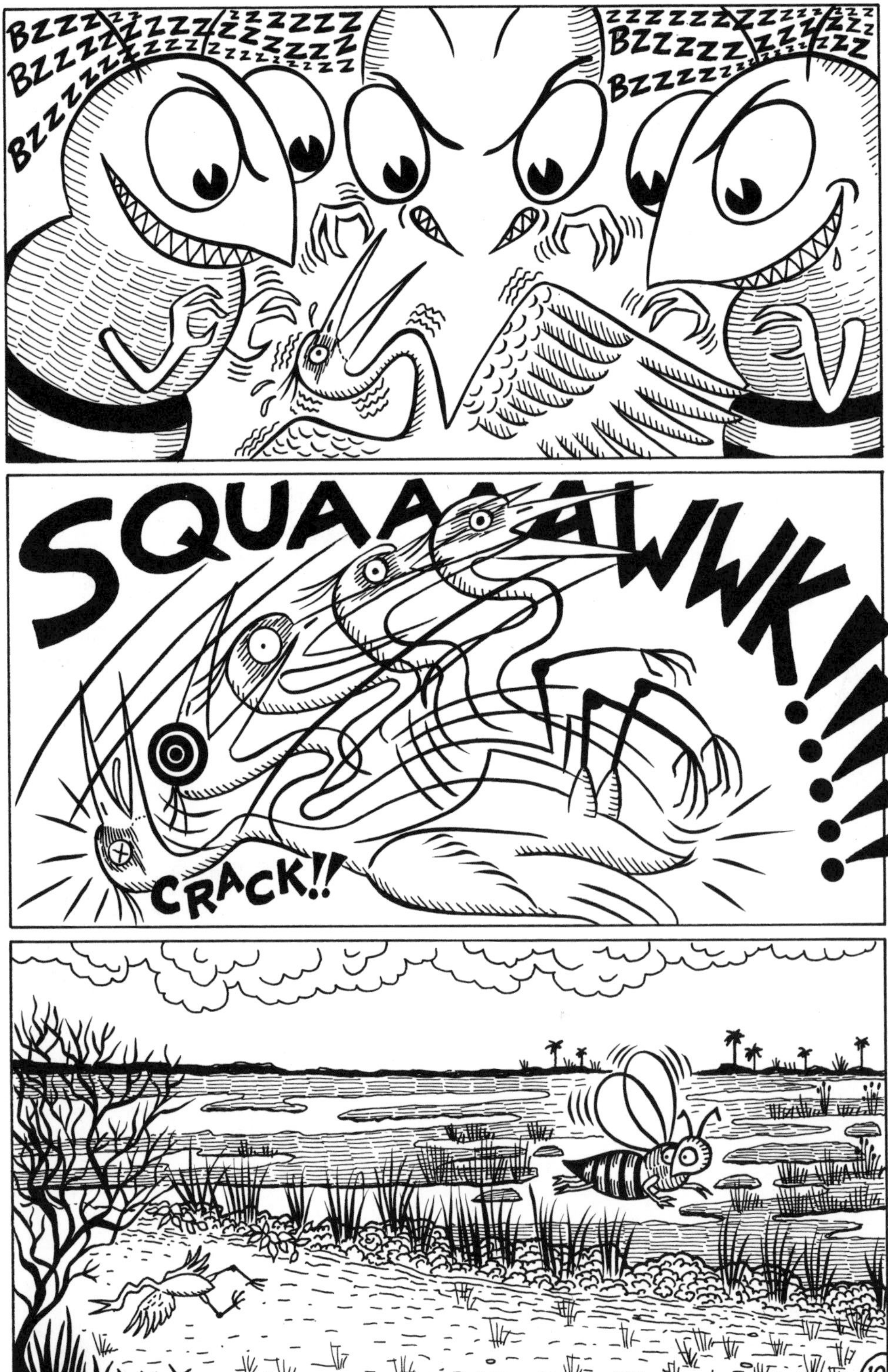
BZZZ
BZZZZ
BZZZZ
BZZZZZ
BZZZZZ
SQUAAAAWWK!!!!!
CRACK!!

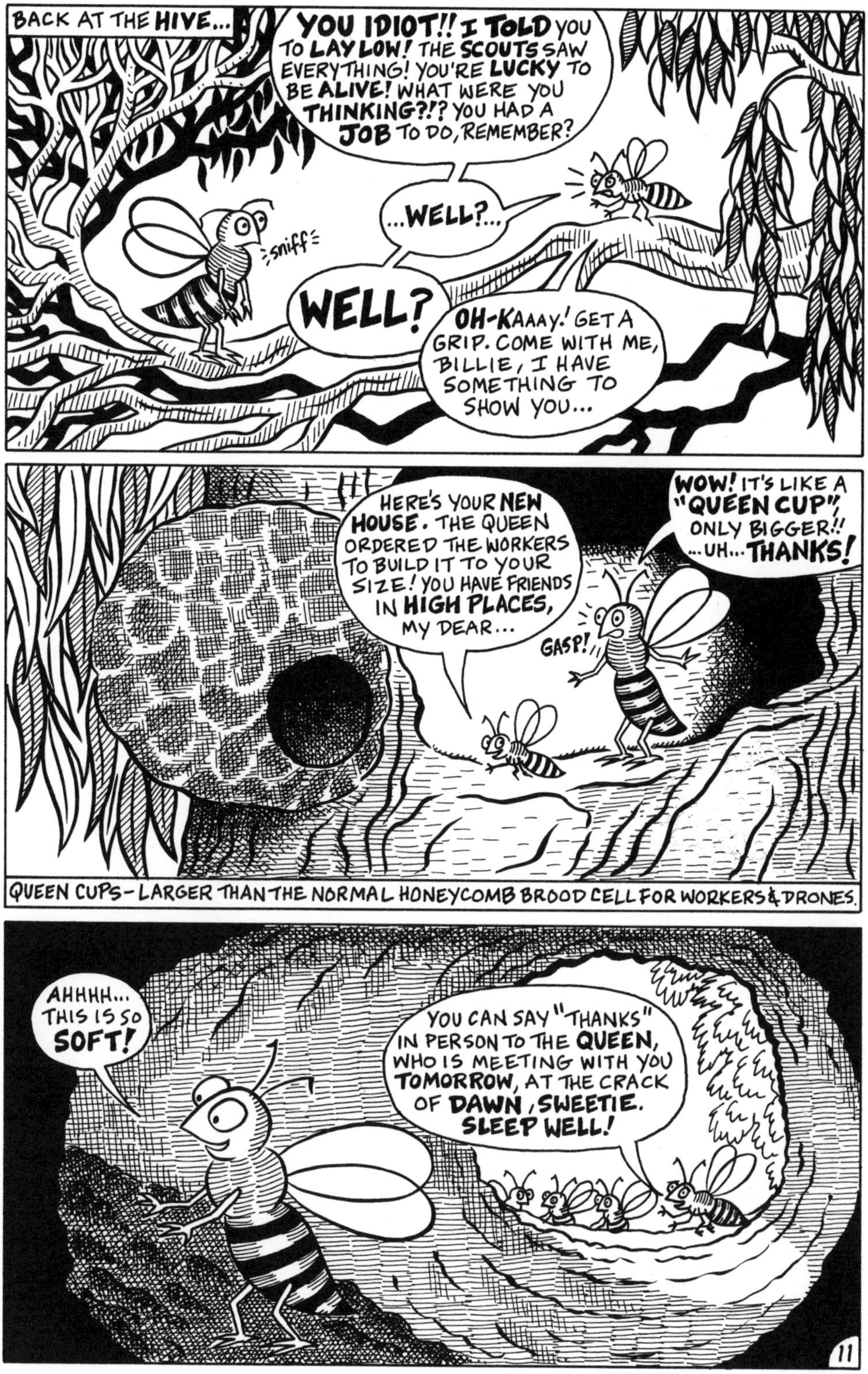
BACK AT THE HIVE...
YOU IDIOT!! I TOLD YOU TO LAY LOW! THE SCOUTS SAW EVERYTHING! YOU'RE LUCKY TO BE ALIVE! WHAT WERE YOU THINKING?!? YOU HAD A JOB TO DO, REMEMBER?
...WELL?...
sniff
WELL?
OH-KAAAY! GET A GRIP. COME WITH ME, BILLIE, I HAVE SOMETHING TO SHOW YOU...
HERE'S YOUR NEW HOUSE. THE QUEEN ORDERED THE WORKERS TO BUILD IT TO YOUR SIZE! YOU HAVE FRIENDS IN HIGH PLACES, MY DEAR...
GASP!
WOW! IT'S LIKE A "QUEEN CUP", ONLY BIGGER!! ...UH... THANKS!
QUEEN CUPS - LARGER THAN THE NORMAL HONEYCOMB BROOD CELL FOR WORKERS & DRONES.
AHHHH... THIS IS SO SOFT!
YOU CAN SAY "THANKS" IN PERSON TO THE QUEEN, WHO IS MEETING WITH YOU TOMORROW, AT THE CRACK OF DAWN, SWEETIE. SLEEP WELL!
11

2

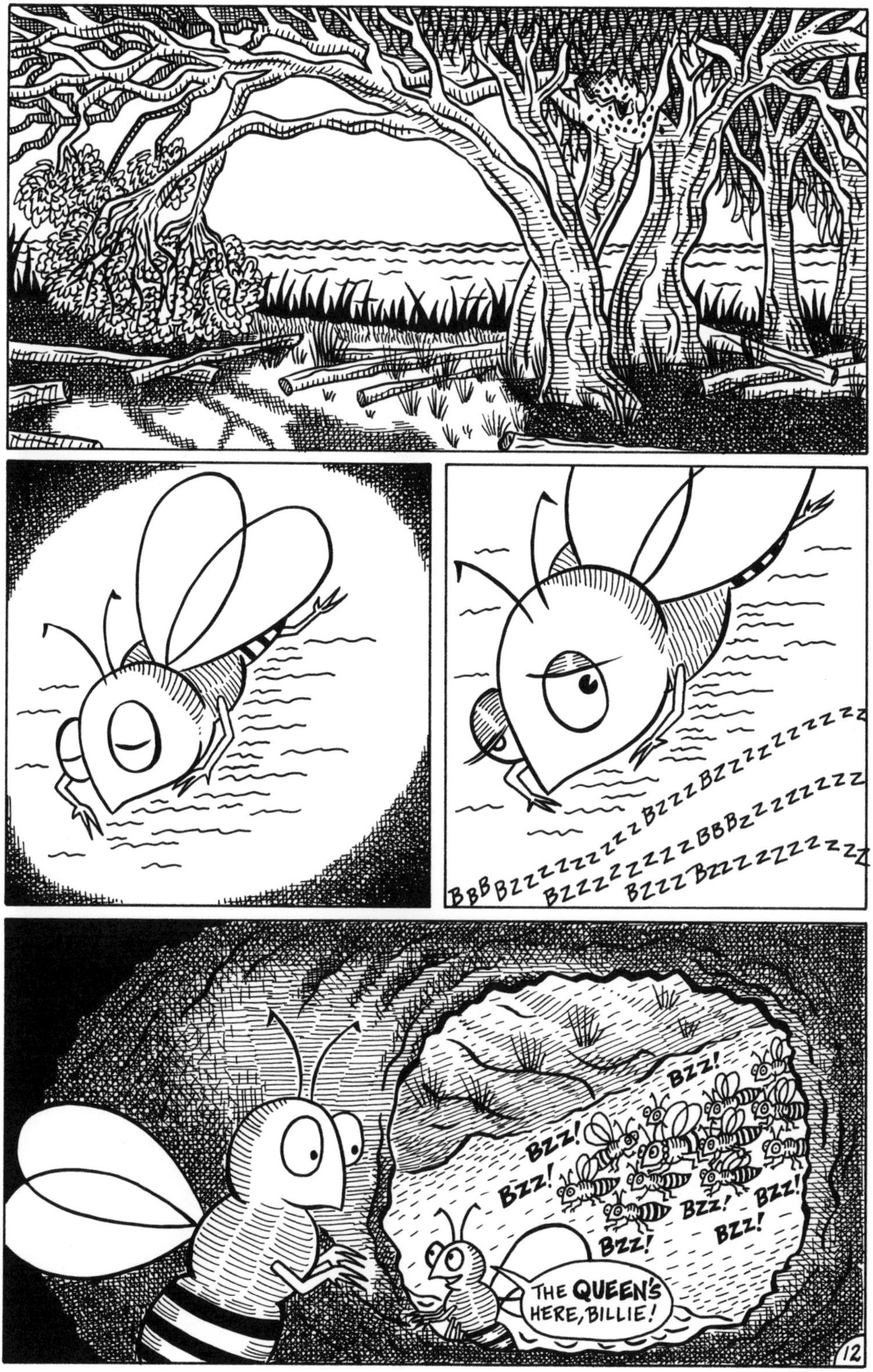
BBBBzzzzzzzzzzzBzzzzBzzzzzzzzzzzzz
BzzzzzzzzzBBBzzzzzzzzzzz
BzzzzBzzzzzzzzzzz
Bzz!
Bzz!
Bzz!
Bzz!
Bzz!
Bzz!
Bzz!
THE QUEEN'S HERE, BILLIE!

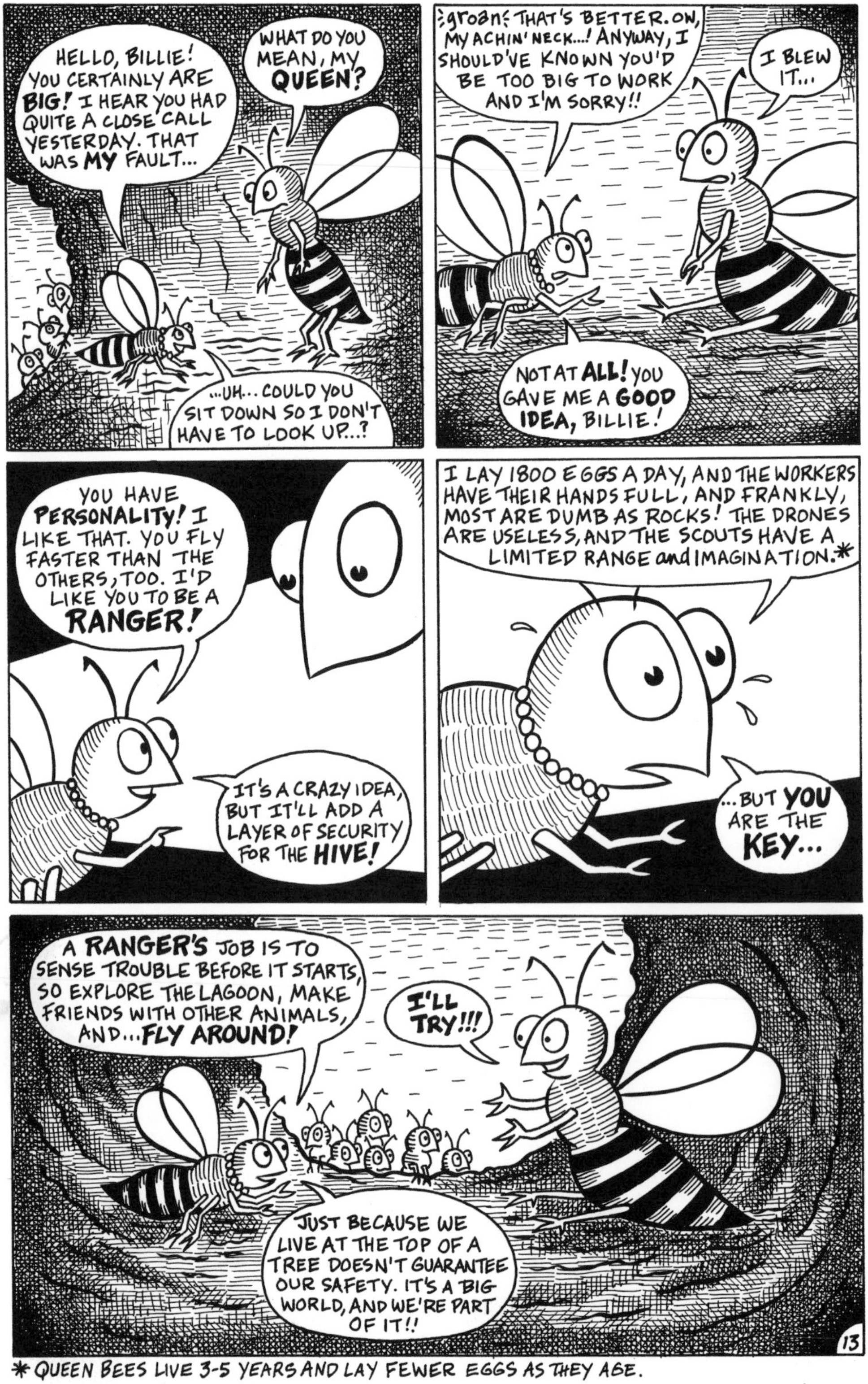
HELLO, BILLIE! YOU CERTAINLY ARE BIG! I HEAR YOU HAD QUITE A CLOSE CALL YESTERDAY. THAT WAS MY FAULT...
WHAT DO YOU MEAN, MY QUEEN?
...UH... COULD YOU SIT DOWN SO I DON'T HAVE TO LOOK UP...?
groan THAT'S BETTER. OW, MY ACHIN' NECK...! ANYWAY, I SHOULD'VE KNOWN YOU'D BE TOO BIG TO WORK AND I'M SORRY!!
I BLEW IT...
NOT AT ALL! YOU GAVE ME A GOOD IDEA, BILLIE!
YOU HAVE PERSONALITY! I LIKE THAT. YOU FLY FASTER THAN THE OTHERS, TOO. I'D LIKE YOU TO BE A RANGER!
IT'S A CRAZY IDEA, BUT IT'LL ADD A LAYER OF SECURITY FOR THE HIVE!
I LAY 1800 EGGS A DAY, AND THE WORKERS HAVE THEIR HANDS FULL, AND FRANKLY, MOST ARE DUMB AS ROCKS! THE DRONES ARE USELESS, AND THE SCOUTS HAVE A LIMITED RANGE and IMAGINATION.*
...BUT YOU ARE THE KEY...
A RANGER'S JOB IS TO SENSE TROUBLE BEFORE IT STARTS, SO EXPLORE THE LAGOON, MAKE FRIENDS WITH OTHER ANIMALS, AND... FLY AROUND!
I'LL TRY!!!
JUST BECAUSE WE LIVE AT THE TOP OF A TREE DOESN'T GUARANTEE OUR SAFETY. IT'S A BIG WORLD, AND WE'RE PART OF IT!!

* QUEEN BEES LIVE 3-5 YEARS AND LAY FEWER EGGS AS THEY AGE.

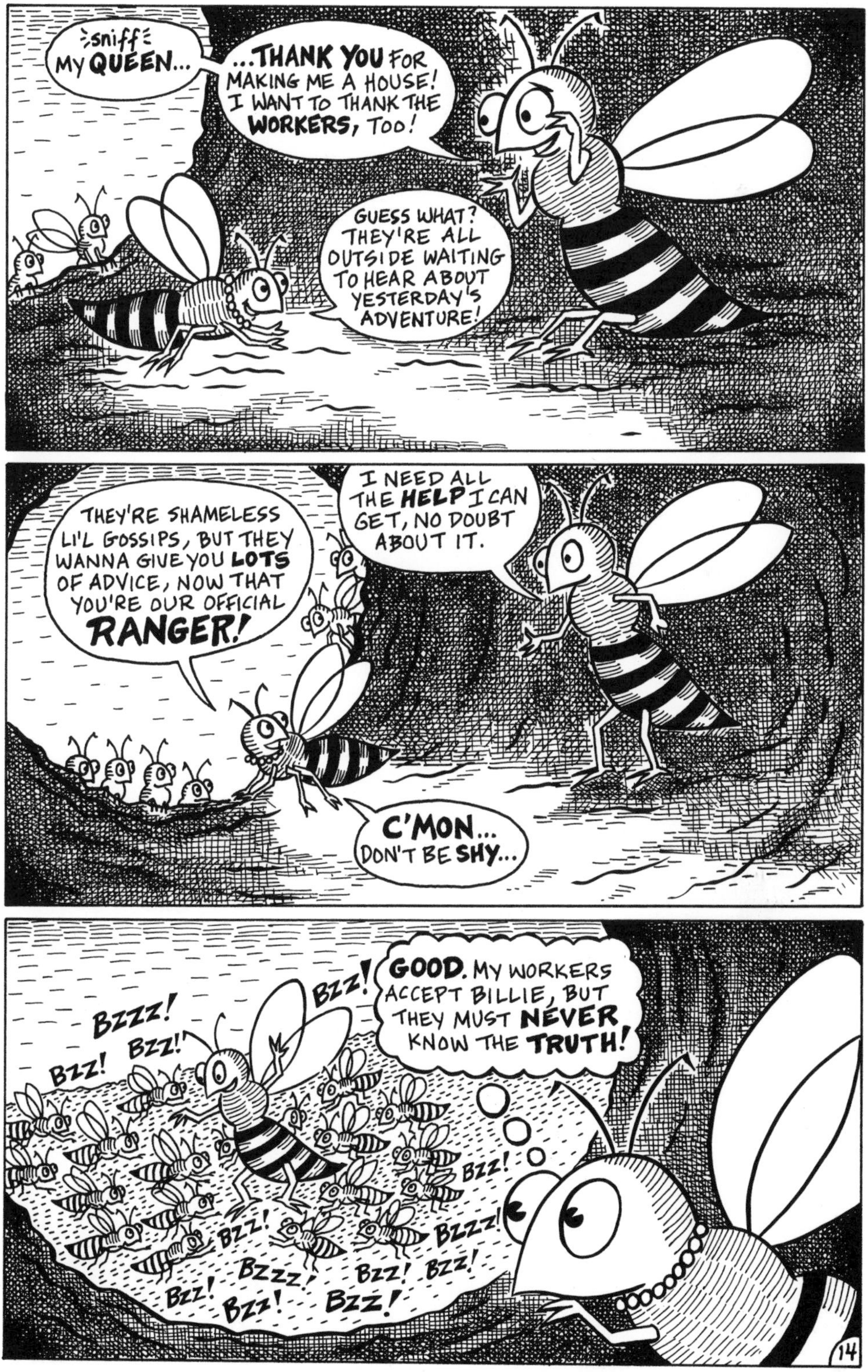
sniff
My QUEEN...
...THANK YOU FOR MAKING ME A HOUSE! I WANT TO THANK THE WORKERS, TOO!
GUESS WHAT? THEY'RE ALL OUTSIDE WAITING TO HEAR ABOUT YESTERDAY'S ADVENTURE!
THEY'RE SHAMELESS LI'L GOSSIPS, BUT THEY WANNA GIVE YOU LOTS OF ADVICE, NOW THAT YOU'RE OUR OFFICIAL RANGER!
I NEED ALL THE HELP I CAN GET, NO DOUBT ABOUT IT.
C'MON... DON'T BE SHY...
BZZZ! BZZ! BZZ! BZZ!
GOOD. MY WORKERS ACCEPT BILLIE, BUT THEY MUST NEVER KNOW THE TRUTH!
BZZ! BZZ! BZZZ! BZZZ! BZZ! BZZ! BZZ! BZZ! BZZ!

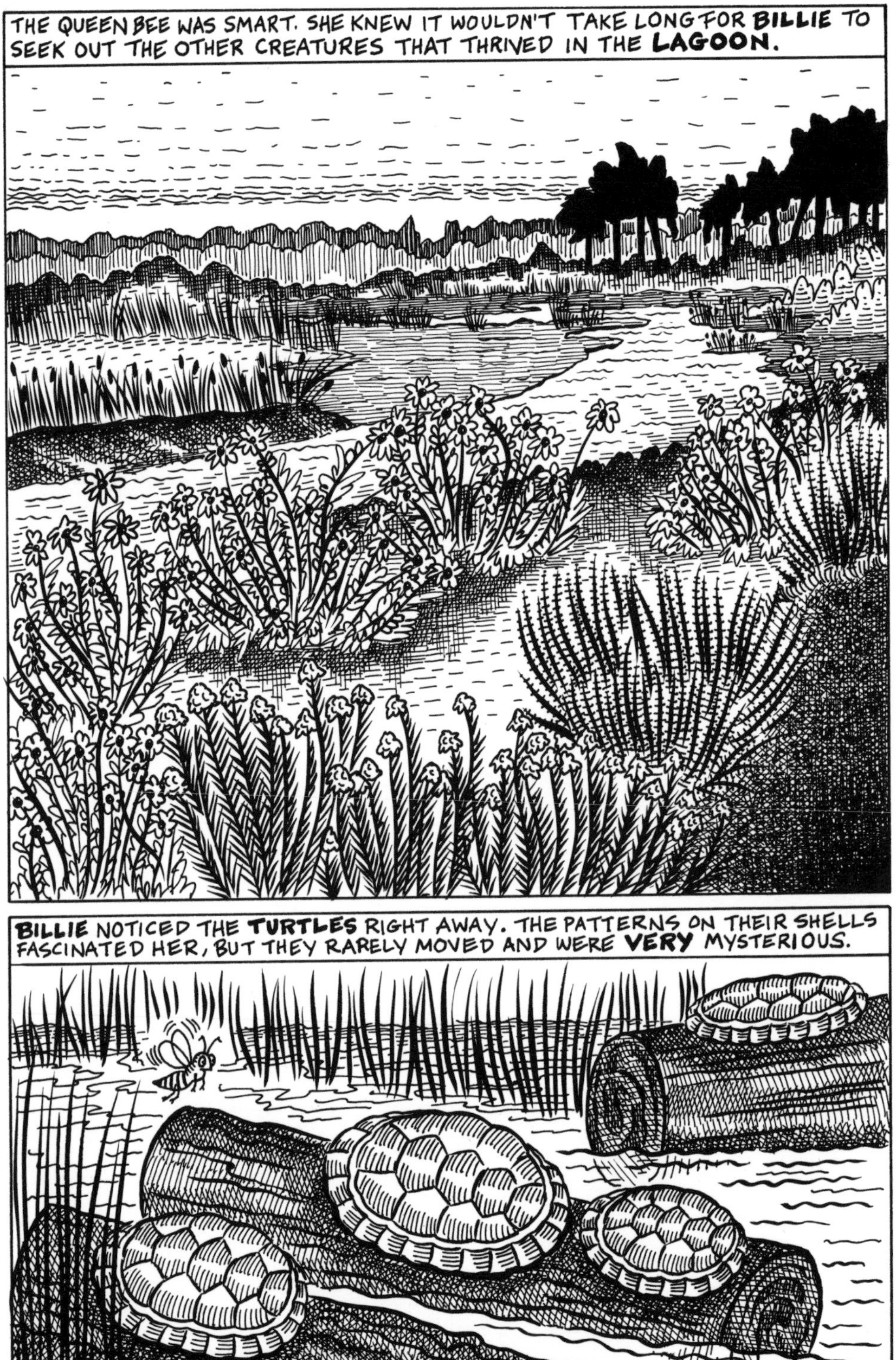
THE QUEEN BEE WAS SMART. SHE KNEW IT WOULDN'T TAKE LONG FOR BILLIE TO SEEK OUT THE OTHER CREATURES THAT THRIVED IN THE LAGOON.
BILLIE NOTICED THE TURTLES RIGHT AWAY. THE PATTERNS ON THEIR SHELLS FASCINATED HER, BUT THEY RARELY MOVED AND WERE VERY MYSTERIOUS.

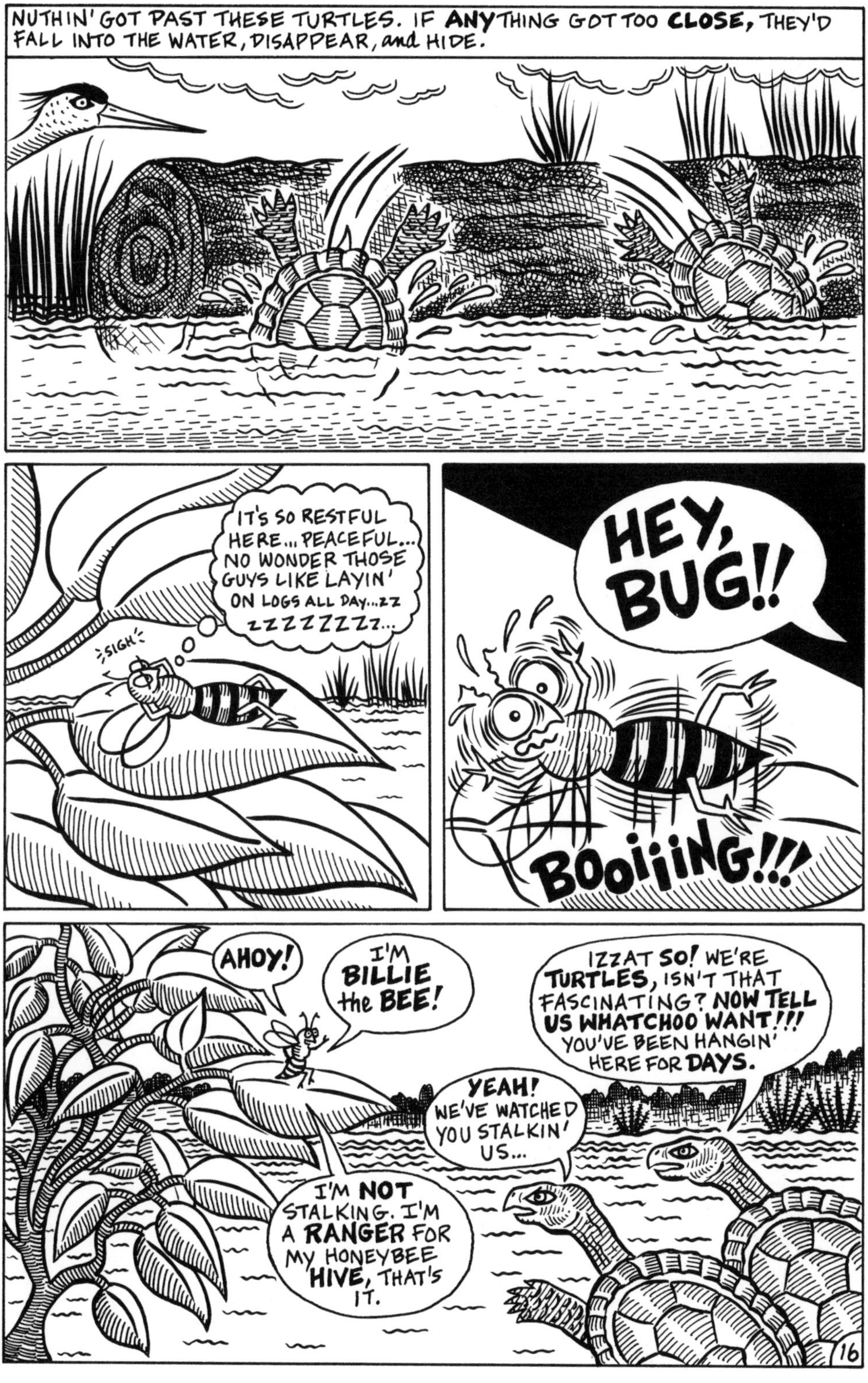
NUTHIN' GOT PAST THESE TURTLES. IF ANYTHING GOT TOO CLOSE, THEY'D FALL INTO THE WATER, DISAPPEAR, and HIDE.
IT'S SO RESTFUL HERE... PEACEFUL... NO WONDER THOSE GUYS LIKE LAYIN' ON LOGS ALL DAY...zz zzzzzzzz...
SIGH
HEY, BUG!!
BOOIIING!!!
AHOY!
I'M BILLIE the BEE!
IZZAT SO! WE'RE TURTLES, ISN'T THAT FASCINATING? NOW TELL US WHATCHOO WANT!!! YOU'VE BEEN HANGIN' HERE FOR DAYS.
YEAH! WE'VE WATCHED YOU STALKIN' US...
I'M NOT STALKING. I'M A RANGER FOR MY HONEYBEE HIVE, THAT'S IT.

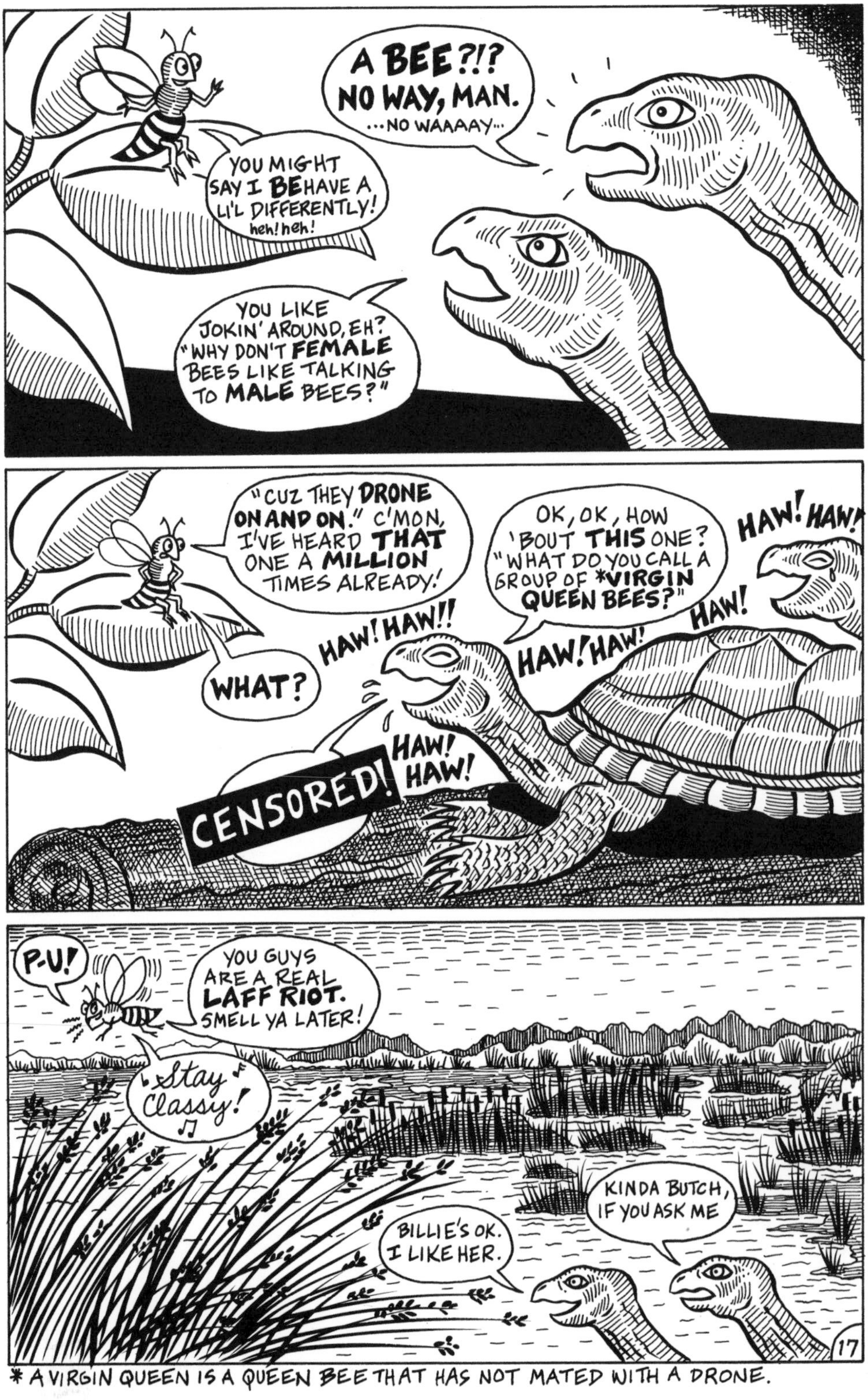
A BEE?!? NO WAY, MAN. ...NO WAAAAY...
YOU MIGHT SAY I BEHAVE A LI'L DIFFERENTLY! heh! heh!
YOU LIKE JOKIN' AROUND, EH? "WHY DON'T FEMALE BEES LIKE TALKING TO MALE BEES?"
"CUZ THEY DRONE ON AND ON." C'MON, I'VE HEARD THAT ONE A MILLION TIMES ALREADY!
OK, OK, HOW 'BOUT THIS ONE? "WHAT DO YOU CALL A GROUP OF *VIRGIN QUEEN BEES?"
HAW! HAW!
HAW!
HAW! HAW!
HAW! HAW!!
WHAT?
CENSORED!
HAW! HAW!
P-U!
YOU GUYS ARE A REAL LAFF RIOT. SMELL YA LATER!
Stay Classy!
KINDA BUTCH, IF YOU ASK ME
BILLIE'S OK. I LIKE HER.

* A VIRGIN QUEEN IS A QUEEN BEE THAT HAS NOT MATED WITH A DRONE.

3

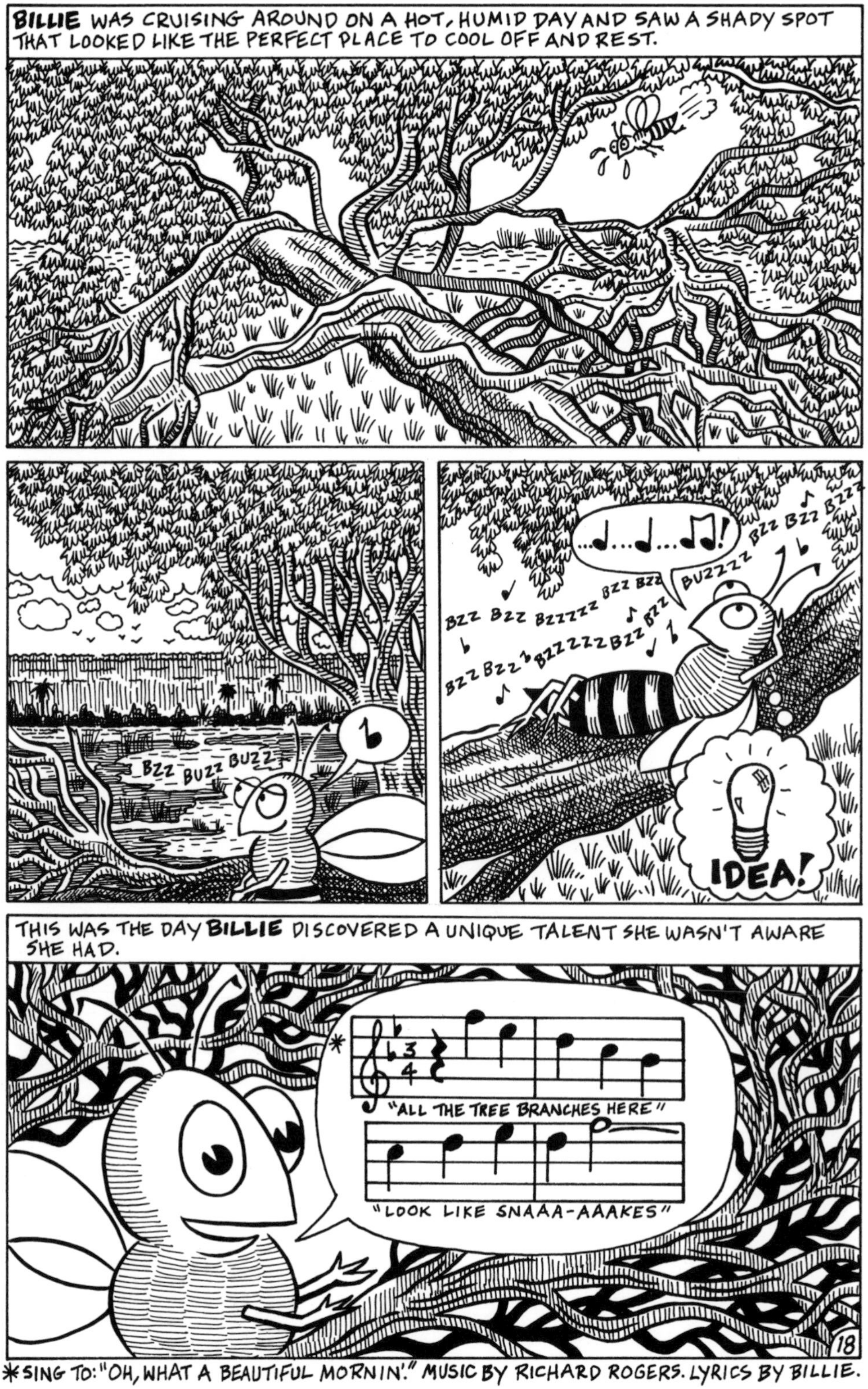
BILLIE WAS CRUISING AROUND ON A HOT, HUMID DAY AND SAW A SHADY SPOT THAT LOOKED LIKE THE PERFECT PLACE TO COOL OFF AND REST.
BZZ BUZZ BUZZ
BZZ BZZ BZZZZZZ BZZ BZZ
BZZ BZZ BZZZZZZBZZ BZZ
BUZZZZZ BZZ BZZ BZZZZ
IDEA!
THIS WAS THE DAY BILLIE DISCOVERED A UNIQUE TALENT SHE WASN'T AWARE SHE HAD.
"ALL THE TREE BRANCHES HERE"
"LOOK LIKE SNAAA-AAAKES"

*SING TO: "OH, WHAT A BEAUTIFUL MORNIN'." MUSIC BY RICHARD ROGERS. LYRICS BY BILLIE.

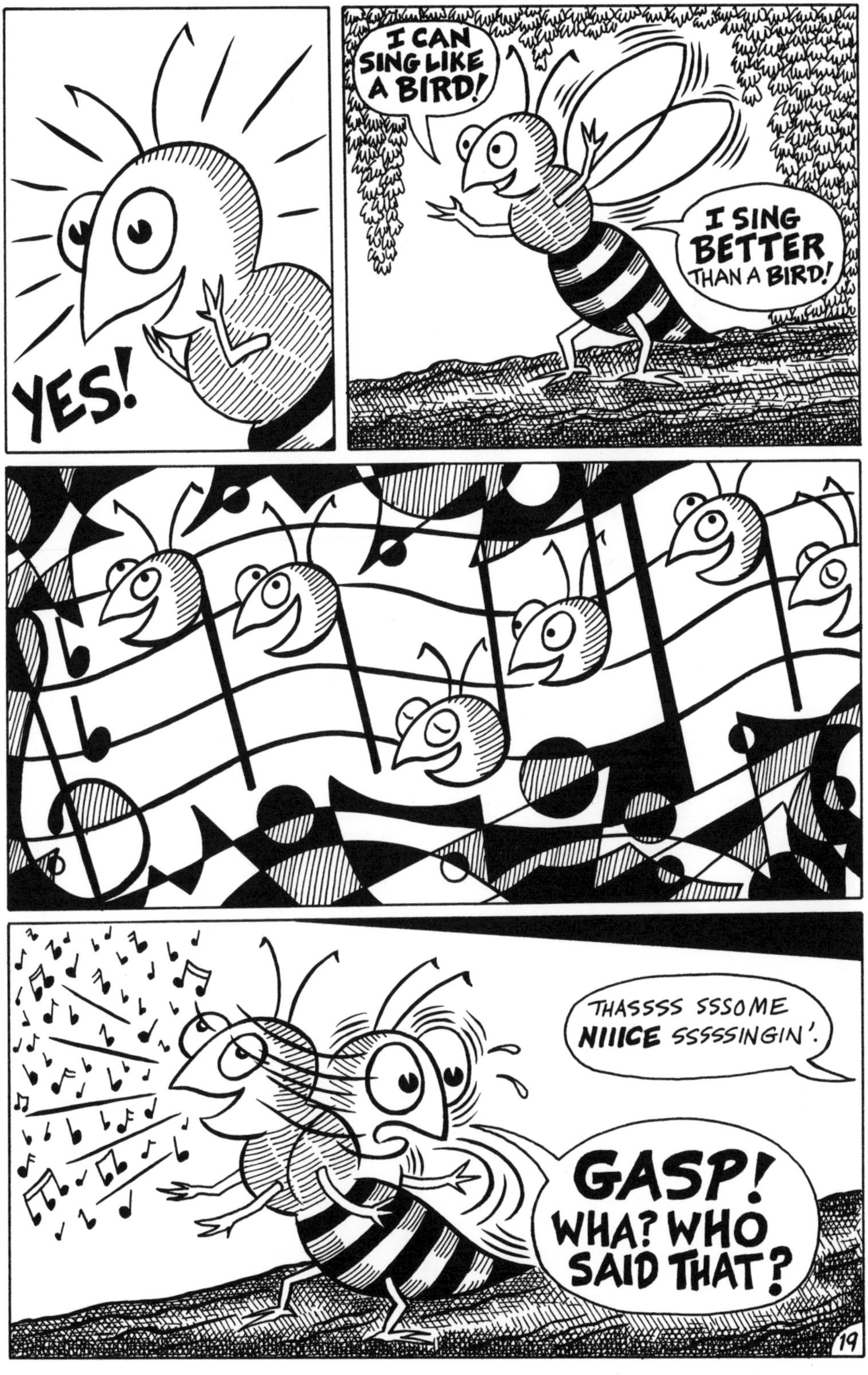
YES!
I CAN SING LIKE A BIRD!
I SING BETTER THAN A BIRD!
THASSSS SSSOME NIIICE SSSSSINGIN'.
GASP! WHA? WHO SAID THAT?

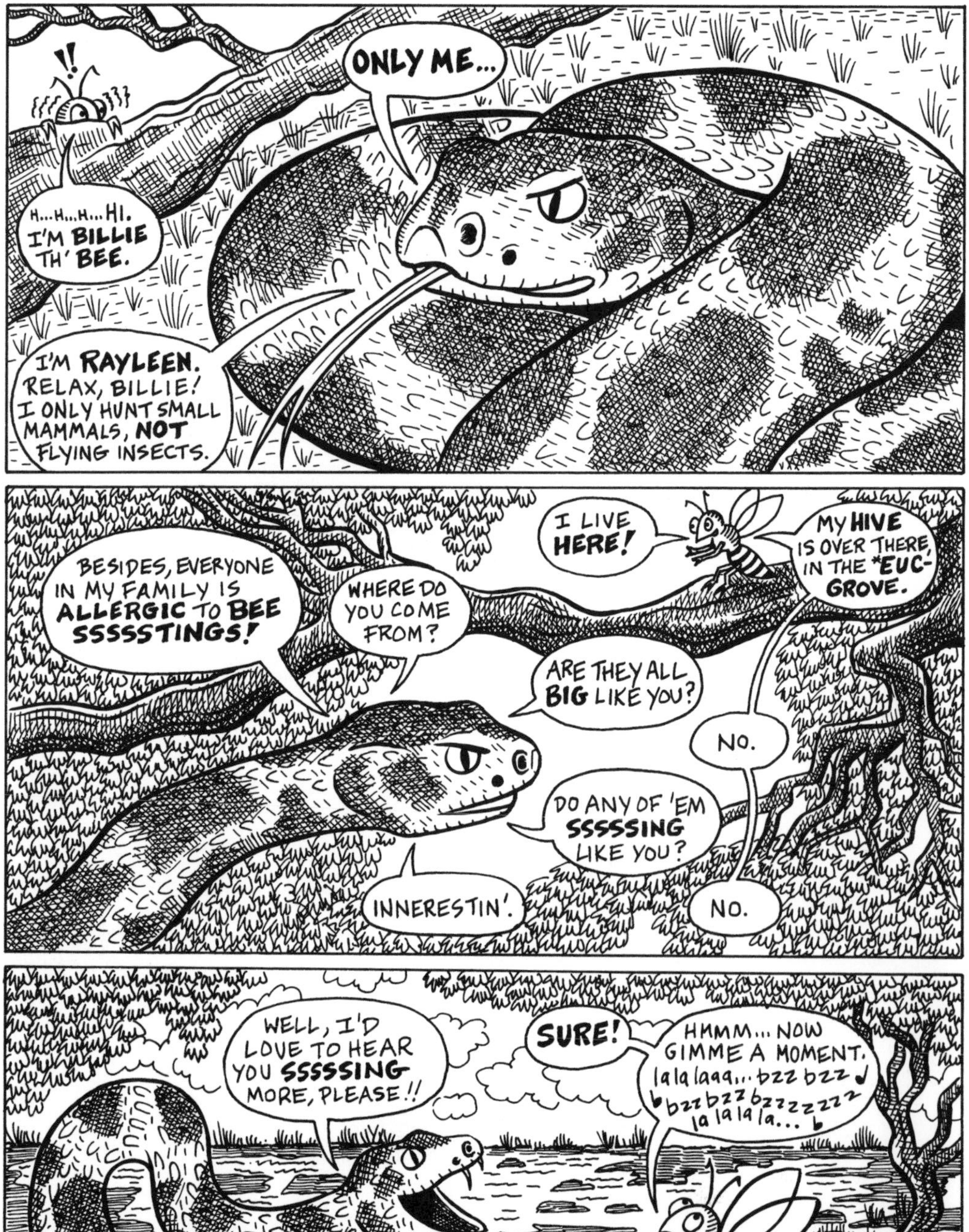

ONLY ME...
H...H...H...HI. I'M BILLIE TH' BEE.
I'M RAYLEEN. RELAX, BILLIE! I ONLY HUNT SMALL MAMMALS, NOT FLYING INSECTS.
BESIDES, EVERYONE IN MY FAMILY IS ALLERGIC TO BEE SSSSSTINGS!
WHERE DO YOU COME FROM?
I LIVE HERE!
MY HIVE IS OVER THERE, IN THE *EUC-GROVE.
ARE THEY ALL BIG LIKE YOU?
NO.
DO ANY OF 'EM SSSSSING LIKE YOU?
NO.
INNERESTIN'.
WELL, I'D LOVE TO HEAR YOU SSSSSING MORE, PLEASE!!
SURE!
HMMM... NOW GIMME A MOMENT. la la laaa... bzz bzz bzz bzz bzzzzzzz la la la la...
OK! SOMETHING JAZZY...

*EUCALYPTUS

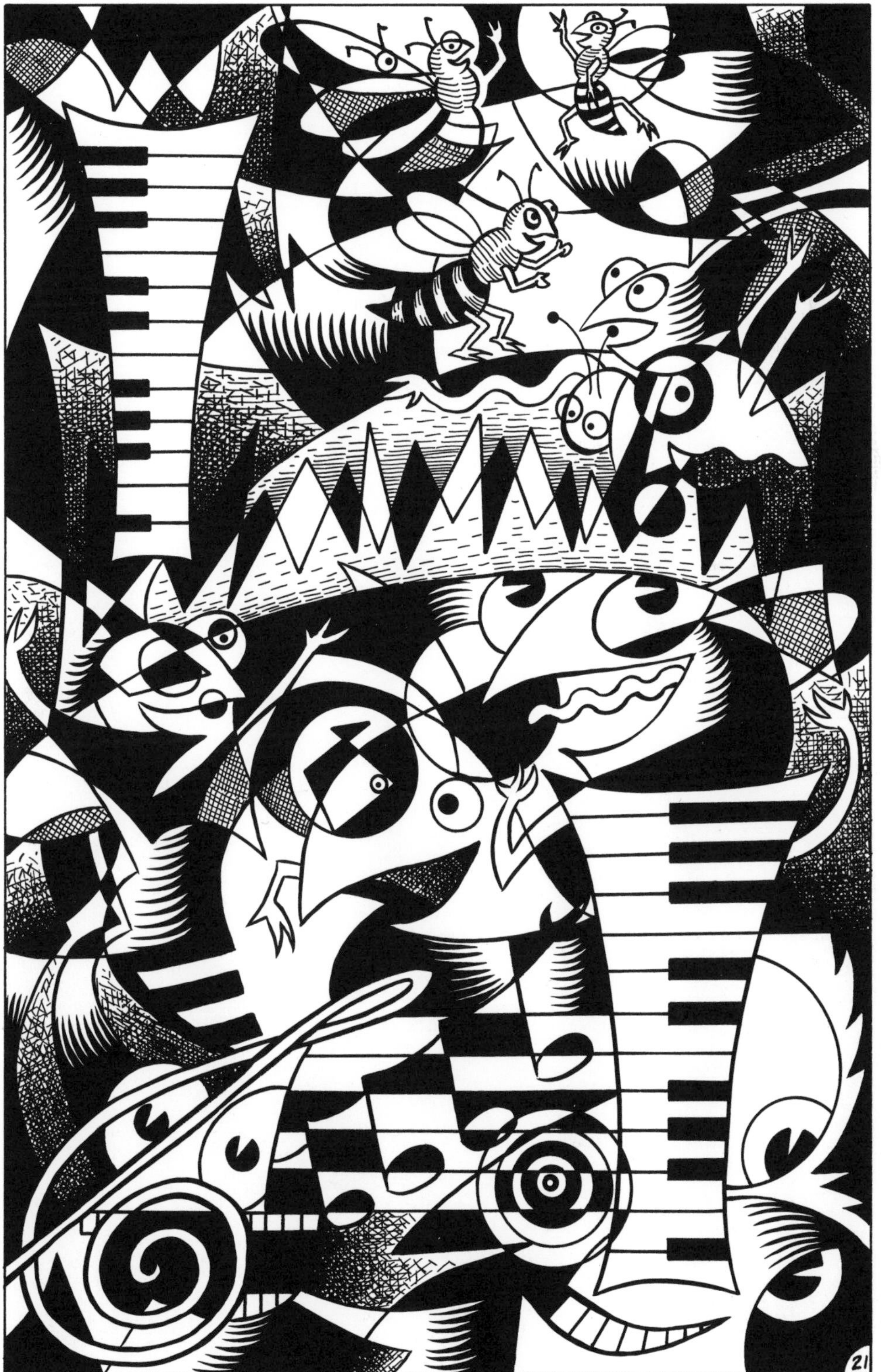

* THINK ELLA FITZGERALD JAMMIN' W/ THELONIOUS MONK.

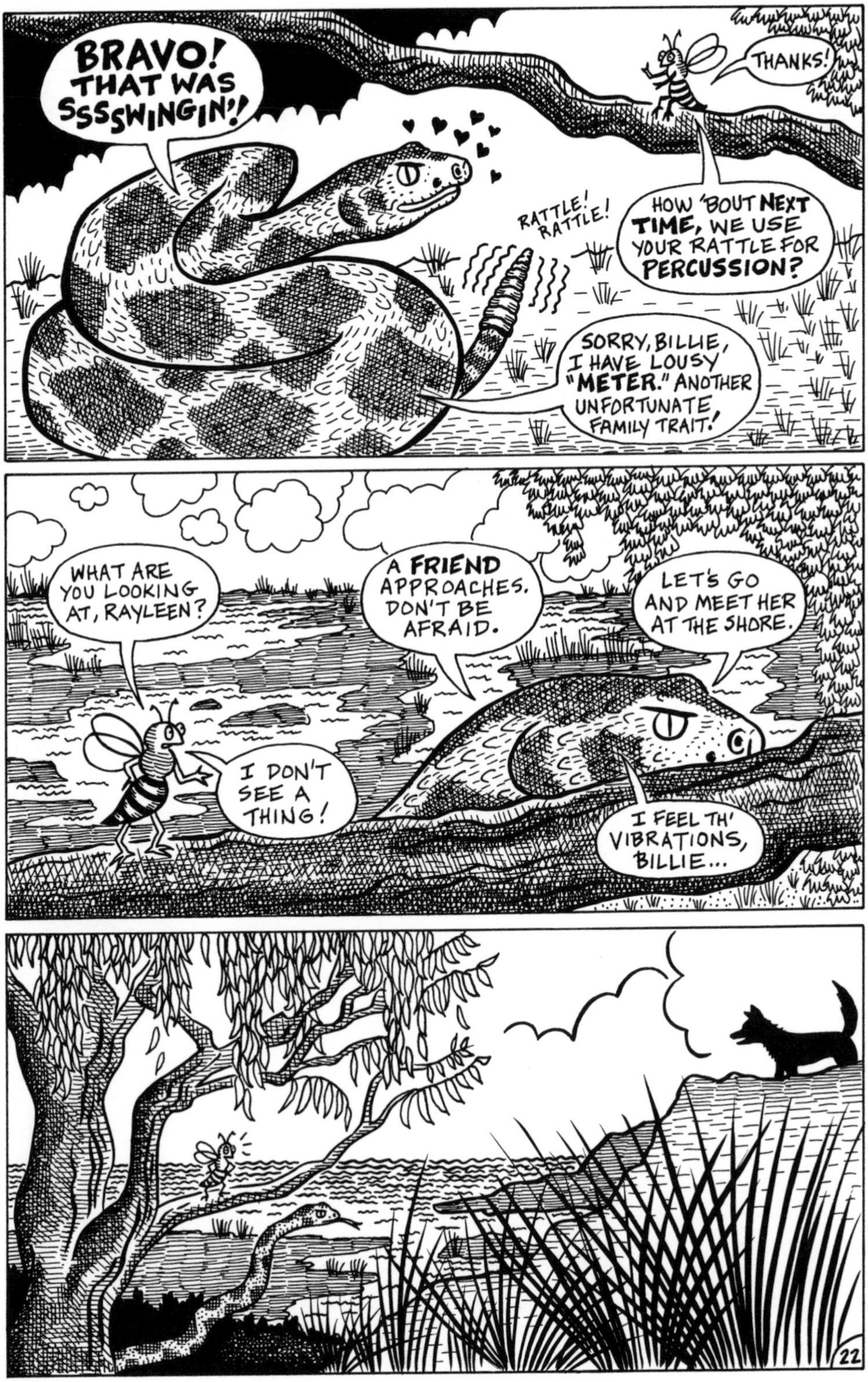
BRAVO! THAT WAS SSSSWINGIN'!
THANKS!
RATTLE! RATTLE!
HOW 'BOUT NEXT TIME, WE USE YOUR RATTLE FOR PERCUSSION?
SORRY, BILLIE, I HAVE LOUSY "METER." ANOTHER UNFORTUNATE FAMILY TRAIT!
WHAT ARE YOU LOOKING AT, RAYLEEN?
A FRIEND APPROACHES. DON'T BE AFRAID.
LET'S GO AND MEET HER AT THE SHORE.
I DON'T SEE A THING!
I FEEL TH' VIBRATIONS, BILLIE...
22

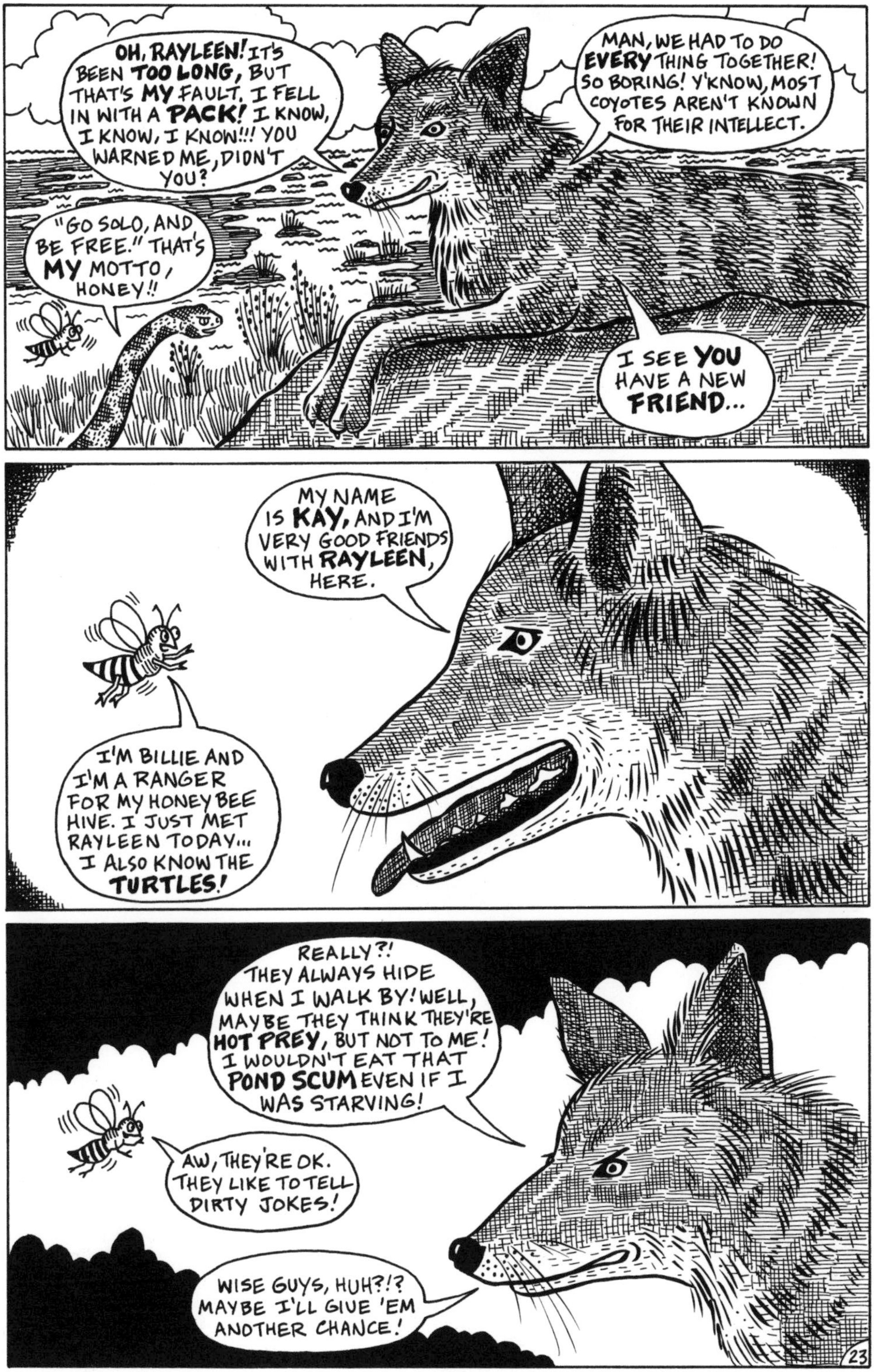
OH, RAYLEEN! IT'S BEEN TOO LONG, BUT THAT'S MY FAULT. I FELL IN WITH A PACK! I KNOW, I KNOW, I KNOW!!! YOU WARNED ME, DIDN'T YOU?
"GO SOLO, AND BE FREE." THAT'S MY MOTTO, HONEY!!
MAN, WE HAD TO DO EVERY THING TOGETHER! SO BORING! Y'KNOW, MOST COYOTES AREN'T KNOWN FOR THEIR INTELLECT.
I SEE YOU HAVE A NEW FRIEND...
MY NAME IS KAY, AND I'M VERY GOOD FRIENDS WITH RAYLEEN, HERE.
I'M BILLIE AND I'M A RANGER FOR MY HONEY BEE HIVE. I JUST MET RAYLEEN TODAY... I ALSO KNOW THE TURTLES!
REALLY?! THEY ALWAYS HIDE WHEN I WALK BY! WELL, MAYBE THEY THINK THEY'RE HOT PREY, BUT NOT TO ME! I WOULDN'T EAT THAT POND SCUM EVEN IF I WAS STARVING!
AW, THEY'RE OK. THEY LIKE TO TELL DIRTY JOKES!
WISE GUYS, HUH?!? MAYBE I'LL GIVE 'EM ANOTHER CHANCE!

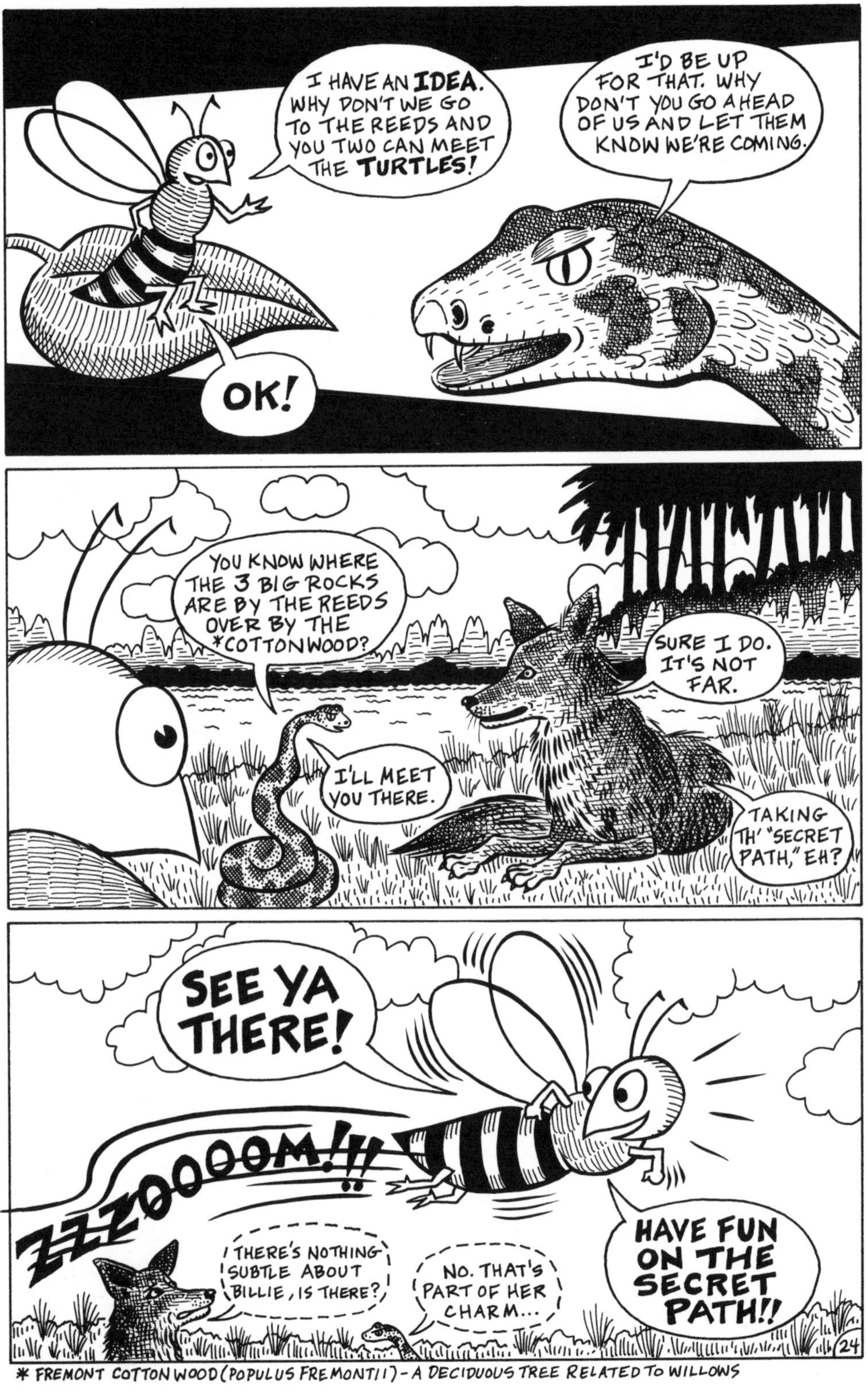

I HAVE AN **IDEA**. WHY DON'T WE GO TO THE REEDS AND YOU TWO CAN MEET THE **TURTLES**!
I'D BE UP FOR THAT. WHY DON'T YOU GO AHEAD OF US AND LET THEM KNOW WE'RE COMING.
OK!
YOU KNOW WHERE THE 3 BIG ROCKS ARE BY THE REEDS OVER BY THE *COTTONWOOD?
SURE I DO. IT'S NOT FAR.
I'LL MEET YOU THERE.
TAKING TH' "SECRET PATH," EH?
SEE YA THERE!
ZZZOOOOOM!!!
HAVE FUN ON THE SECRET PATH!!
THERE'S NOTHING SUBTLE ABOUT BILLIE, IS THERE?
NO. THAT'S PART OF HER CHARM...

* FREMONT COTTONWOOD (POPULUS FREMONTII) - A DECIDUOUS TREE RELATED TO WILLOWS

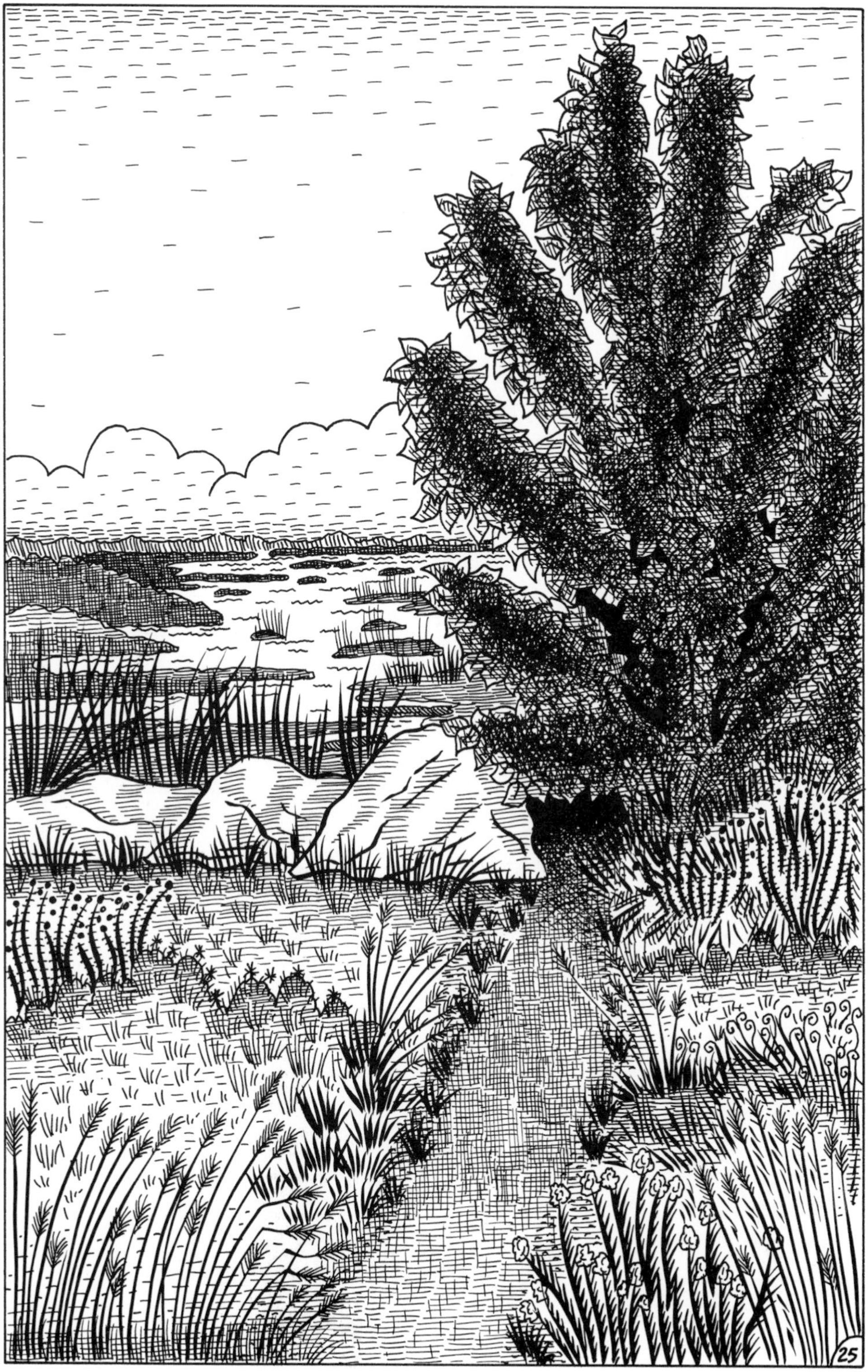

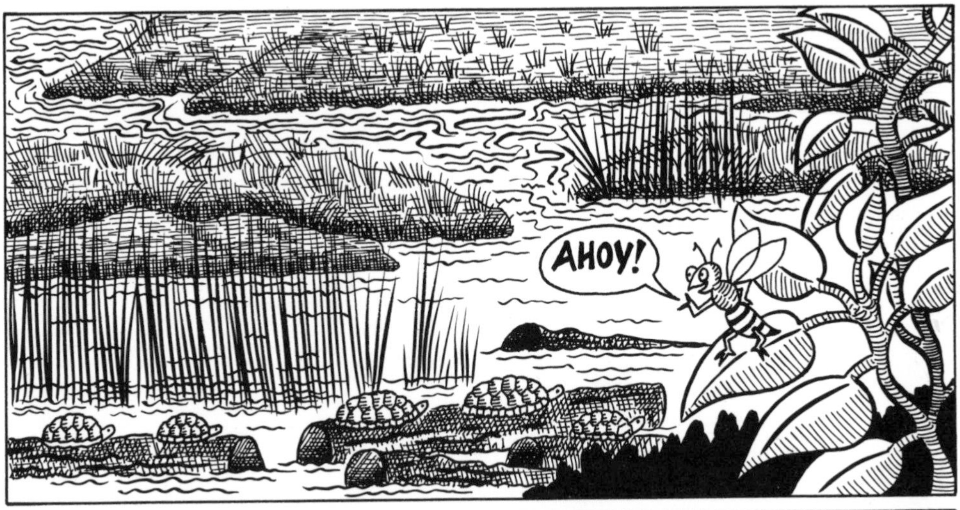
AHOY!

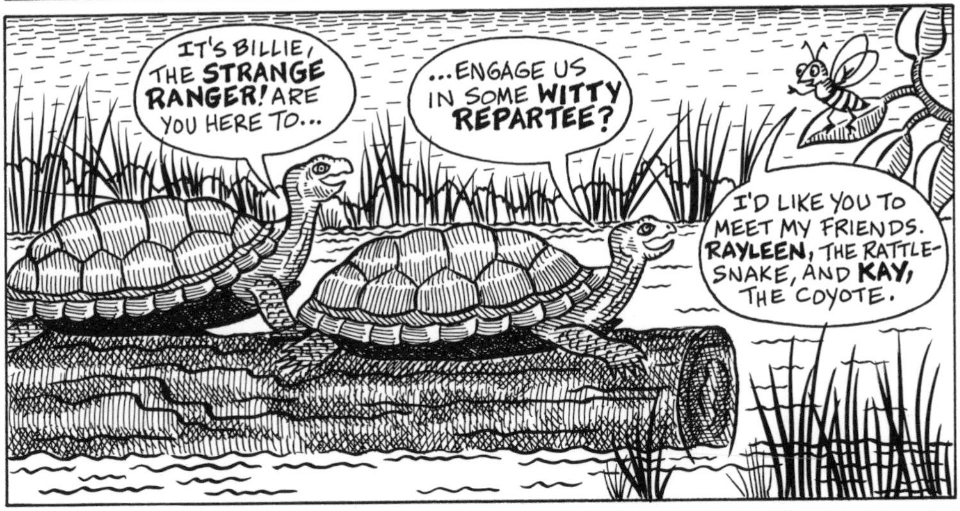
IT'S BILLIE, THE **STRANGE RANGER!** ARE YOU HERE TO...
...ENGAGE US IN SOME **WITTY REPARTEE?**
I'D LIKE YOU TO MEET MY FRIENDS. **RAYLEEN,** THE RATTLE-SNAKE, AND **KAY,** THE COYOTE.

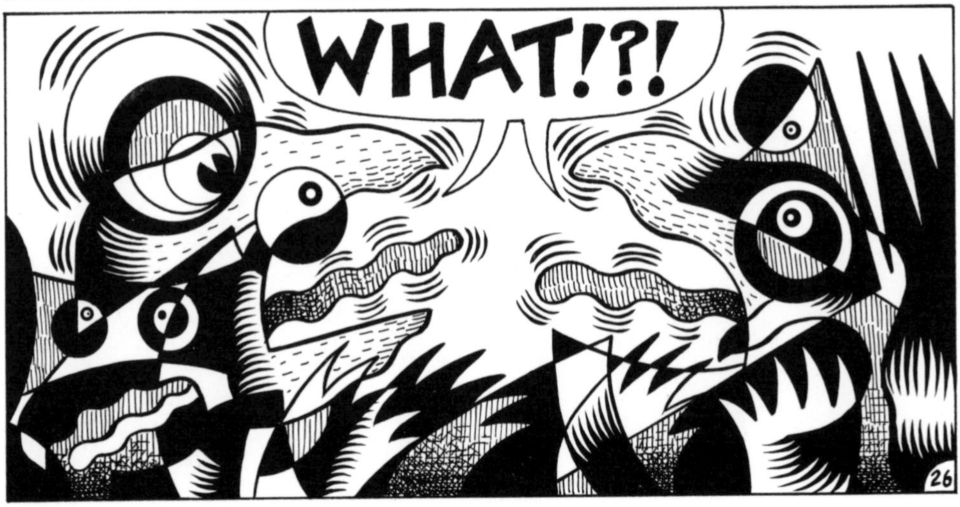
WHAT!?!

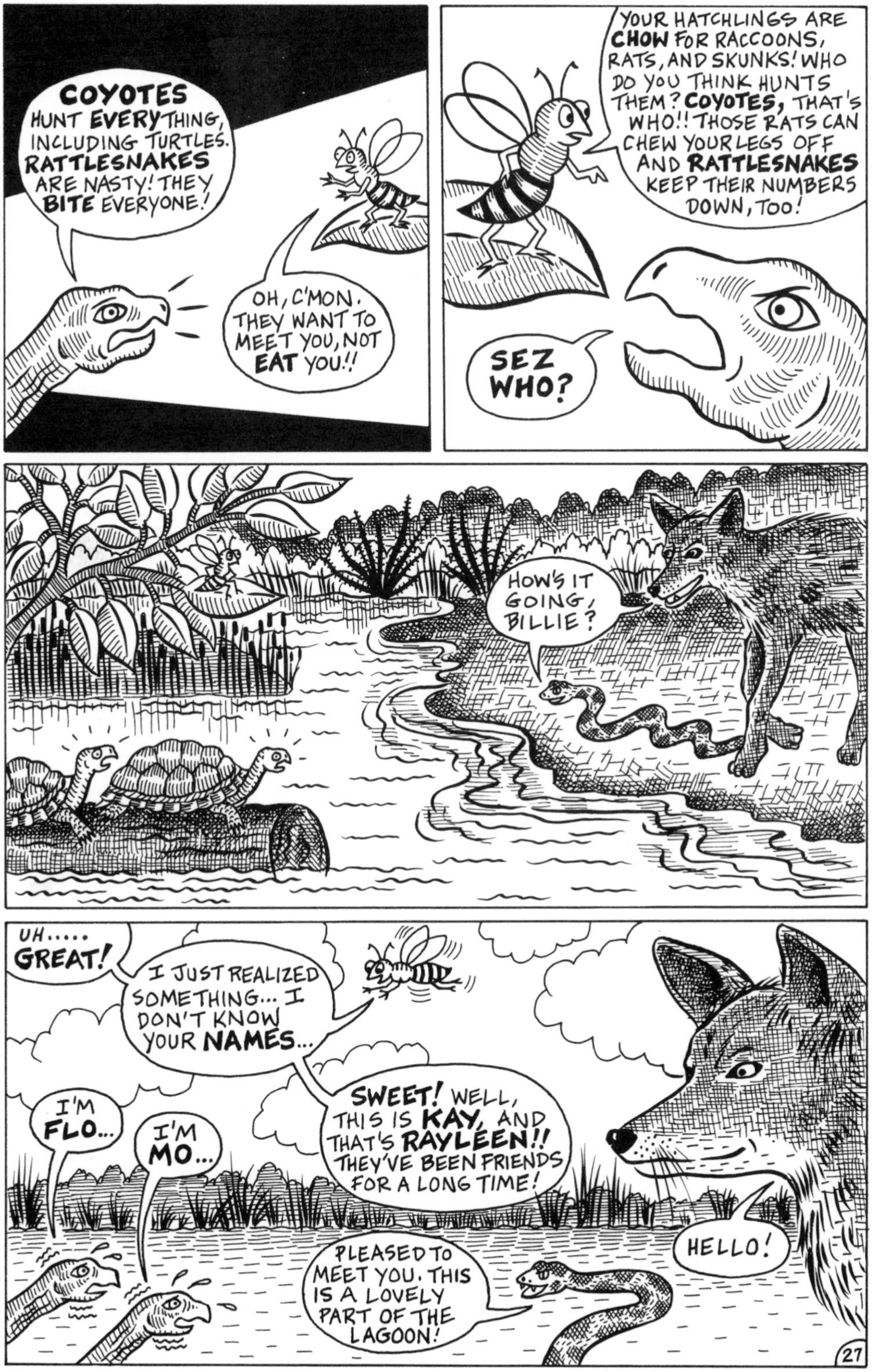
COYOTES HUNT EVERYTHING, INCLUDING TURTLES. RATTLESNAKES ARE NASTY! THEY BITE EVERYONE!
OH, C'MON. THEY WANT TO MEET YOU, NOT EAT YOU!!
YOUR HATCHLINGS ARE CHOW FOR RACCOONS, RATS, AND SKUNKS! WHO DO YOU THINK HUNTS THEM? COYOTES, THAT'S WHO!! THOSE RATS CAN CHEW YOUR LEGS OFF AND RATTLESNAKES KEEP THEIR NUMBERS DOWN, TOO!
SEZ WHO?
HOW'S IT GOING, BILLIE?
UH..... GREAT!
I JUST REALIZED SOMETHING... I DON'T KNOW YOUR NAMES...
I'M FLO...
I'M MO...
SWEET! WELL, THIS IS KAY, AND THAT'S RAYLEEN!! THEY'VE BEEN FRIENDS FOR A LONG TIME!
HELLO!
PLEASED TO MEET YOU. THIS IS A LOVELY PART OF THE LAGOON!

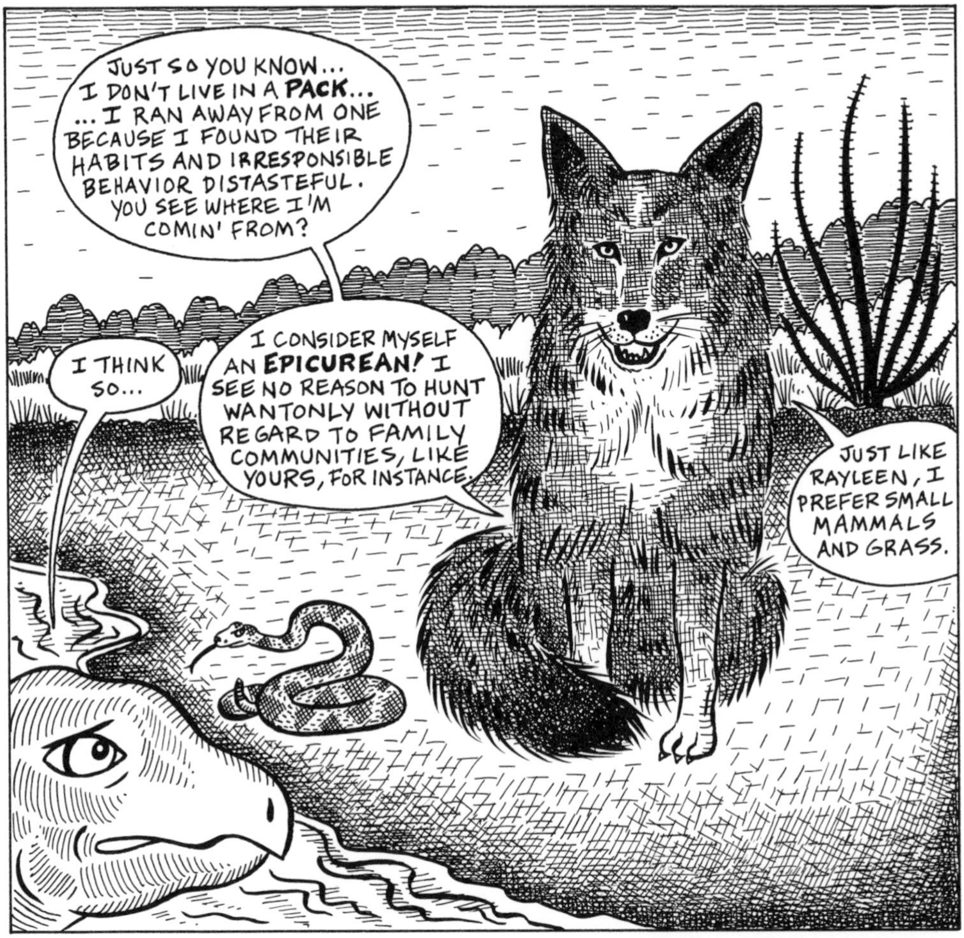
JUST SO YOU KNOW... I DON'T LIVE IN A PACK... ...I RAN AWAY FROM ONE BECAUSE I FOUND THEIR HABITS AND IRRESPONSIBLE BEHAVIOR DISTASTEFUL. YOU SEE WHERE I'M COMIN' FROM?
I THINK SO...
I CONSIDER MYSELF AN EPICUREAN! I SEE NO REASON TO HUNT WANTONLY WITHOUT REGARD TO FAMILY COMMUNITIES, LIKE YOURS, FOR INSTANCE.
JUST LIKE RAYLEEN, I PREFER SMALL MAMMALS AND GRASS.

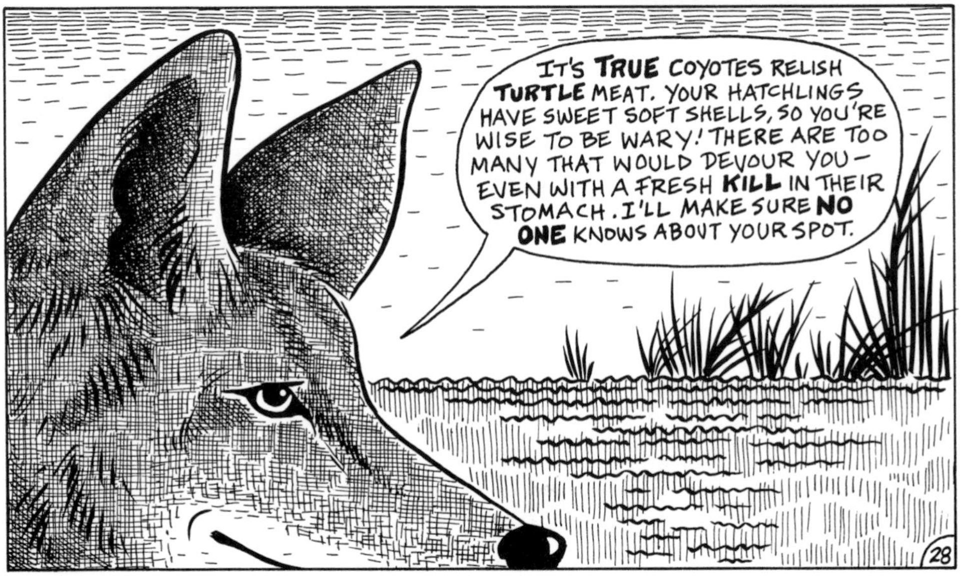
IT'S TRUE COYOTES RELISH TURTLE MEAT. YOUR HATCHLINGS HAVE SWEET SOFT SHELLS, SO YOU'RE WISE TO BE WARY! THERE ARE TOO MANY THAT WOULD DEVOUR YOU— EVEN WITH A FRESH KILL IN THEIR STOMACH. I'LL MAKE SURE NO ONE KNOWS ABOUT YOUR SPOT.

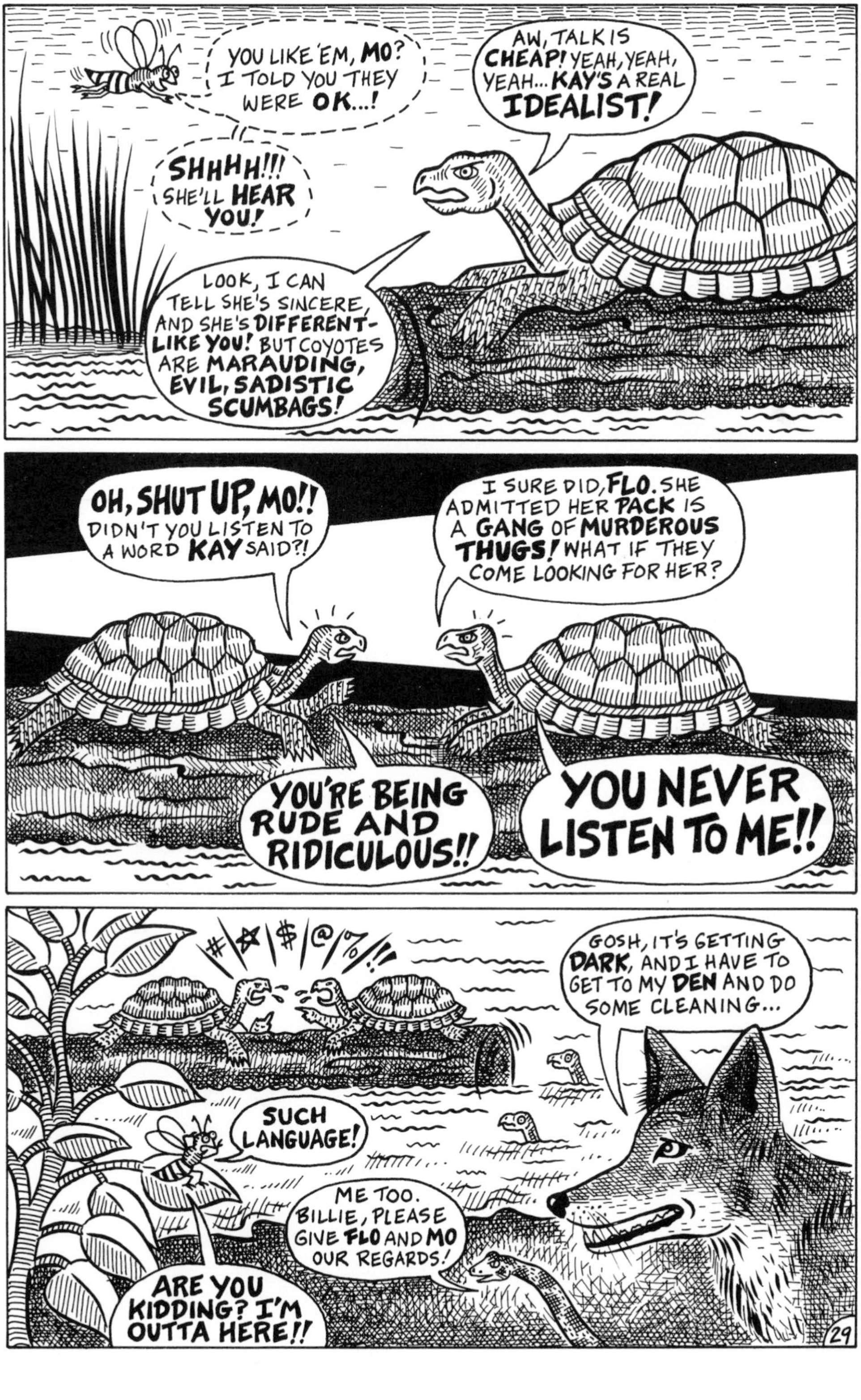
YOU LIKE 'EM, MO? I TOLD YOU THEY WERE OK...!
AW, TALK IS CHEAP! YEAH, YEAH, YEAH... KAY'S A REAL IDEALIST!
SHHHH!!! SHE'LL HEAR YOU!
LOOK, I CAN TELL SHE'S SINCERE, AND SHE'S DIFFERENT- LIKE YOU! BUT COYOTES ARE MARAUDING, EVIL, SADISTIC SCUMBAGS!
OH, SHUT UP, MO!! DIDN'T YOU LISTEN TO A WORD KAY SAID?!
I SURE DID, FLO. SHE ADMITTED HER PACK IS A GANG OF MURDEROUS THUGS! WHAT IF THEY COME LOOKING FOR HER?
YOU'RE BEING RUDE AND RIDICULOUS!!
YOU NEVER LISTEN TO ME!!
✡ $ @ % !!
GOSH, IT'S GETTING DARK, AND I HAVE TO GET TO MY DEN AND DO SOME CLEANING...
SUCH LANGUAGE!
ME TOO. BILLIE, PLEASE GIVE FLO AND MO OUR REGARDS!
ARE YOU KIDDING? I'M OUTTA HERE!!

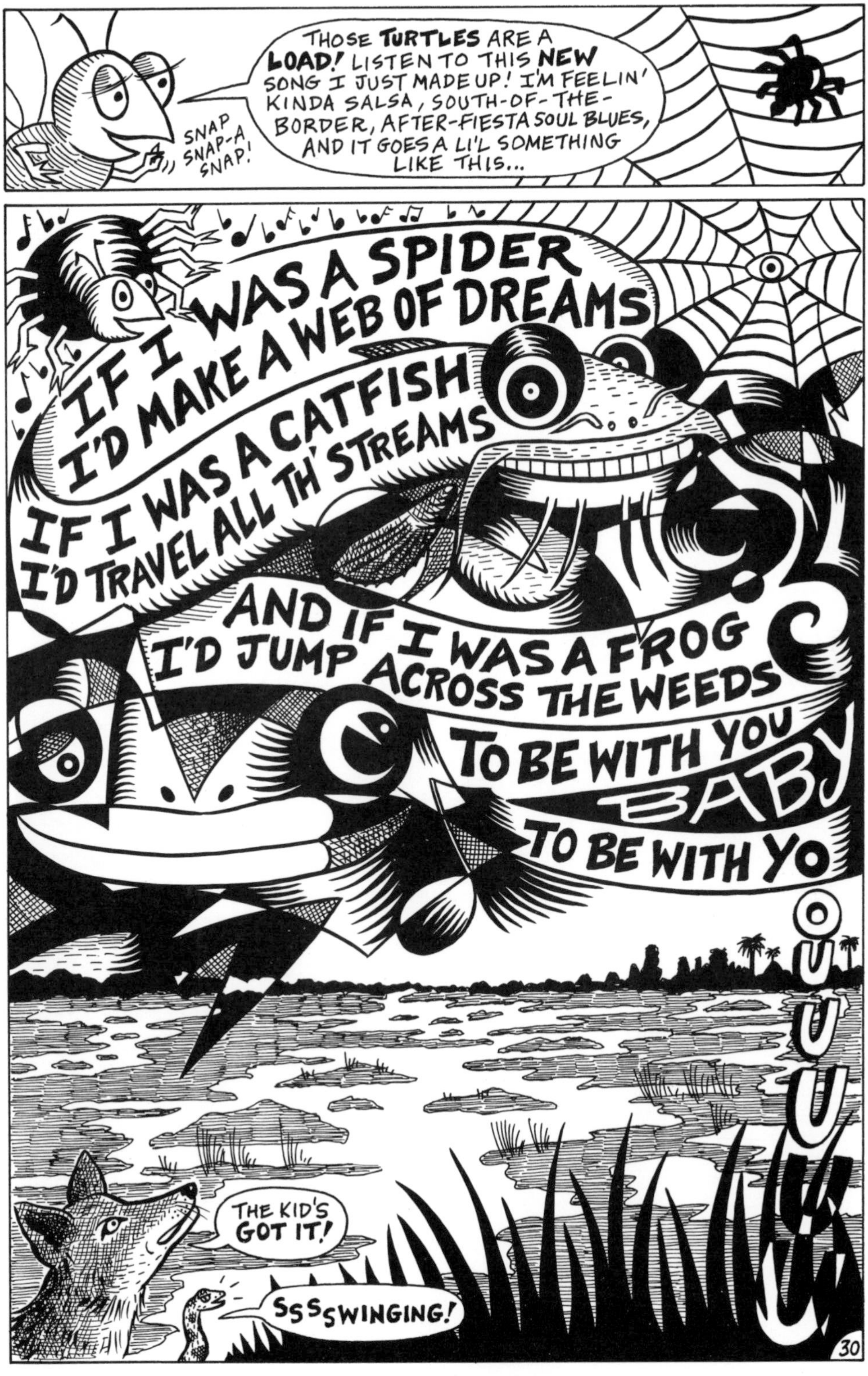
THOSE TURTLES ARE A LOAD! LISTEN TO THIS NEW SONG I JUST MADE UP! I'M FEELIN' KINDA SALSA, SOUTH-OF-THE-BORDER, AFTER-FIESTA SOUL BLUES, AND IT GOES A LI'L SOMETHING LIKE THIS...
SNAP SNAP-A SNAP!
IF I WAS A SPIDER
I'D MAKE A WEB OF DREAMS
IF I WAS A CATFISH
I'D TRAVEL ALL TH' STREAMS
AND IF I WAS A FROG
I'D JUMP ACROSS THE WEEDS
TO BE WITH YOU
BABY
TO BE WITH YOUUUUUUU
THE KID'S GOT IT!
SSSSWINGING!

4

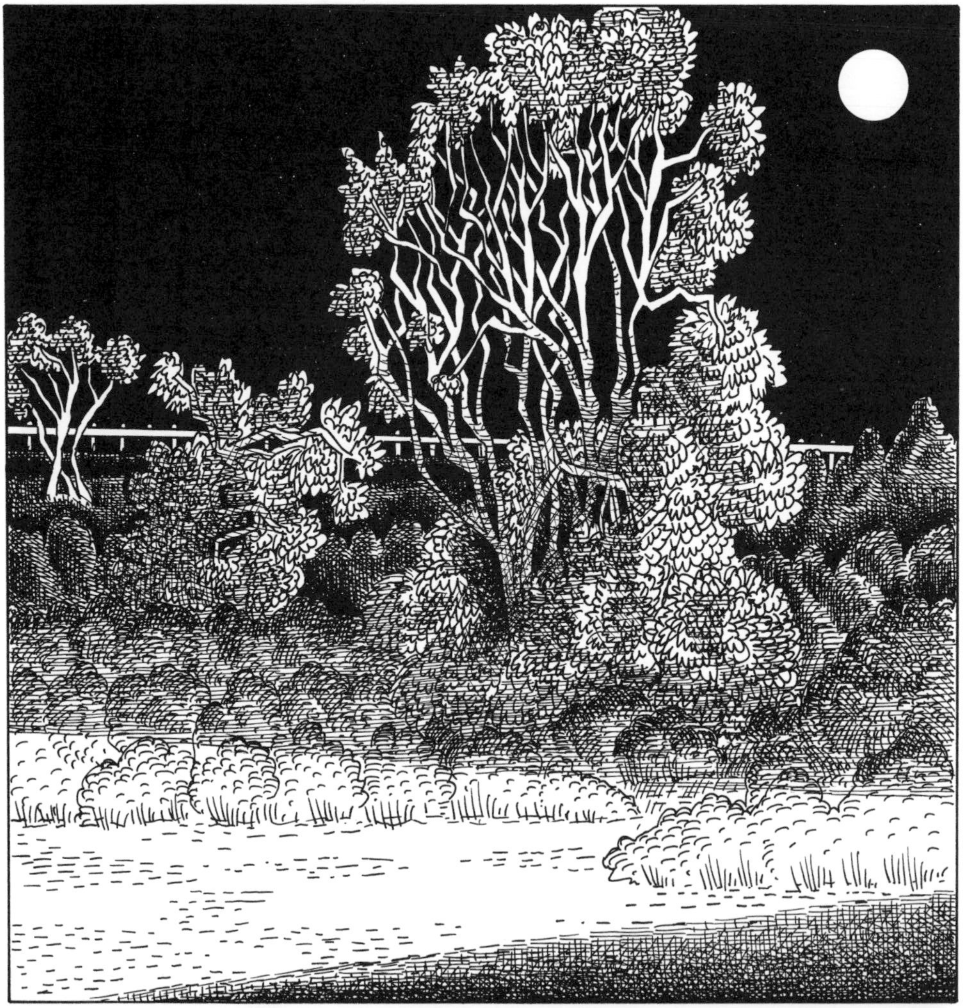

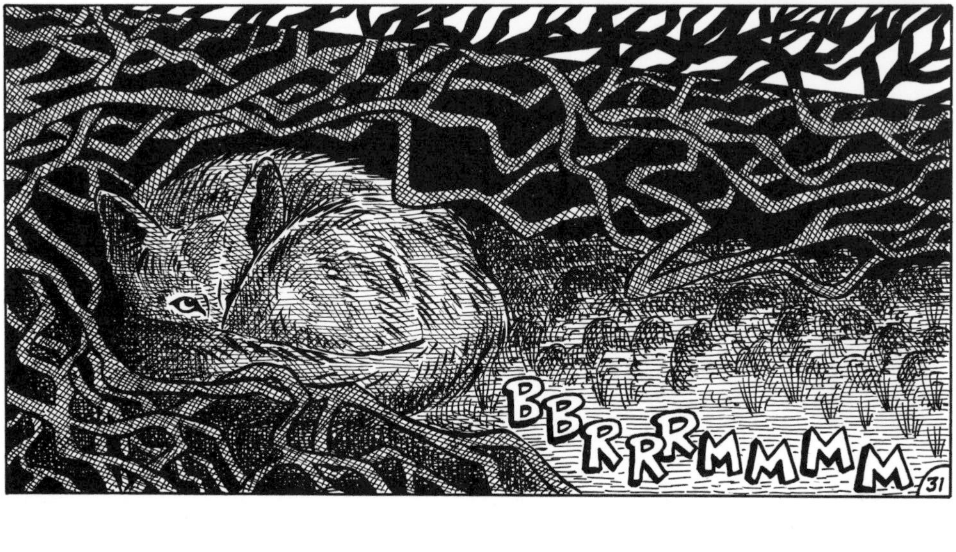
BBRRRRMMMMM

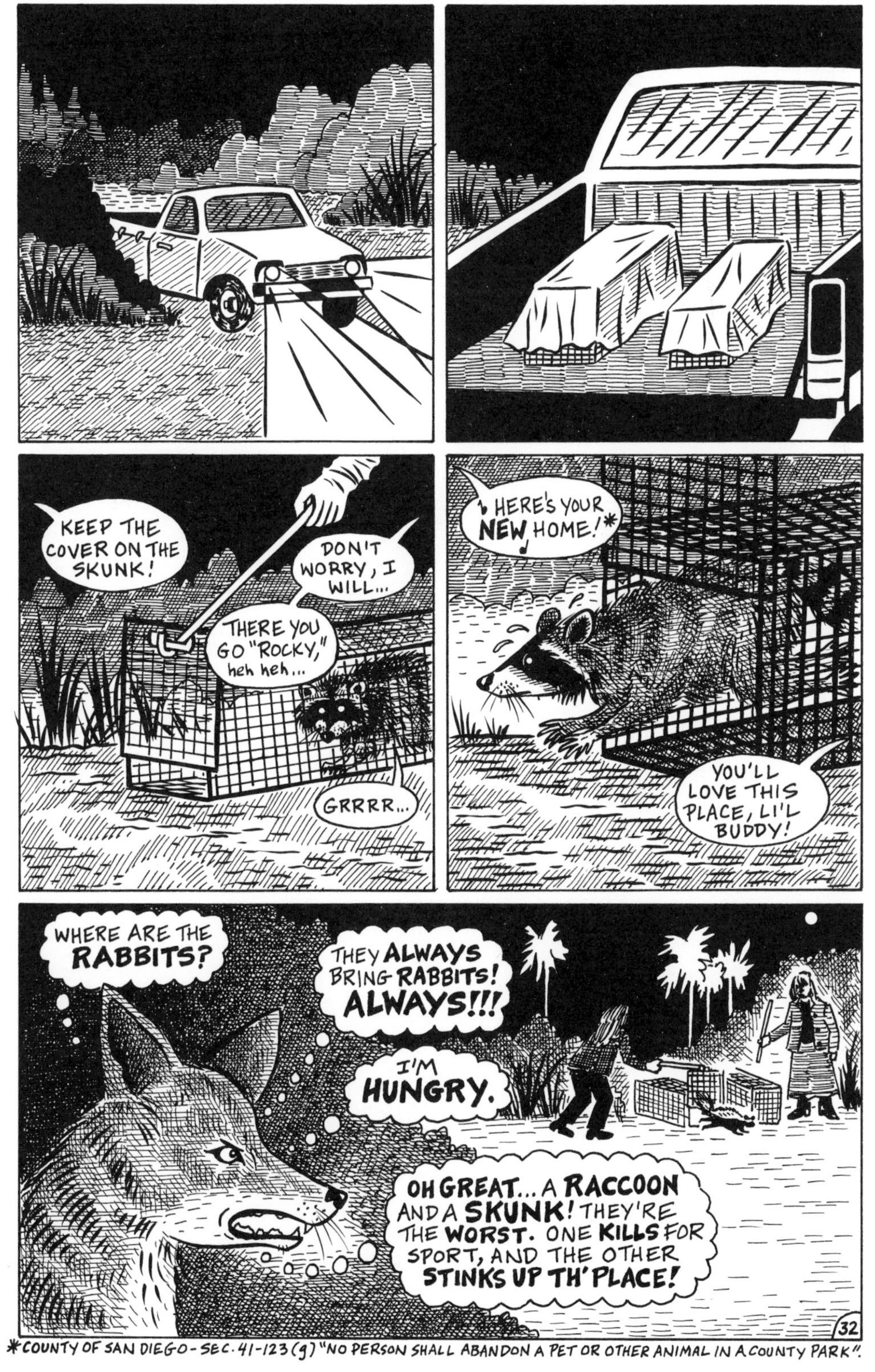
KEEP THE COVER ON THE SKUNK!
DON'T WORRY, I WILL...
THERE YOU GO "ROCKY," heh heh...
GRRRR...
HERE'S YOUR NEW HOME!*
YOU'LL LOVE THIS PLACE, LI'L BUDDY!
WHERE ARE THE RABBITS?
THEY ALWAYS BRING RABBITS! ALWAYS!!!
I'M HUNGRY.
OH GREAT... A RACCOON AND A SKUNK! THEY'RE THE WORST. ONE KILLS FOR SPORT, AND THE OTHER STINKS UP TH' PLACE!
32

*COUNTY OF SAN DIEGO - SEC. 41-123 (g) "NO PERSON SHALL ABANDON A PET OR OTHER ANIMAL IN A COUNTY PARK".

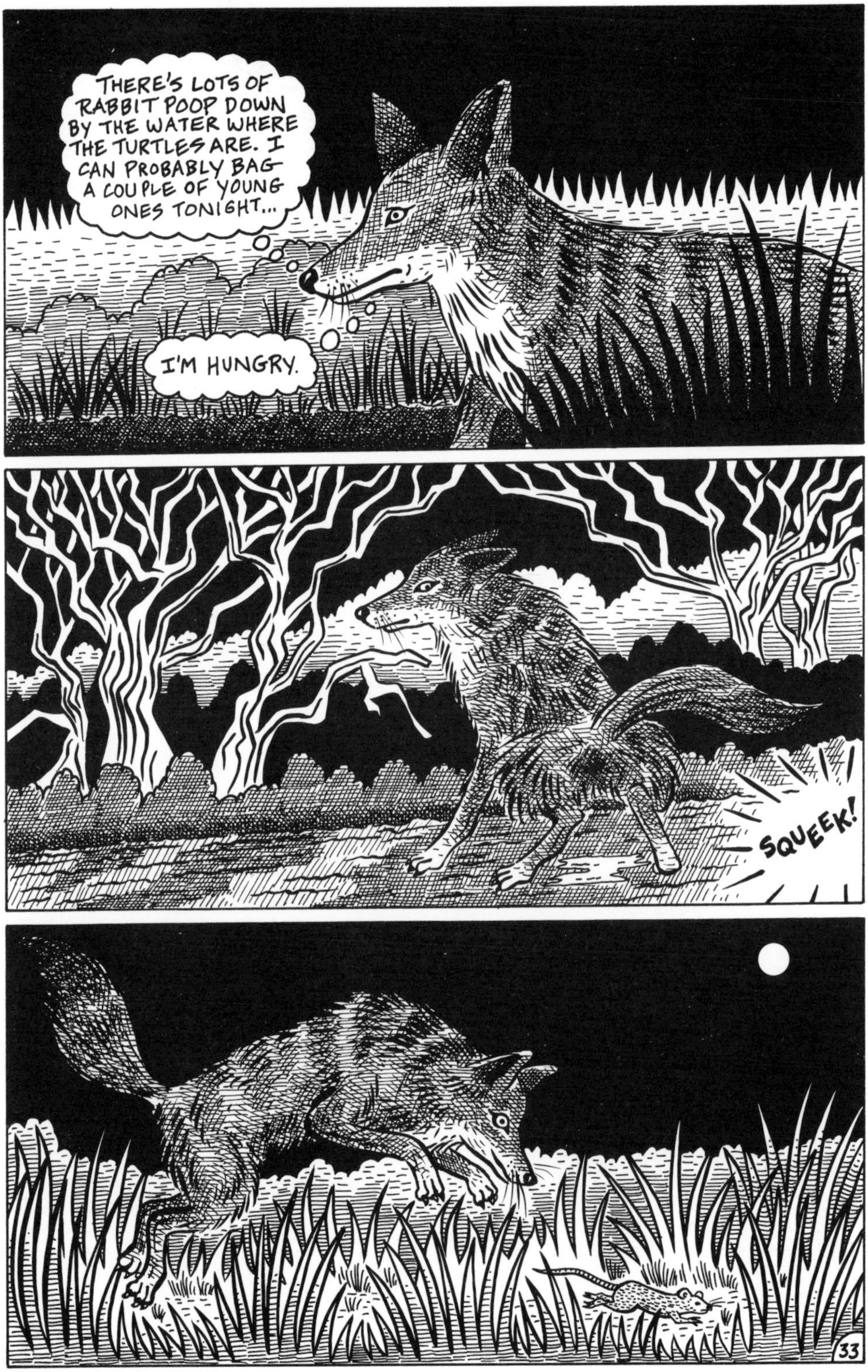
THERE'S LOTS OF RABBIT POOP DOWN BY THE WATER WHERE THE TURTLES ARE. I CAN PROBABLY BAG A COUPLE OF YOUNG ONES TONIGHT...
I'M HUNGRY.
SQUEEK!

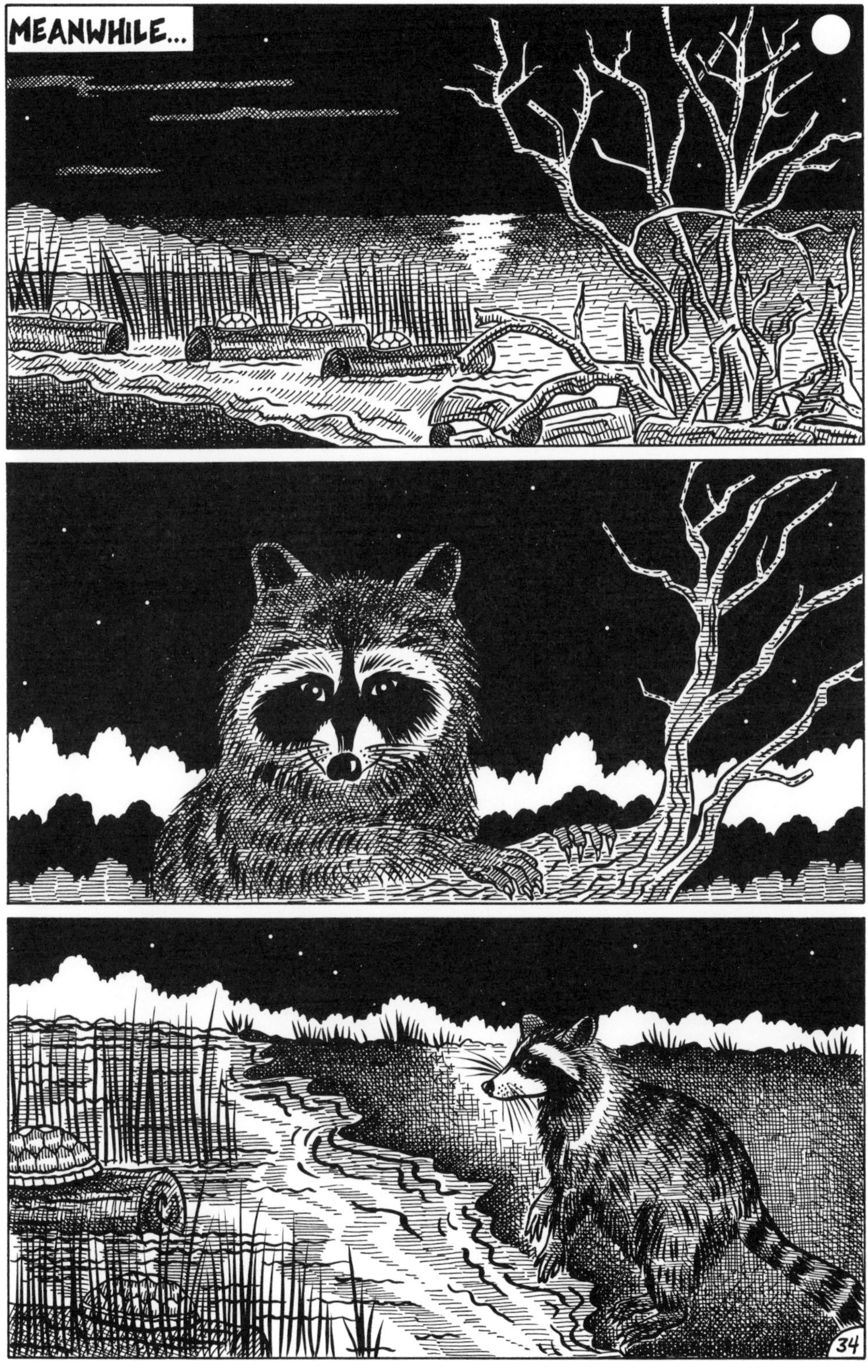
MEANWHILE...
34

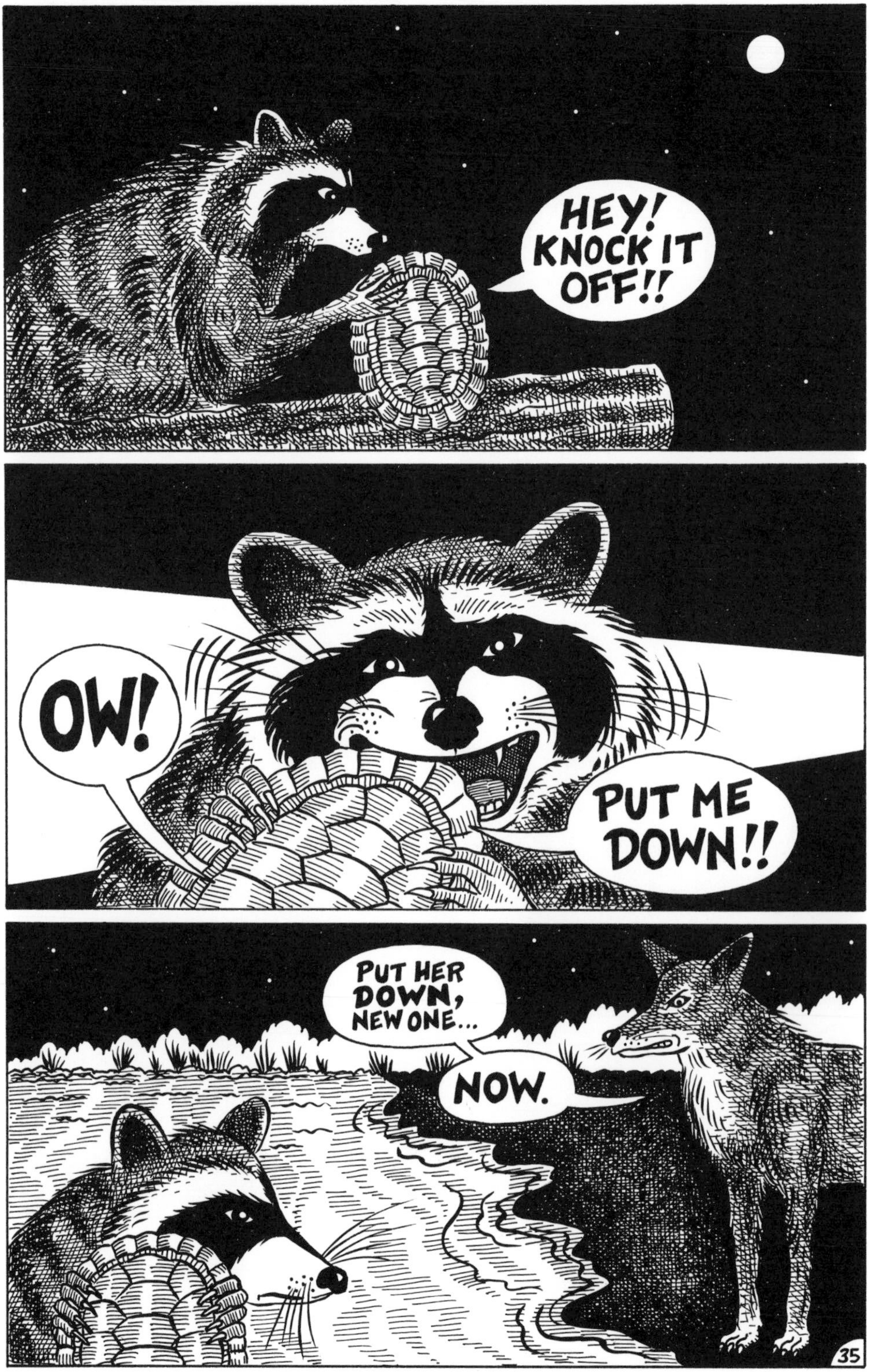
HEY! KNOCK IT OFF!!
OW!
PUT ME DOWN!!
PUT HER DOWN, NEW ONE...
NOW.
35

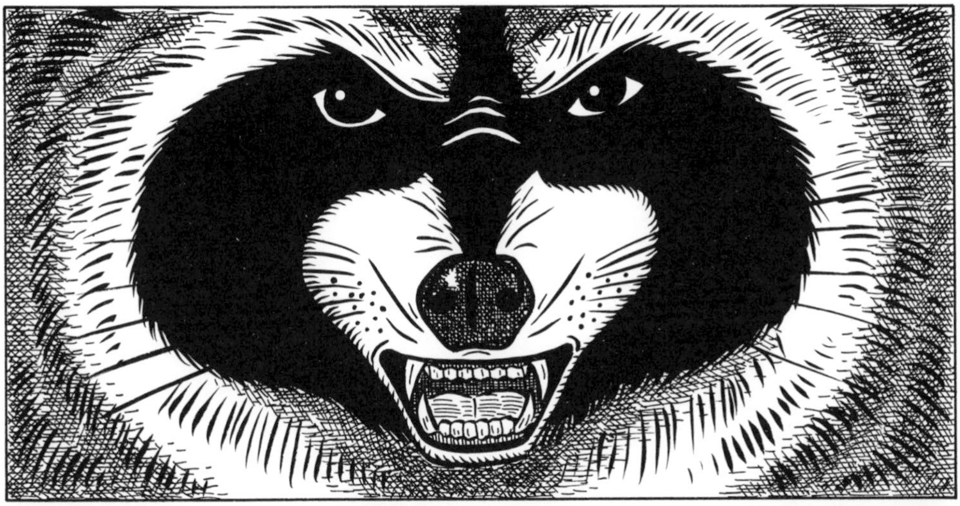

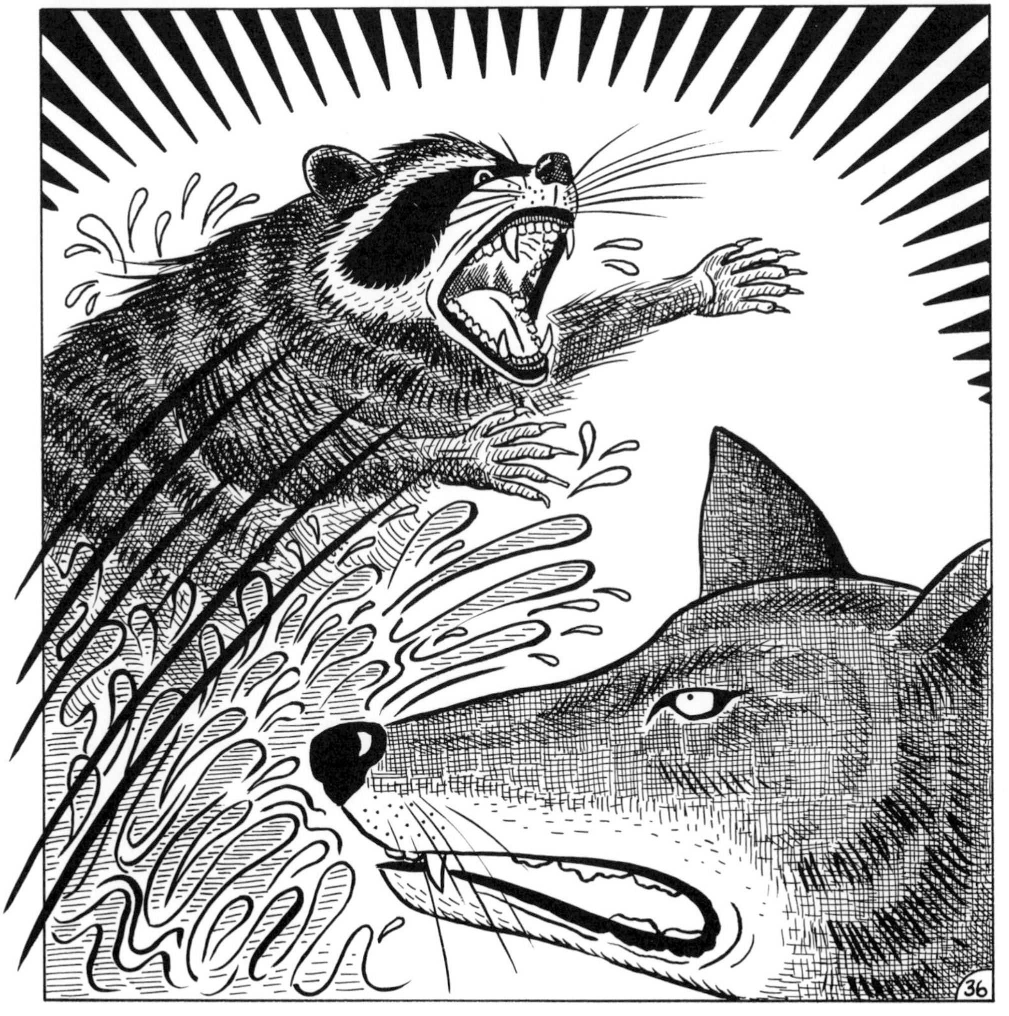

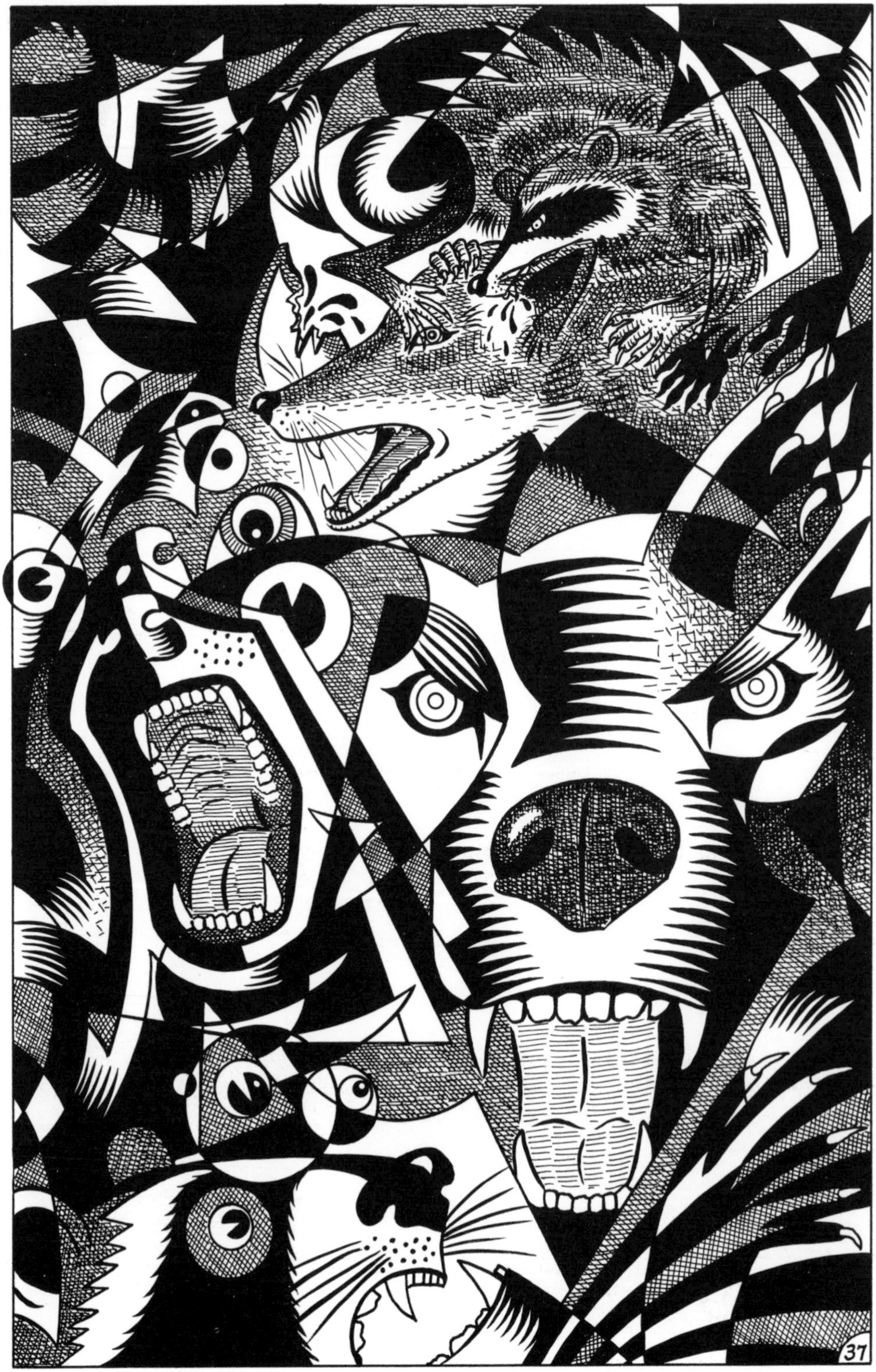

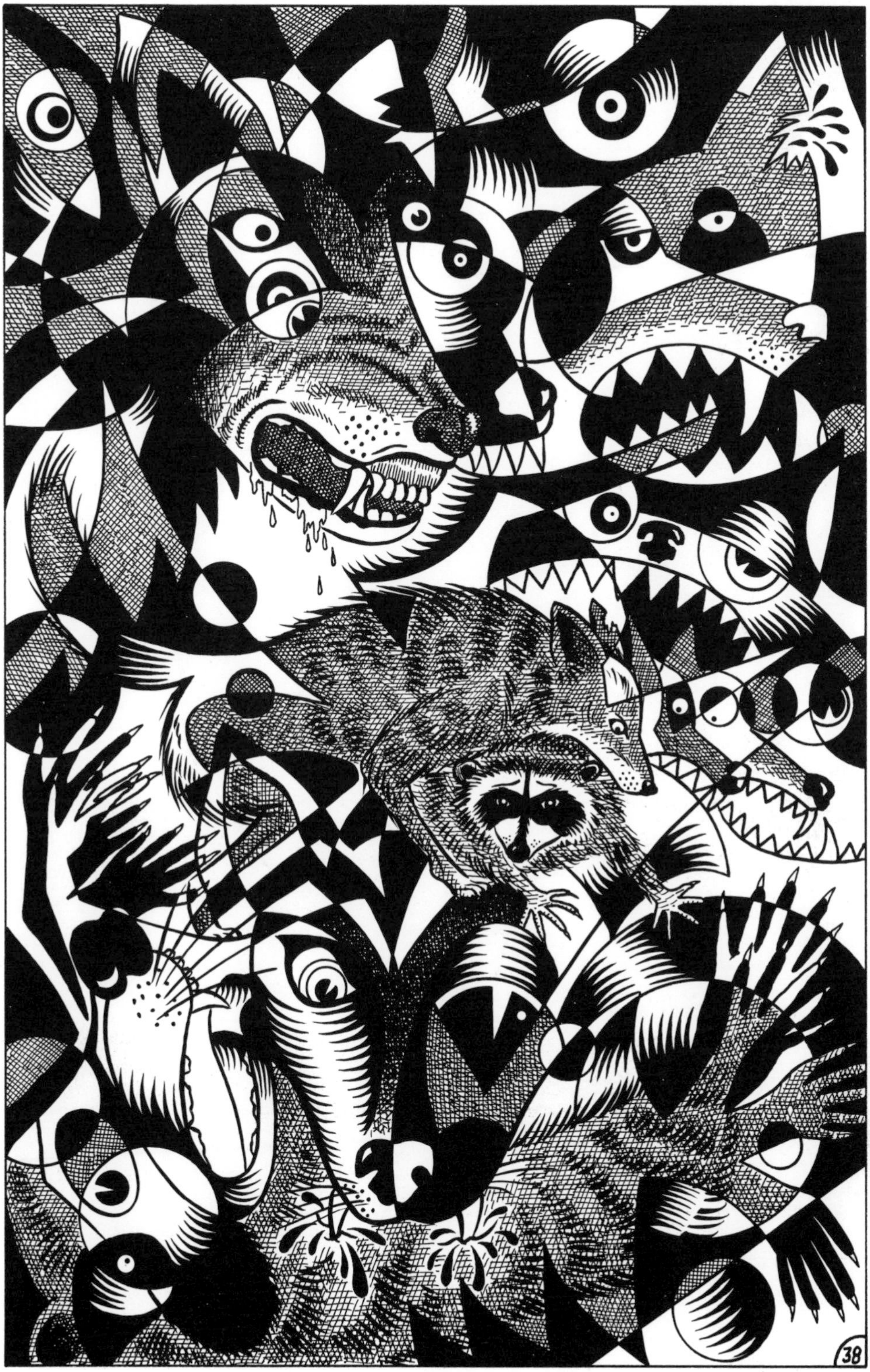

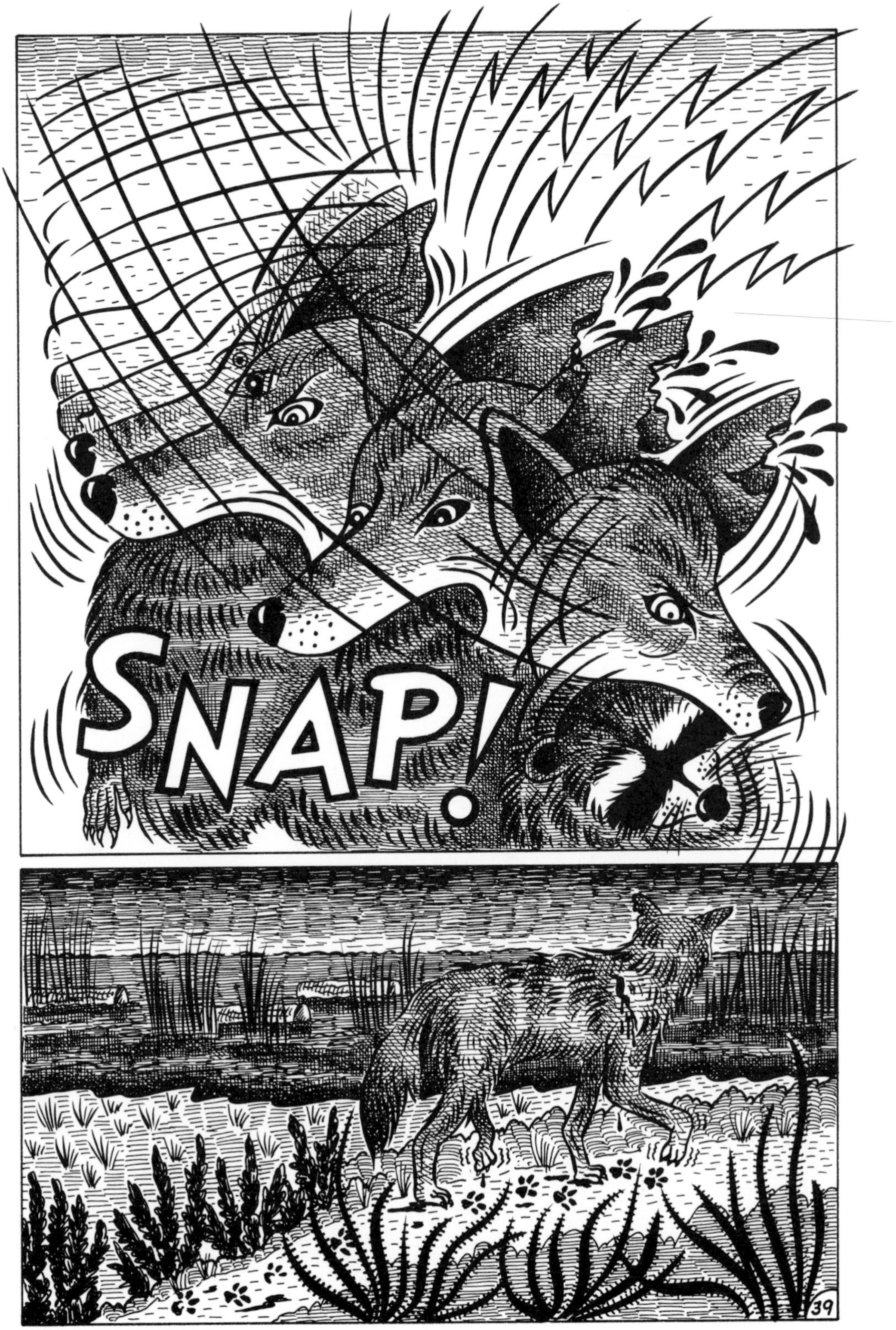
SNAP!

5

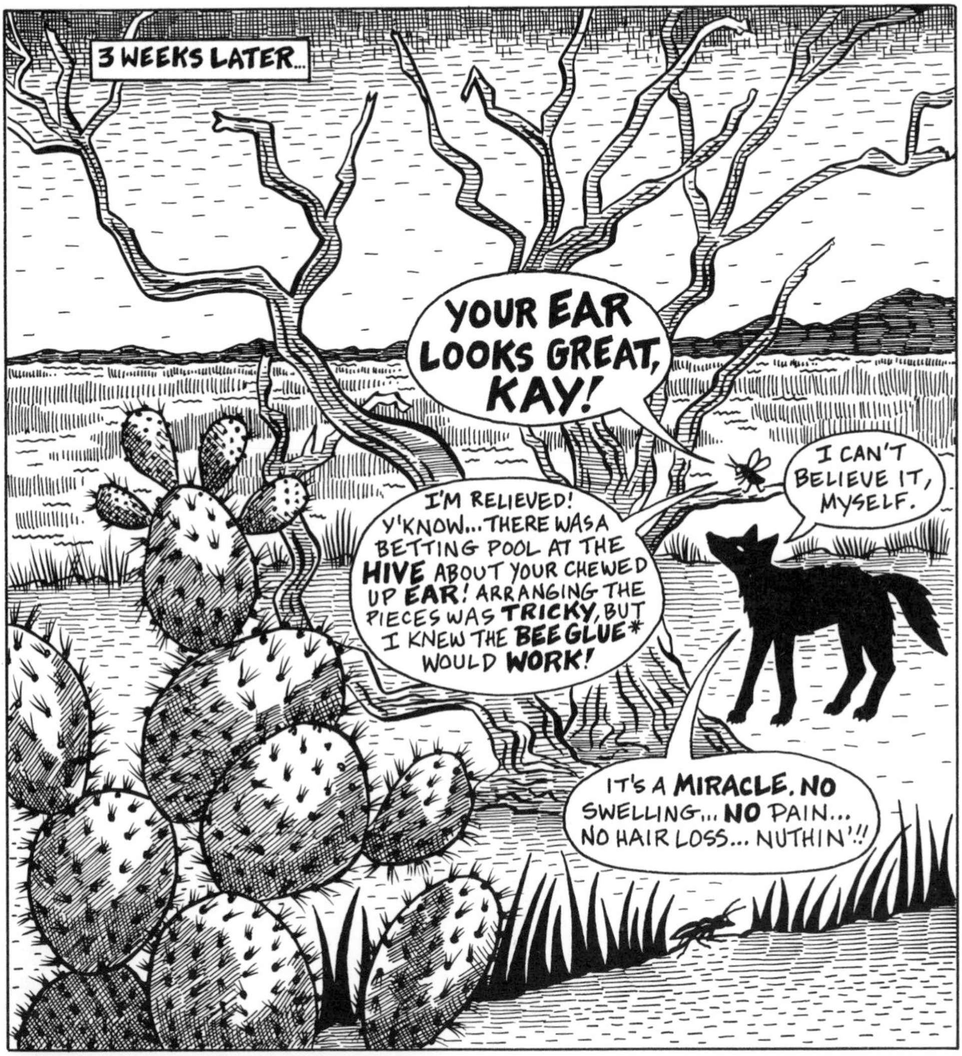

3 WEEKS LATER...
YOUR EAR LOOKS GREAT, KAY!
I CAN'T BELIEVE IT, MYSELF.
I'M RELIEVED! Y'KNOW... THERE WAS A BETTING POOL AT THE HIVE ABOUT YOUR CHEWED UP EAR! ARRANGING THE PIECES WAS TRICKY, BUT I KNEW THE BEE GLUE* WOULD WORK!
IT'S A MIRACLE. NO SWELLING... NO PAIN... NO HAIR LOSS... NUTHIN'!!

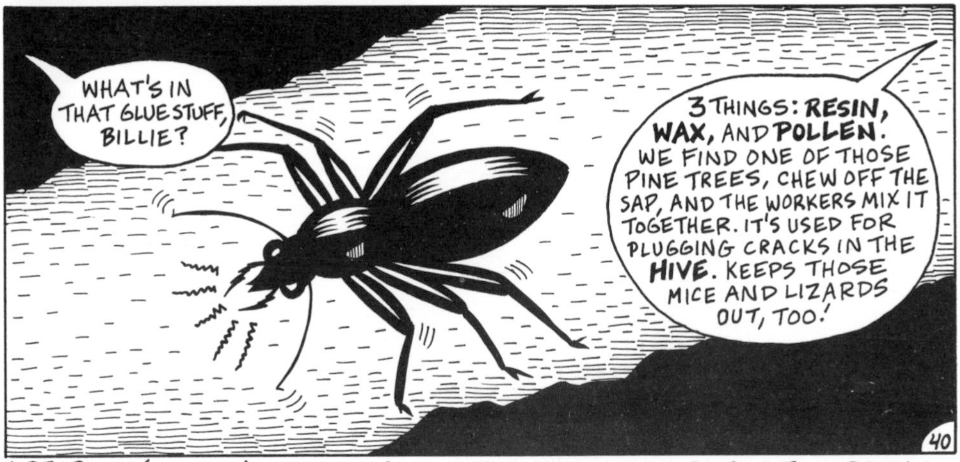

WHAT'S IN THAT GLUE STUFF, BILLIE?
3 THINGS: RESIN, WAX, AND POLLEN. WE FIND ONE OF THOSE PINE TREES, CHEW OFF THE SAP, AND THE WORKERS MIX IT TOGETHER. IT'S USED FOR PLUGGING CRACKS IN THE HIVE. KEEPS THOSE MICE AND LIZARDS OUT, TOO!

* **PROPOLIS** (BEE GLUE) - MADE BY BEES TO SEAL THE HIVE AND PROTECT FROM PREDATORS AND CONTAMINATION. THE NAME COMES FROM **GREEK** MEANING "DEFENSE OF CITY."

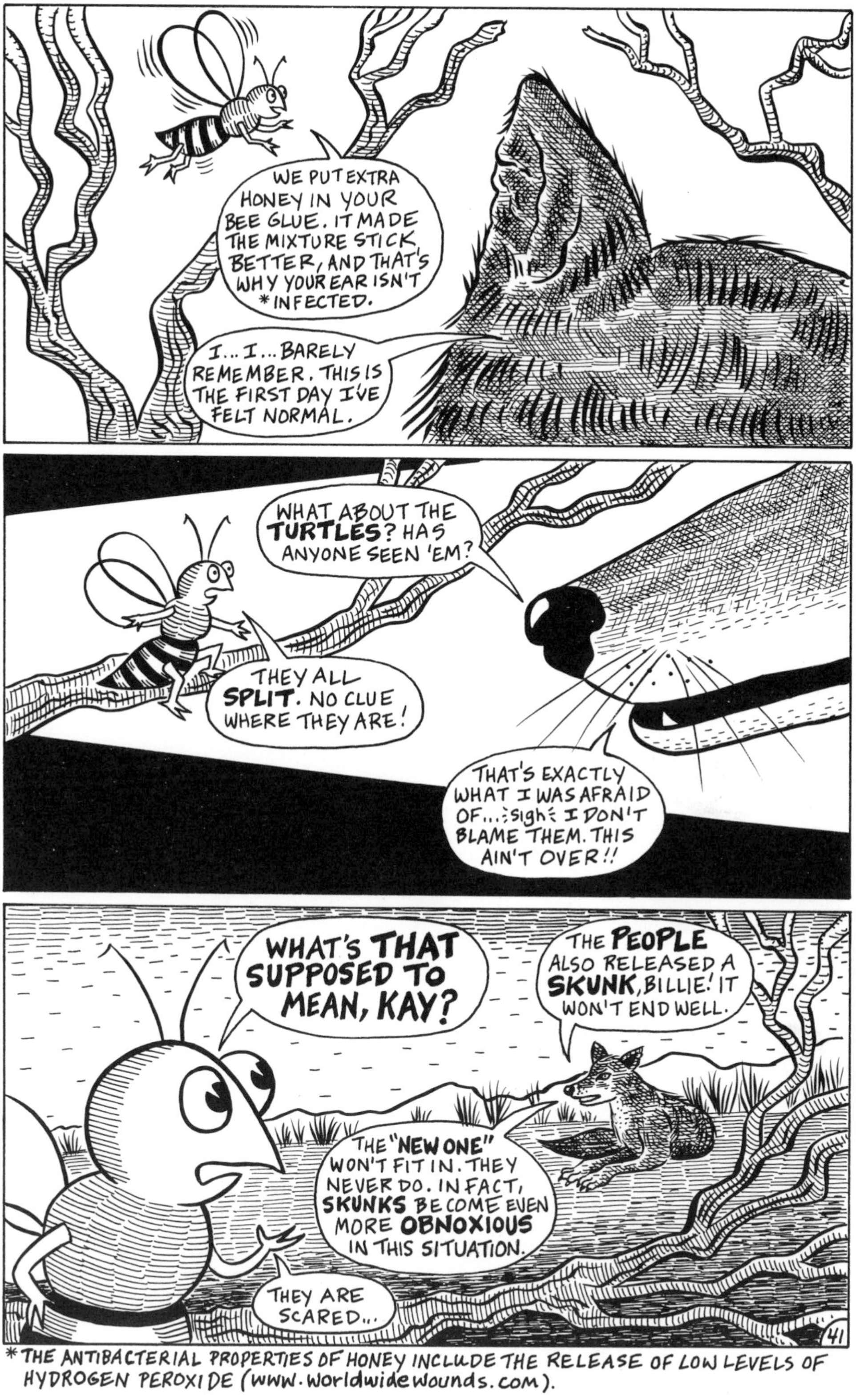
WE PUT EXTRA HONEY IN YOUR BEE GLUE. IT MADE THE MIXTURE STICK BETTER, AND THAT'S WHY YOUR EAR ISN'T *INFECTED.
I... I... BARELY REMEMBER. THIS IS THE FIRST DAY I'VE FELT NORMAL.
WHAT ABOUT THE **TURTLES**? HAS ANYONE SEEN 'EM?
THEY ALL **SPLIT**. NO CLUE WHERE THEY ARE!
THAT'S EXACTLY WHAT I WAS AFRAID OF... :sigh: I DON'T BLAME THEM. THIS AIN'T OVER!!
WHAT'S **THAT** SUPPOSED TO MEAN, KAY?
THE **PEOPLE** ALSO RELEASED A **SKUNK**, BILLIE! IT WON'T END WELL.
THE "**NEW ONE**" WON'T FIT IN. THEY NEVER DO. IN FACT, **SKUNKS** BECOME EVEN MORE **OBNOXIOUS** IN THIS SITUATION.
THEY ARE SCARED...

* THE ANTIBACTERIAL PROPERTIES OF HONEY INCLUDE THE RELEASE OF LOW LEVELS OF HYDROGEN PEROXIDE (www.worldwidewounds.com).

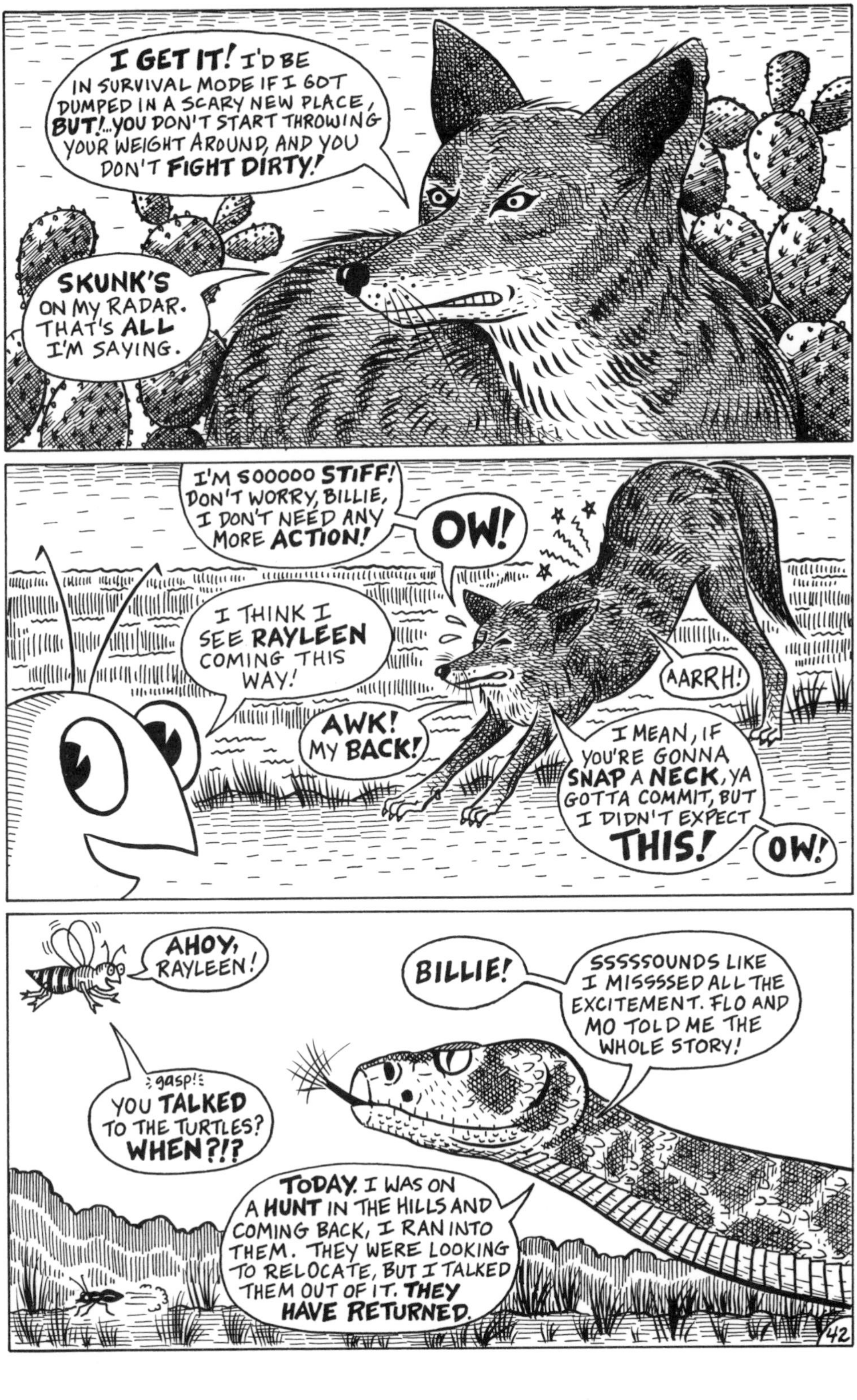
I GET IT! I'D BE IN SURVIVAL MODE IF I GOT DUMPED IN A SCARY NEW PLACE, BUT!...YOU DON'T START THROWING YOUR WEIGHT AROUND, AND YOU DON'T FIGHT DIRTY!
SKUNK'S ON MY RADAR. THAT'S ALL I'M SAYING.
I'M SOOOOO STIFF! DON'T WORRY, BILLIE, I DON'T NEED ANY MORE ACTION!
OW!
I THINK I SEE RAYLEEN COMING THIS WAY!
AARRH!
AWK! MY BACK!
I MEAN, IF YOU'RE GONNA SNAP A NECK, YA GOTTA COMMIT, BUT I DIDN'T EXPECT THIS!
OW!
AHOY, RAYLEEN!
BILLIE!
SSSSSOUNDS LIKE I MISSSSED ALL THE EXCITEMENT. FLO AND MO TOLD ME THE WHOLE STORY!
gasp! YOU TALKED TO THE TURTLES? WHEN?!?
TODAY. I WAS ON A HUNT IN THE HILLS AND COMING BACK, I RAN INTO THEM. THEY WERE LOOKING TO RELOCATE, BUT I TALKED THEM OUT OF IT. THEY HAVE RETURNED.

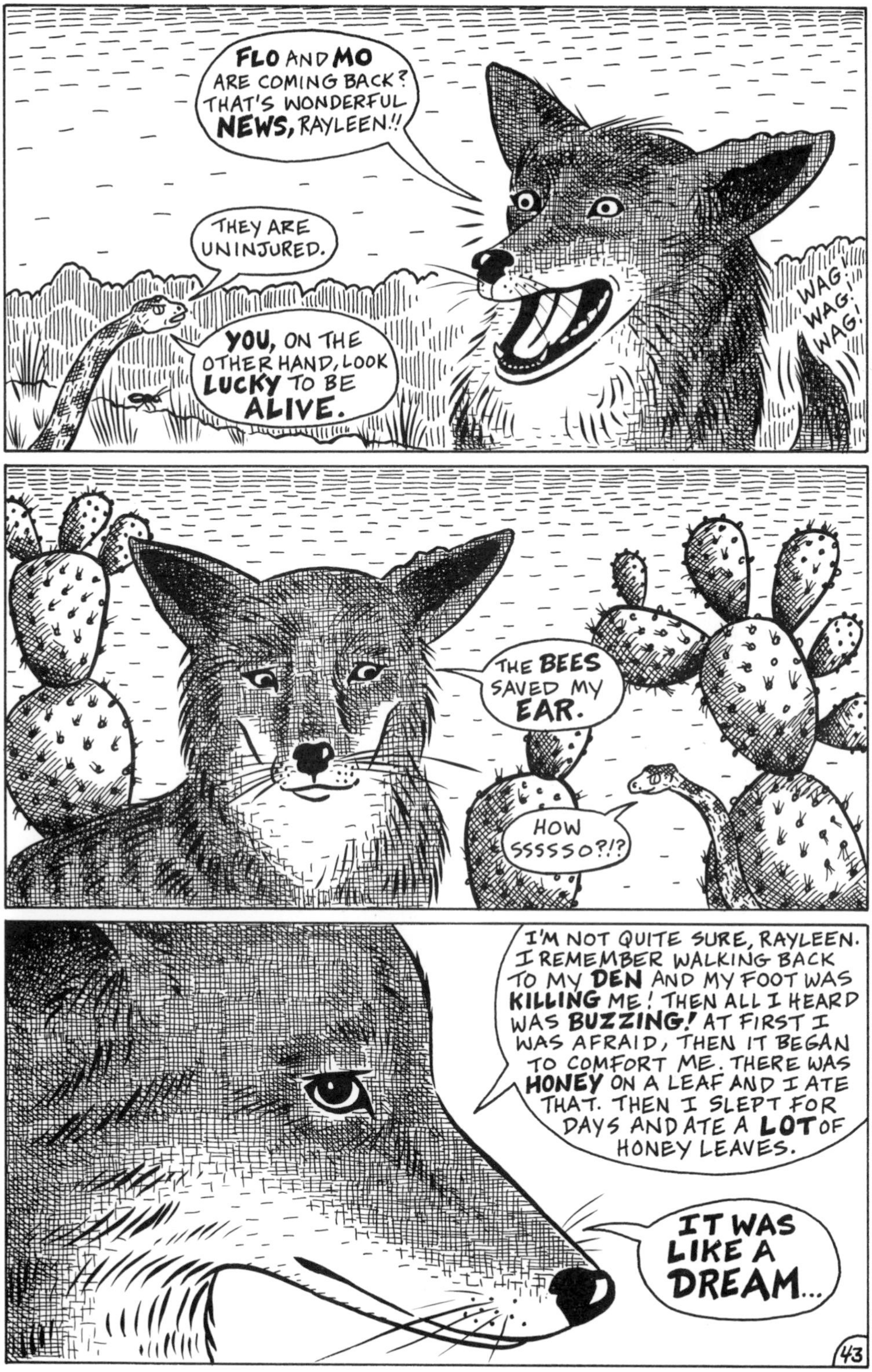
FLO AND MO ARE COMING BACK? THAT'S WONDERFUL NEWS, RAYLEEN!!
THEY ARE UNINJURED.
YOU, ON THE OTHER HAND, LOOK LUCKY TO BE ALIVE.
WAG! WAG! WAG!
THE BEES SAVED MY EAR.
HOW SSSSSO?!?
I'M NOT QUITE SURE, RAYLEEN. I REMEMBER WALKING BACK TO MY DEN AND MY FOOT WAS KILLING ME! THEN ALL I HEARD WAS BUZZING! AT FIRST I WAS AFRAID, THEN IT BEGAN TO COMFORT ME. THERE WAS HONEY ON A LEAF AND I ATE THAT. THEN I SLEPT FOR DAYS AND ATE A LOT OF HONEY LEAVES.
IT WAS LIKE A DREAM...

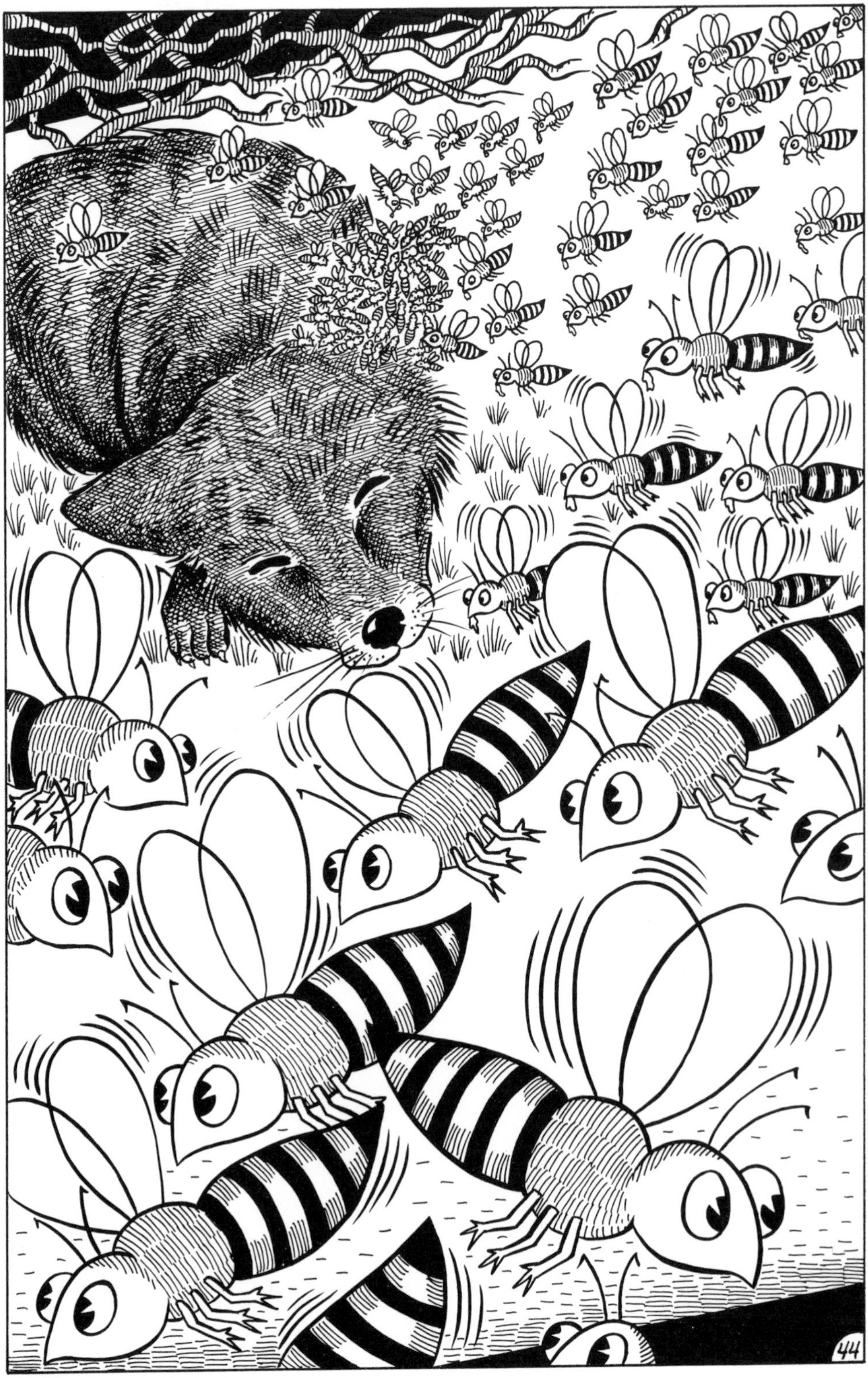
44

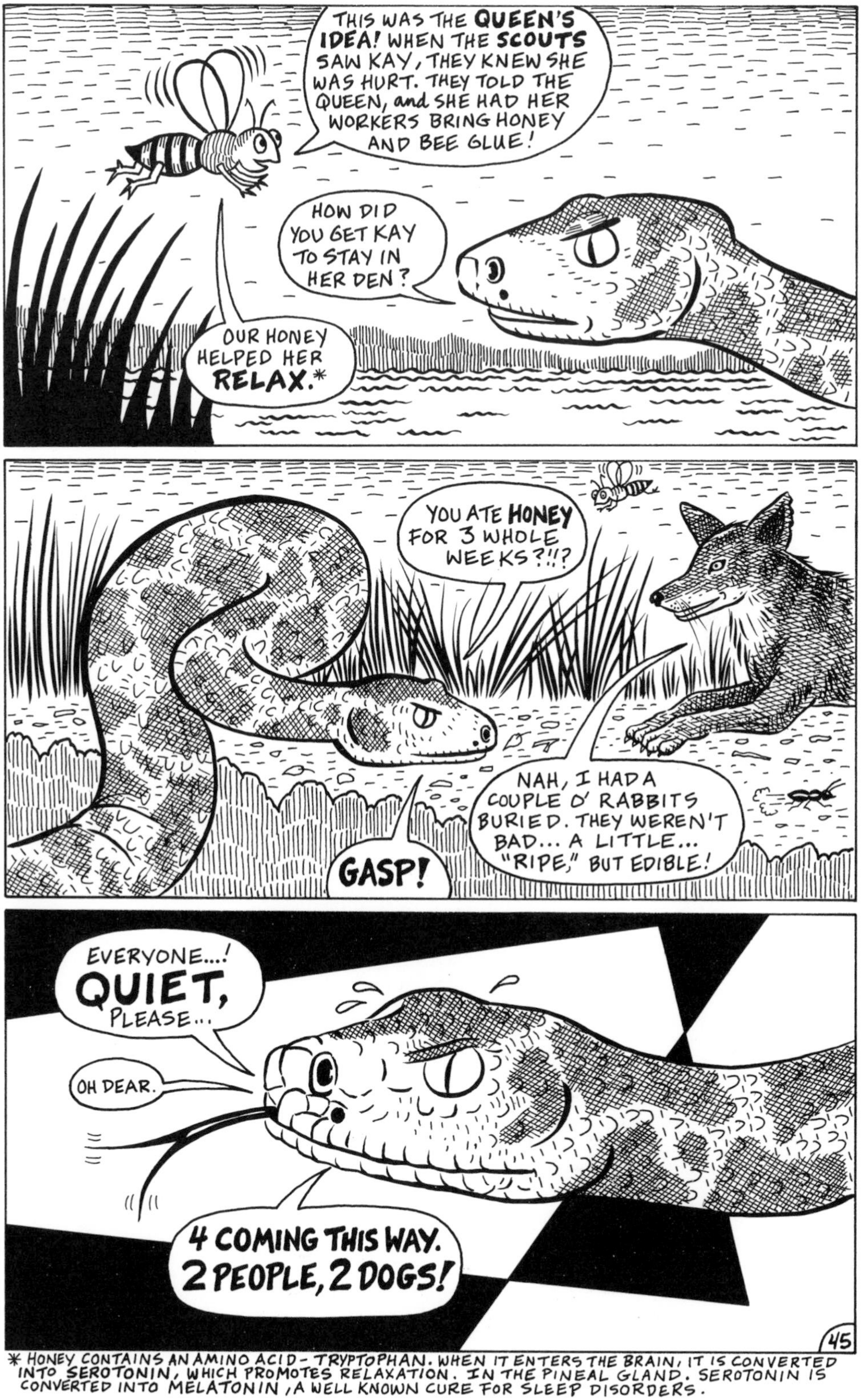
THIS WAS THE QUEEN'S IDEA! WHEN THE SCOUTS SAW KAY, THEY KNEW SHE WAS HURT. THEY TOLD THE QUEEN, and SHE HAD HER WORKERS BRING HONEY AND BEE GLUE!
HOW DID YOU GET KAY TO STAY IN HER DEN?
OUR HONEY HELPED HER RELAX.*
YOU ATE HONEY FOR 3 WHOLE WEEKS?!!?
NAH, I HAD A COUPLE O' RABBITS BURIED. THEY WEREN'T BAD... A LITTLE... "RIPE," BUT EDIBLE!
GASP!
EVERYONE...! QUIET, PLEASE...
OH DEAR.
4 COMING THIS WAY. 2 PEOPLE, 2 DOGS!

* HONEY CONTAINS AN AMINO ACID - TRYPTOPHAN. WHEN IT ENTERS THE BRAIN, IT IS CONVERTED INTO SEROTONIN, WHICH PROMOTES RELAXATION. IN THE PINEAL GLAND, SEROTONIN IS CONVERTED INTO MELATONIN, A WELL KNOWN CURE FOR SLEEP DISORDERS.

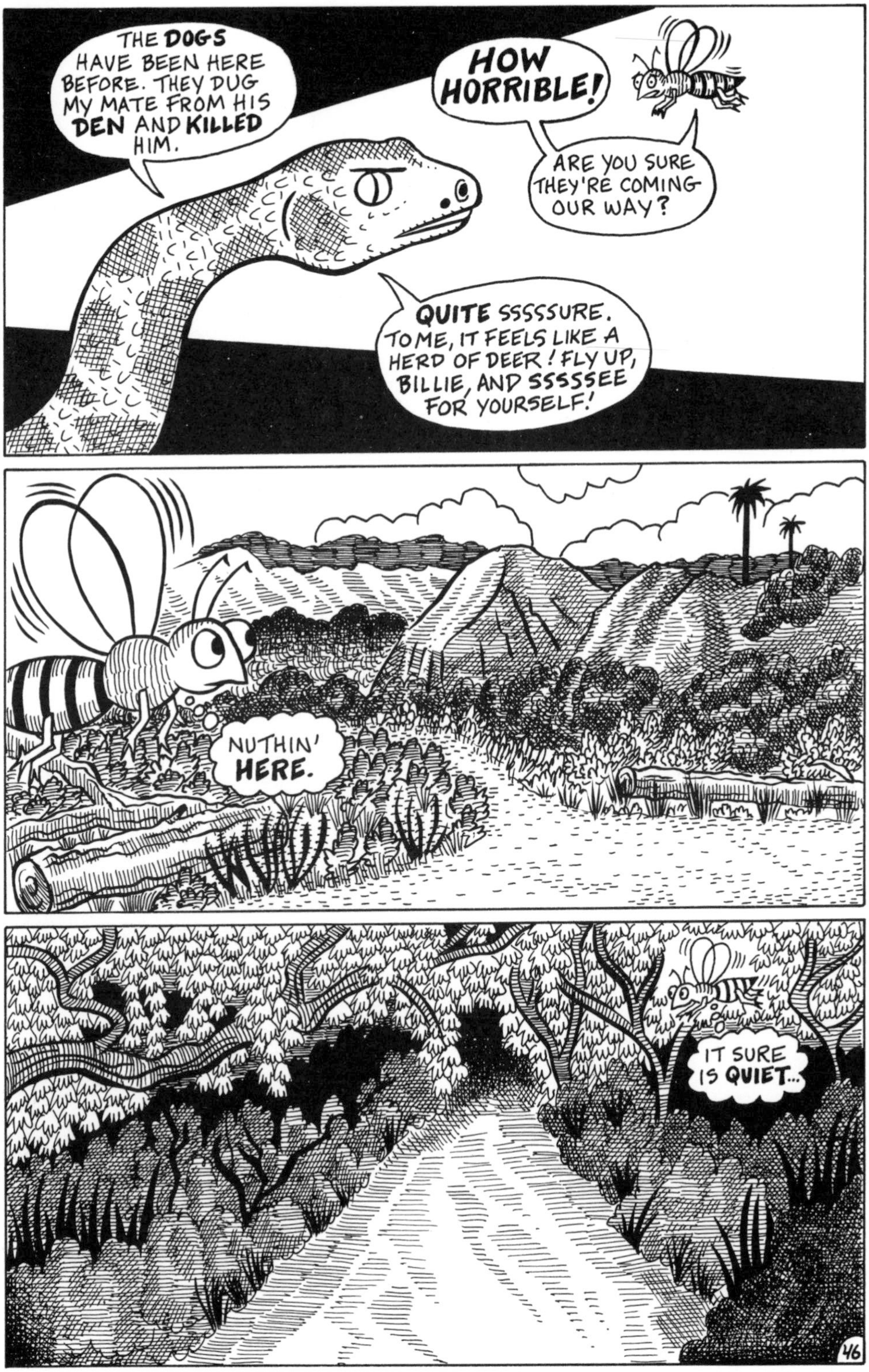

THE DOGS HAVE BEEN HERE BEFORE. THEY DUG MY MATE FROM HIS DEN AND KILLED HIM.
HOW HORRIBLE!
ARE YOU SURE THEY'RE COMING OUR WAY?
QUITE SSSSSURE. TO ME, IT FEELS LIKE A HERD OF DEER! FLY UP, BILLIE, AND SSSSSEE FOR YOURSELF!
NUTHIN' HERE.
IT SURE IS QUIET...
46

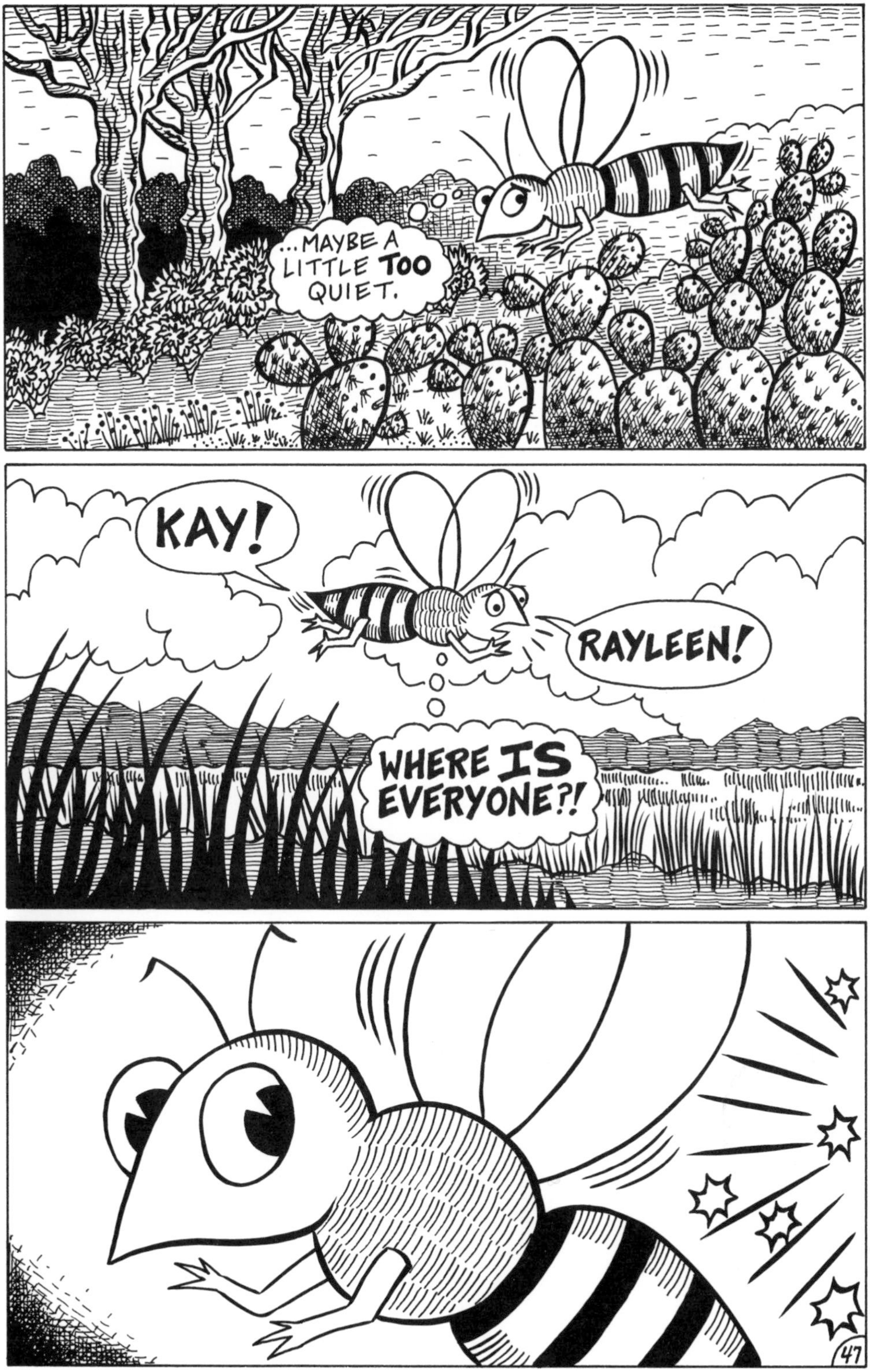
...MAYBE A LITTLE TOO QUIET.
KAY!
RAYLEEN!
WHERE IS EVERYONE?!

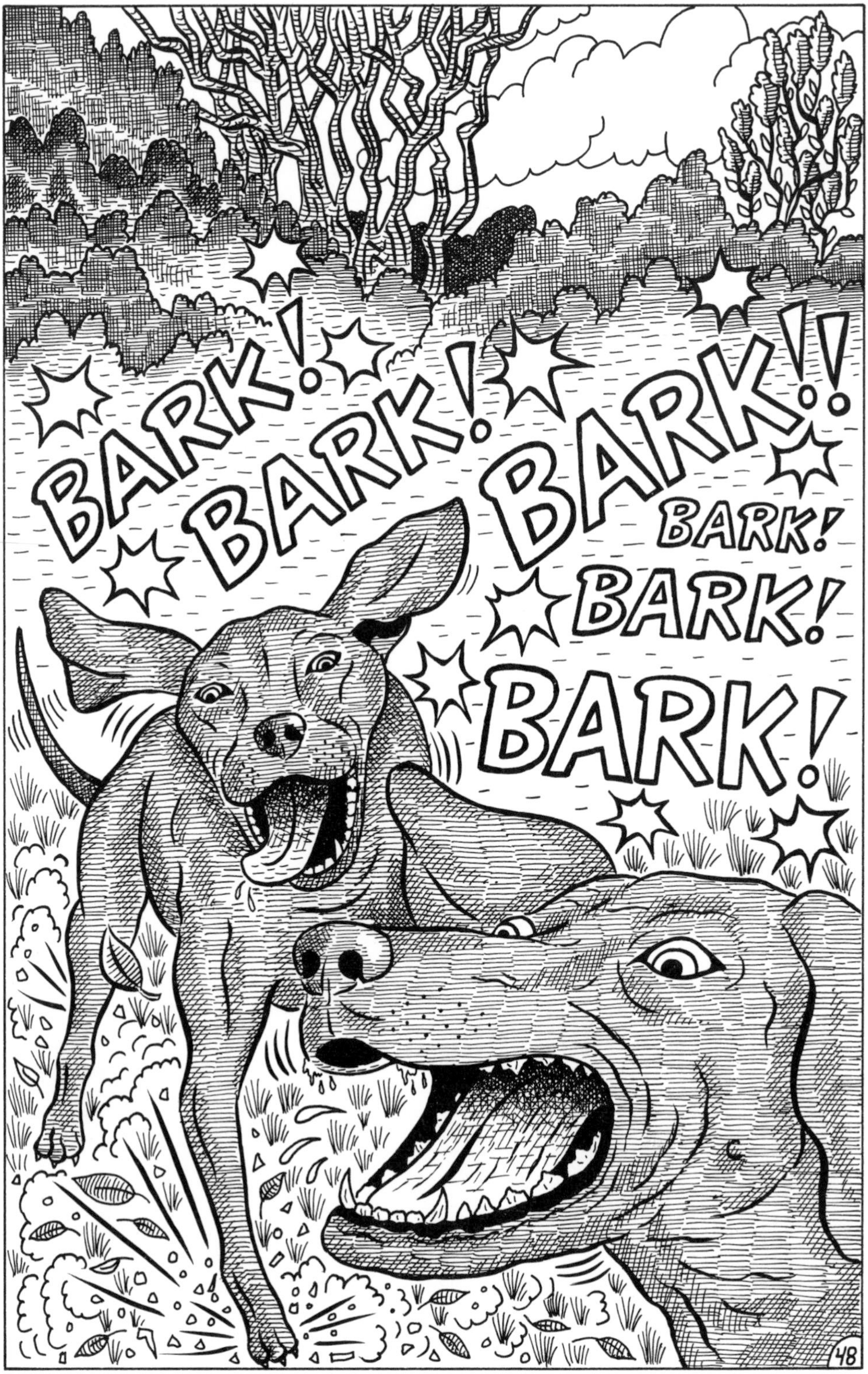
BARK!
BARK!
BARK!!
BARK!
BARK!
BARK!

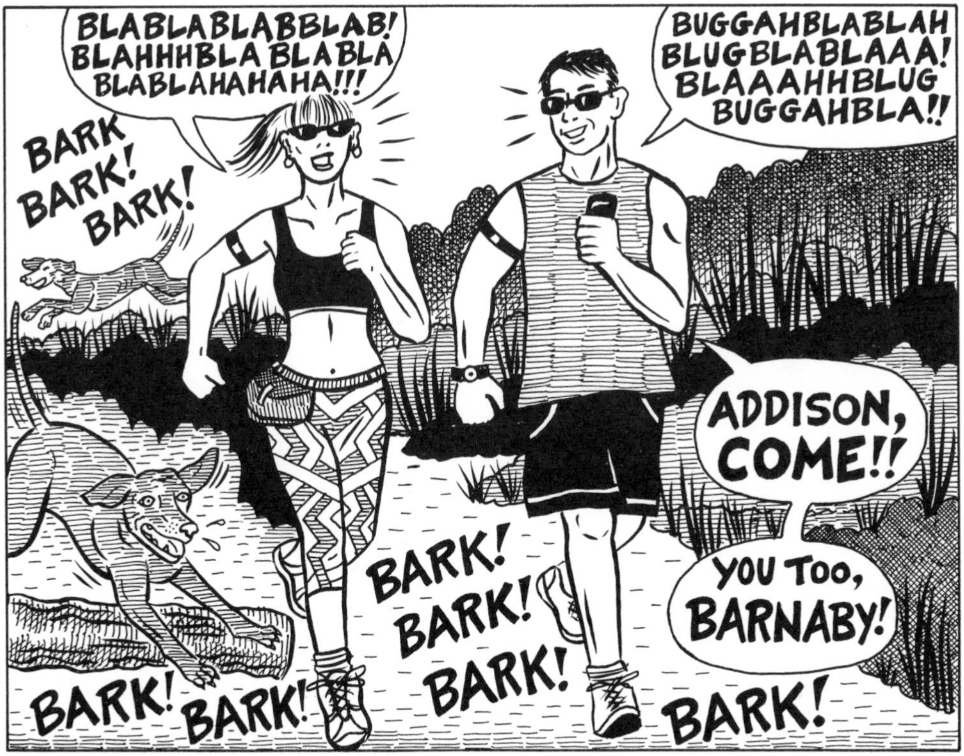
BLABLABLABBLAB! BLAHHHBLA BLABLA BLABLAHAHAHA!!!
BUGGAHBLABLAH BLUGBLABLAAA! BLAAAHHBLUG BUGGAHBLA!!
BARK BARK! BARK!
ADDISON, COME!!
YOU TOO, BARNABY!
BARK! BARK! BARK!
BARK! BARK!
BARK!
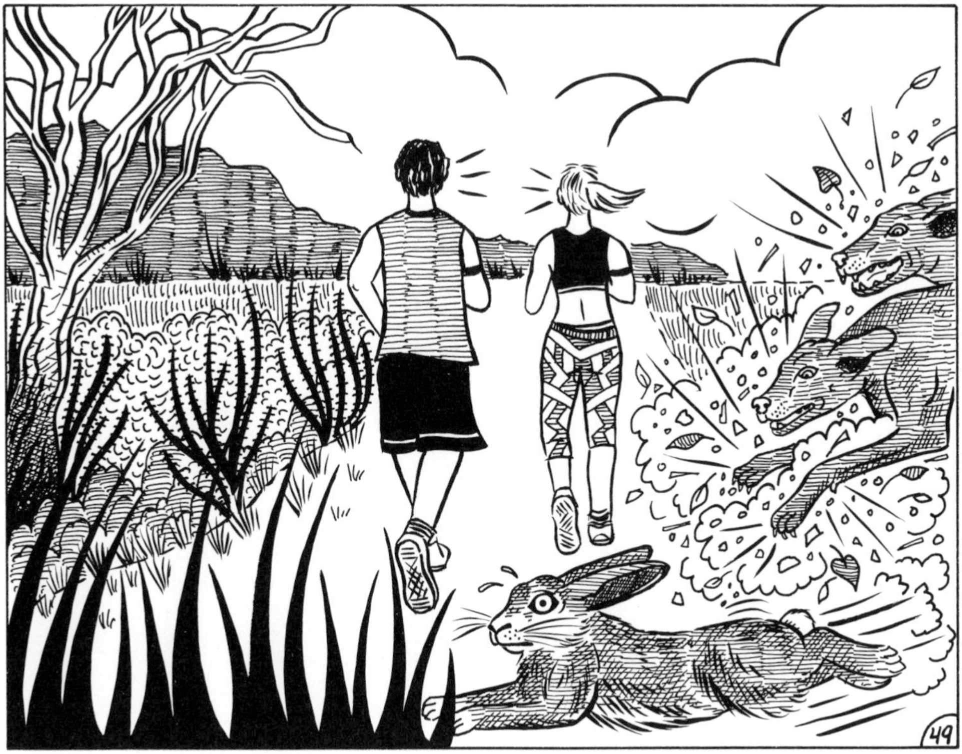

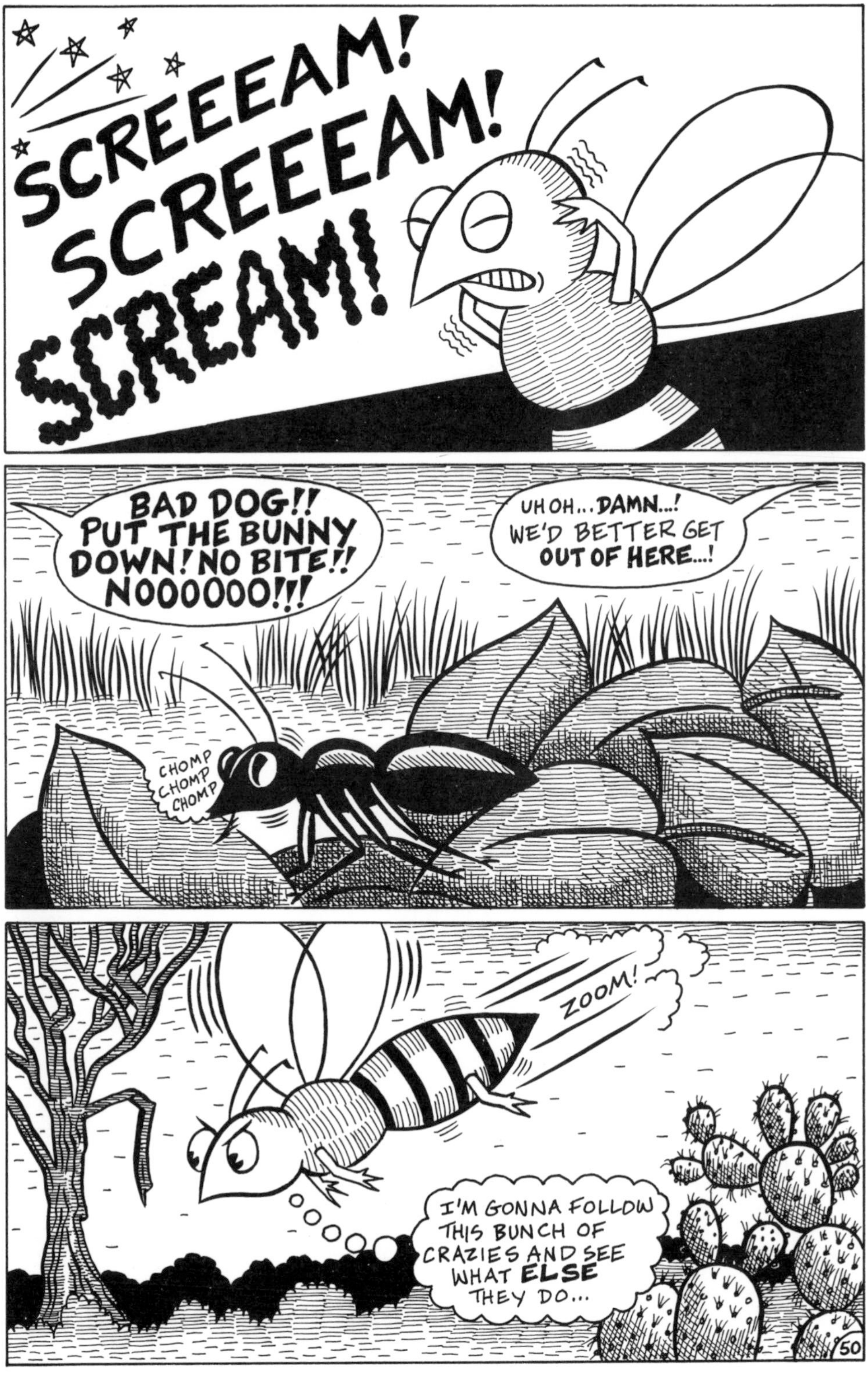
SCREEEAM!
SCREEEAM!
SCREAM!
BAD DOG!! PUT THE BUNNY DOWN! NO BITE!! NOOOOOO!!!
UH OH... DAMN...! WE'D BETTER GET OUT OF HERE...!
CHOMP CHOMP CHOMP
ZOOM!
I'M GONNA FOLLOW THIS BUNCH OF CRAZIES AND SEE WHAT ELSE THEY DO...

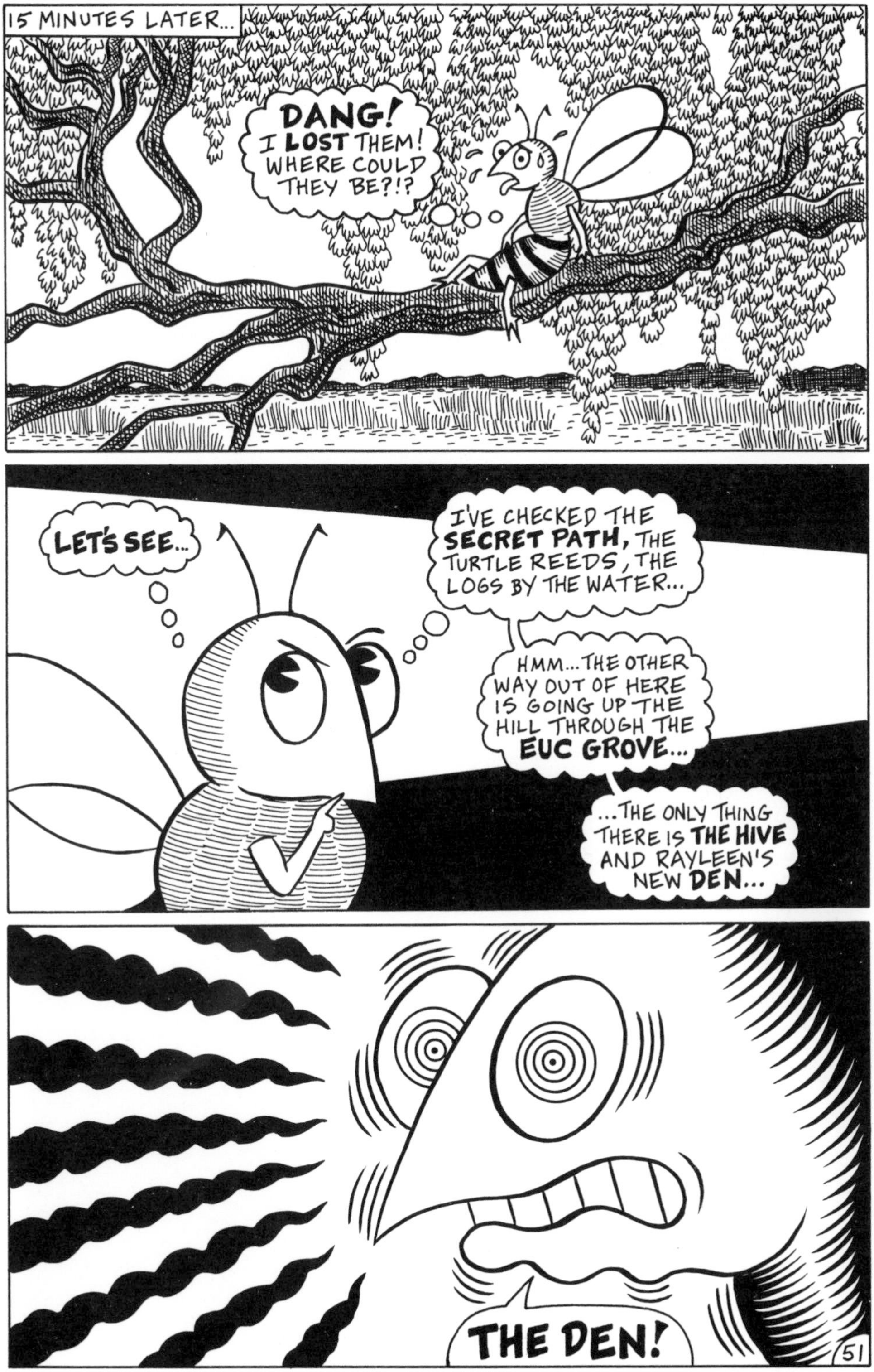
15 MINUTES LATER...
DANG! I LOST THEM! WHERE COULD THEY BE?!?
LET'S SEE...
I'VE CHECKED THE SECRET PATH, THE TURTLE REEDS, THE LOGS BY THE WATER...
HMM... THE OTHER WAY OUT OF HERE IS GOING UP THE HILL THROUGH THE EUC GROVE...
...THE ONLY THING THERE IS THE HIVE AND RAYLEEN'S NEW DEN...
THE DEN!

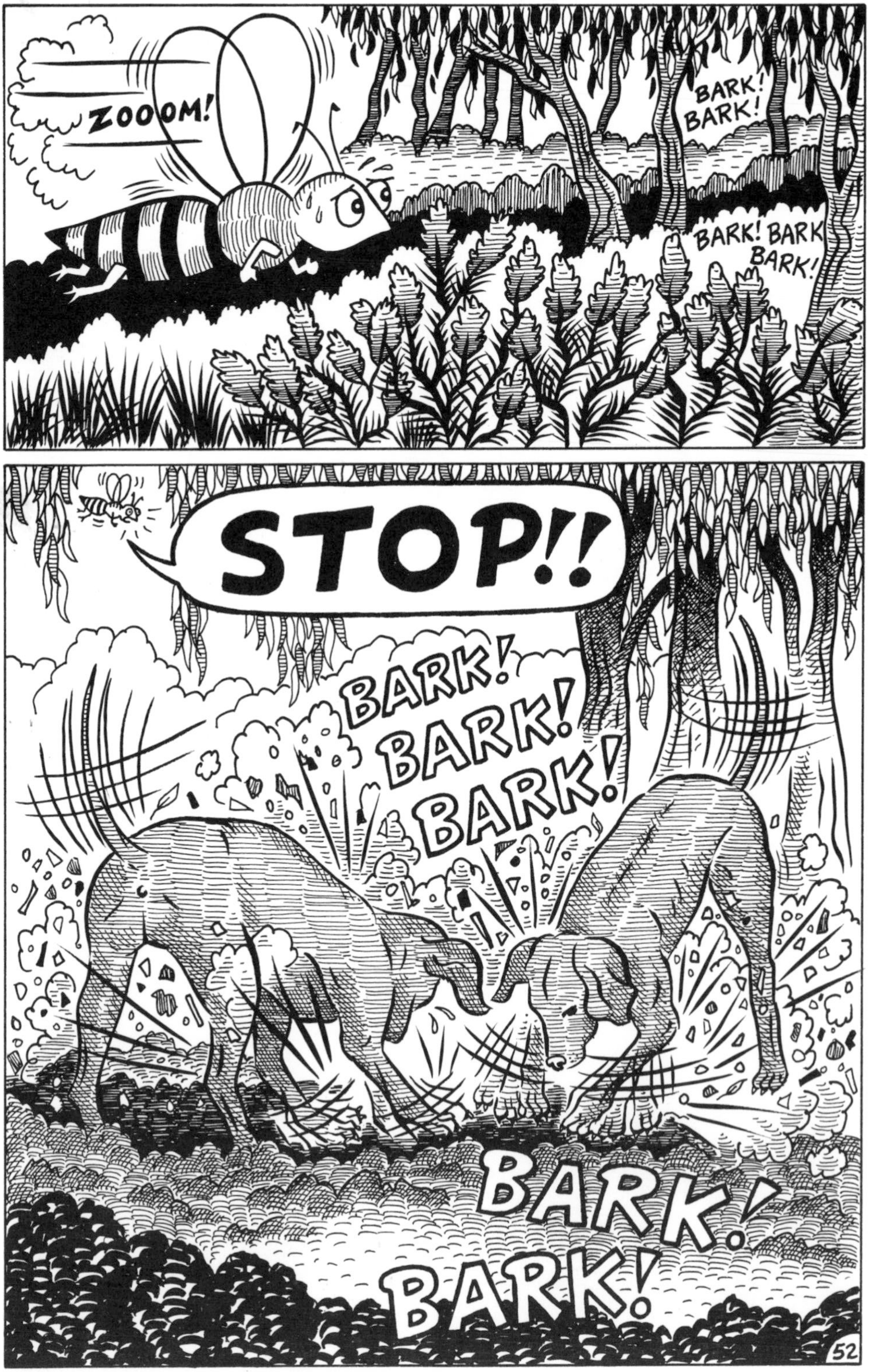
ZOOOM!
BARK! BARK!
BARK! BARK BARK!
STOP!!
BARK! BARK! BARK!
BARK! BARK!

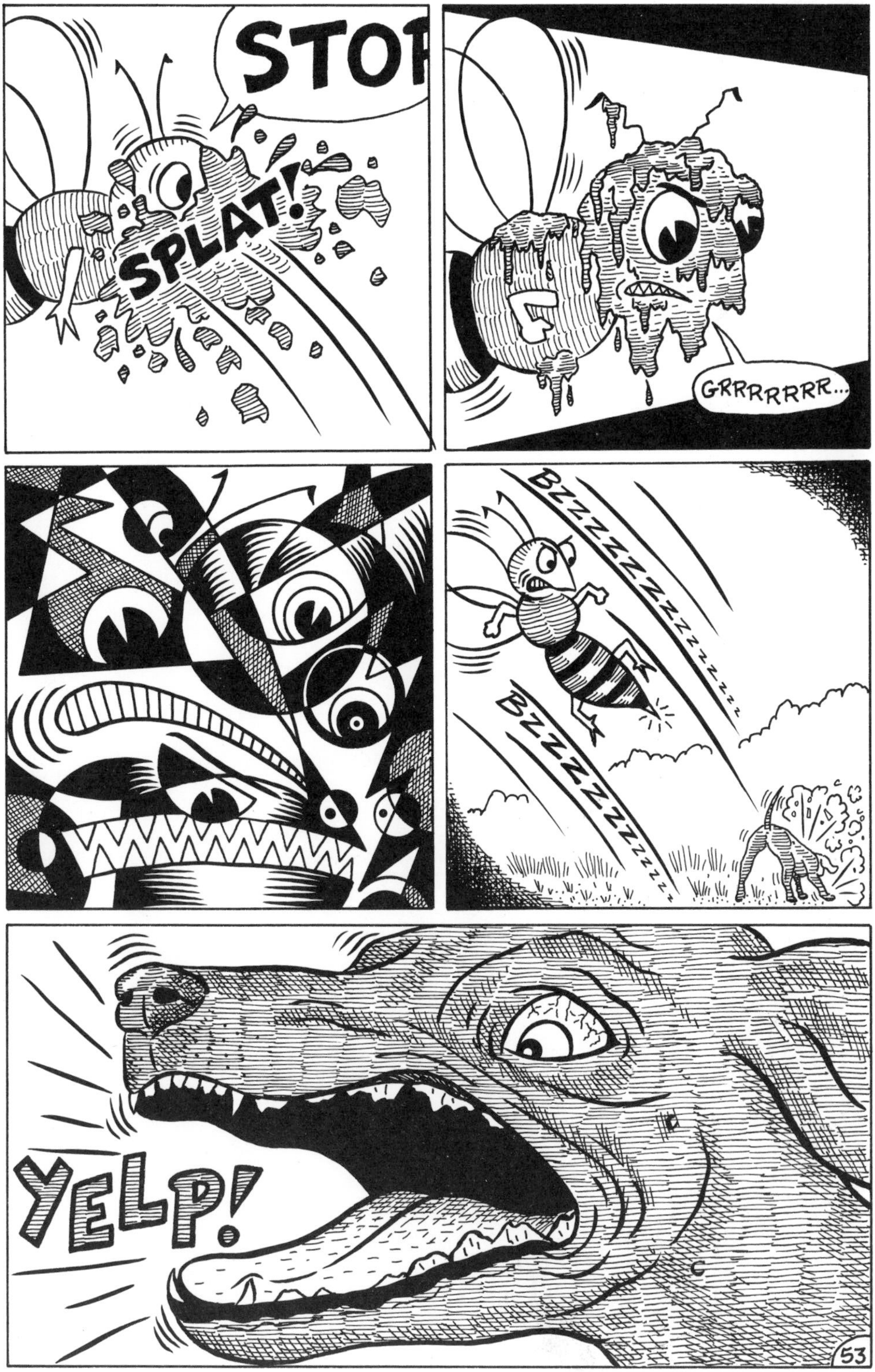
STOP
SPLAT!
GRRRRRRR...
BZZZZZZZZZZZZZZZZZZ
BZZZZZZZZZZZZ
YELP!

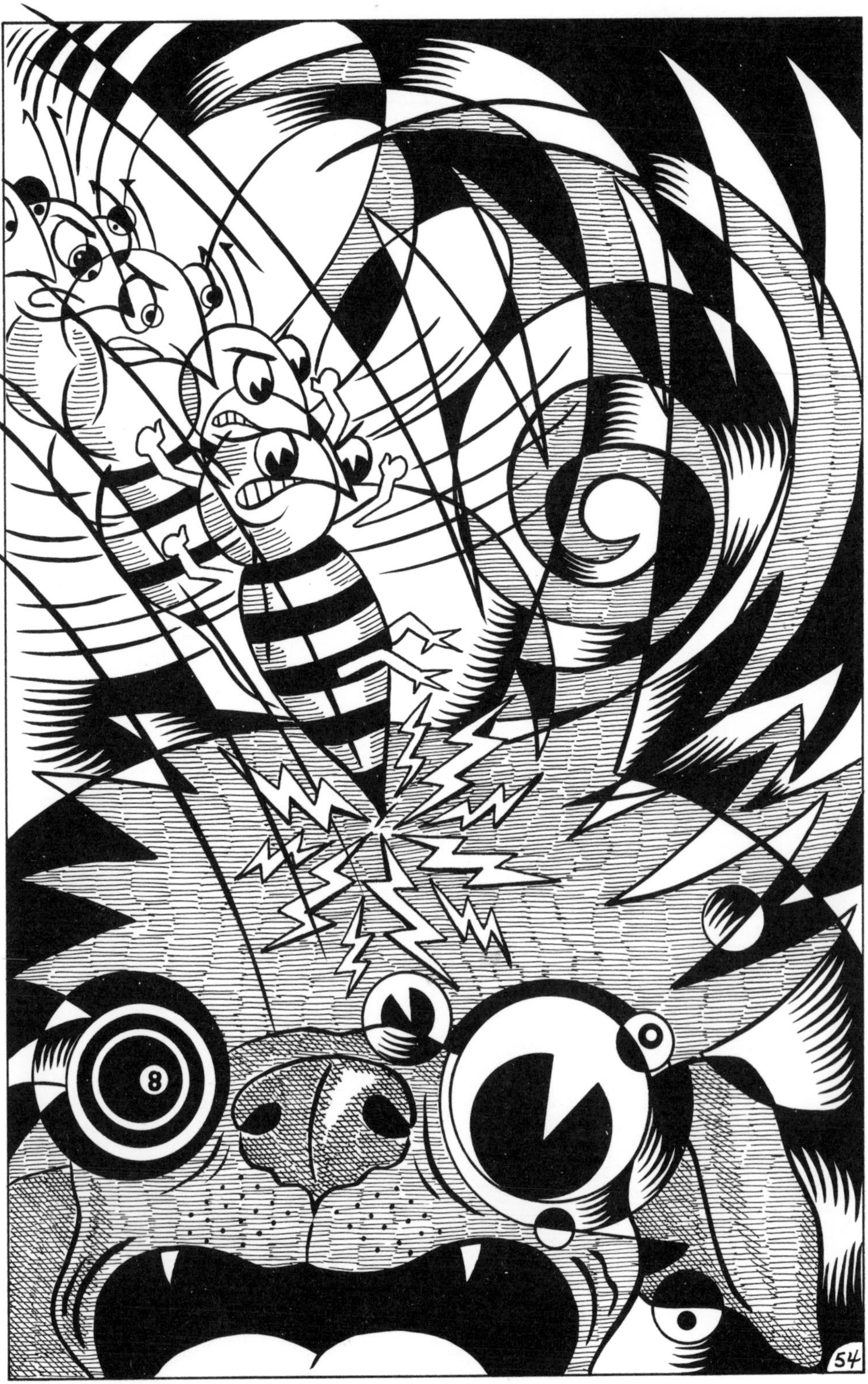
8

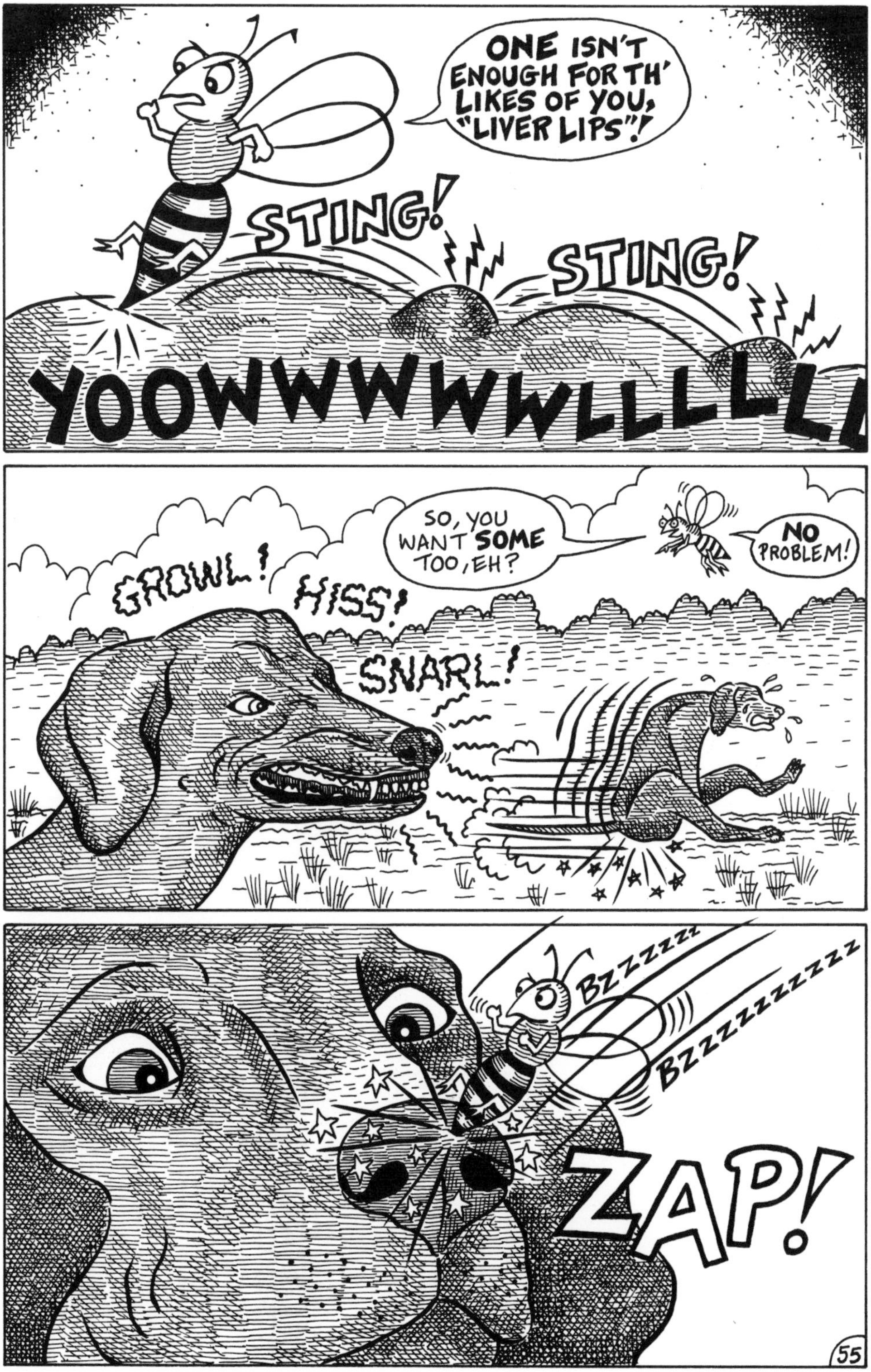
ONE ISN'T ENOUGH FOR TH' LIKES OF YOU, "LIVER LIPS"!
STING!
STING!
YOOWWWWWLLLLL
SO, YOU WANT SOME TOO, EH?
NO PROBLEM!
GROWL!
HISS!
SNARL!
BZZZZZZ
BZZZZZZZZZZ
ZAP!

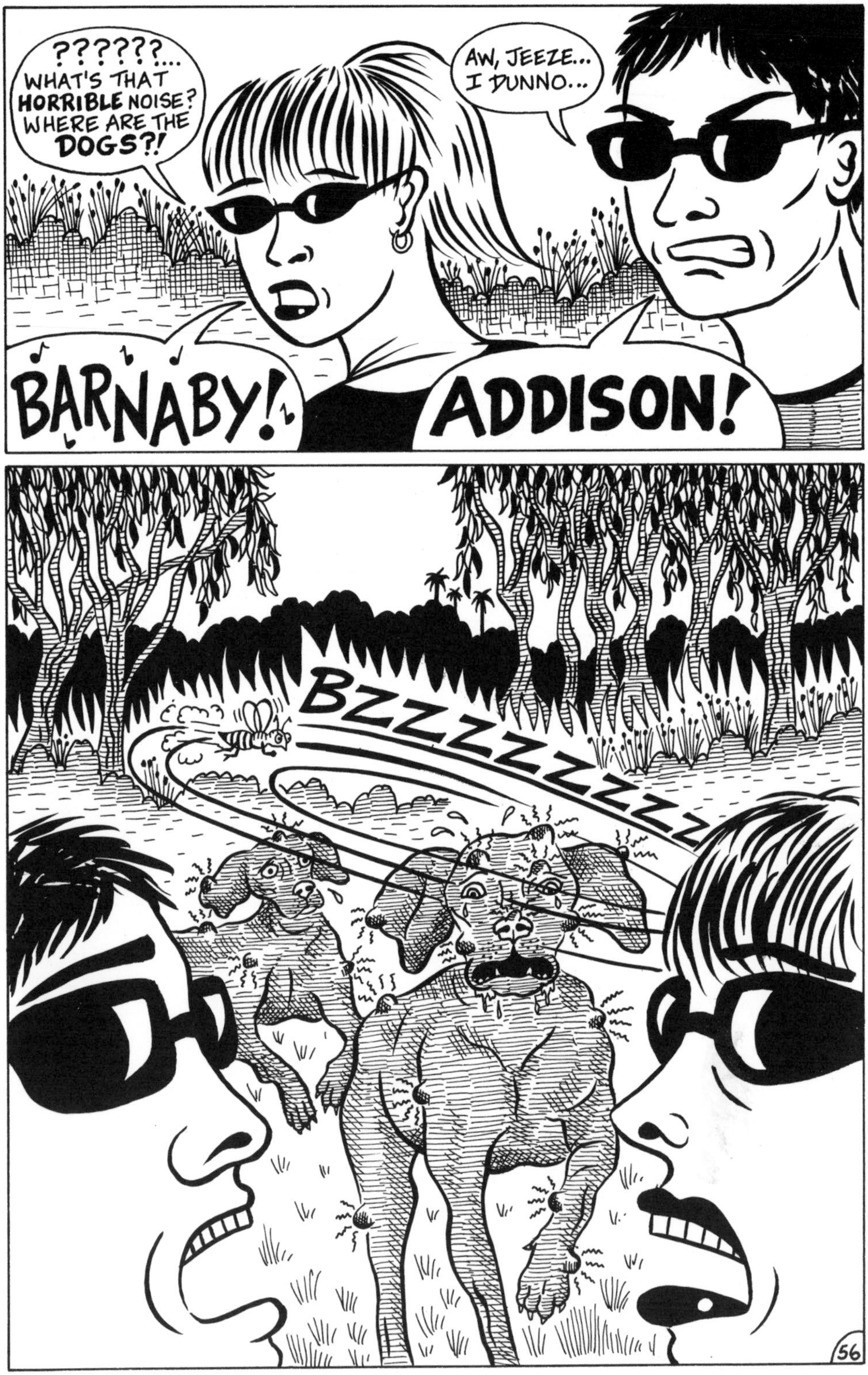
??????... WHAT'S THAT HORRIBLE NOISE? WHERE ARE THE DOGS?!
AW, JEEZE... I DUNNO...
BARNABY!
ADDISON!
BZZZZZZZZZZ

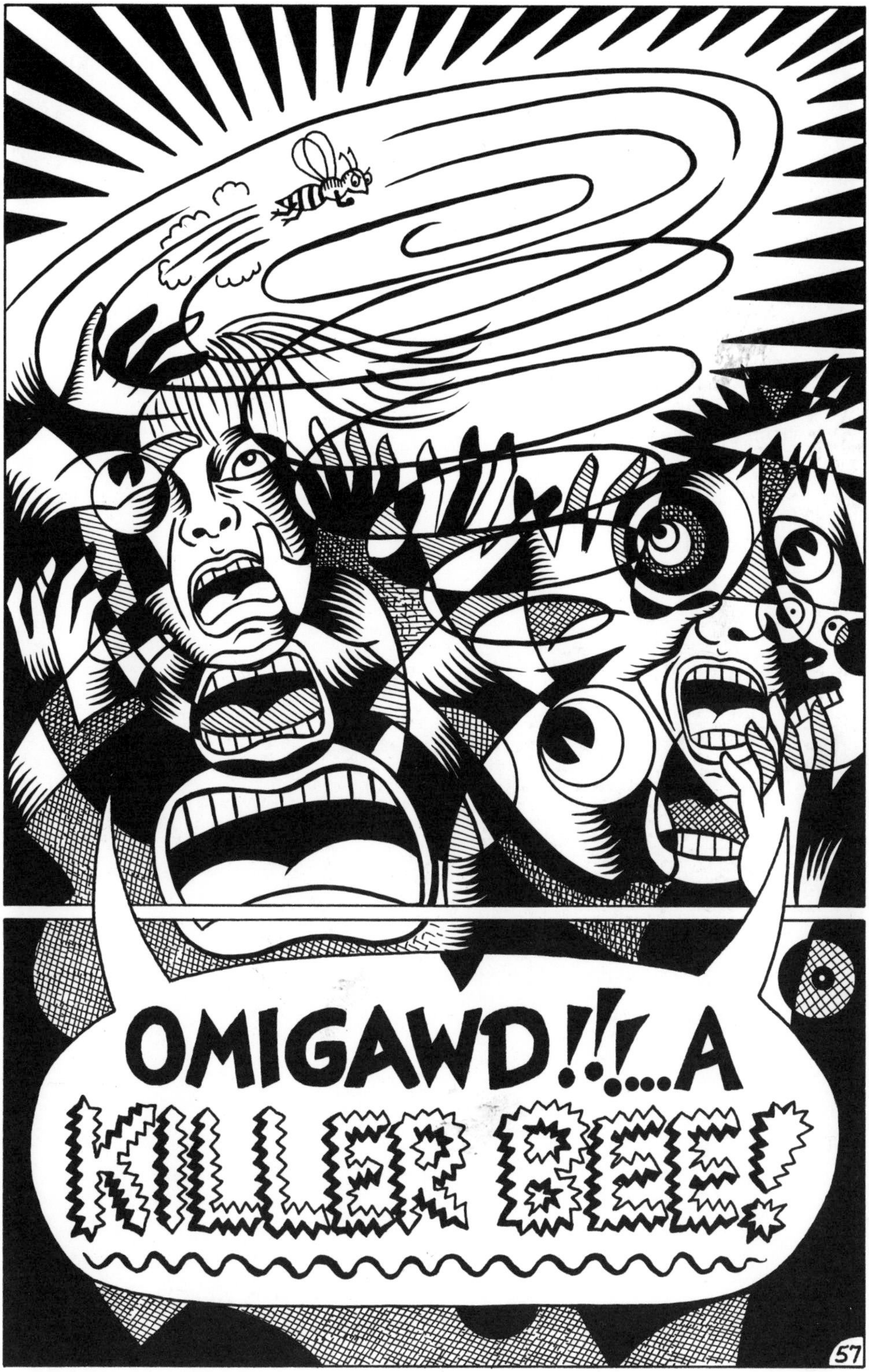
OMIGAWD!!!...A
KILLER BEE!

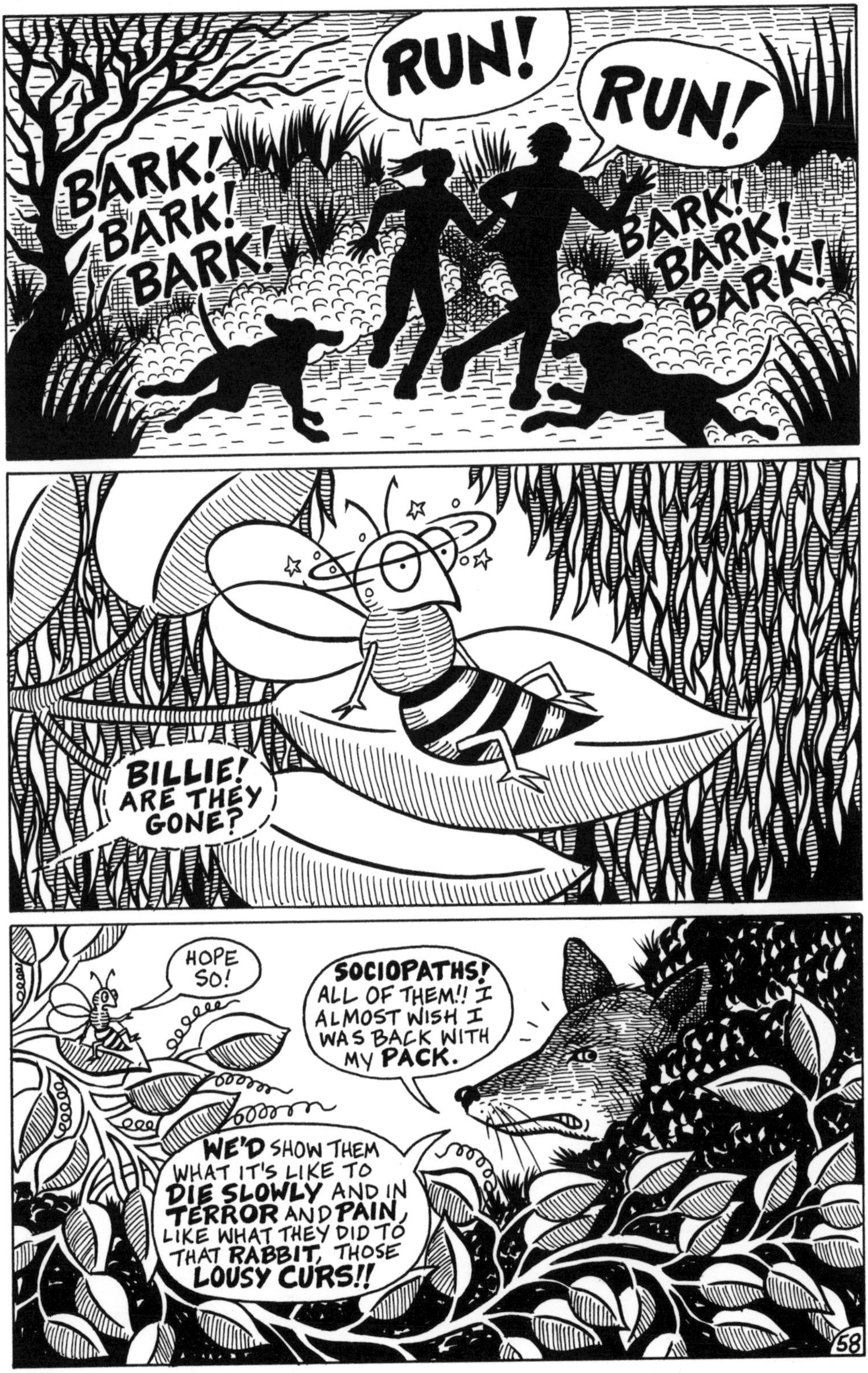
RUN!
RUN!
BARK! BARK! BARK!
BARK! BARK! BARK!
BILLIE! ARE THEY GONE?
HOPE SO!
SOCIOPATHS! ALL OF THEM!! I ALMOST WISH I WAS BACK WITH MY PACK.
WE'D SHOW THEM WHAT IT'S LIKE TO DIE SLOWLY AND IN TERROR AND PAIN, LIKE WHAT THEY DID TO THAT RABBIT, THOSE LOUSY CURS!!
58

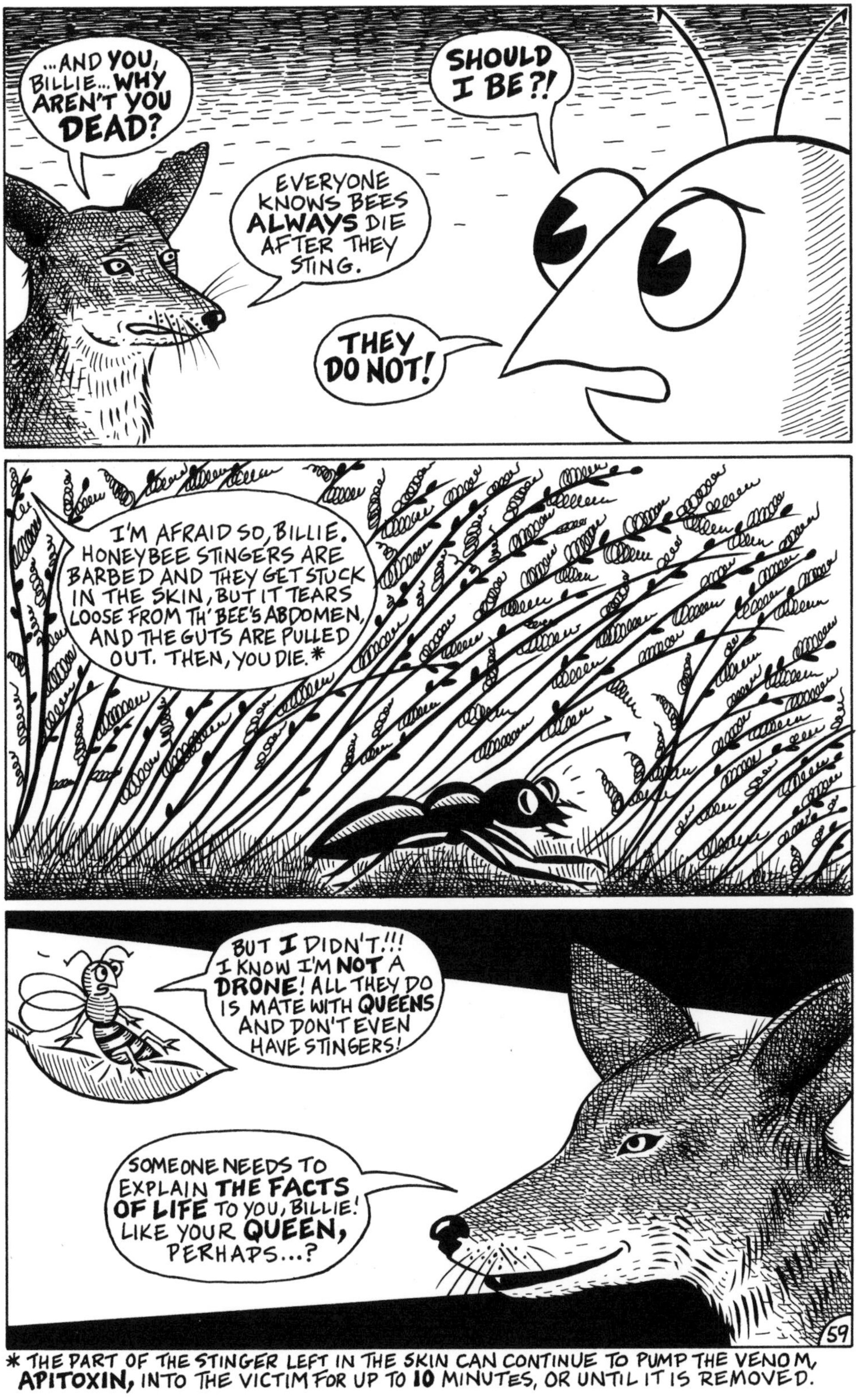
...AND YOU, BILLIE... WHY AREN'T YOU DEAD?
SHOULD I BE?!
EVERYONE KNOWS BEES ALWAYS DIE AFTER THEY STING.
THEY DO NOT!
I'M AFRAID SO, BILLIE. HONEYBEE STINGERS ARE BARBED AND THEY GET STUCK IN THE SKIN, BUT IT TEARS LOOSE FROM TH' BEE'S ABDOMEN, AND THE GUTS ARE PULLED OUT. THEN, YOU DIE.*
BUT I DIDN'T!!! I KNOW I'M NOT A DRONE! ALL THEY DO IS MATE WITH QUEENS AND DON'T EVEN HAVE STINGERS!
SOMEONE NEEDS TO EXPLAIN THE FACTS OF LIFE TO YOU, BILLIE! LIKE YOUR QUEEN, PERHAPS...?

* THE PART OF THE STINGER LEFT IN THE SKIN CAN CONTINUE TO PUMP THE VENOM, **APITOXIN,** INTO THE VICTIM FOR UP TO **10** MINUTES, OR UNTIL IT IS REMOVED.

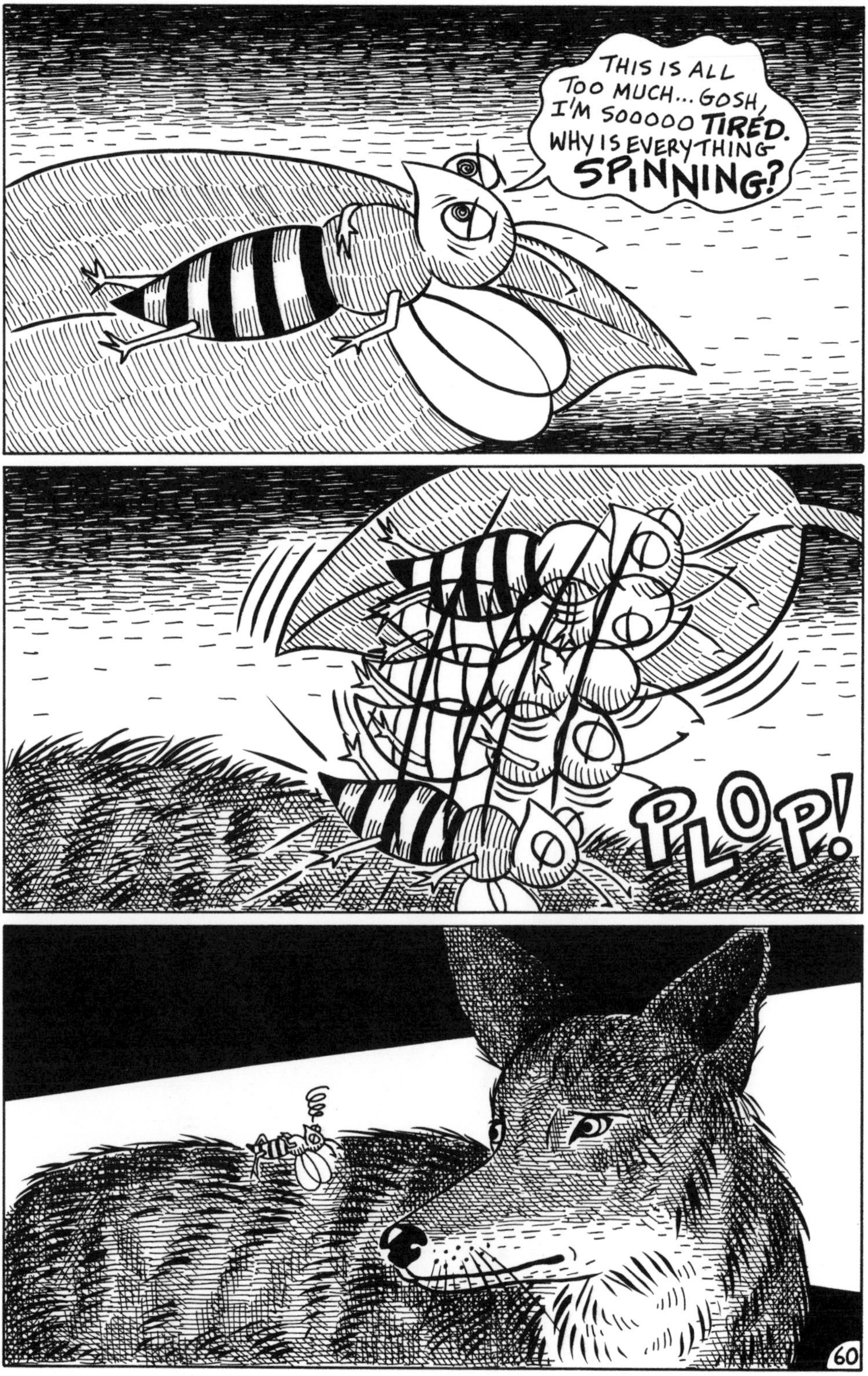

THIS IS ALL TOO MUCH... GOSH, I'M SOOOOO TIRED. WHY IS EVERYTHING SPINNING?
PLOP!

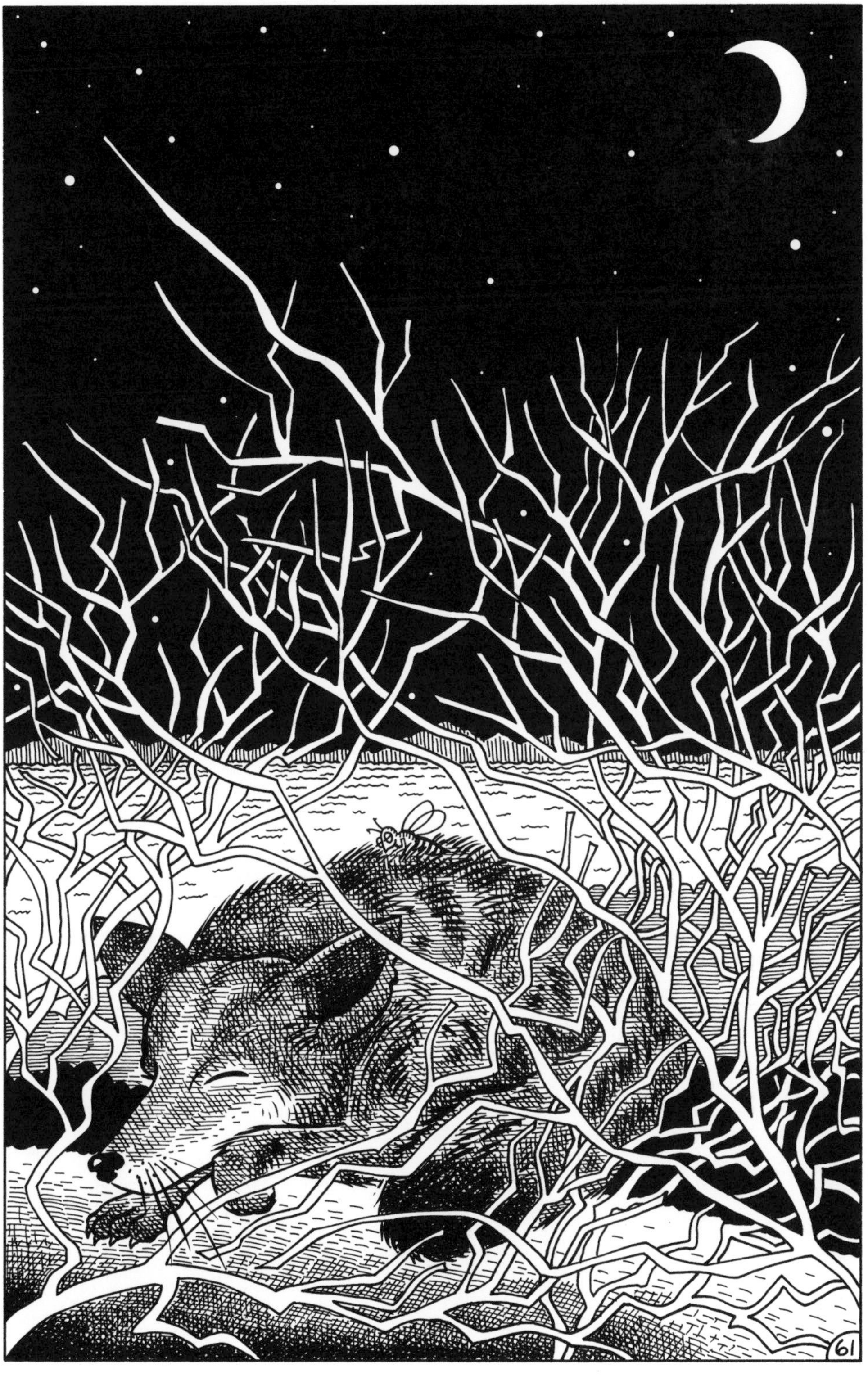

6

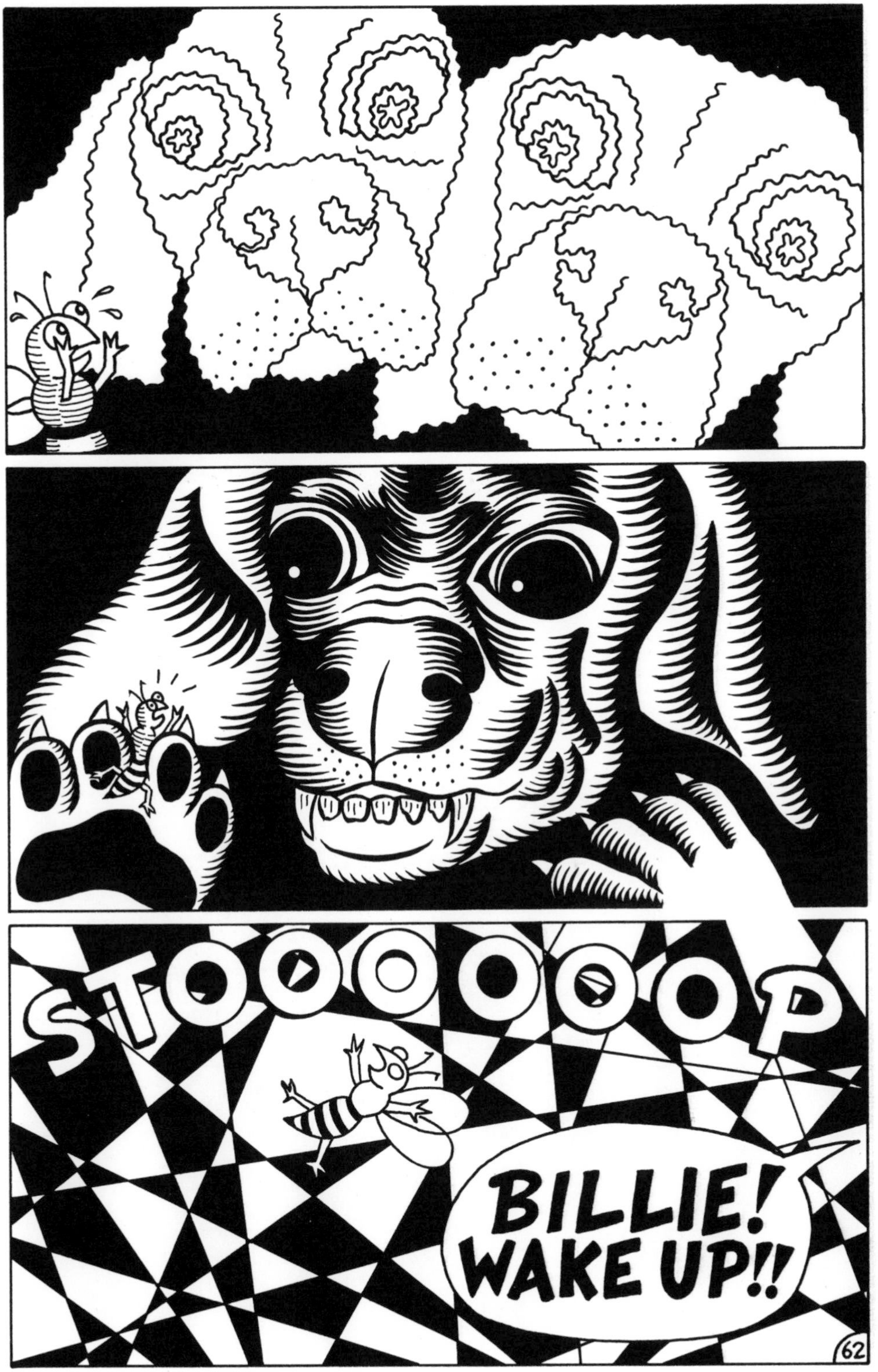
STOOOOOOP
BILLIE! WAKE UP!!
62

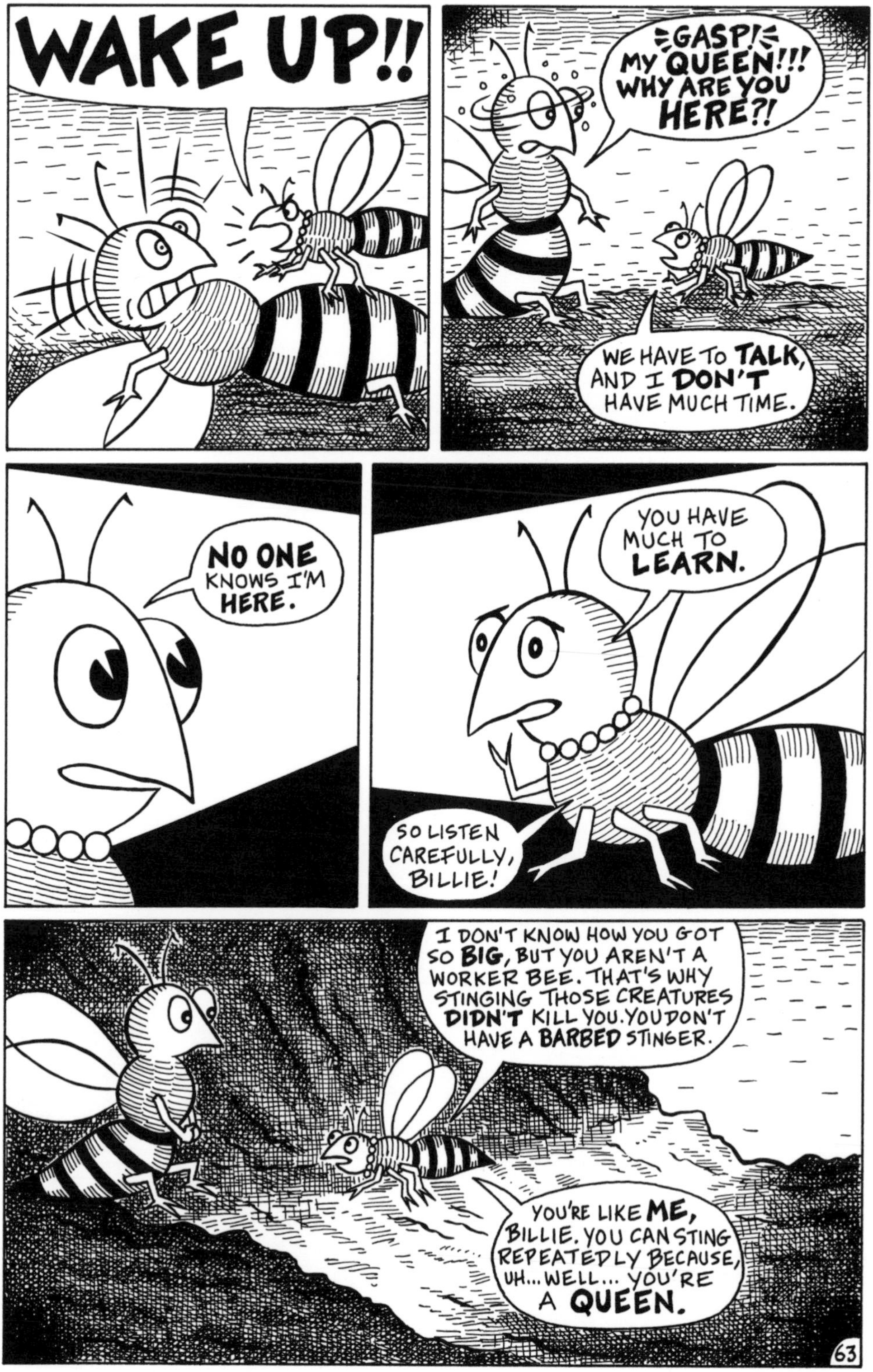
WAKE UP!!
GASP! MY QUEEN!!! WHY ARE YOU HERE?!
WE HAVE TO TALK, AND I DON'T HAVE MUCH TIME.
NO ONE KNOWS I'M HERE.
YOU HAVE MUCH TO LEARN.
SO LISTEN CAREFULLY, BILLIE!
I DON'T KNOW HOW YOU GOT SO BIG, BUT YOU AREN'T A WORKER BEE. THAT'S WHY STINGING THOSE CREATURES DIDN'T KILL YOU. YOU DON'T HAVE A BARBED STINGER.
YOU'RE LIKE ME, BILLIE. YOU CAN STING REPEATEDLY BECAUSE, UH... WELL... YOU'RE A QUEEN.
63

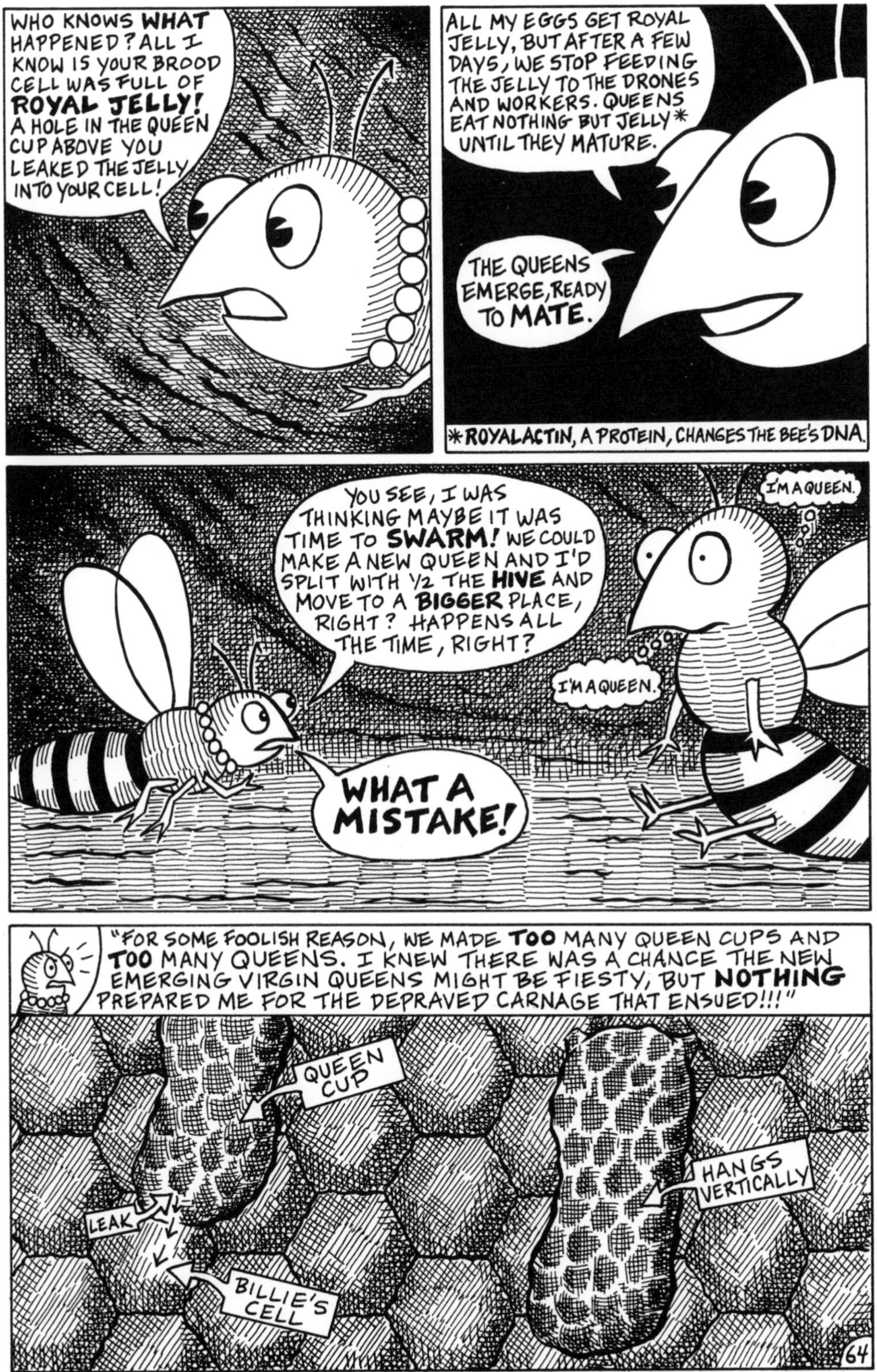
WHO KNOWS WHAT HAPPENED? ALL I KNOW IS YOUR BROOD CELL WAS FULL OF ROYAL JELLY! A HOLE IN THE QUEEN CUP ABOVE YOU LEAKED THE JELLY INTO YOUR CELL!
ALL MY EGGS GET ROYAL JELLY, BUT AFTER A FEW DAYS, WE STOP FEEDING THE JELLY TO THE DRONES AND WORKERS. QUEENS EAT NOTHING BUT JELLY* UNTIL THEY MATURE.
THE QUEENS EMERGE, READY TO MATE.
*ROYALACTIN, A PROTEIN, CHANGES THE BEE'S DNA.
YOU SEE, I WAS THINKING MAYBE IT WAS TIME TO SWARM! WE COULD MAKE A NEW QUEEN AND I'D SPLIT WITH 1/2 THE HIVE AND MOVE TO A BIGGER PLACE, RIGHT? HAPPENS ALL THE TIME, RIGHT?
I'M A QUEEN.
I'M A QUEEN.
WHAT A MISTAKE!
"FOR SOME FOOLISH REASON, WE MADE TOO MANY QUEEN CUPS AND TOO MANY QUEENS. I KNEW THERE WAS A CHANCE THE NEW EMERGING VIRGIN QUEENS MIGHT BE FIESTY, BUT NOTHING PREPARED ME FOR THE DEPRAVED CARNAGE THAT ENSUED!!!"
QUEEN CUP
HANGS VERTICALLY
LEAK
BILLIE'S CELL

*ROYAL JELLY IS A PROTEIN/SUGAR SUBSTANCE SECRETED FROM THE HYPOPHARYNGEAL GLANDS LOCATED ON THE HEADS OF "NURSE" WORKER BEES.

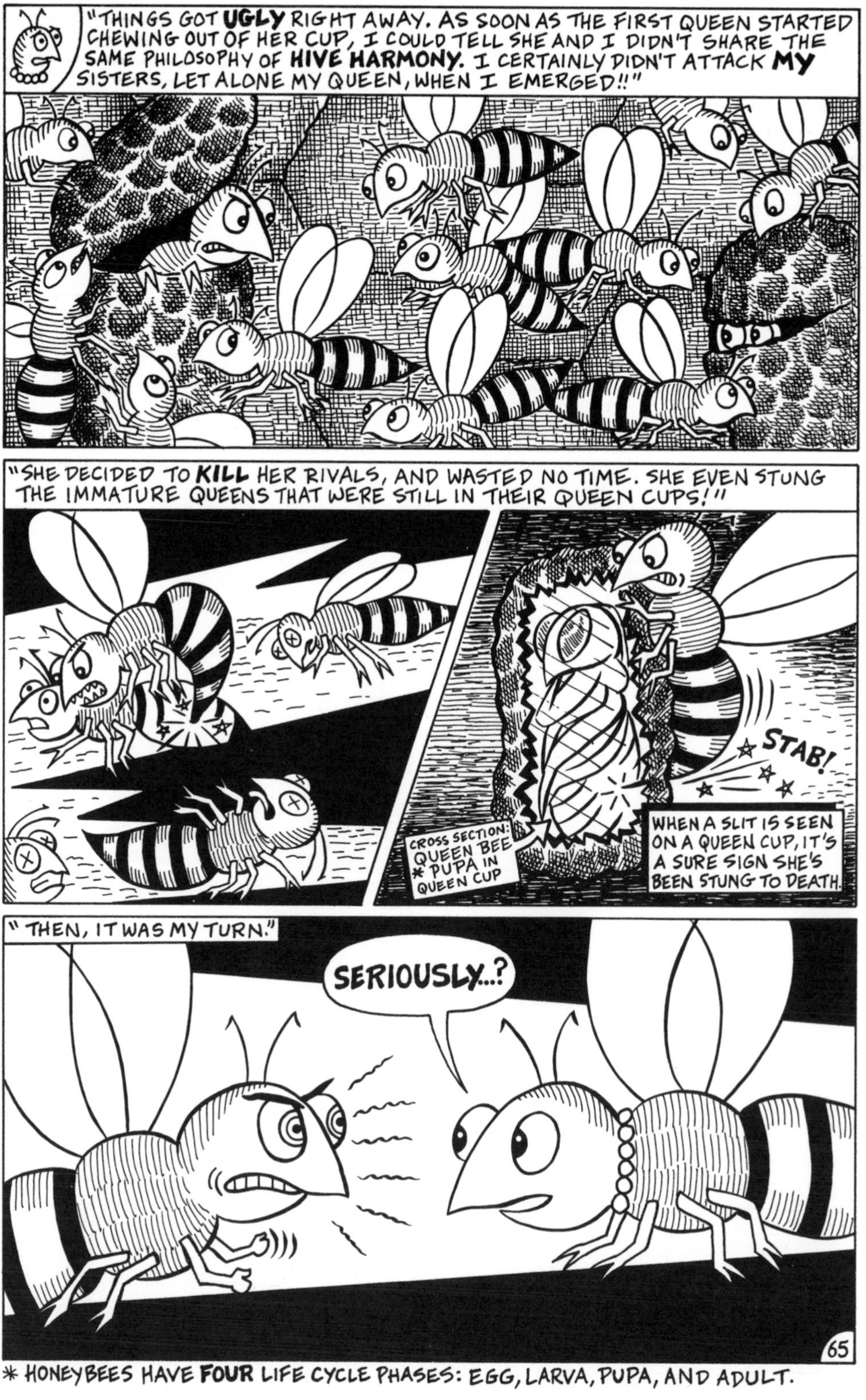

"THINGS GOT UGLY RIGHT AWAY. AS SOON AS THE FIRST QUEEN STARTED CHEWING OUT OF HER CUP, I COULD TELL SHE AND I DIDN'T SHARE THE SAME PHILOSOPHY OF HIVE HARMONY. I CERTAINLY DIDN'T ATTACK MY SISTERS, LET ALONE MY QUEEN, WHEN I EMERGED!!"
"SHE DECIDED TO KILL HER RIVALS, AND WASTED NO TIME. SHE EVEN STUNG THE IMMATURE QUEENS THAT WERE STILL IN THEIR QUEEN CUPS!"
STAB!
CROSS SECTION: QUEEN BEE * PUPA IN QUEEN CUP
WHEN A SLIT IS SEEN ON A QUEEN CUP, IT'S A SURE SIGN SHE'S BEEN STUNG TO DEATH.
"THEN, IT WAS MY TURN."
SERIOUSLY...?

* HONEYBEES HAVE **FOUR** LIFE CYCLE PHASES: EGG, LARVA, PUPA, AND ADULT.

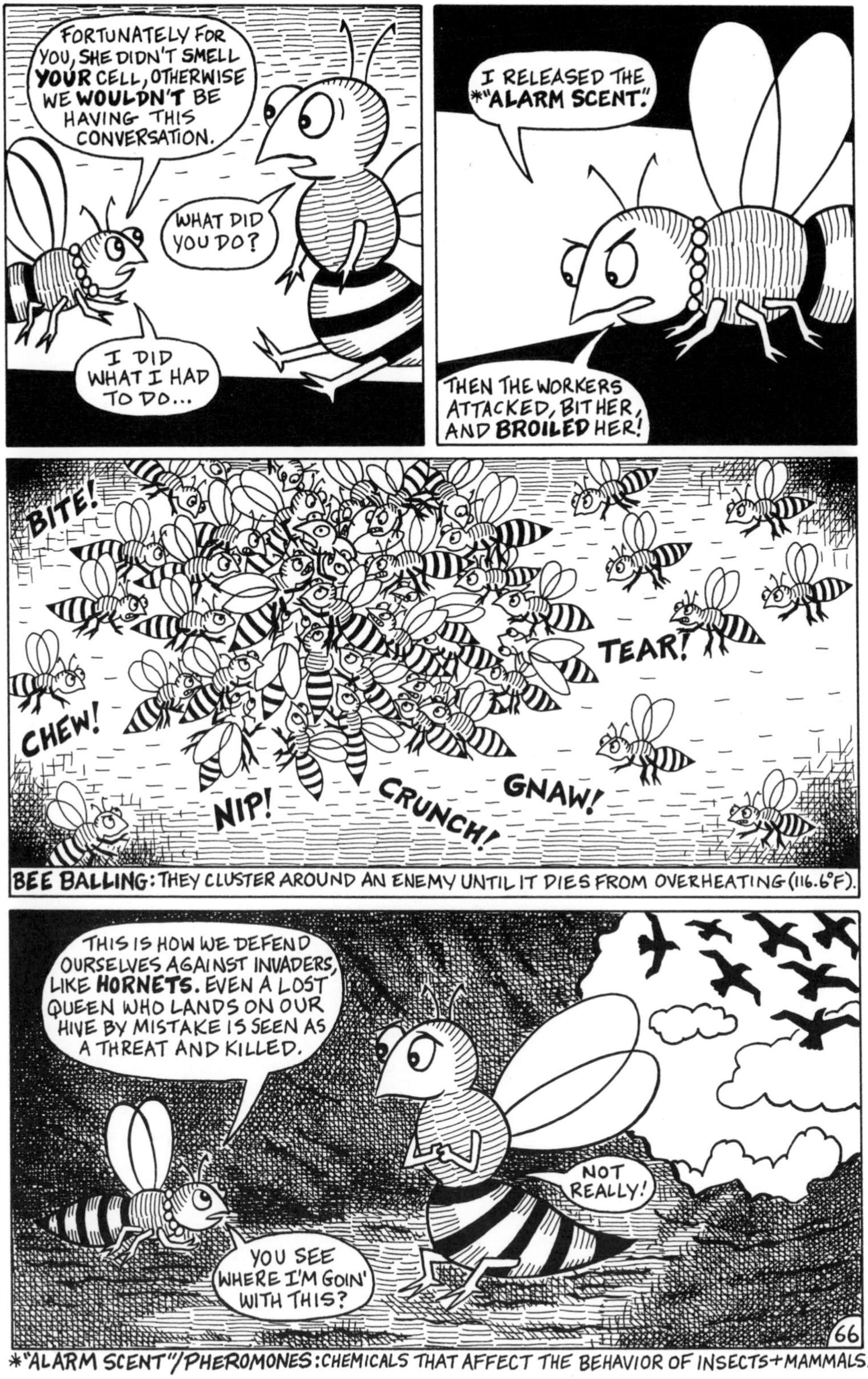

FORTUNATELY FOR YOU, SHE DIDN'T SMELL YOUR CELL, OTHERWISE WE WOULDN'T BE HAVING THIS CONVERSATION.
WHAT DID YOU DO?
I DID WHAT I HAD TO DO...
I RELEASED THE *"ALARM SCENT."
THEN THE WORKERS ATTACKED, BIT HER, AND BROILED HER!
BITE!
TEAR!
CHEW!
NIP!
CRUNCH!
GNAW!
BEE BALLING: THEY CLUSTER AROUND AN ENEMY UNTIL IT DIES FROM OVERHEATING (116.6°F).
THIS IS HOW WE DEFEND OURSELVES AGAINST INVADERS, LIKE HORNETS. EVEN A LOST QUEEN WHO LANDS ON OUR HIVE BY MISTAKE IS SEEN AS A THREAT AND KILLED.
NOT REALLY!
YOU SEE WHERE I'M GOIN' WITH THIS?

*"ALARM SCENT"/PHEROMONES: CHEMICALS THAT AFFECT THE BEHAVIOR OF INSECTS+MAMMALS.

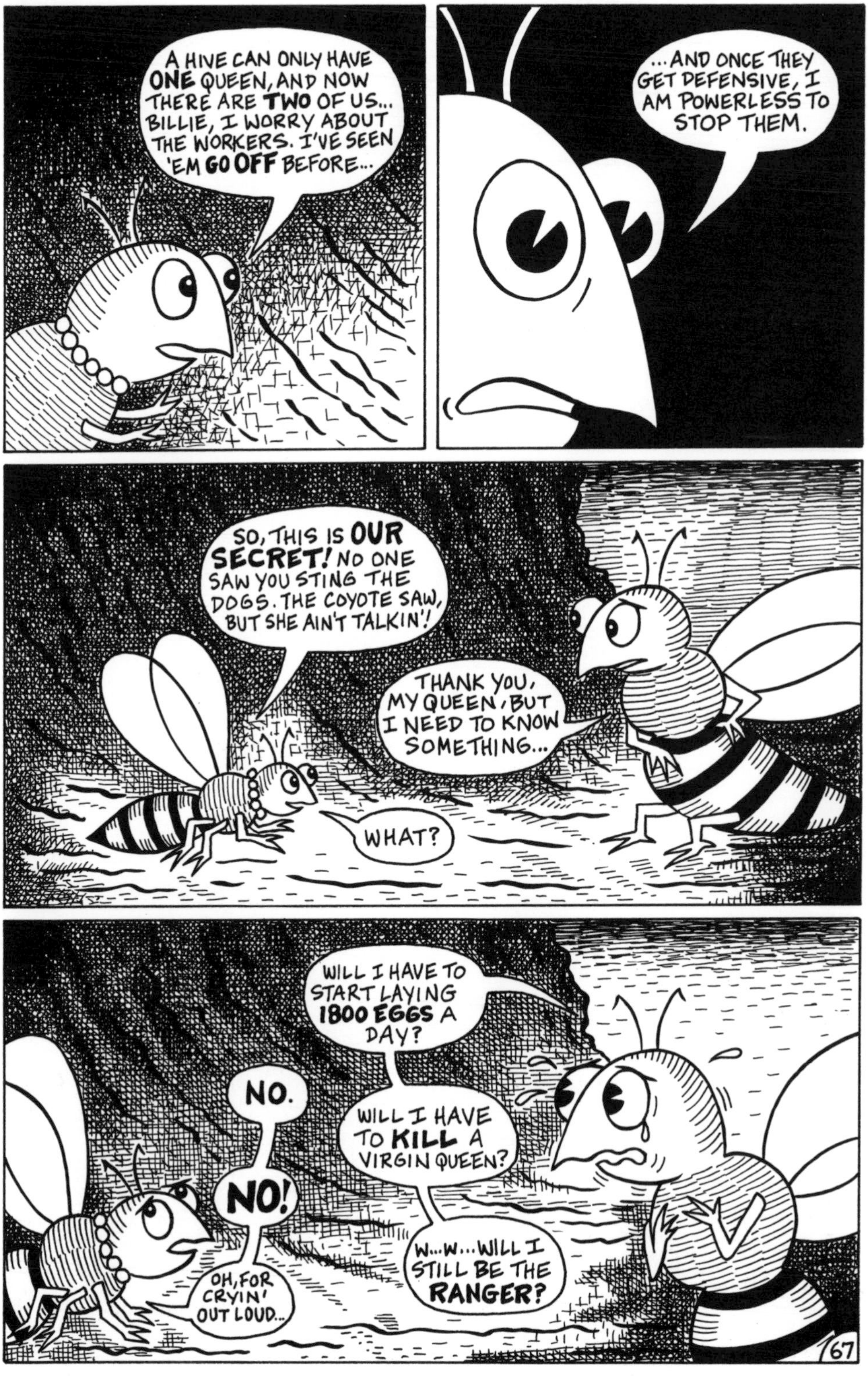
A HIVE CAN ONLY HAVE ONE QUEEN, AND NOW THERE ARE TWO OF US... BILLIE, I WORRY ABOUT THE WORKERS. I'VE SEEN 'EM GO OFF BEFORE...
...AND ONCE THEY GET DEFENSIVE, I AM POWERLESS TO STOP THEM.
SO, THIS IS OUR SECRET! NO ONE SAW YOU STING THE DOGS. THE COYOTE SAW, BUT SHE AIN'T TALKIN'!
THANK YOU, MY QUEEN, BUT I NEED TO KNOW SOMETHING...
WHAT?
WILL I HAVE TO START LAYING 1800 EGGS A DAY?
NO.
WILL I HAVE TO KILL A VIRGIN QUEEN?
NO!
W...W...WILL I STILL BE THE RANGER?
OH, FOR CRYIN' OUT LOUD...

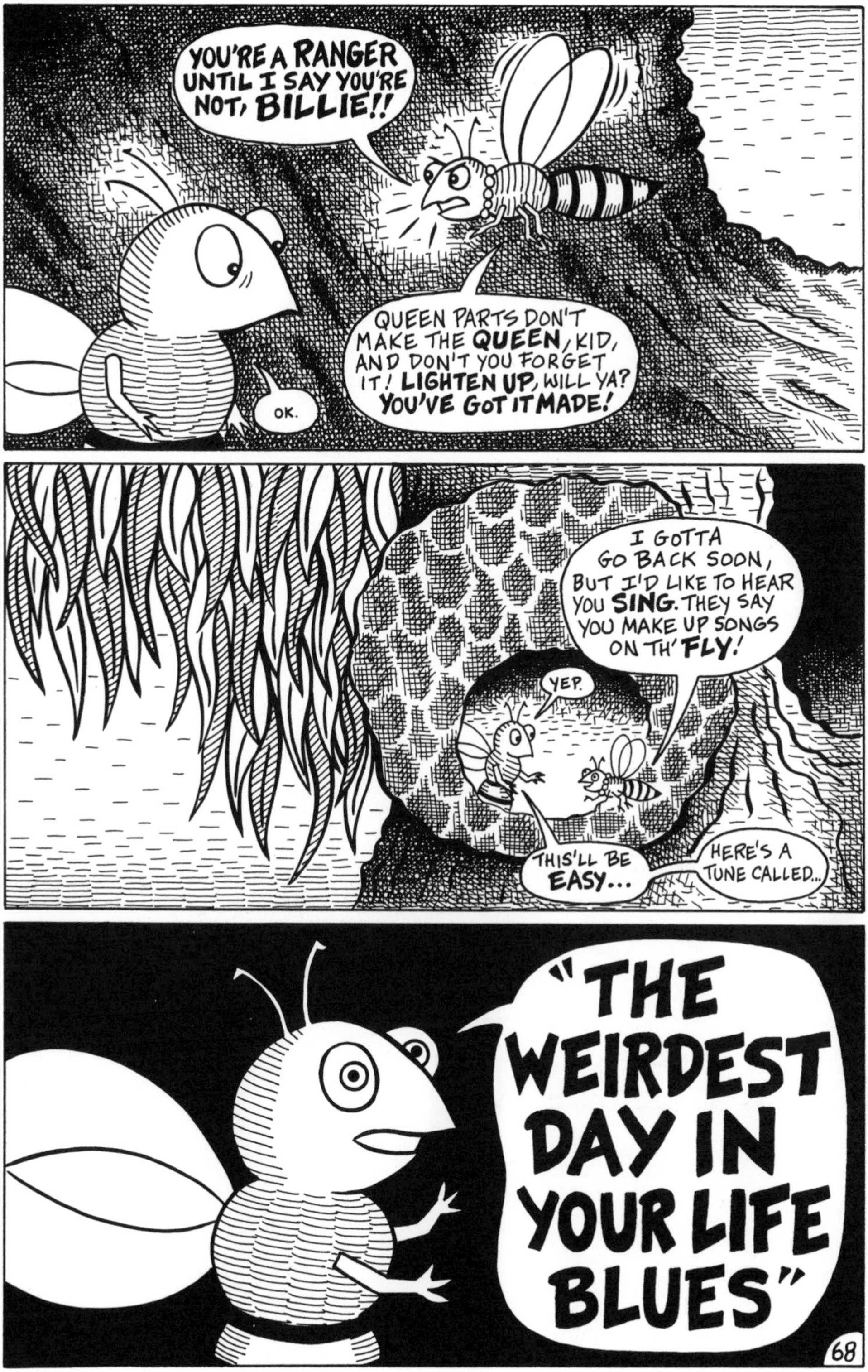
YOU'RE A RANGER UNTIL I SAY YOU'RE NOT, BILLIE!!
QUEEN PARTS DON'T MAKE THE QUEEN, KID, AND DON'T YOU FORGET IT! LIGHTEN UP, WILL YA? YOU'VE GOT IT MADE!
OK.
I GOTTA GO BACK SOON, BUT I'D LIKE TO HEAR YOU SING. THEY SAY YOU MAKE UP SONGS ON TH' FLY!
YEP.
THIS'LL BE EASY...
HERE'S A TUNE CALLED...
"THE WEIRDEST DAY IN YOUR LIFE BLUES"
68

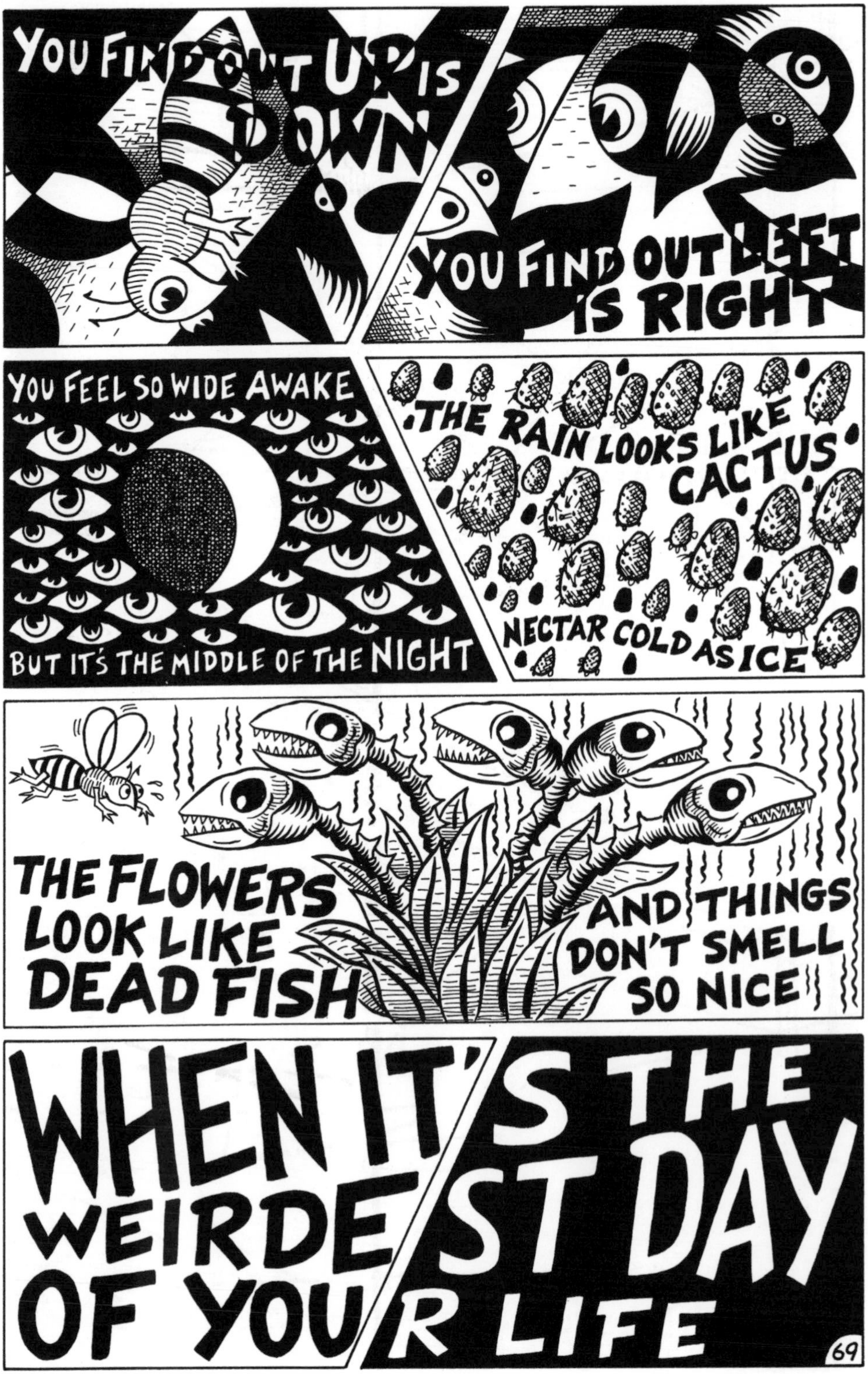
YOU FIND OUT UP IS DOWN
YOU FIND OUT LEFT IS RIGHT
YOU FEEL SO WIDE AWAKE
BUT IT'S THE MIDDLE OF THE NIGHT
THE RAIN LOOKS LIKE CACTUS
NECTAR COLD AS ICE
THE FLOWERS LOOK LIKE DEAD FISH
AND THINGS DON'T SMELL SO NICE
WHEN IT'S THE WEIRDEST DAY OF YOUR LIFE

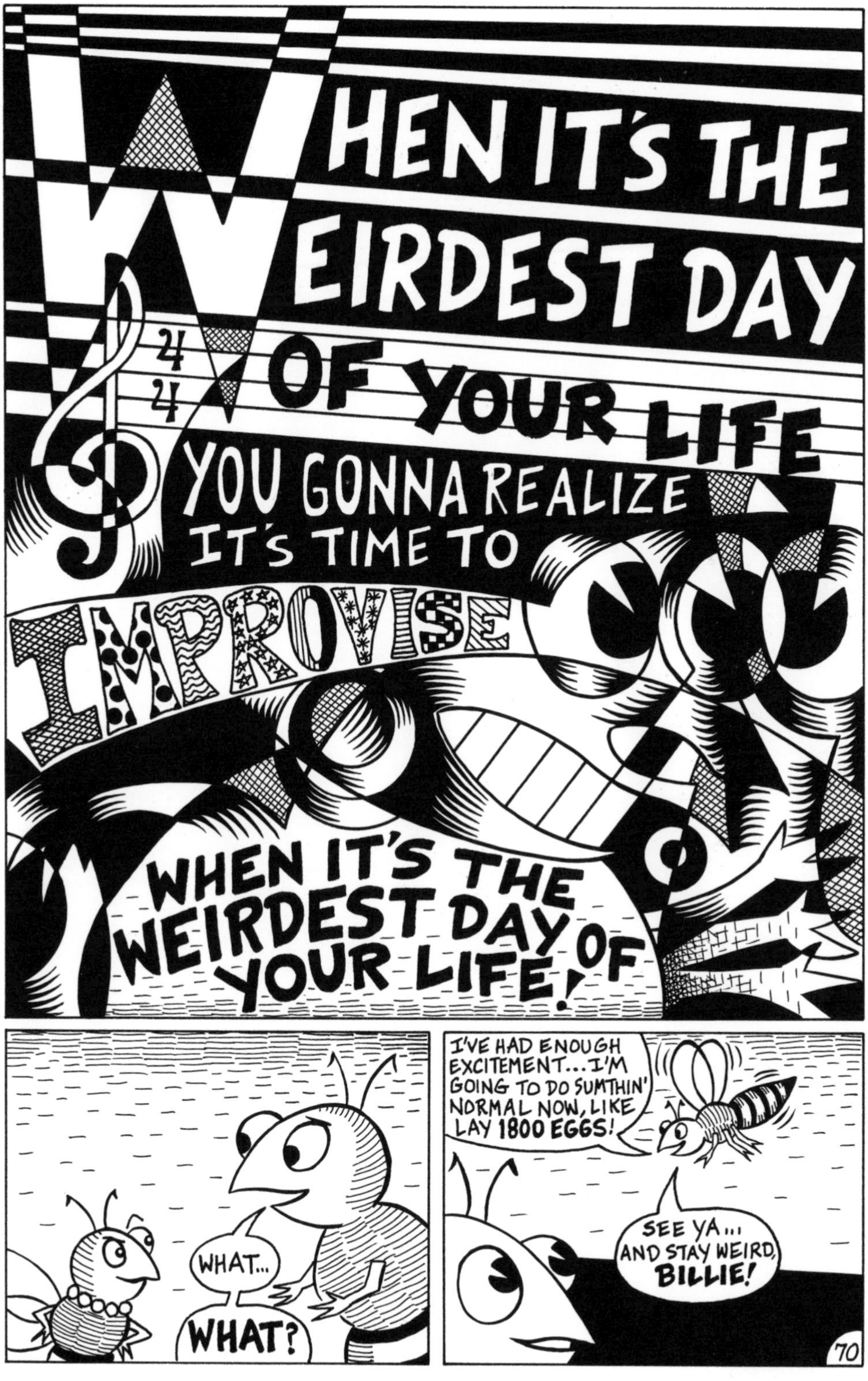
WHEN IT'S THE WEIRDEST DAY OF YOUR LIFE
YOU GONNA REALIZE IT'S TIME TO
IMPROVISE
WHEN IT'S THE WEIRDEST DAY OF YOUR LIFE!
WHAT...
WHAT?
I'VE HAD ENOUGH EXCITEMENT... I'M GOING TO DO SUMTHIN' NORMAL NOW, LIKE LAY 1800 EGGS!
SEE YA... AND STAY WEIRD, BILLIE!

7

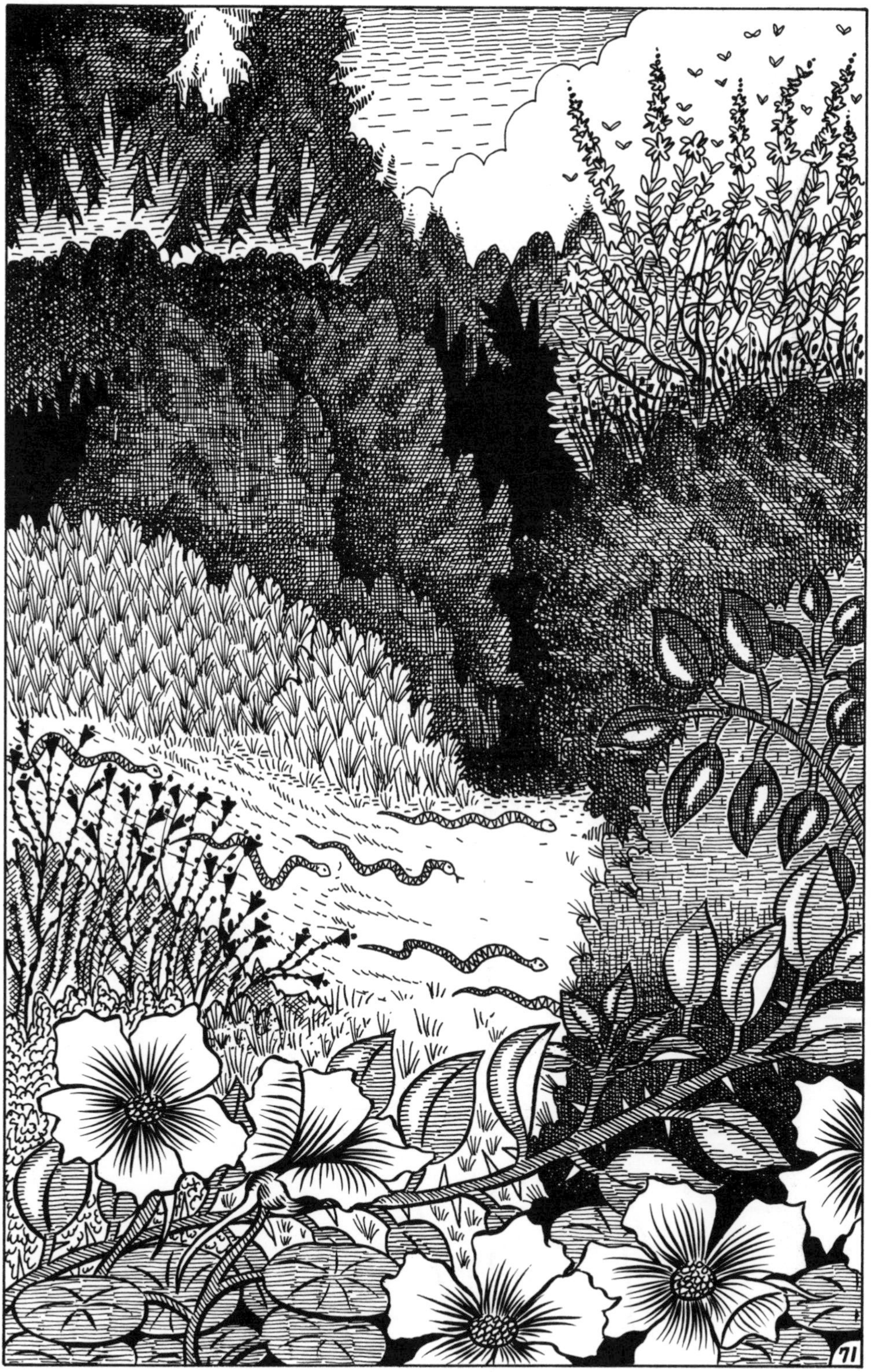

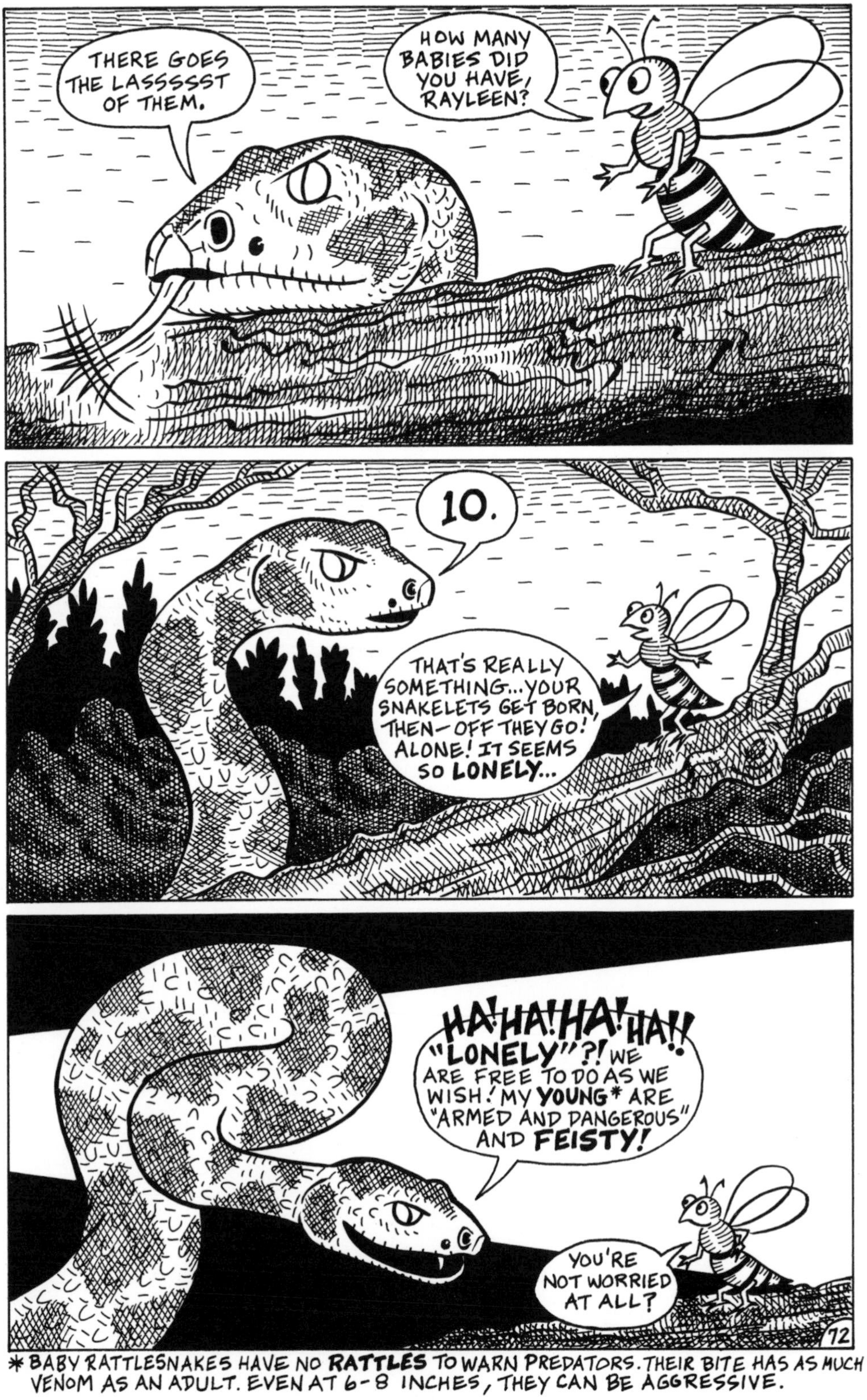
THERE GOES THE LASSSSST OF THEM.
HOW MANY BABIES DID YOU HAVE, RAYLEEN?
10.
THAT'S REALLY SOMETHING... YOUR SNAKELETS GET BORN, THEN—OFF THEY GO! ALONE! IT SEEMS SO LONELY...
HA!HA!HA!HA!!
"LONELY"?! WE ARE FREE TO DO AS WE WISH! MY YOUNG* ARE "ARMED AND DANGEROUS" AND FEISTY!
YOU'RE NOT WORRIED AT ALL?

* BABY RATTLESNAKES HAVE NO **RATTLES** TO WARN PREDATORS. THEIR BITE HAS AS MUCH VENOM AS AN ADULT. EVEN AT 6-8 INCHES, THEY CAN BE AGGRESSIVE.

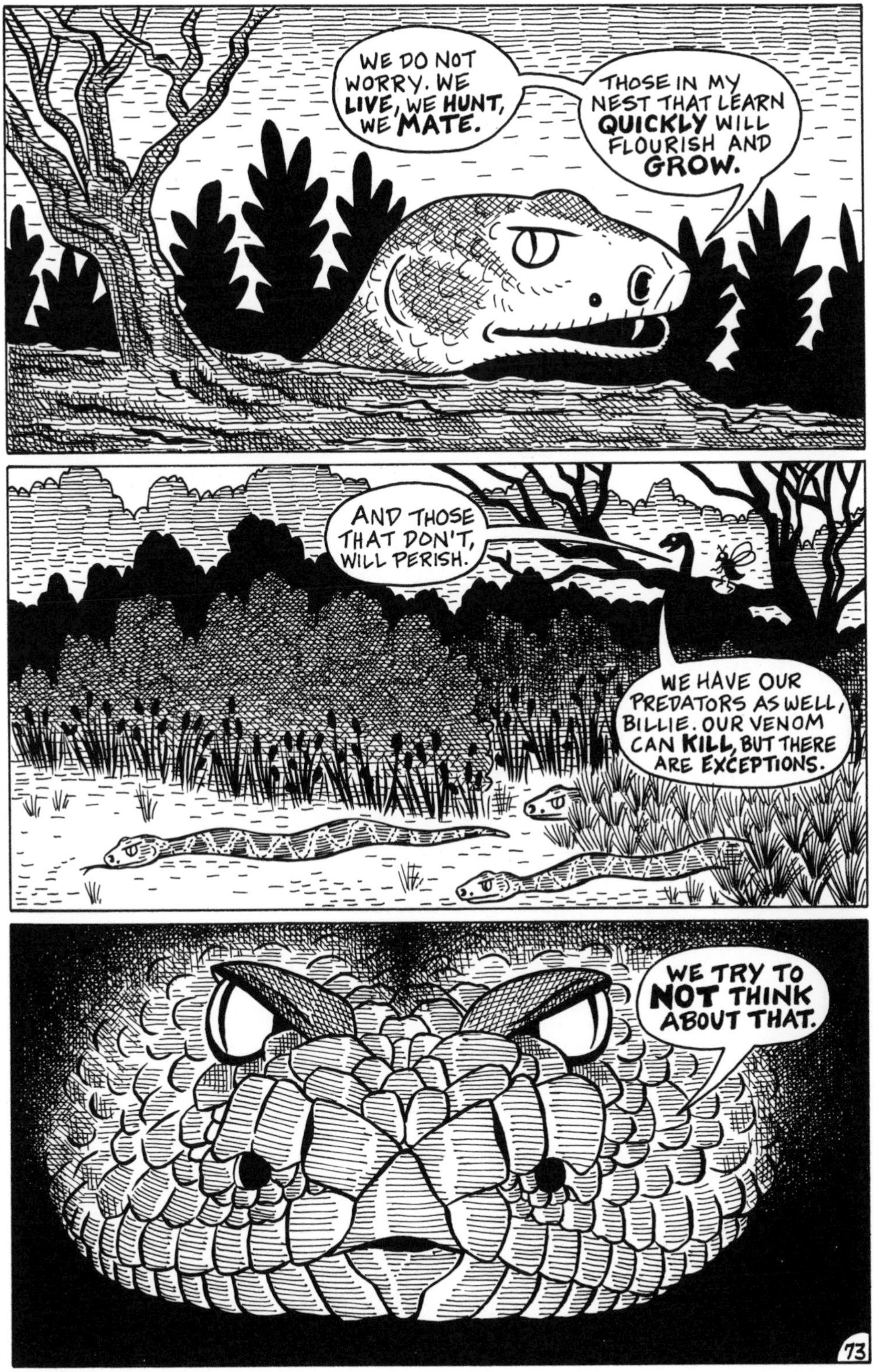
WE DO NOT WORRY. WE LIVE, WE HUNT, WE MATE.
THOSE IN MY NEST THAT LEARN QUICKLY WILL FLOURISH AND GROW.
AND THOSE THAT DON'T, WILL PERISH.
WE HAVE OUR PREDATORS AS WELL, BILLIE. OUR VENOM CAN KILL, BUT THERE ARE EXCEPTIONS.
WE TRY TO NOT THINK ABOUT THAT.

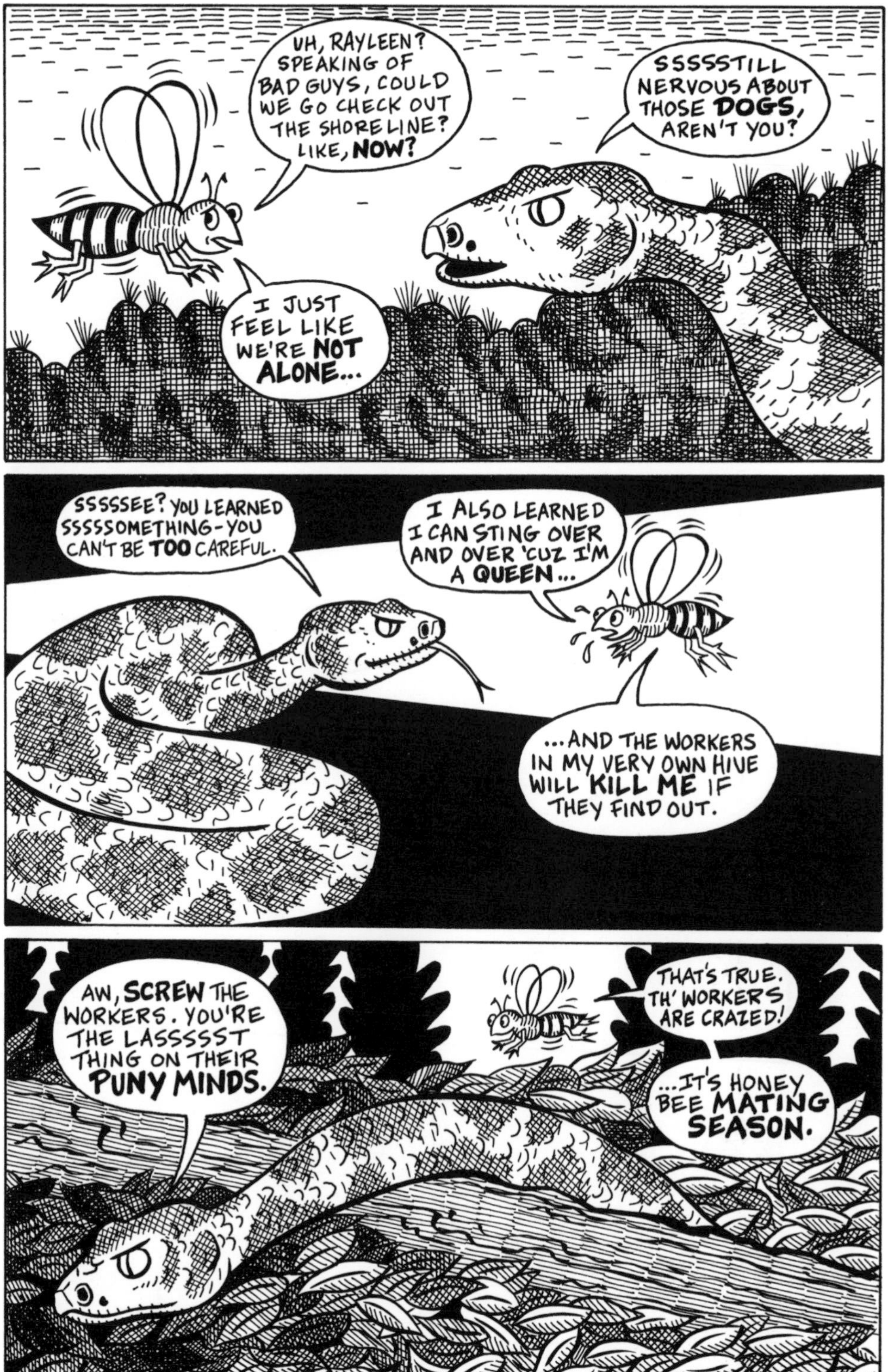
UH, RAYLEEN? SPEAKING OF BAD GUYS, COULD WE GO CHECK OUT THE SHORELINE? LIKE, **NOW?**
SSSSSTILL NERVOUS ABOUT THOSE **DOGS**, AREN'T YOU?
I JUST FEEL LIKE WE'RE **NOT ALONE...**
SSSSSEE? YOU LEARNED SSSSSOMETHING - YOU CAN'T BE **TOO** CAREFUL.
I ALSO LEARNED I CAN STING OVER AND OVER 'CUZ I'M A **QUEEN...**
...AND THE WORKERS IN MY VERY OWN HIVE WILL **KILL ME** IF THEY FIND OUT.
AW, **SCREW** THE WORKERS. YOU'RE THE LASSSSST THING ON THEIR **PUNY MINDS.**
THAT'S TRUE. TH' WORKERS ARE CRAZED!
...IT'S HONEY BEE **MATING SEASON.**

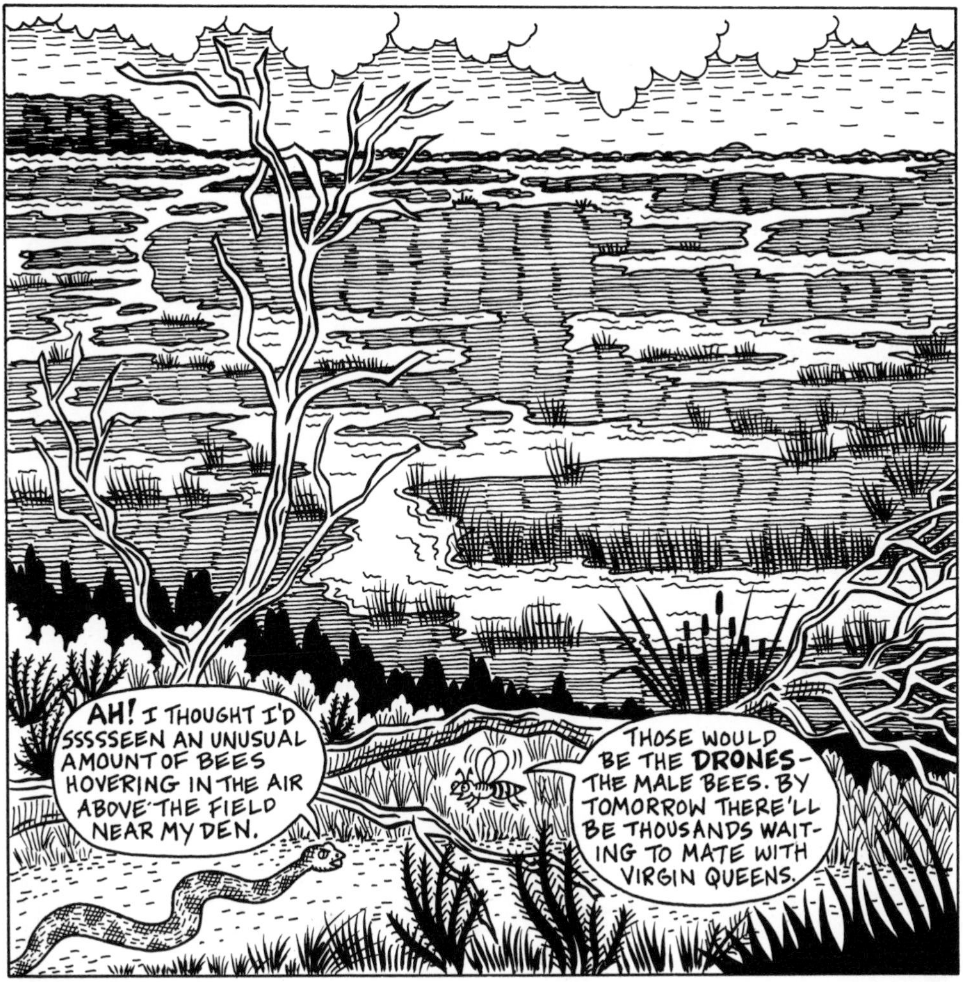
AH! I THOUGHT I'D SSSSSEEN AN UNUSUAL AMOUNT OF BEES HOVERING IN THE AIR ABOVE THE FIELD NEAR MY DEN.
THOSE WOULD BE THE **DRONES**- THE MALE BEES. BY TOMORROW THERE'LL BE THOUSANDS WAITING TO MATE WITH VIRGIN QUEENS.

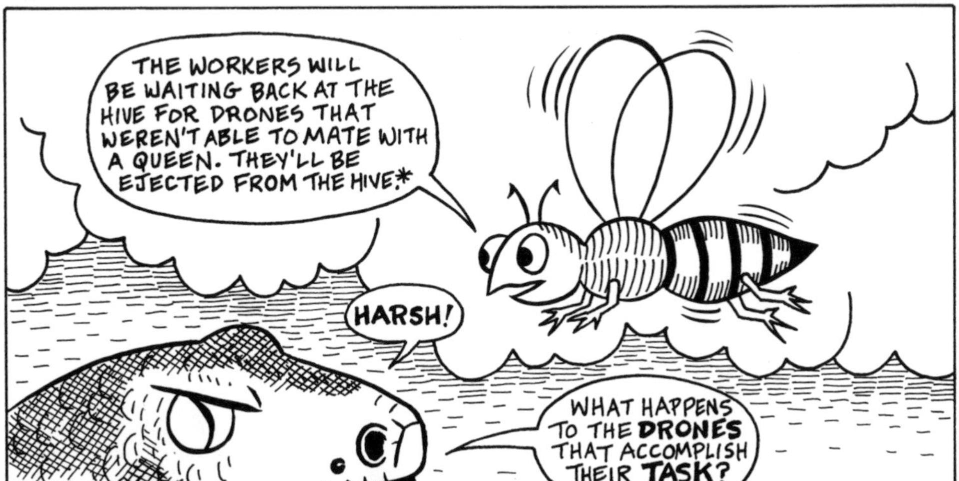
THE WORKERS WILL BE WAITING BACK AT THE HIVE FOR DRONES THAT WEREN'T ABLE TO MATE WITH A QUEEN. THEY'LL BE EJECTED FROM THE HIVE.*
HARSH!
WHAT HAPPENS TO THE **DRONES** THAT ACCOMPLISH THEIR **TASK**?

*ALL DRONES ARE DRIVEN FROM THE HIVE IN AUTUMN. THEIR LIFESPAN IS 90 DAYS.

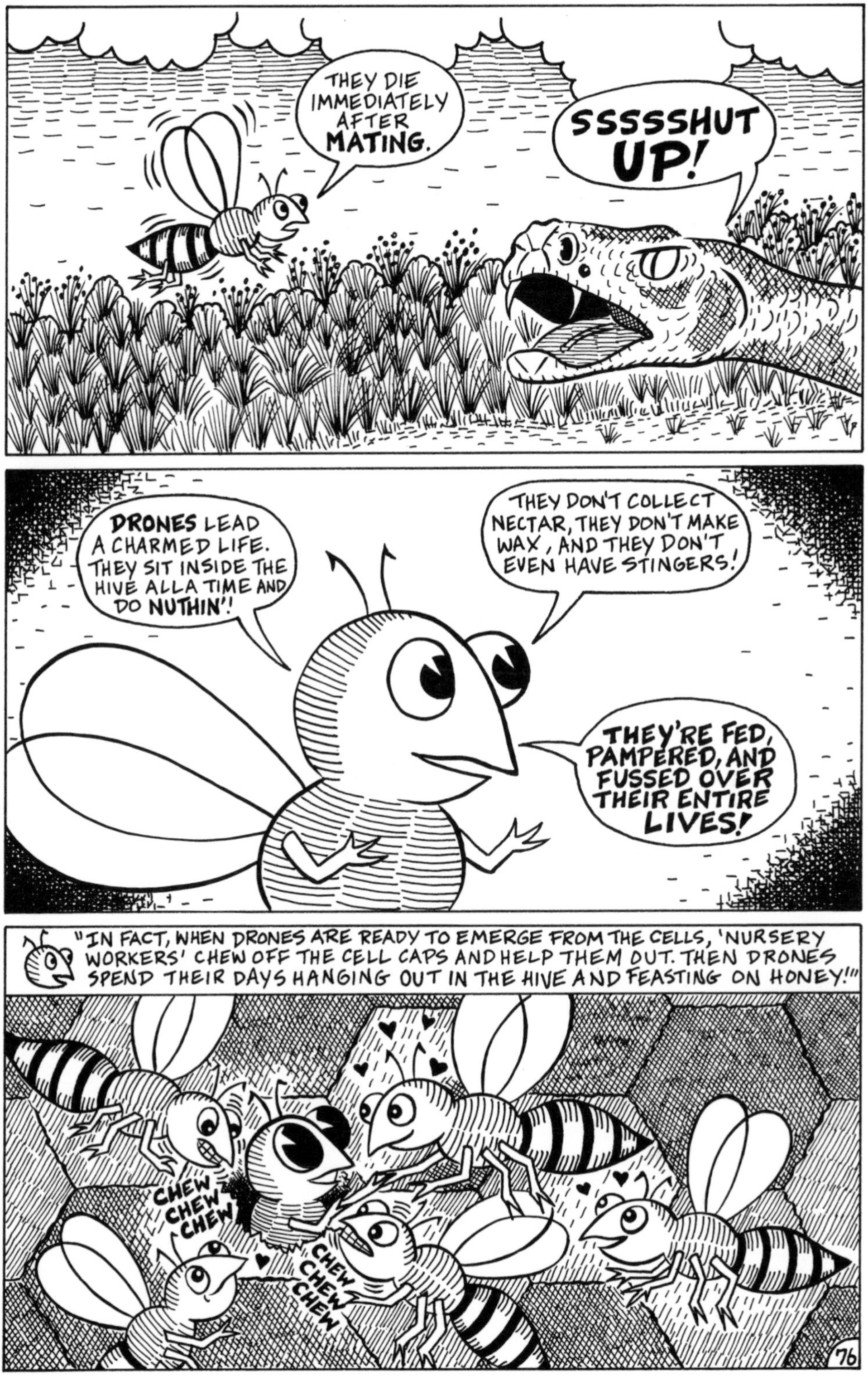
THEY DIE IMMEDIATELY AFTER MATING.
SSSSSHUT UP!
DRONES LEAD A CHARMED LIFE. THEY SIT INSIDE THE HIVE ALLA TIME AND DO NUTHIN'!
THEY DON'T COLLECT NECTAR, THEY DON'T MAKE WAX, AND THEY DON'T EVEN HAVE STINGERS!
THEY'RE FED, PAMPERED, AND FUSSED OVER THEIR ENTIRE LIVES!
"IN FACT, WHEN DRONES ARE READY TO EMERGE FROM THE CELLS, 'NURSERY WORKERS' CHEW OFF THE CELL CAPS AND HELP THEM OUT. THEN DRONES SPEND THEIR DAYS HANGING OUT IN THE HIVE AND FEASTING ON HONEY!"
CHEW CHEW CHEW
CHEW CHEW CHEW

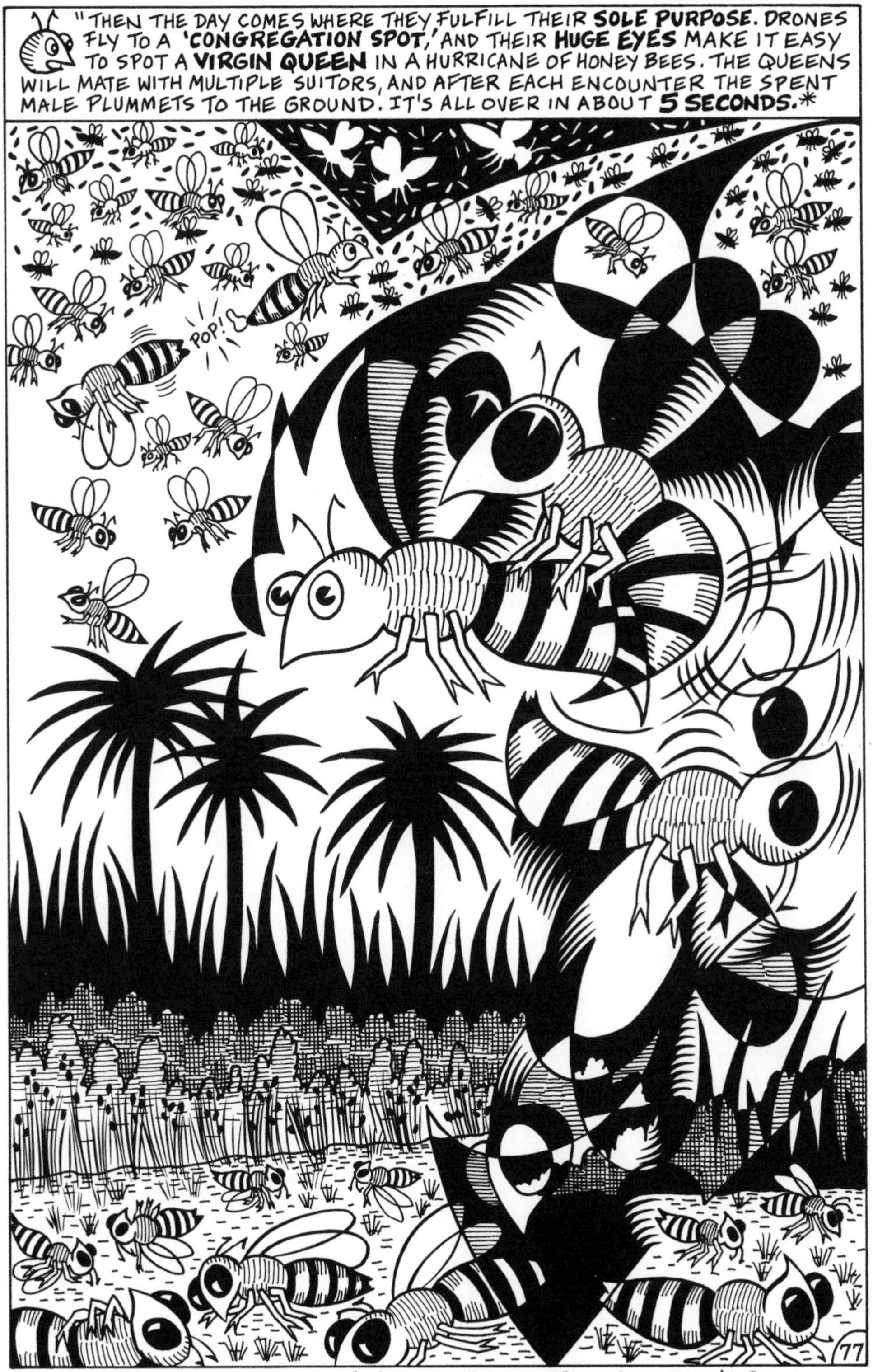
"THEN THE DAY COMES WHERE THEY FULFILL THEIR **SOLE PURPOSE**. DRONES FLY TO A **'CONGREGATION SPOT,'** AND THEIR **HUGE EYES** MAKE IT EASY TO SPOT A **VIRGIN QUEEN** IN A HURRICANE OF HONEY BEES. THE QUEENS WILL MATE WITH MULTIPLE SUITORS, AND AFTER EACH ENCOUNTER THE SPENT MALE PLUMMETS TO THE GROUND. IT'S ALL OVER IN ABOUT **5 SECONDS**.*
POP!

*AFTER EJACULATION, THE ENDOPHALLUS IS RIPPED FROM THE DRONE'S BODY.

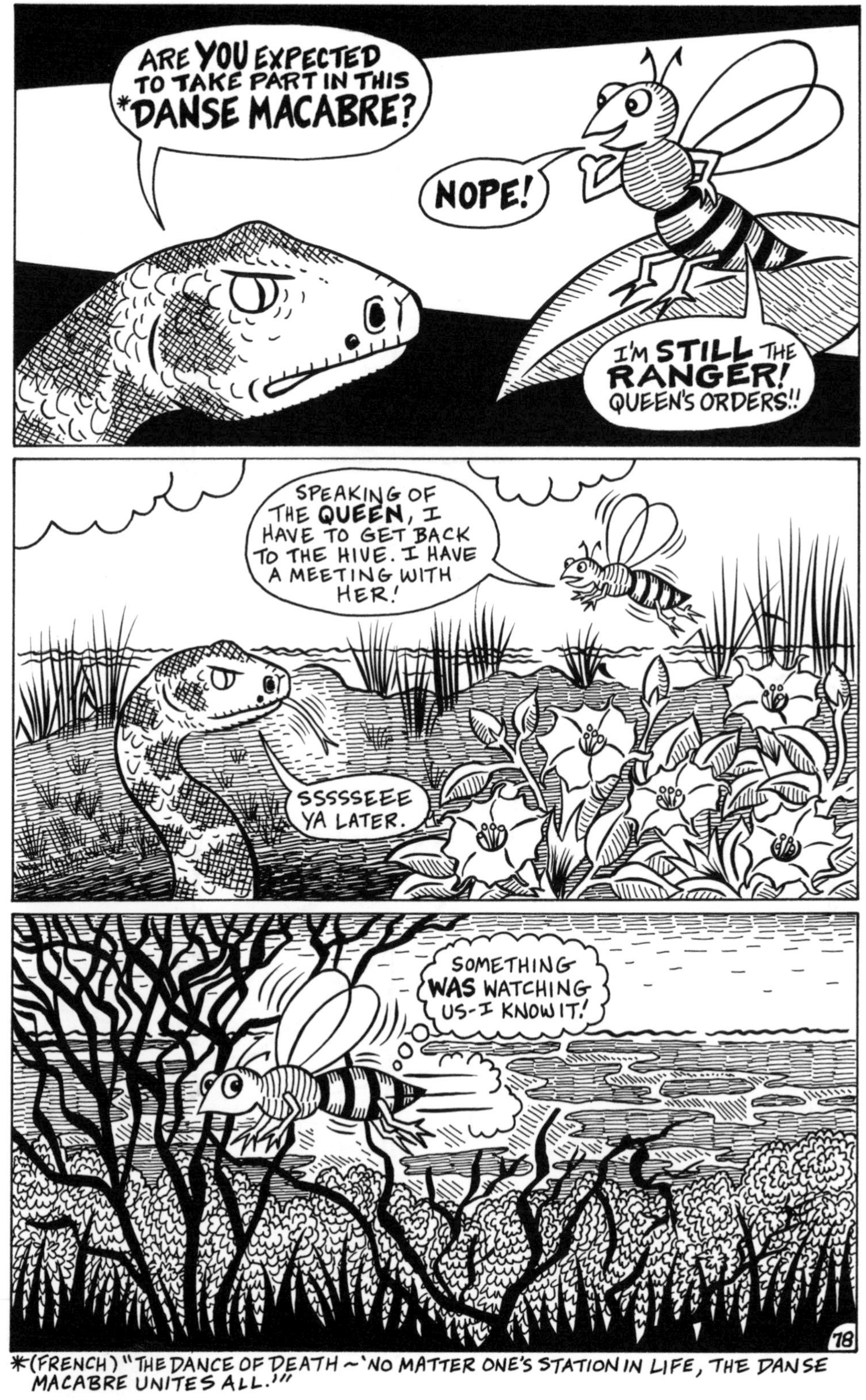
ARE YOU EXPECTED TO TAKE PART IN THIS *DANSE MACABRE?
NOPE!
I'M STILL THE RANGER! QUEEN'S ORDERS!!
SPEAKING OF THE QUEEN, I HAVE TO GET BACK TO THE HIVE. I HAVE A MEETING WITH HER!
SSSSSEEE YA LATER.
SOMETHING WAS WATCHING US-I KNOW IT!

*(FRENCH) "THE DANCE OF DEATH ~ 'NO MATTER ONE'S STATION IN LIFE, THE DANSE MACABRE UNITES ALL.'"

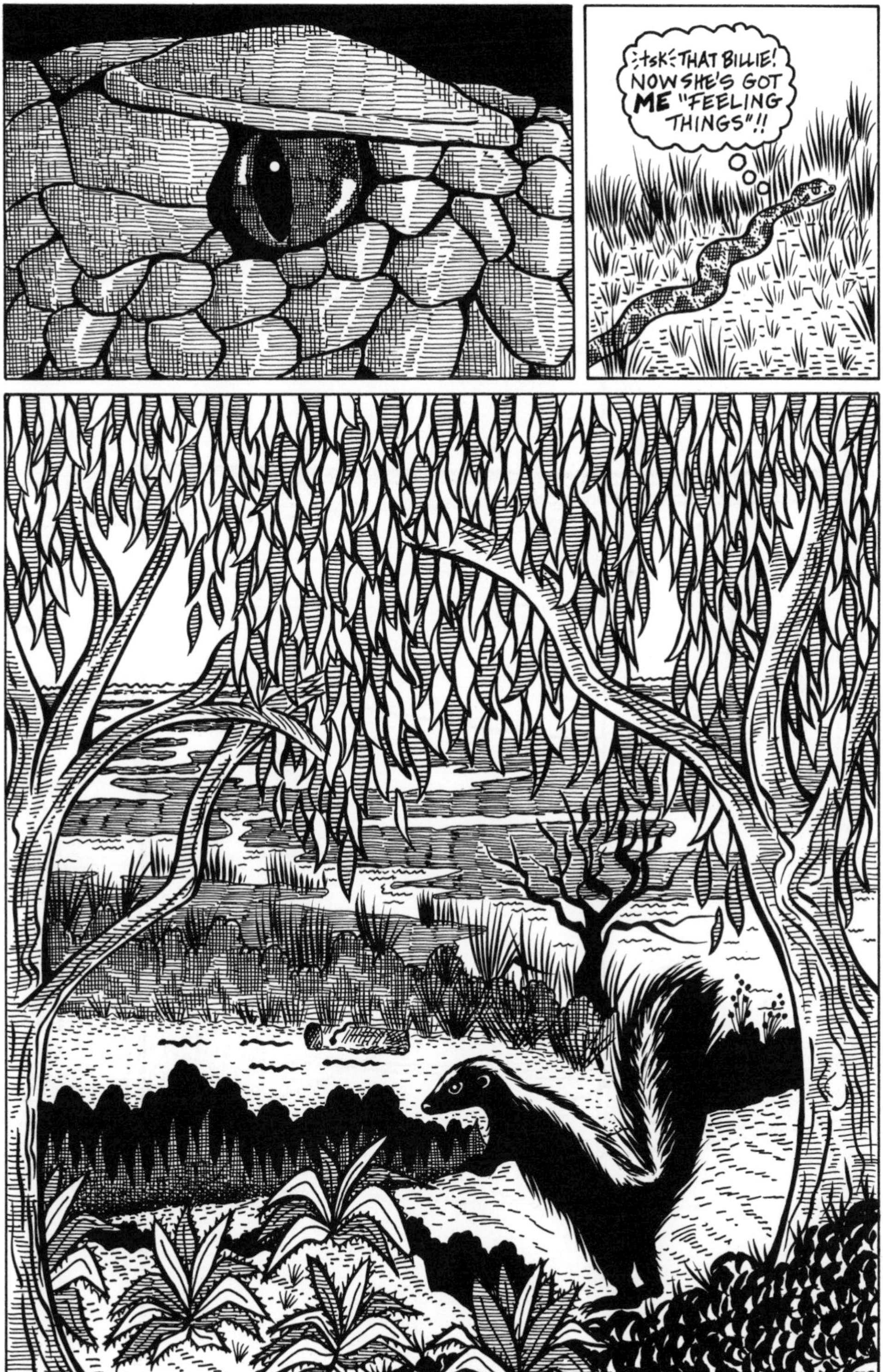
tsk THAT BILLIE! NOW SHE'S GOT ME "FEELING THINGS"!!

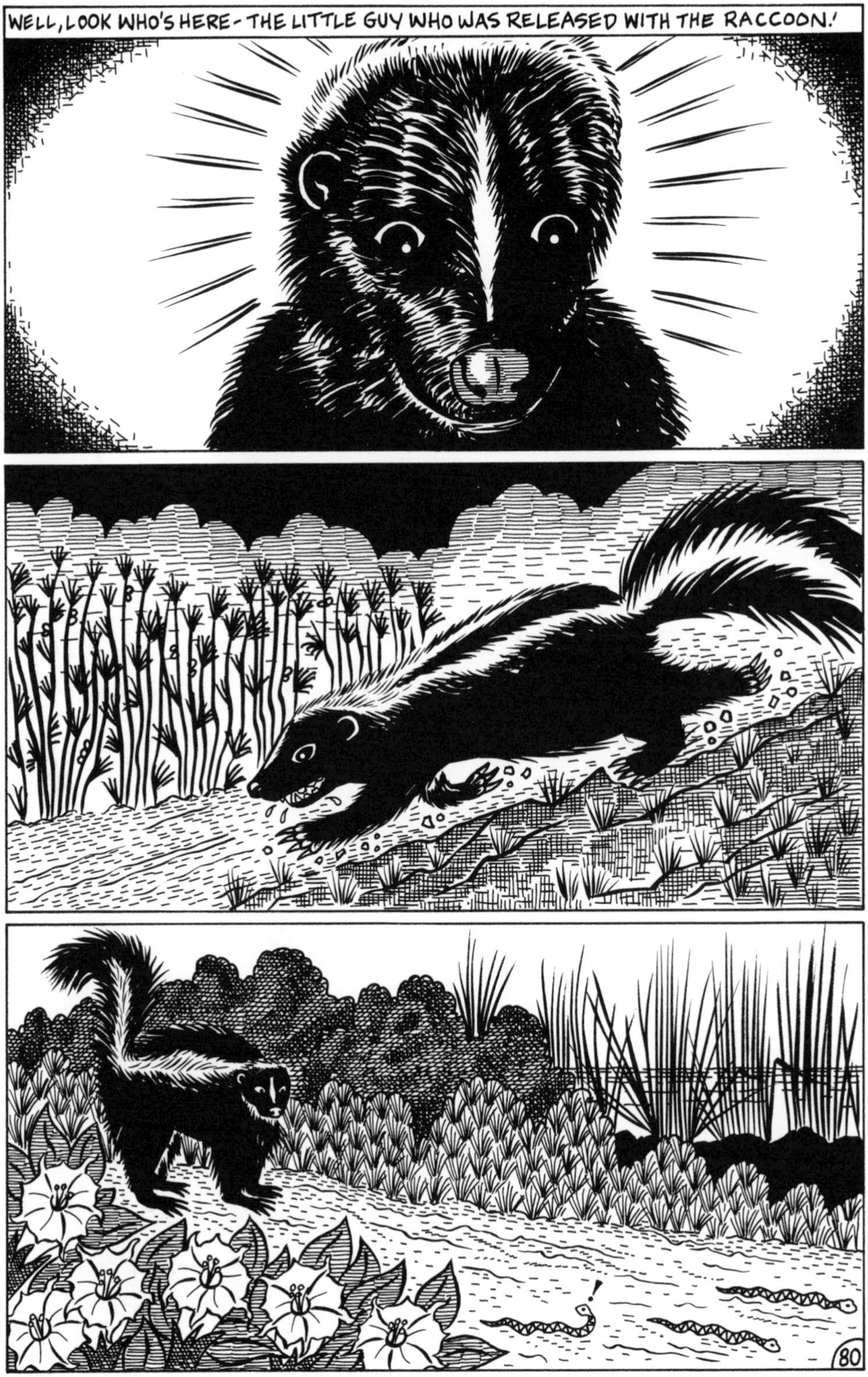
WELL, LOOK WHO'S HERE - THE LITTLE GUY WHO WAS RELEASED WITH THE RACCOON!
!

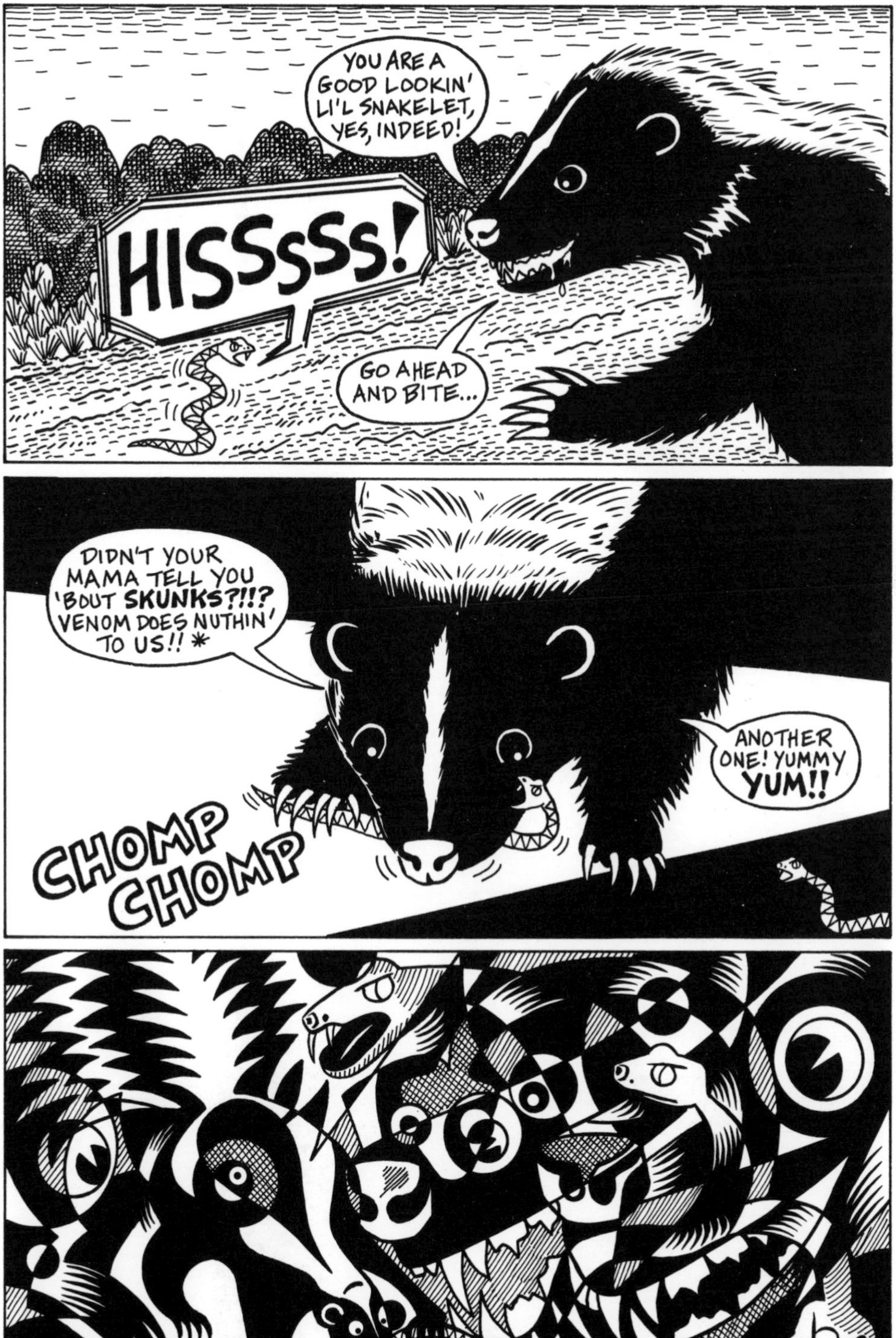
YOU ARE A GOOD LOOKIN' LI'L SNAKELET, YES, INDEED!
HISSSSSS!
GO AHEAD AND BITE...
DIDN'T YOUR MAMA TELL YOU 'BOUT SKUNKS?!!? VENOM DOES NUTHIN' TO US!! *
ANOTHER ONE! YUMMY YUM!!
CHOMP CHOMP
AND SO ON...

* SKUNKS ARE IMMUNE TO RATTLESNAKE VENOM.

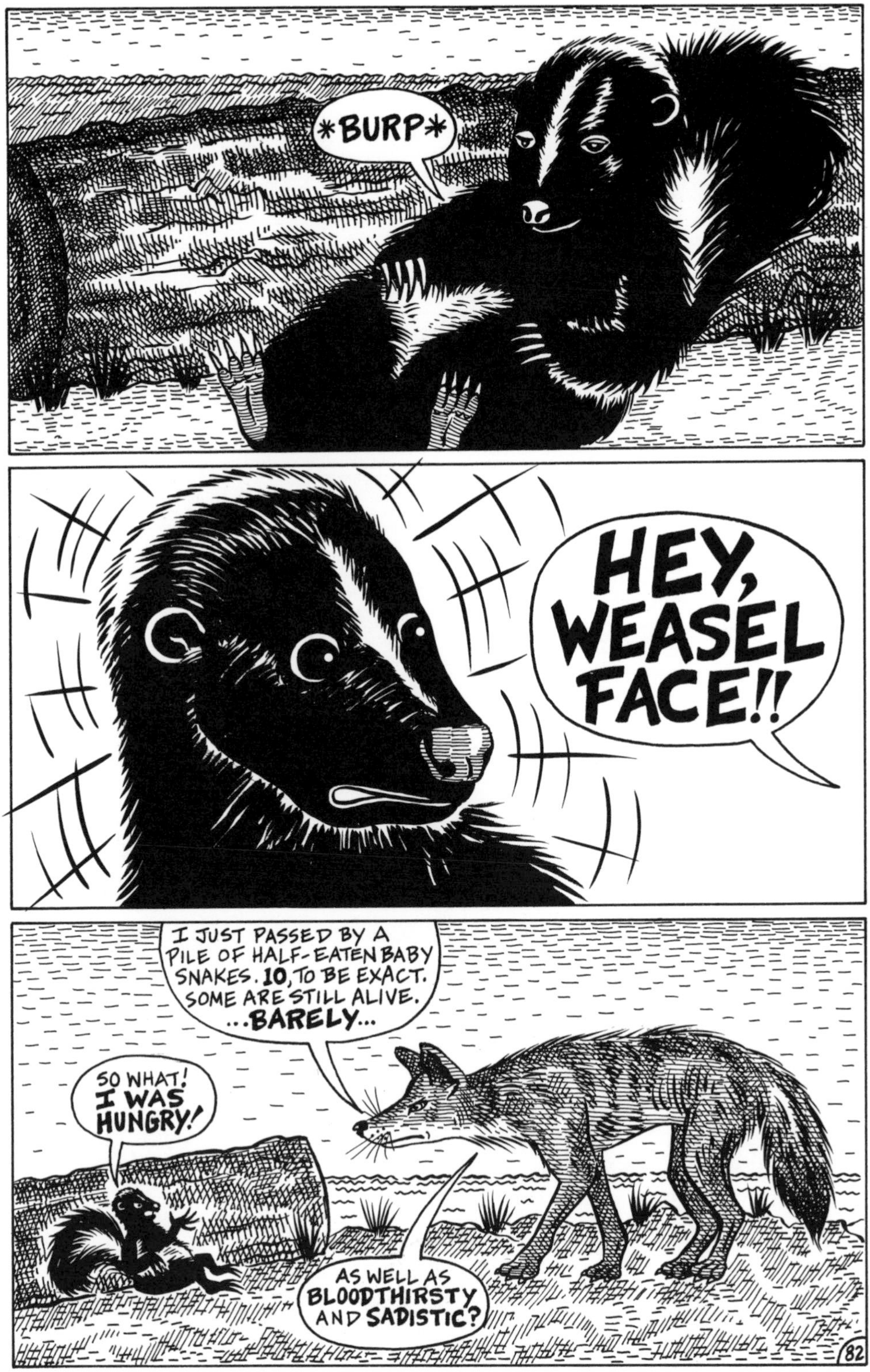
BURP
HEY, WEASEL FACE!!
I JUST PASSED BY A PILE OF HALF-EATEN BABY SNAKES. 10, TO BE EXACT. SOME ARE STILL ALIVE. ...BARELY...
SO WHAT! I WAS HUNGRY!
AS WELL AS BLOODTHIRSTY AND SADISTIC?

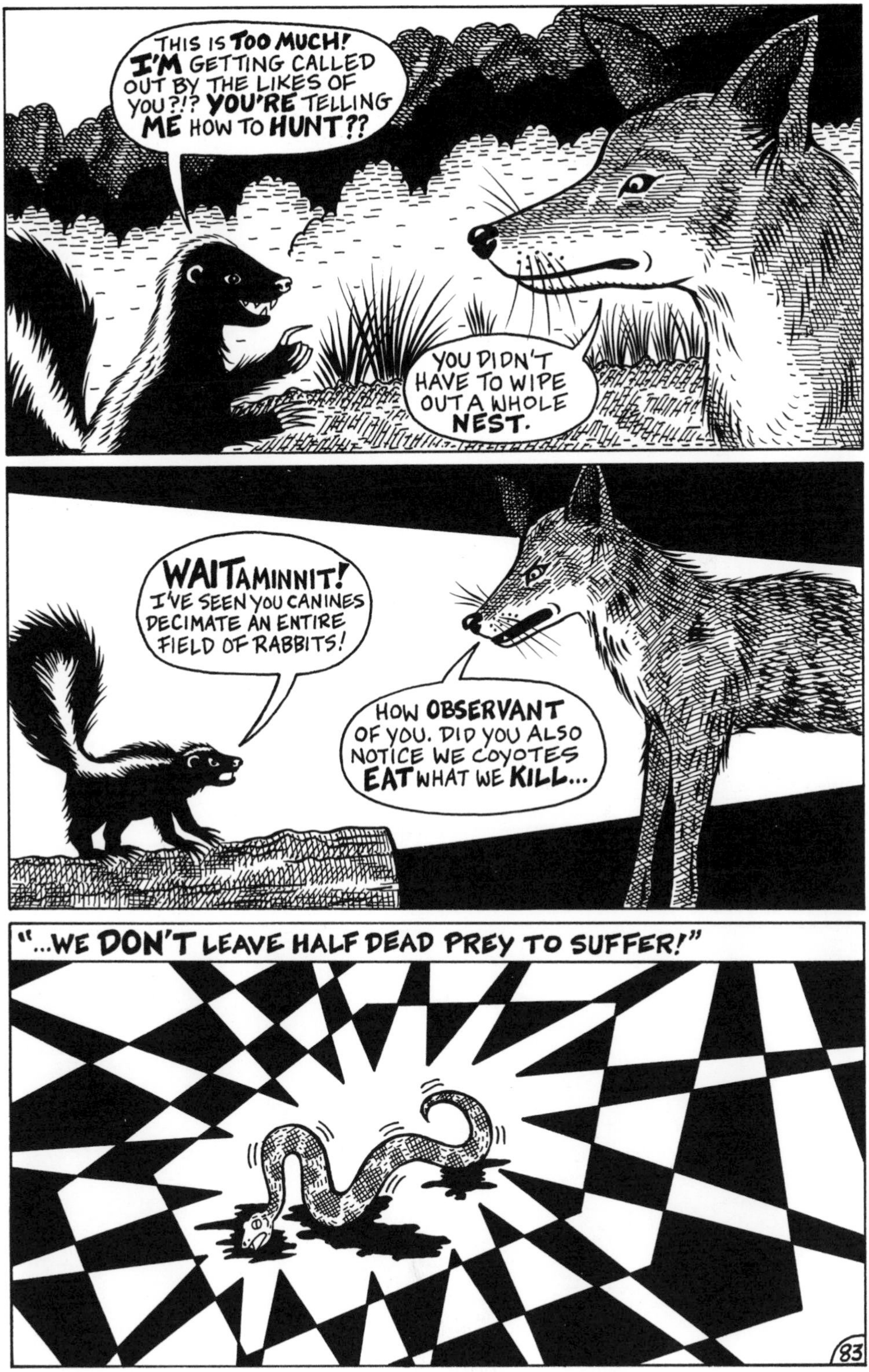
THIS IS TOO MUCH! I'M GETTING CALLED OUT BY THE LIKES OF YOU?!? YOU'RE TELLING ME HOW TO HUNT??
YOU DIDN'T HAVE TO WIPE OUT A WHOLE NEST.
WAITAMINNIT! I'VE SEEN YOU CANINES DECIMATE AN ENTIRE FIELD OF RABBITS!
HOW OBSERVANT OF YOU. DID YOU ALSO NOTICE WE COYOTES EAT WHAT WE KILL...
"...WE DON'T LEAVE HALF DEAD PREY TO SUFFER!"

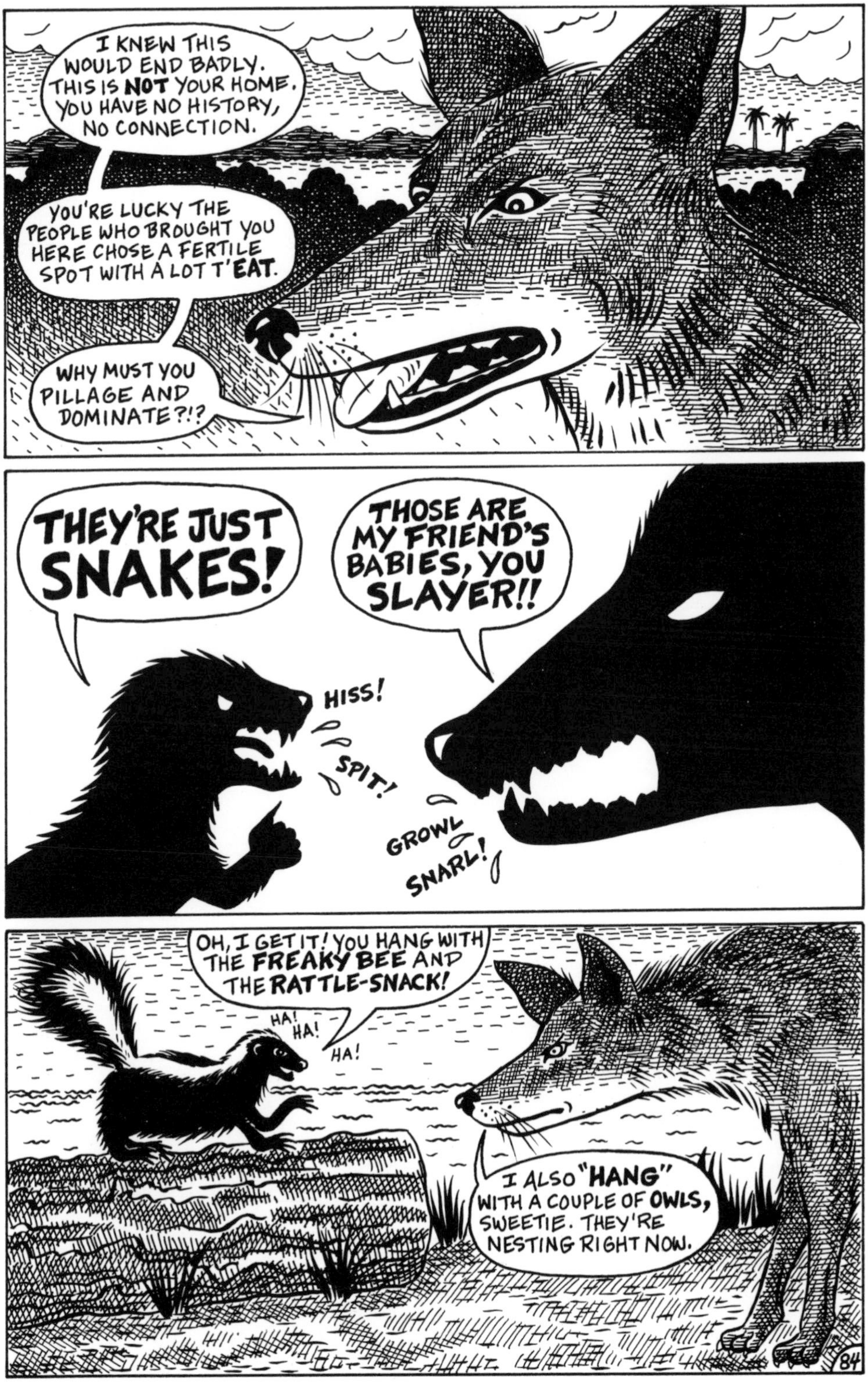
I KNEW THIS WOULD END BADLY. THIS IS **NOT** YOUR HOME. YOU HAVE NO HISTORY, NO CONNECTION.
YOU'RE LUCKY THE PEOPLE WHO BROUGHT YOU HERE CHOSE A FERTILE SPOT WITH A LOT T'**EAT**.
WHY MUST YOU PILLAGE AND DOMINATE?!?
THEY'RE JUST SNAKES!
THOSE ARE MY FRIEND'S BABIES, YOU SLAYER!!
HISS!
SPIT!
GROWL
SNARL!
OH, I GET IT! YOU HANG WITH THE **FREAKY BEE** AND THE **RATTLE-SNACK**!
HA! HA! HA!
I ALSO "**HANG**" WITH A COUPLE OF **OWLS**, SWEETIE. THEY'RE NESTING RIGHT NOW.

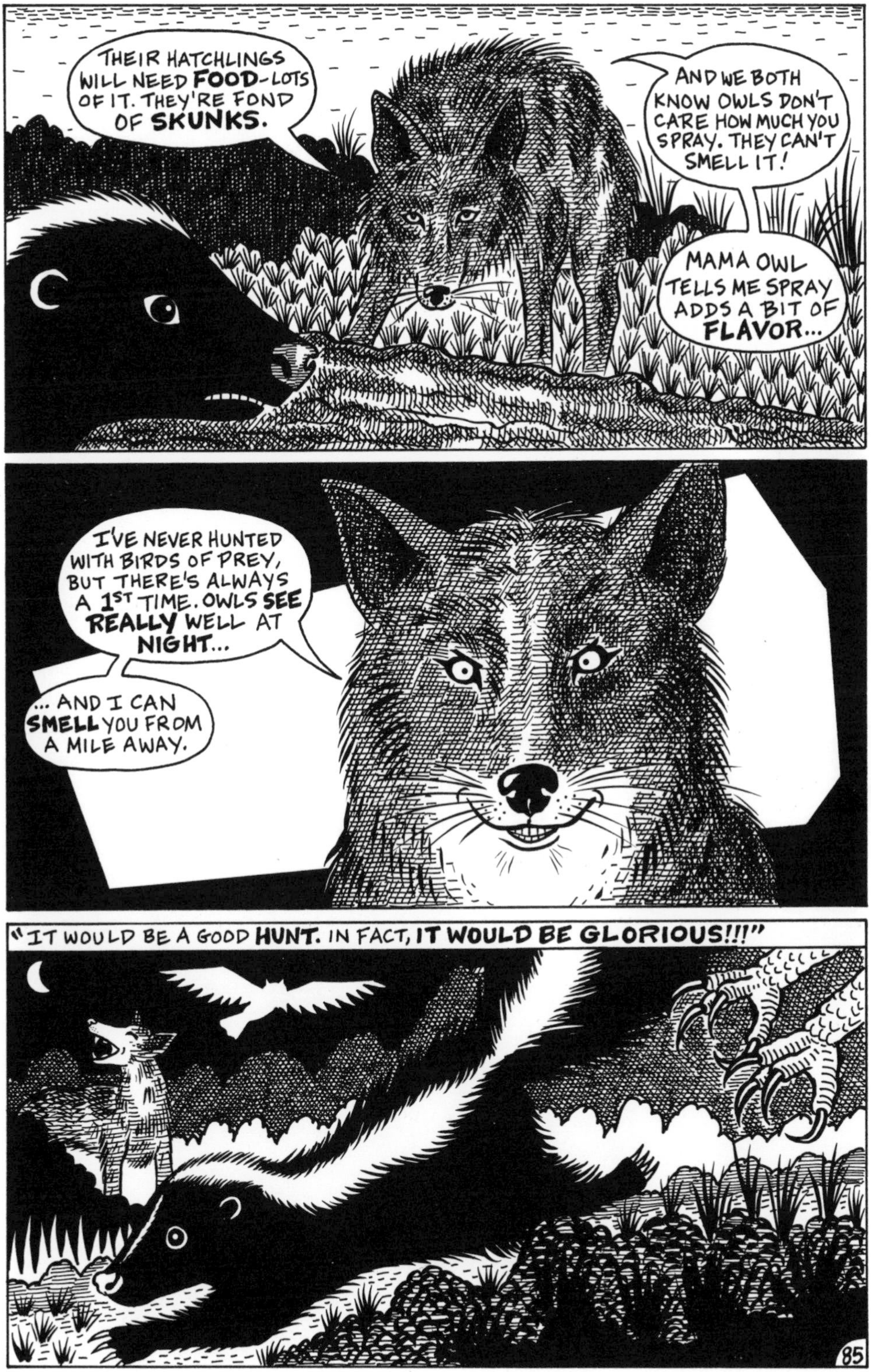
THEIR HATCHLINGS WILL NEED FOOD-LOTS OF IT. THEY'RE FOND OF SKUNKS.
AND WE BOTH KNOW OWLS DON'T CARE HOW MUCH YOU SPRAY. THEY CAN'T SMELL IT!
MAMA OWL TELLS ME SPRAY ADDS A BIT OF FLAVOR...
I'VE NEVER HUNTED WITH BIRDS OF PREY, BUT THERE'S ALWAYS A 1ST TIME. OWLS SEE REALLY WELL AT NIGHT...
... AND I CAN SMELL YOU FROM A MILE AWAY.
"IT WOULD BE A GOOD HUNT. IN FACT, IT WOULD BE GLORIOUS!!!"
85

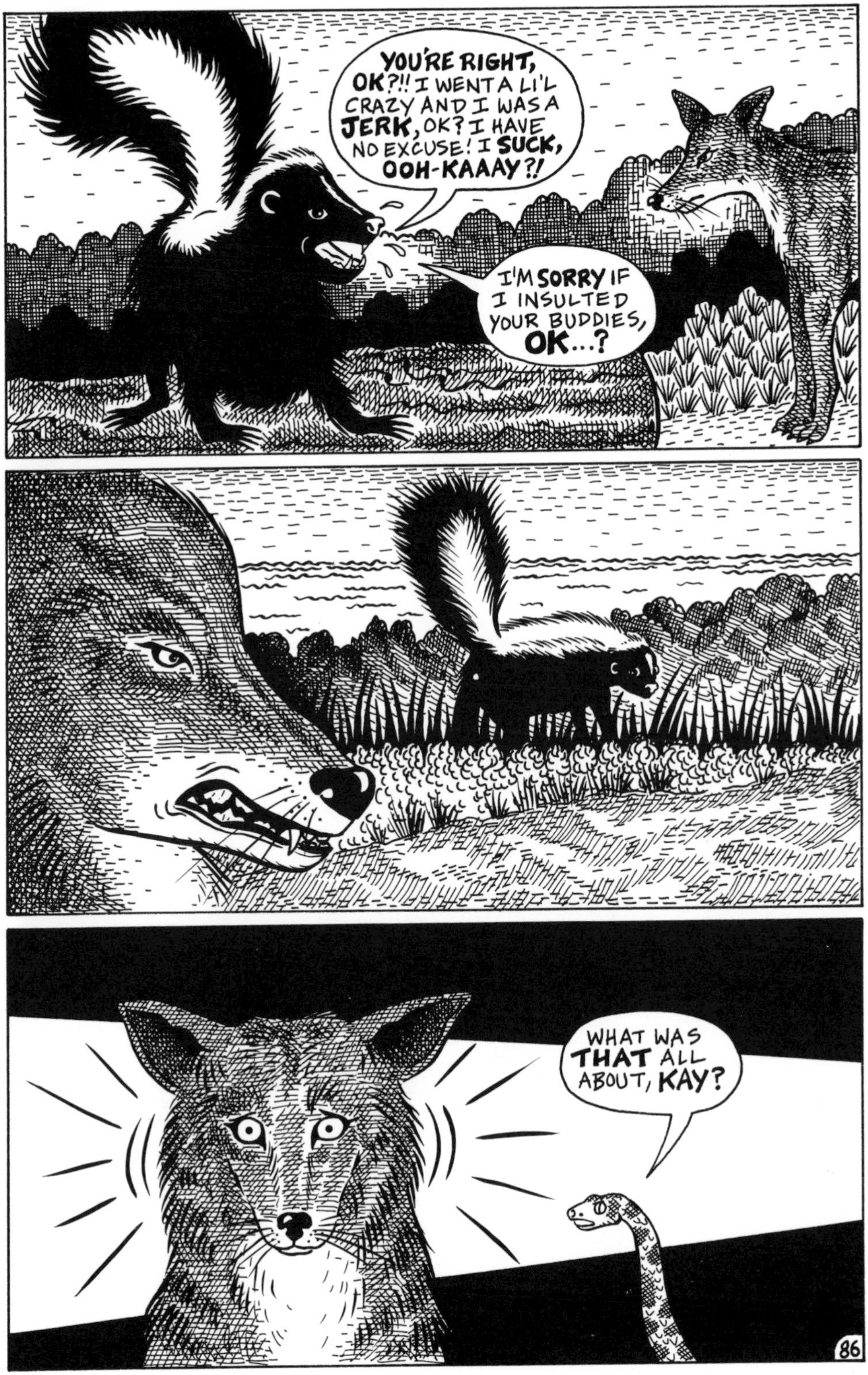
YOU'RE RIGHT, OK?!! I WENT A LI'L CRAZY AND I WAS A JERK, OK? I HAVE NO EXCUSE! I SUCK, OOH-KAAAY?!
I'M SORRY IF I INSULTED YOUR BUDDIES, OK...?
WHAT WAS THAT ALL ABOUT, KAY?

8

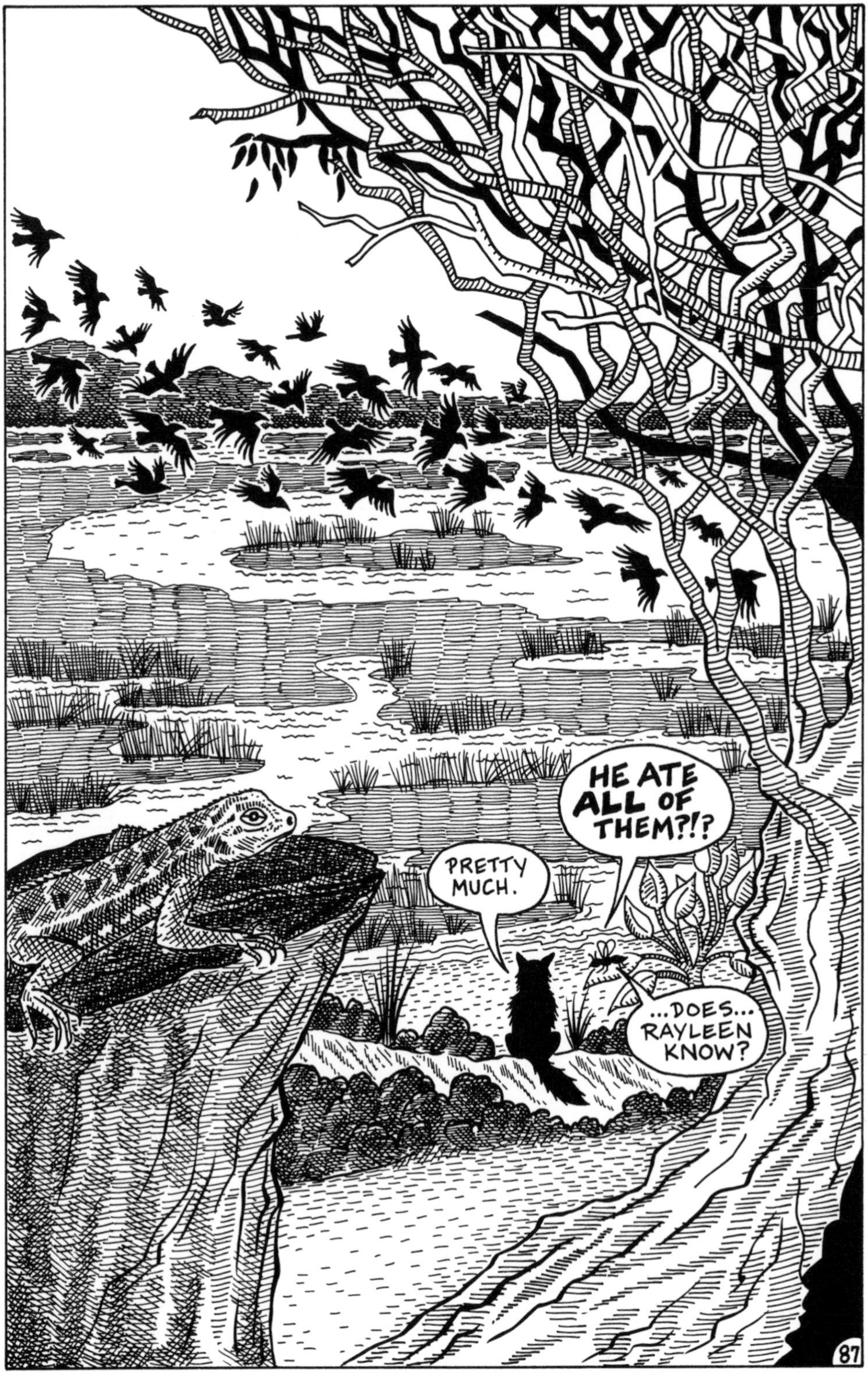
PRETTY MUCH.
HE ATE ALL OF THEM?!?
...DOES... RAYLEEN KNOW?

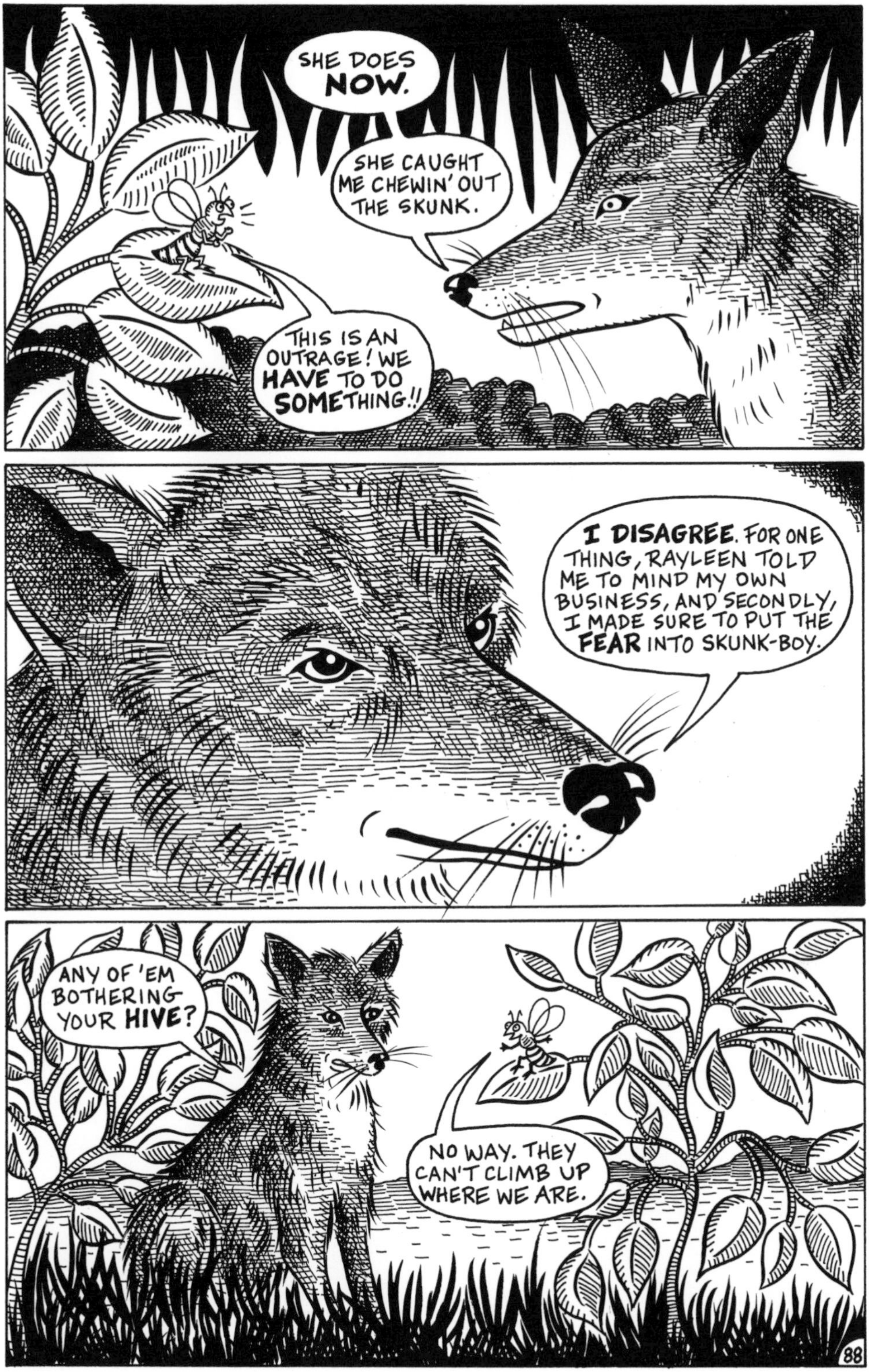
SHE DOES NOW.
SHE CAUGHT ME CHEWIN' OUT THE SKUNK.
THIS IS AN OUTRAGE! WE HAVE TO DO SOMETHING!!
I DISAGREE. FOR ONE THING, RAYLEEN TOLD ME TO MIND MY OWN BUSINESS, AND SECONDLY, I MADE SURE TO PUT THE FEAR INTO SKUNK-BOY.
ANY OF 'EM BOTHERING YOUR HIVE?
NO WAY. THEY CAN'T CLIMB UP WHERE WE ARE.
88

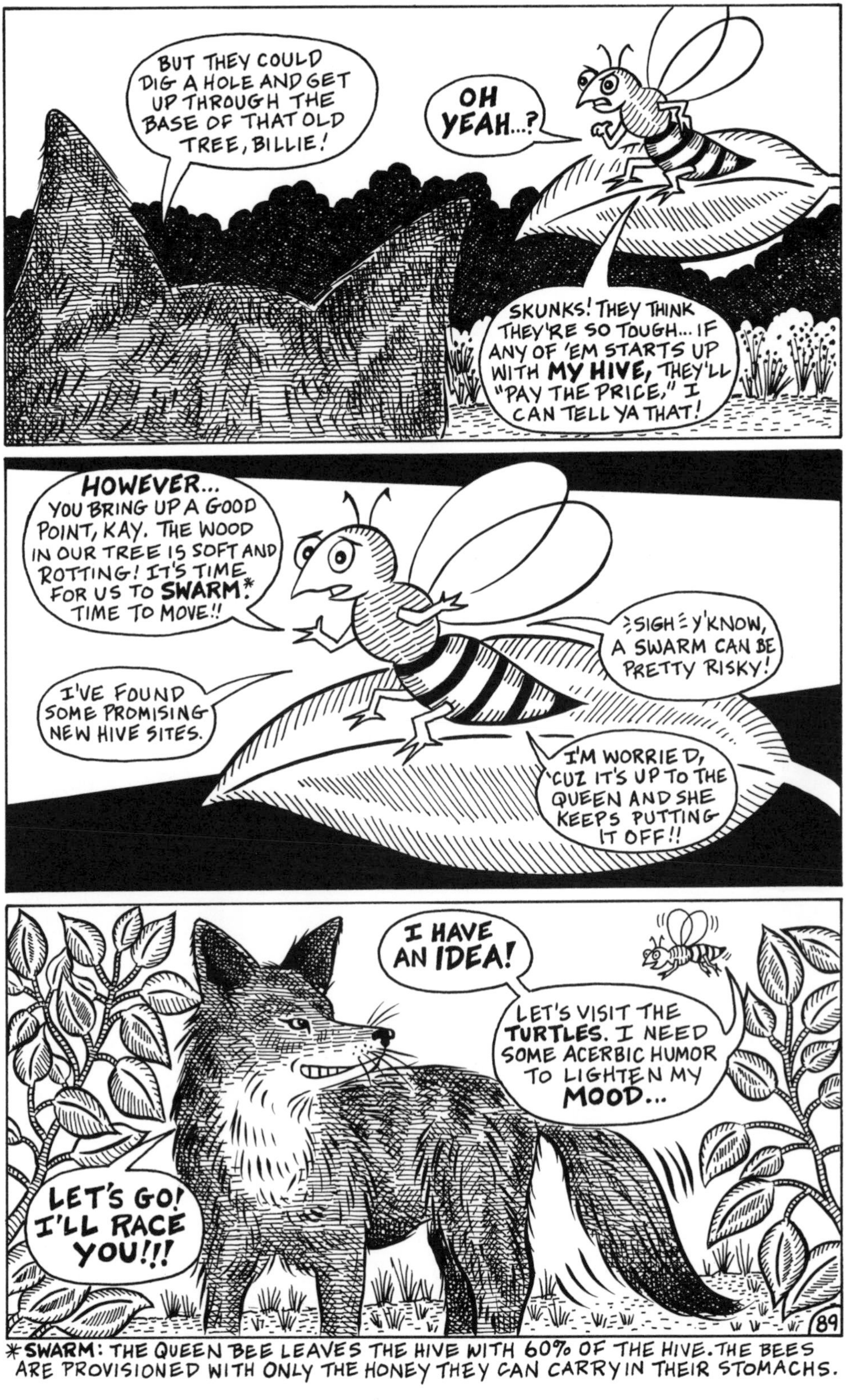

BUT THEY COULD DIG A HOLE AND GET UP THROUGH THE BASE OF THAT OLD TREE, BILLIE!
OH YEAH...?
SKUNKS! THEY THINK THEY'RE SO TOUGH... IF ANY OF 'EM STARTS UP WITH MY HIVE, THEY'LL "PAY THE PRICE," I CAN TELL YA THAT!
HOWEVER... YOU BRING UP A GOOD POINT, KAY. THE WOOD IN OUR TREE IS SOFT AND ROTTING! IT'S TIME FOR US TO SWARM.* TIME TO MOVE!!
I'VE FOUND SOME PROMISING NEW HIVE SITES.
≋SIGH≋ Y'KNOW, A SWARM CAN BE PRETTY RISKY!
I'M WORRIED, 'CUZ IT'S UP TO THE QUEEN AND SHE KEEPS PUTTING IT OFF!!
I HAVE AN IDEA!
LET'S VISIT THE TURTLES. I NEED SOME ACERBIC HUMOR TO LIGHTEN MY MOOD...
LET'S GO! I'LL RACE YOU!!!

CHAPTER EIGHT

*SWARM: THE QUEEN BEE LEAVES THE HIVE WITH 60% OF THE HIVE. THE BEES ARE PROVISIONED WITH ONLY THE HONEY THEY CAN CARRY IN THEIR STOMACHS.

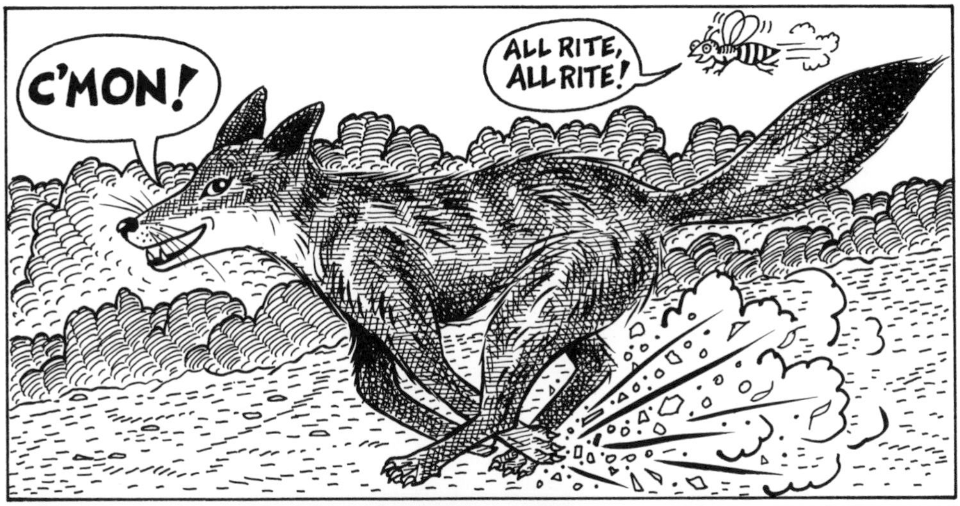
C'MON!
ALL RITE, ALL RITE!

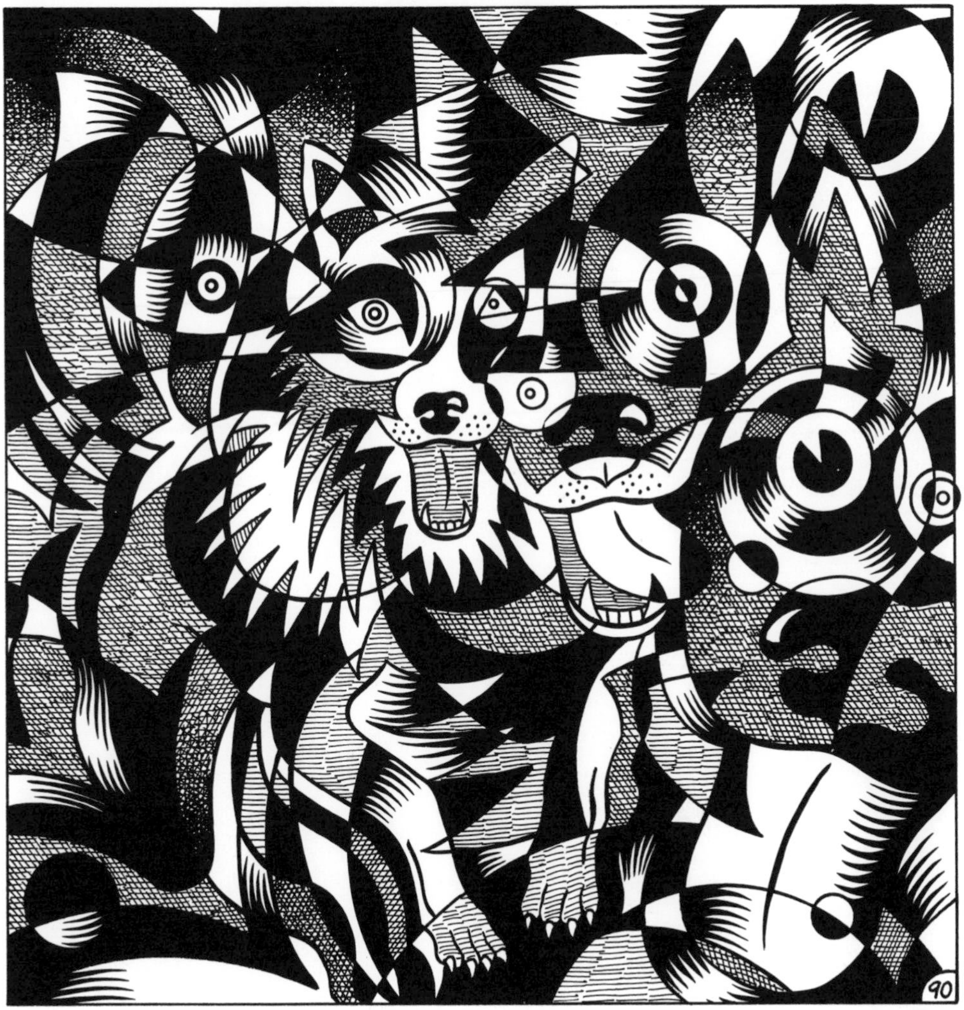

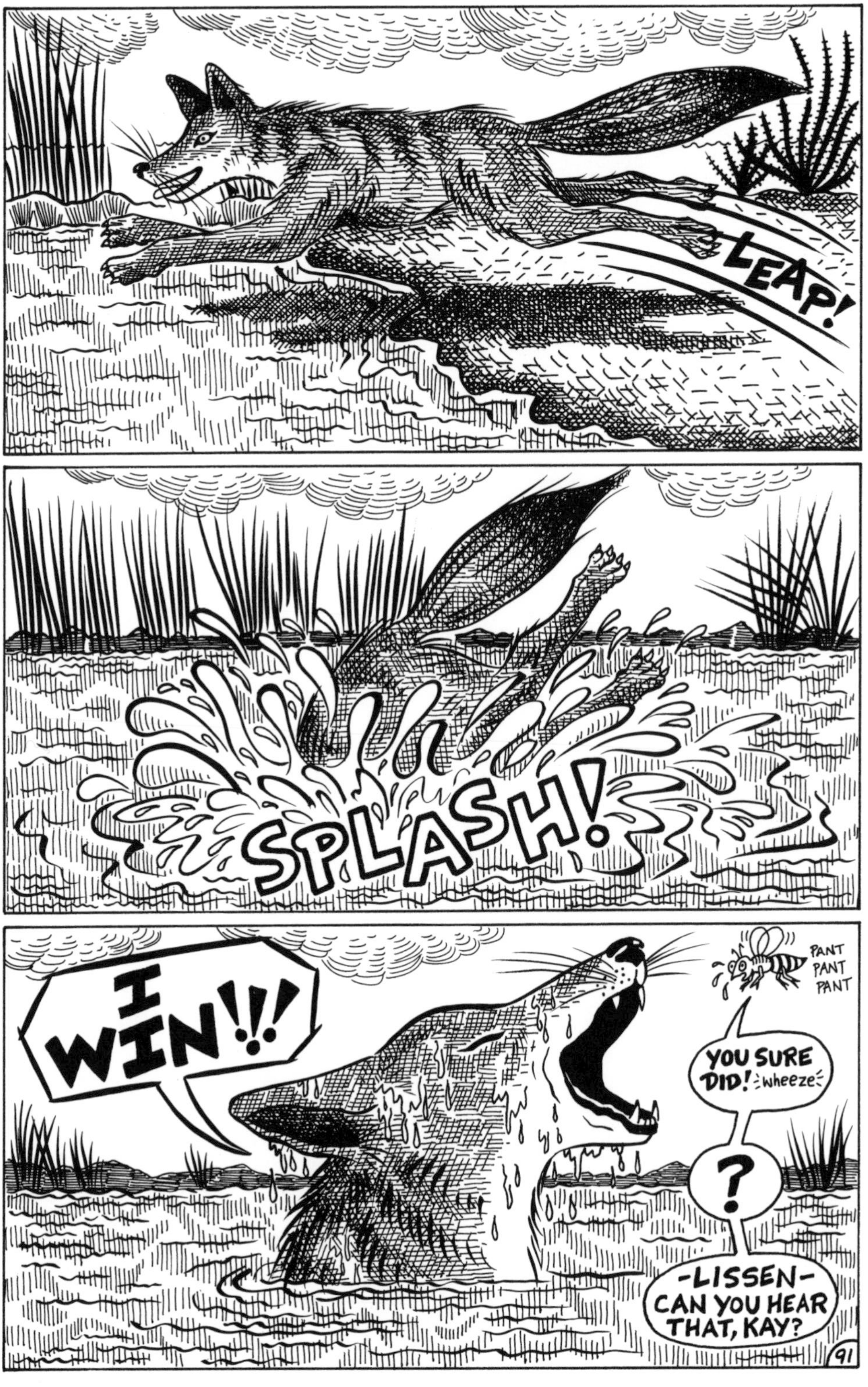
LEAP!
SPLASH!
I WIN!!!
PANT PANT PANT
YOU SURE DID! wheeze
?
-LISSEN- CAN YOU HEAR THAT, KAY?

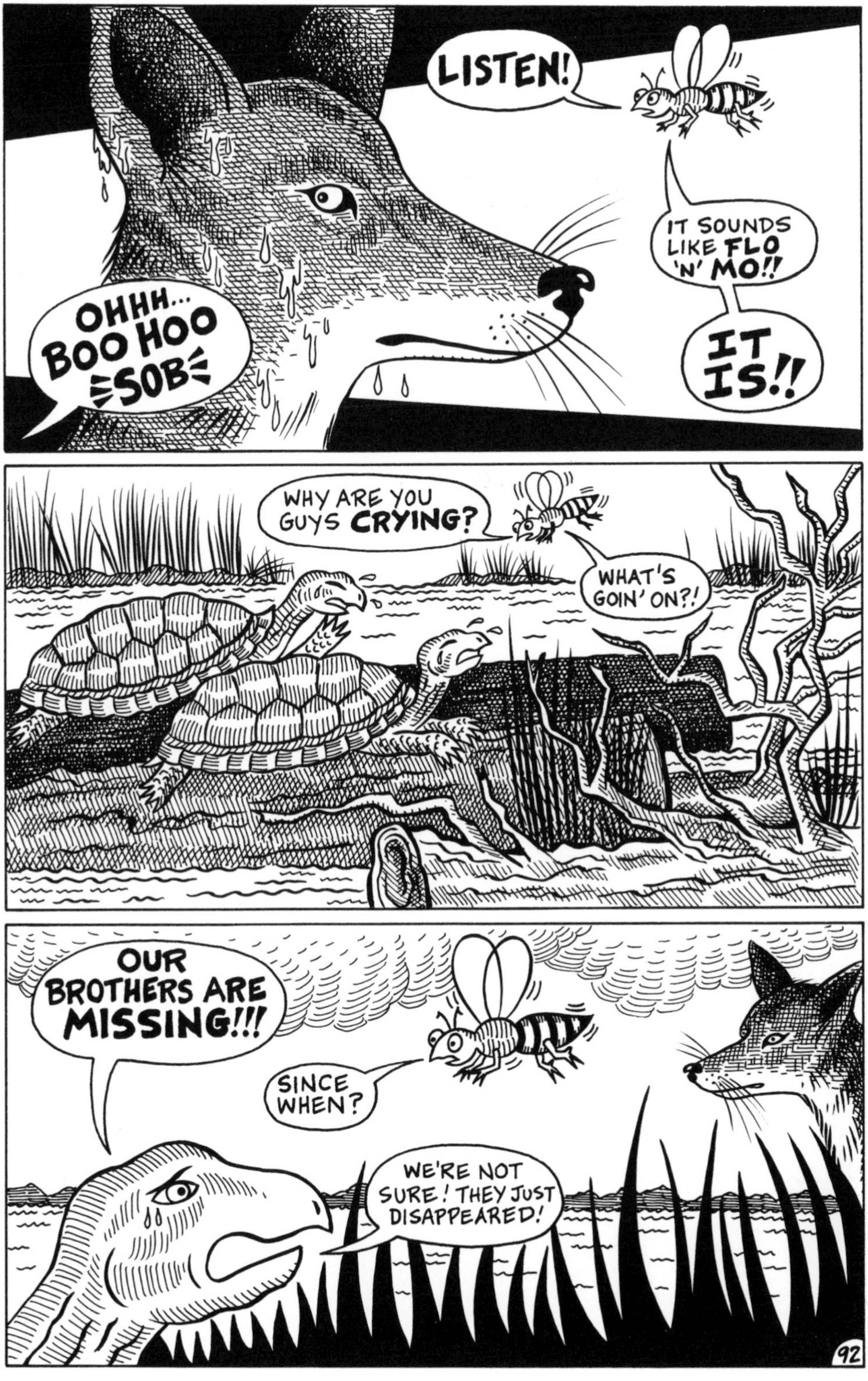
LISTEN!
IT SOUNDS LIKE FLO 'N' MO!!
IT IS!!
OHHH... BOO HOO SOB
WHY ARE YOU GUYS CRYING?
WHAT'S GOIN' ON?!
OUR BROTHERS ARE MISSING!!!
SINCE WHEN?
WE'RE NOT SURE! THEY JUST DISAPPEARED!
92

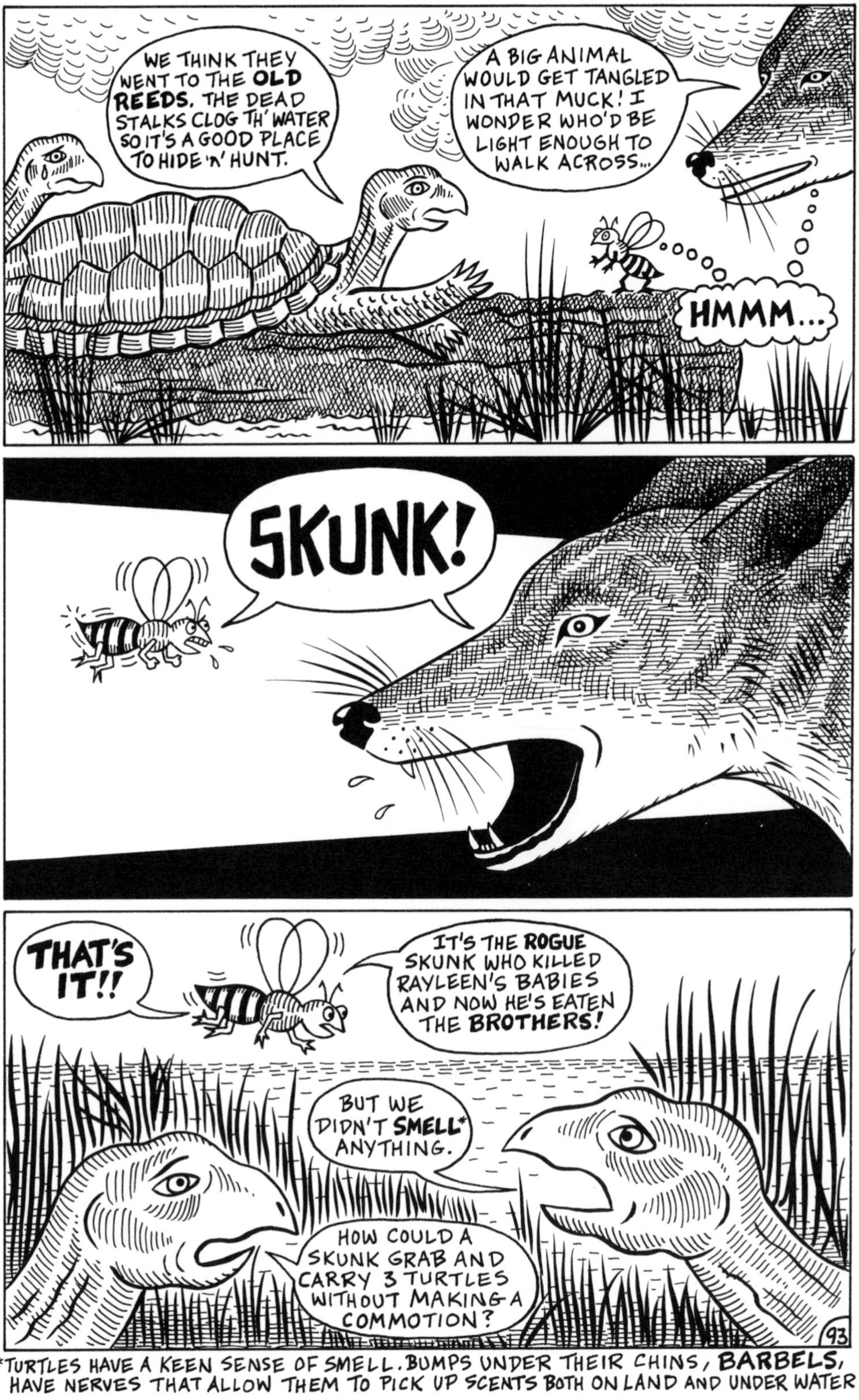

WE THINK THEY WENT TO THE OLD REEDS. THE DEAD STALKS CLOG TH' WATER SO IT'S A GOOD PLACE TO HIDE 'N' HUNT.
A BIG ANIMAL WOULD GET TANGLED IN THAT MUCK! I WONDER WHO'D BE LIGHT ENOUGH TO WALK ACROSS...
HMMM...
SKUNK!
THAT'S IT!!
IT'S THE ROGUE SKUNK WHO KILLED RAYLEEN'S BABIES AND NOW HE'S EATEN THE BROTHERS!
BUT WE DIDN'T SMELL* ANYTHING.
HOW COULD A SKUNK GRAB AND CARRY 3 TURTLES WITHOUT MAKING A COMMOTION?

*TURTLES HAVE A KEEN SENSE OF SMELL. BUMPS UNDER THEIR CHINS, **BARBELS**, HAVE NERVES THAT ALLOW THEM TO PICK UP SCENTS BOTH ON LAND AND UNDER WATER.

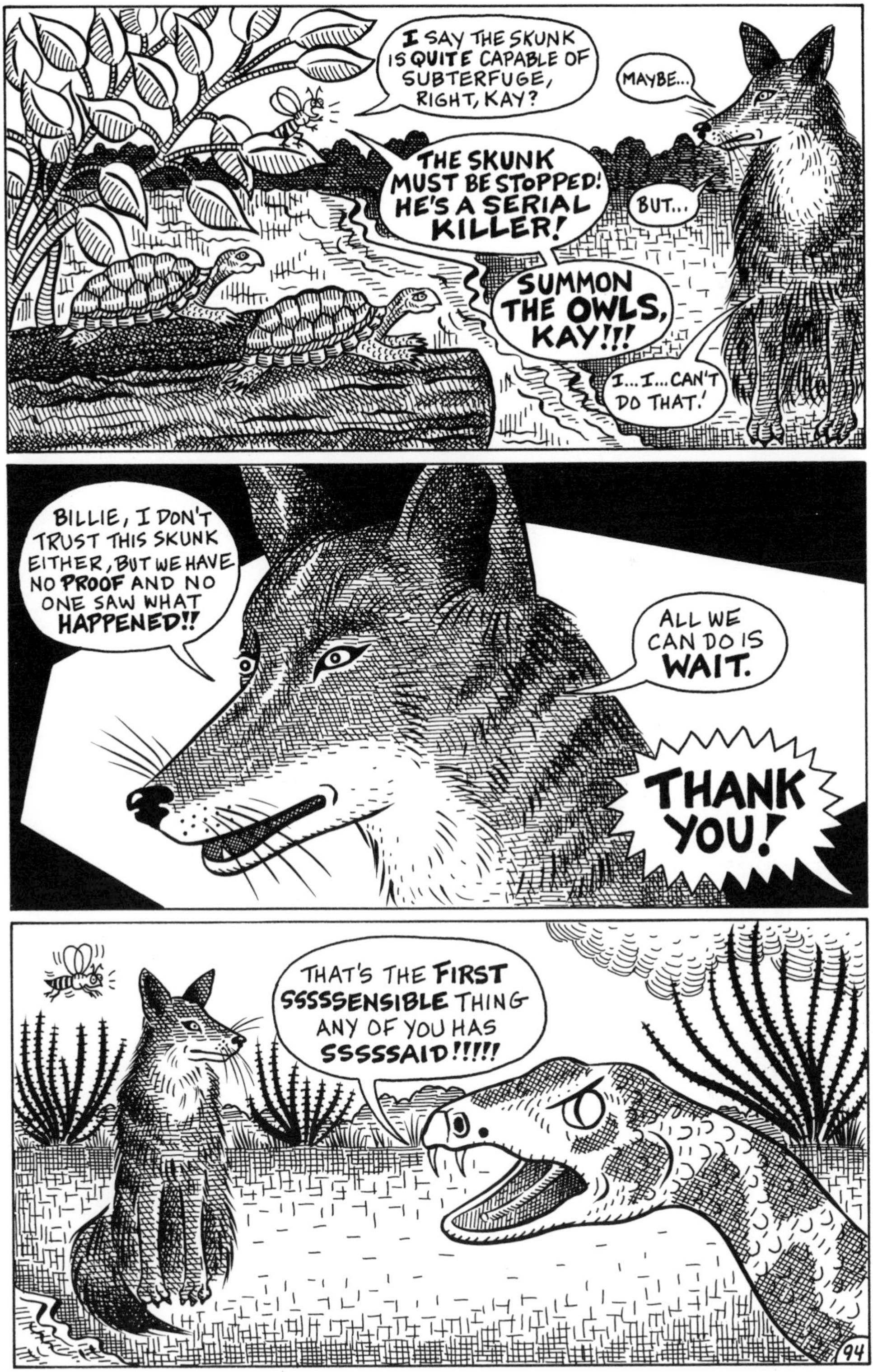
I SAY THE SKUNK IS QUITE CAPABLE OF SUBTERFUGE, RIGHT, KAY?
MAYBE...
THE SKUNK MUST BE STOPPED! HE'S A SERIAL KILLER!
BUT...
SUMMON THE OWLS, KAY!!!
I... I... CAN'T DO THAT.
BILLIE, I DON'T TRUST THIS SKUNK EITHER, BUT WE HAVE NO PROOF AND NO ONE SAW WHAT HAPPENED!!
ALL WE CAN DO IS WAIT.
THANK YOU!
THAT'S THE FIRST SSSSSENSIBLE THING ANY OF YOU HAS SSSSSAID!!!!!
94

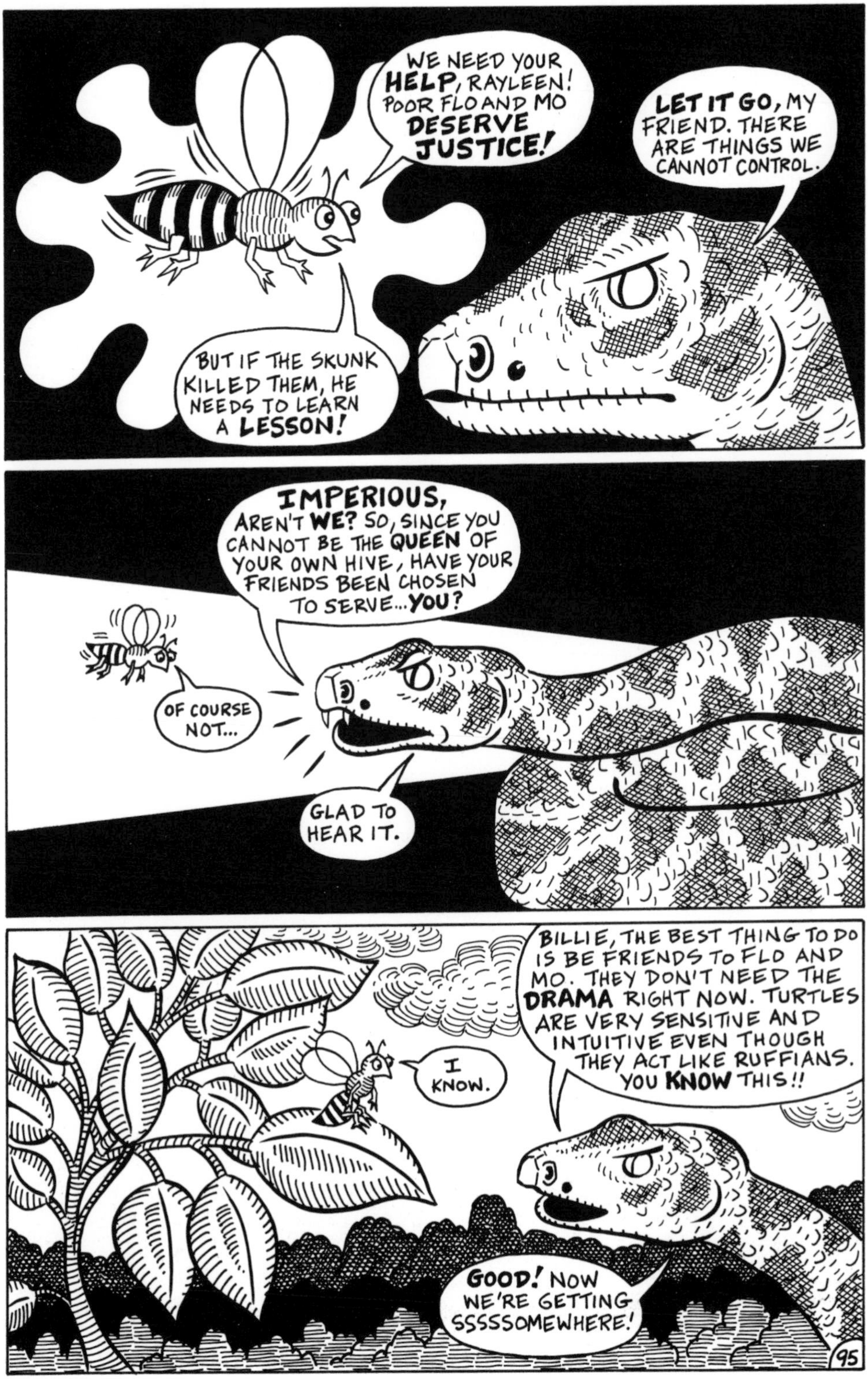
WE NEED YOUR HELP, RAYLEEN! POOR FLO AND MO DESERVE JUSTICE!
LET IT GO, MY FRIEND. THERE ARE THINGS WE CANNOT CONTROL.
BUT IF THE SKUNK KILLED THEM, HE NEEDS TO LEARN A LESSON!
IMPERIOUS, AREN'T WE? SO, SINCE YOU CANNOT BE THE QUEEN OF YOUR OWN HIVE, HAVE YOUR FRIENDS BEEN CHOSEN TO SERVE...YOU?
OF COURSE NOT...
GLAD TO HEAR IT.
BILLIE, THE BEST THING TO DO IS BE FRIENDS TO FLO AND MO. THEY DON'T NEED THE DRAMA RIGHT NOW. TURTLES ARE VERY SENSITIVE AND INTUITIVE EVEN THOUGH THEY ACT LIKE RUFFIANS. YOU KNOW THIS!!
I KNOW.
GOOD! NOW WE'RE GETTING SSSSSOMEWHERE!

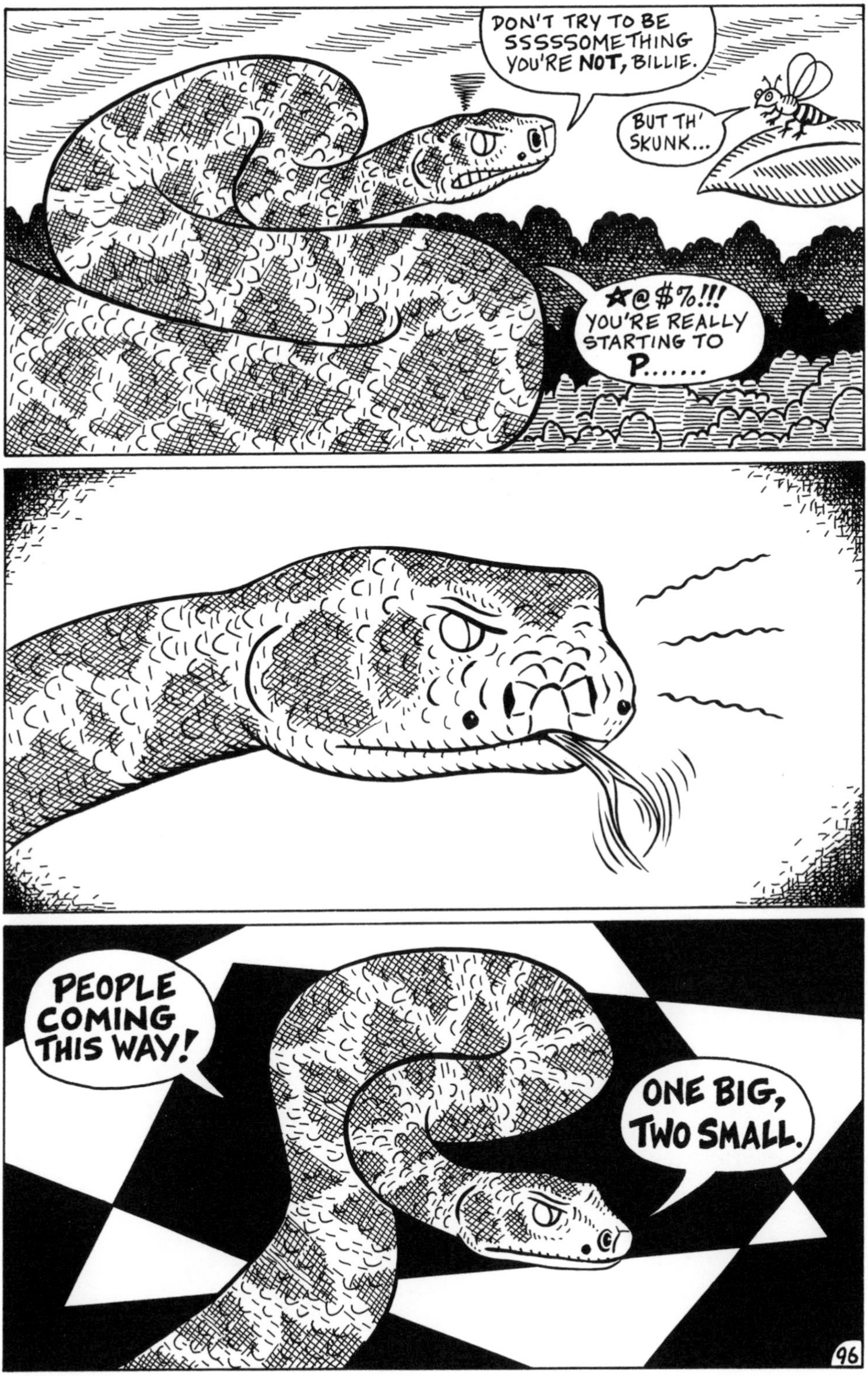
DON'T TRY TO BE SSSSSOMETHING YOU'RE NOT, BILLIE.
BUT TH' SKUNK...
☆@$%!!! YOU'RE REALLY STARTING TO P.......
PEOPLE COMING THIS WAY!
ONE BIG, TWO SMALL.

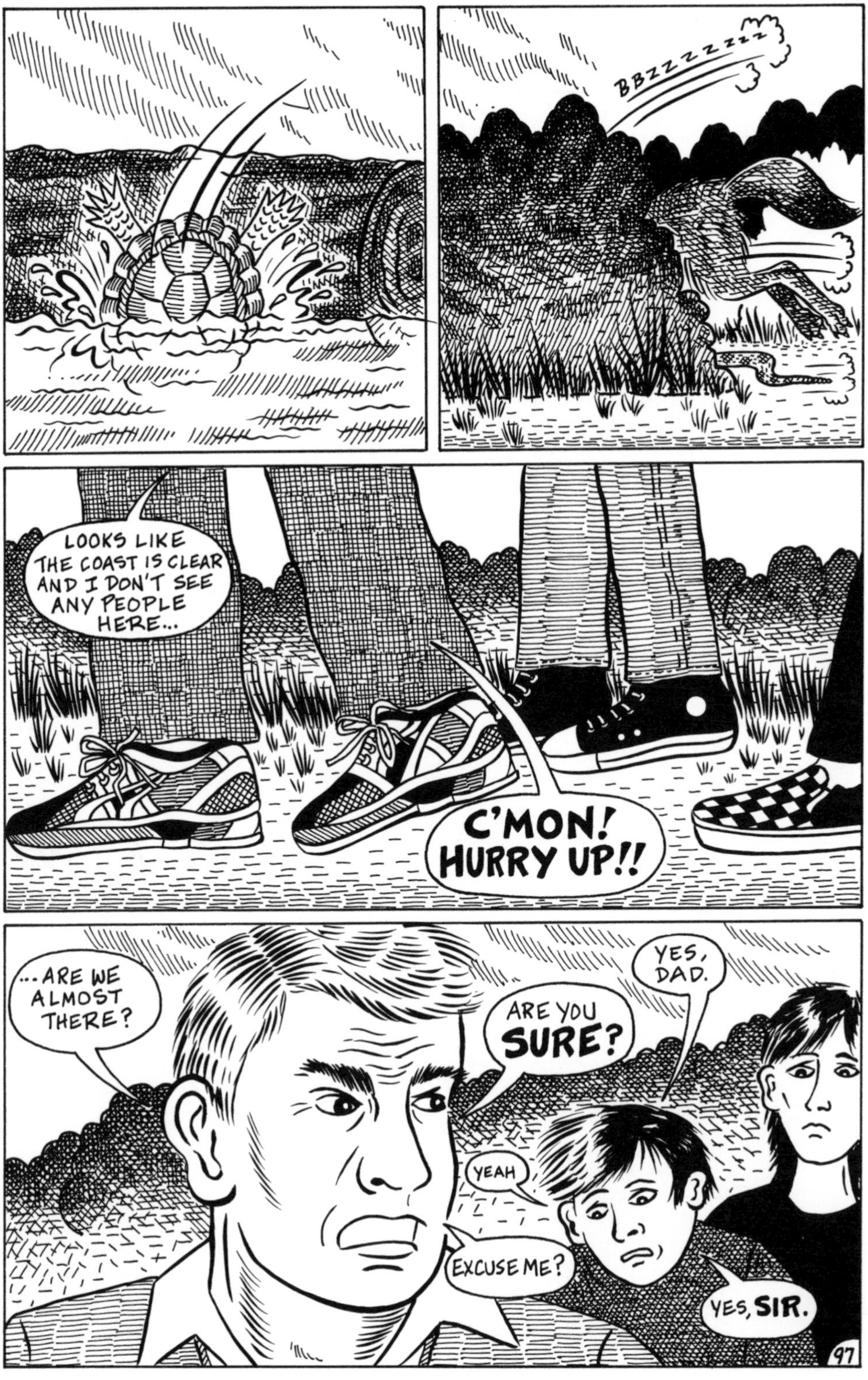
BBZZZZZZZZ
LOOKS LIKE THE COAST IS CLEAR AND I DON'T SEE ANY PEOPLE HERE...
C'MON! HURRY UP!!
...ARE WE ALMOST THERE?
ARE YOU **SURE**?
YES, DAD.
YEAH
EXCUSE ME?
YES, **SIR.**

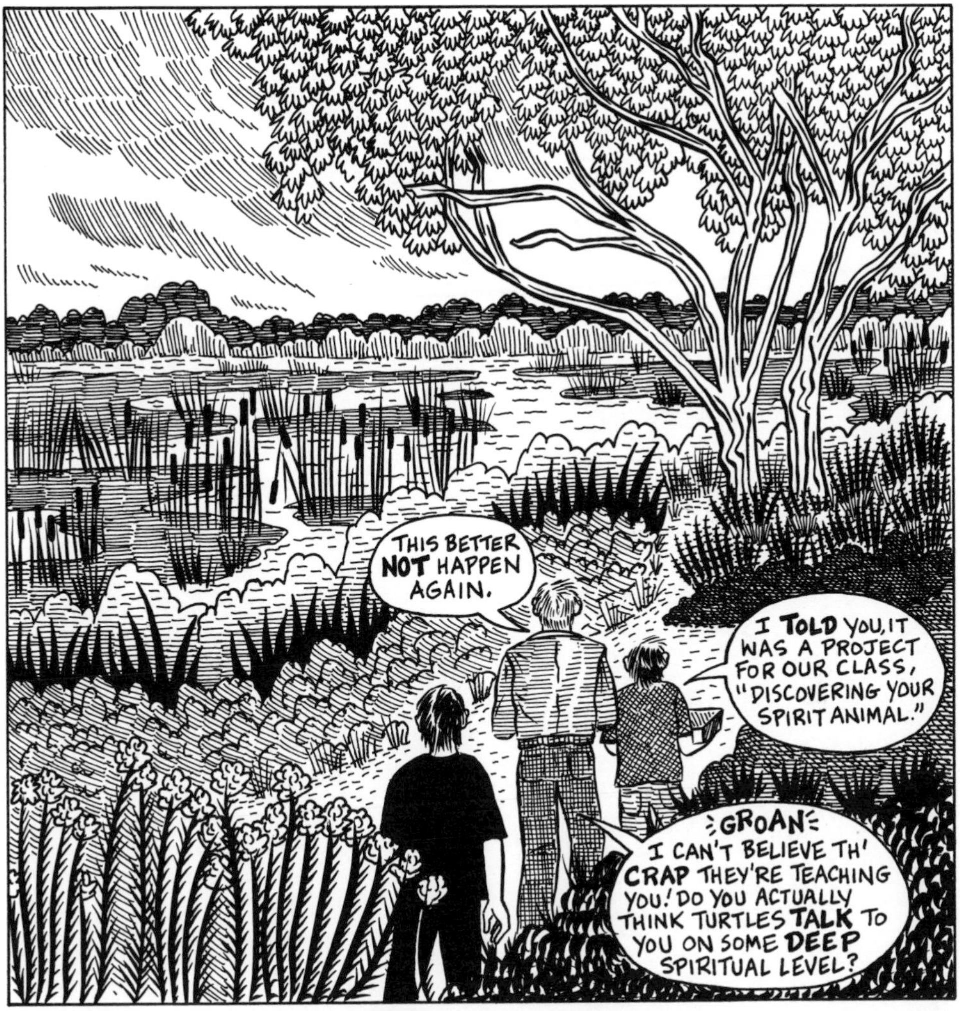
THIS BETTER NOT HAPPEN AGAIN.
I TOLD YOU, IT WAS A PROJECT FOR OUR CLASS, "DISCOVERING YOUR SPIRIT ANIMAL."
GROAN
I CAN'T BELIEVE TH' CRAP THEY'RE TEACHING YOU! DO YOU ACTUALLY THINK TURTLES TALK TO YOU ON SOME DEEP SPIRITUAL LEVEL?

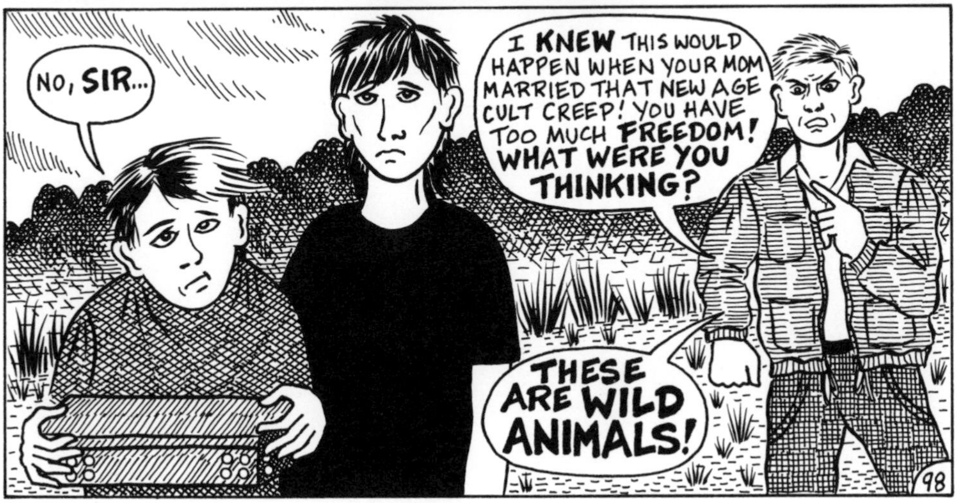
NO, SIR...
I KNEW THIS WOULD HAPPEN WHEN YOUR MOM MARRIED THAT NEW AGE CULT CREEP! YOU HAVE TOO MUCH FREEDOM! WHAT WERE YOU THINKING?
THESE ARE WILD ANIMALS!
98

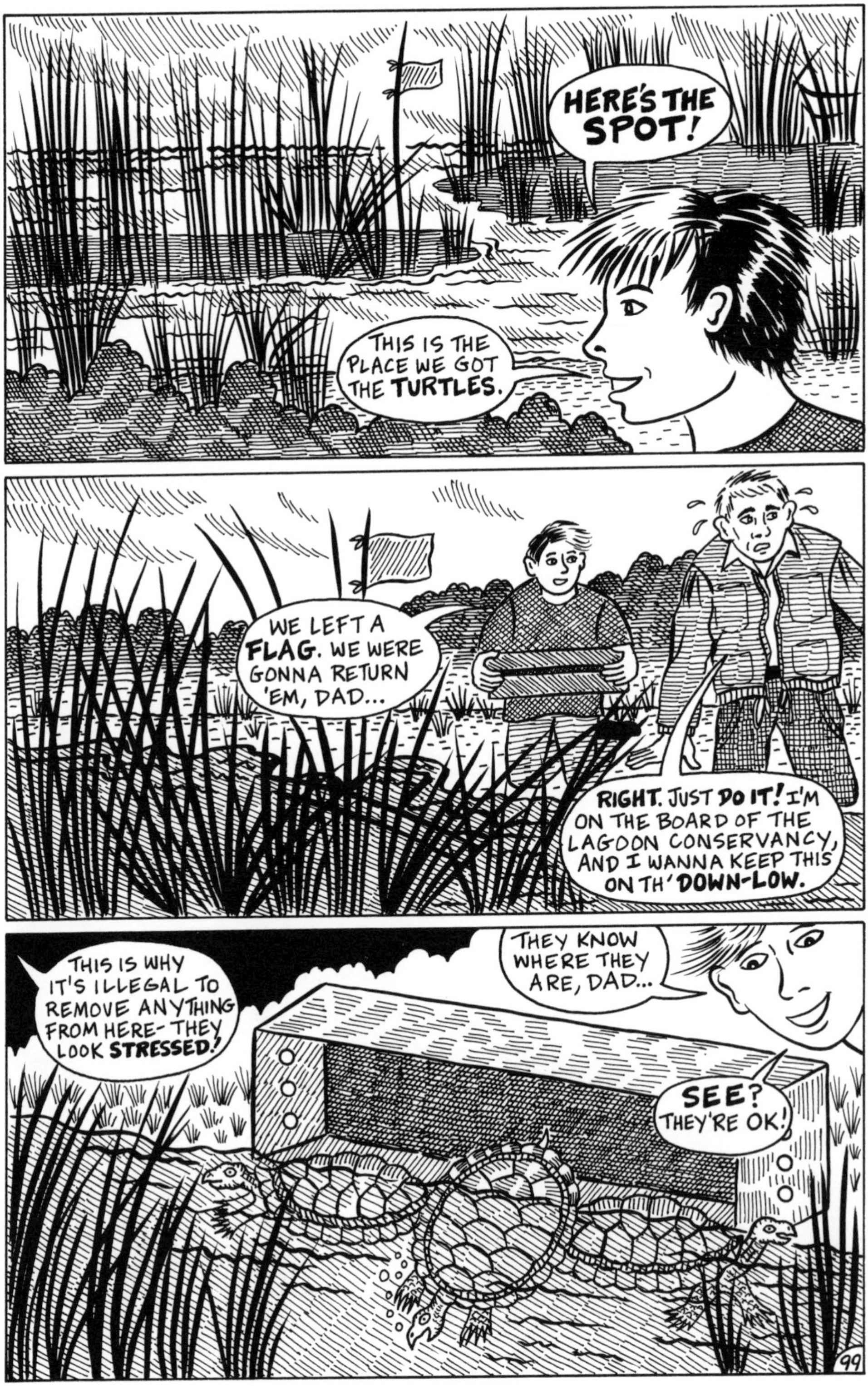
HERE'S THE SPOT!
THIS IS THE PLACE WE GOT THE TURTLES.
WE LEFT A FLAG. WE WERE GONNA RETURN 'EM, DAD...
RIGHT. JUST DO IT! I'M ON THE BOARD OF THE LAGOON CONSERVANCY, AND I WANNA KEEP THIS ON TH' DOWN-LOW.
THIS IS WHY IT'S ILLEGAL TO REMOVE ANYTHING FROM HERE- THEY LOOK STRESSED!
THEY KNOW WHERE THEY ARE, DAD...
SEE? THEY'RE OK!
99

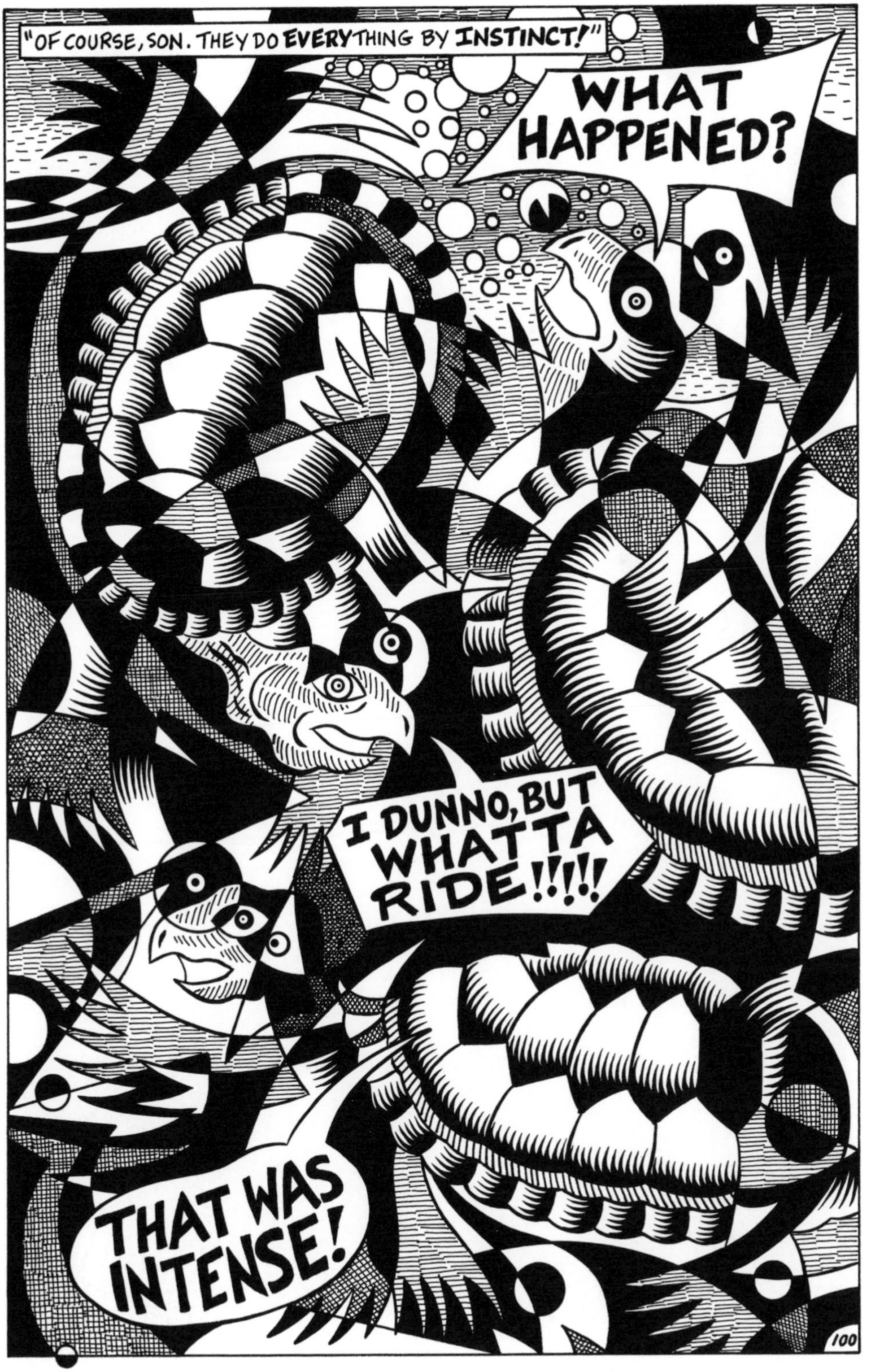
"OF COURSE, SON. THEY DO EVERYTHING BY INSTINCT!"
WHAT HAPPENED?
I DUNNO, BUT WHATTA RIDE!!!!!
THAT WAS INTENSE!

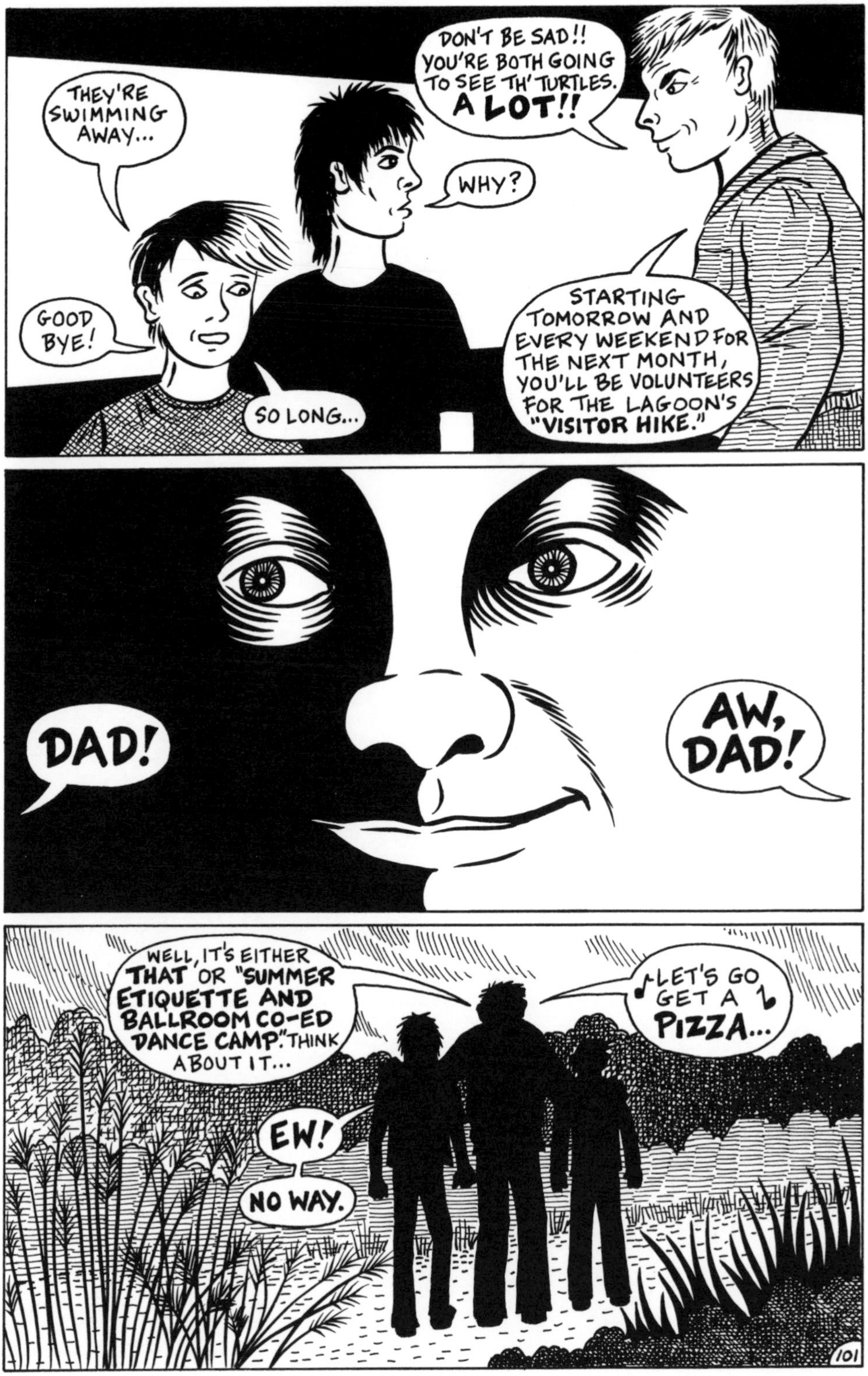
THEY'RE SWIMMING AWAY...
DON'T BE SAD!! YOU'RE BOTH GOING TO SEE TH' TURTLES. A LOT!!
WHY?
GOOD BYE!
SO LONG...
STARTING TOMORROW AND EVERY WEEKEND FOR THE NEXT MONTH, YOU'LL BE VOLUNTEERS FOR THE LAGOON'S "VISITOR HIKE."
DAD!
AW, DAD!
WELL, IT'S EITHER THAT OR "SUMMER ETIQUETTE AND BALLROOM CO-ED DANCE CAMP." THINK ABOUT IT...
LET'S GO GET A PIZZA...
EW!
NO WAY.

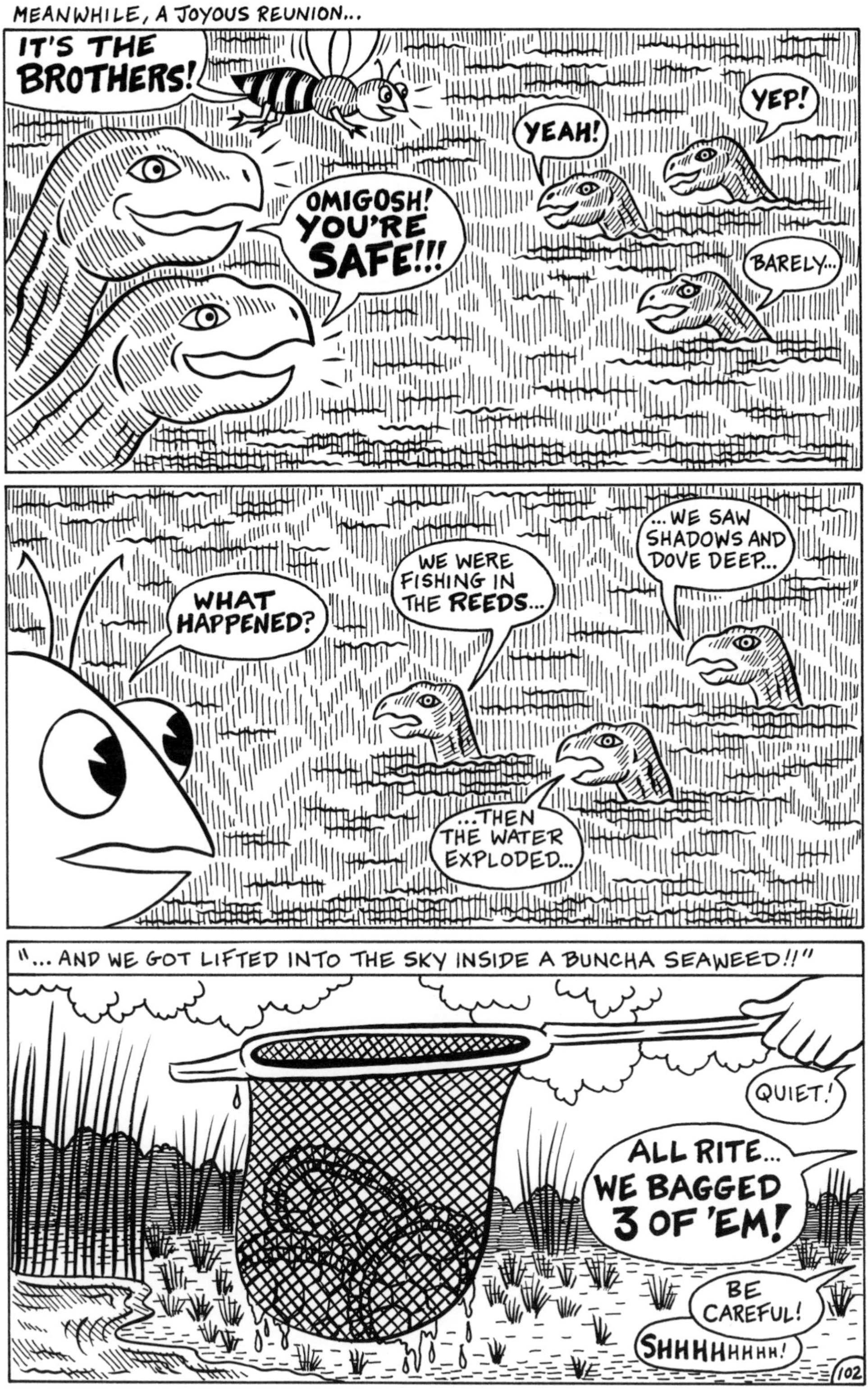
MEANWHILE, A JOYOUS REUNION...
IT'S THE BROTHERS!
OMIGOSH! YOU'RE SAFE!!!
YEAH!
YEP!
BARELY...
WHAT HAPPENED?
WE WERE FISHING IN THE REEDS...
...WE SAW SHADOWS AND DOVE DEEP...
...THEN THE WATER EXPLODED...
"... AND WE GOT LIFTED INTO THE SKY INSIDE A BUNCHA SEAWEED!!"
QUIET!
ALL RITE... WE BAGGED 3 OF 'EM!
BE CAREFUL!
SHHHHHHHH!

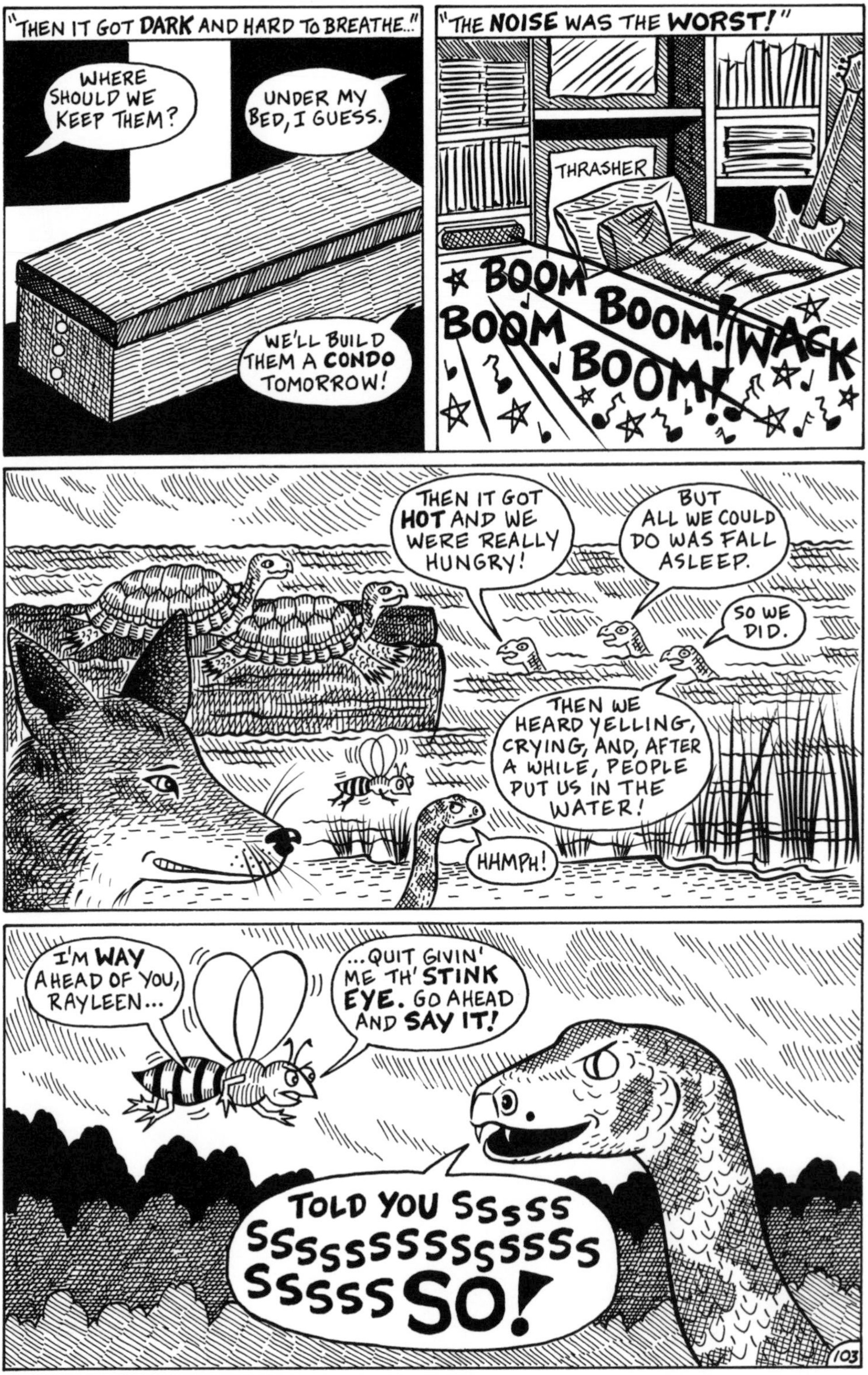
"THEN IT GOT DARK AND HARD TO BREATHE..."
WHERE SHOULD WE KEEP THEM?
UNDER MY BED, I GUESS.
WE'LL BUILD THEM A CONDO TOMORROW!
"THE NOISE WAS THE WORST!"
THRASHER
BOOM BOOM BOOM! BOOM! WACK
THEN IT GOT HOT AND WE WERE REALLY HUNGRY!
BUT ALL WE COULD DO WAS FALL ASLEEP.
SO WE DID.
THEN WE HEARD YELLING, CRYING, AND, AFTER A WHILE, PEOPLE PUT US IN THE WATER!
HHMPH!
I'M WAY AHEAD OF YOU, RAYLEEN...
...QUIT GIVIN' ME TH' STINK EYE. GO AHEAD AND SAY IT!
TOLD YOU SSSSS SSSSSSSSSSSSSSS SSSSS SO!

9

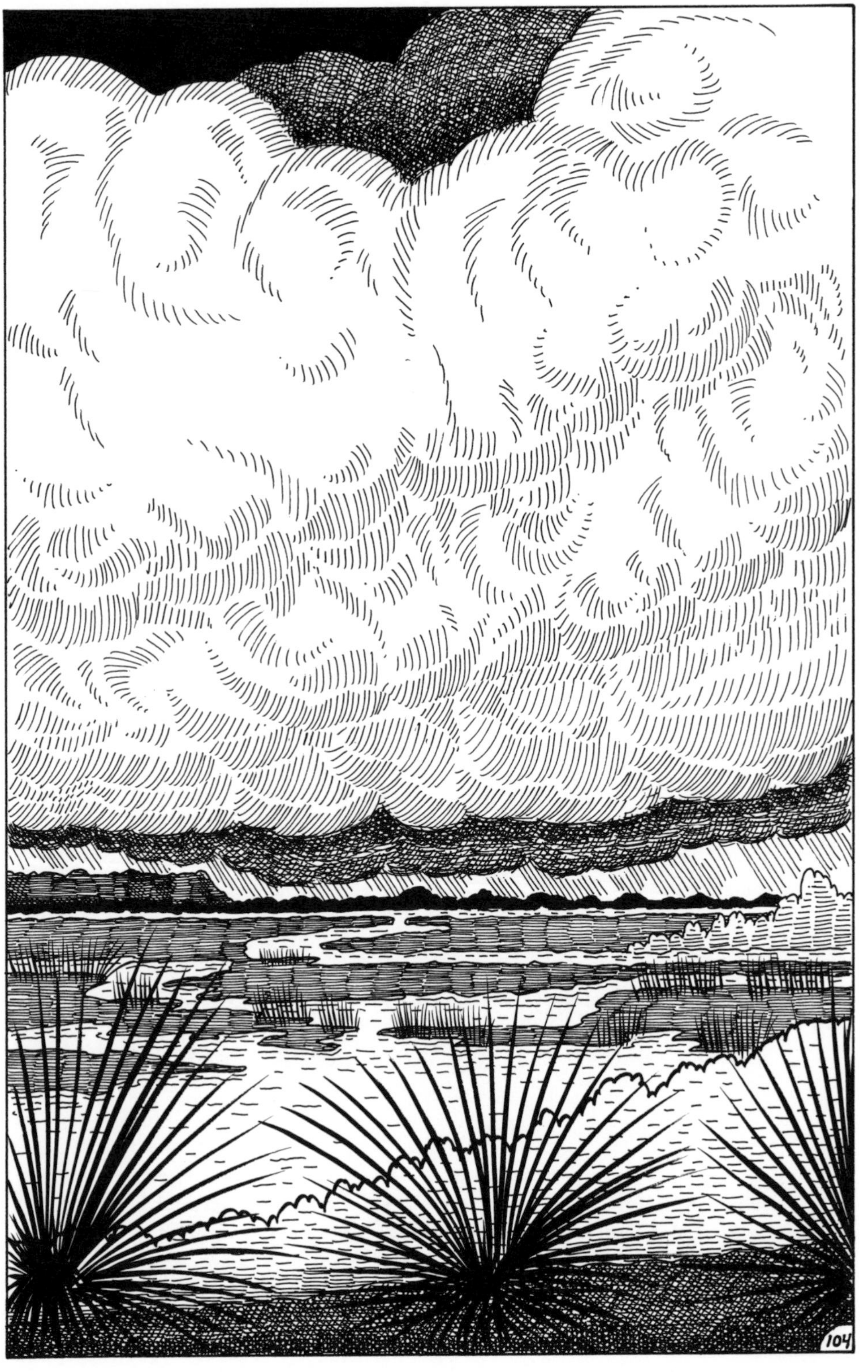
104

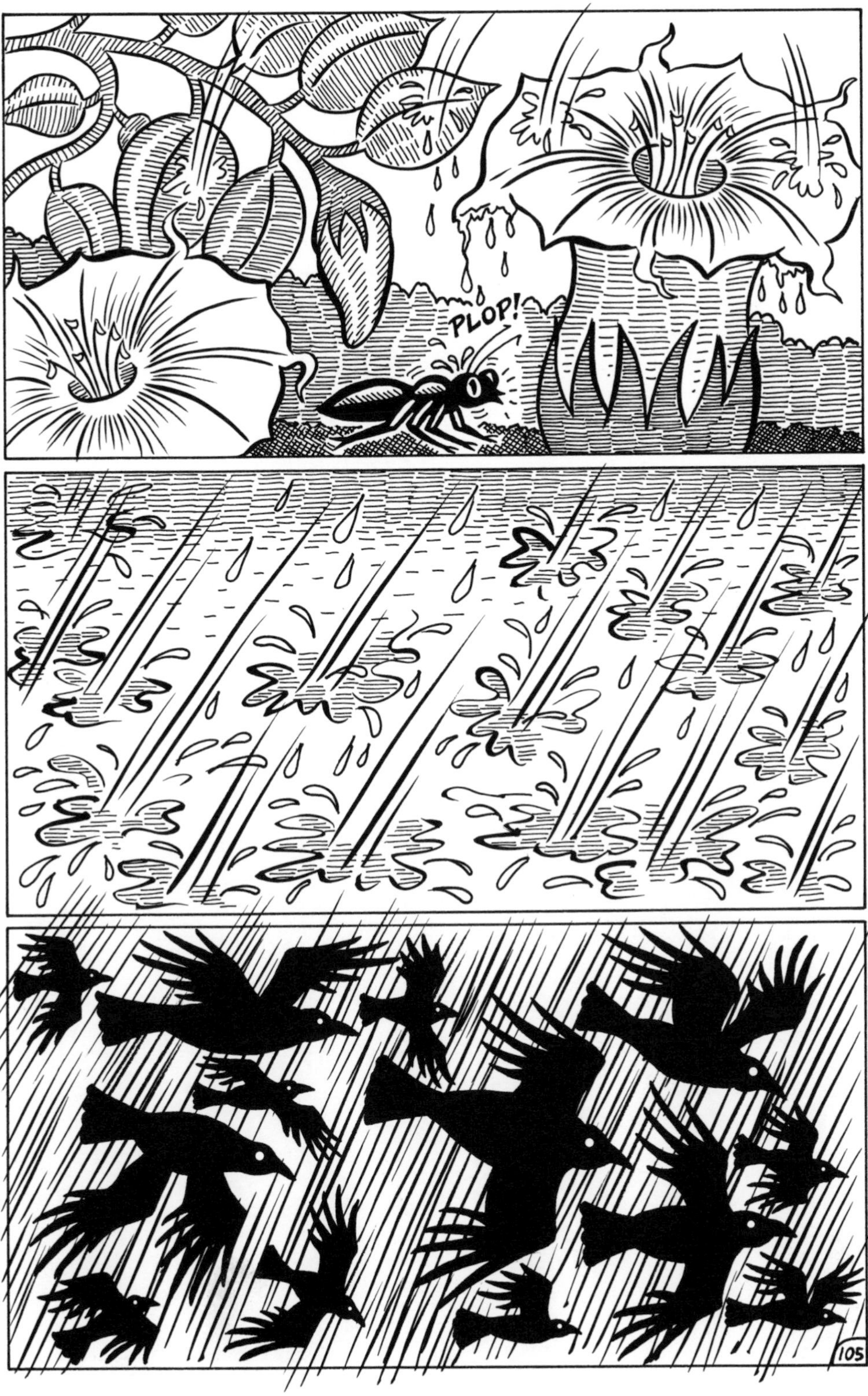
PLOP!

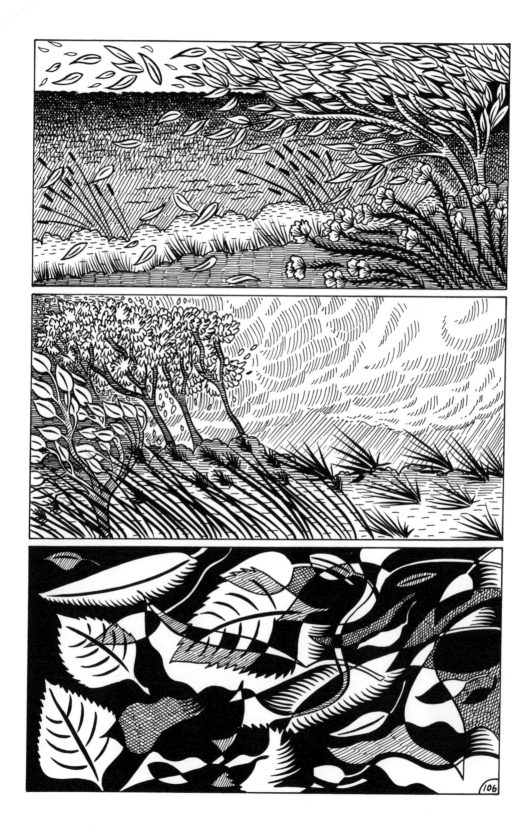

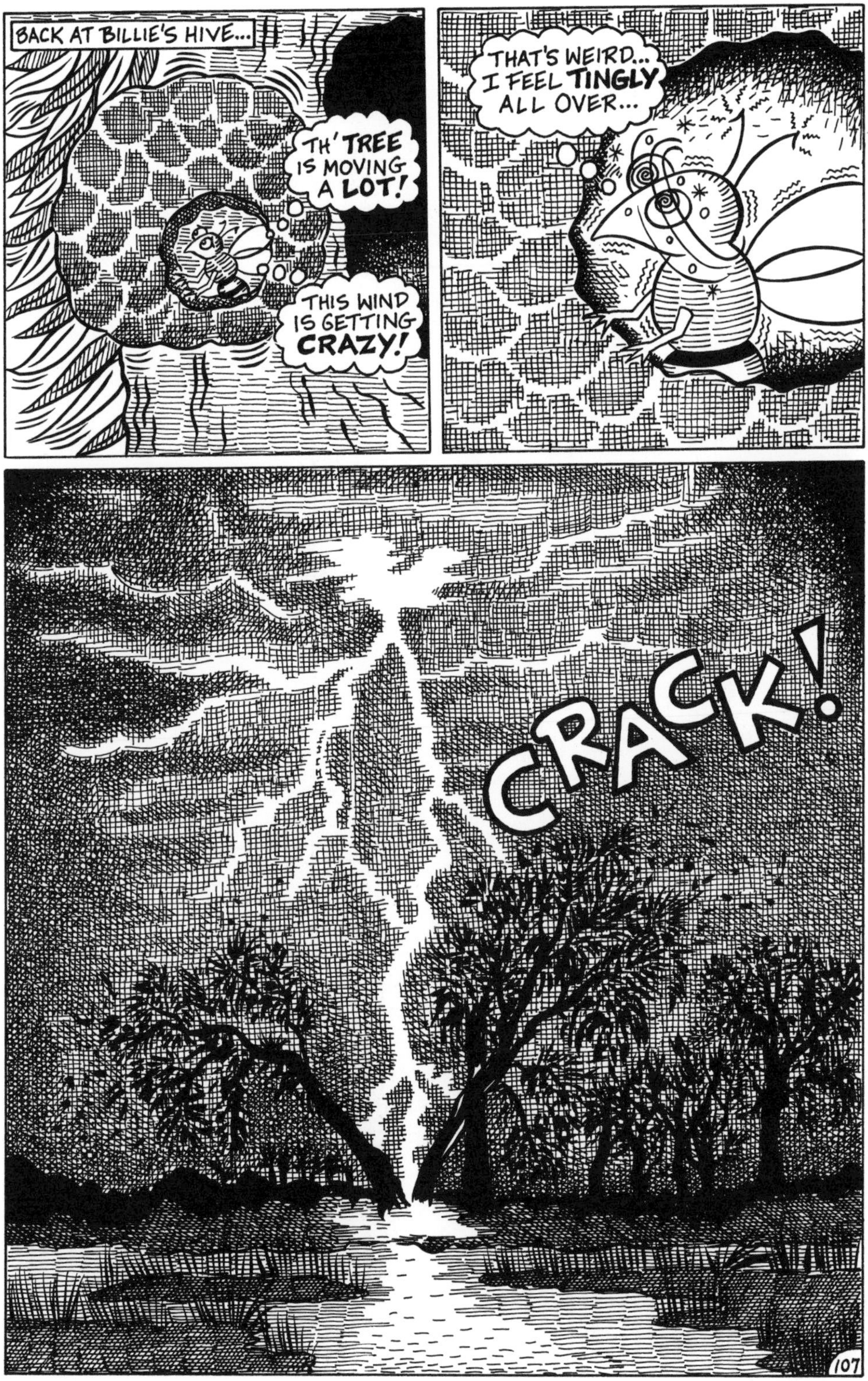
BACK AT BILLIE'S HIVE...
TH' TREE IS MOVING A LOT!
THIS WIND IS GETTING CRAZY!
THAT'S WEIRD... I FEEL TINGLY ALL OVER...
CRACK!
107

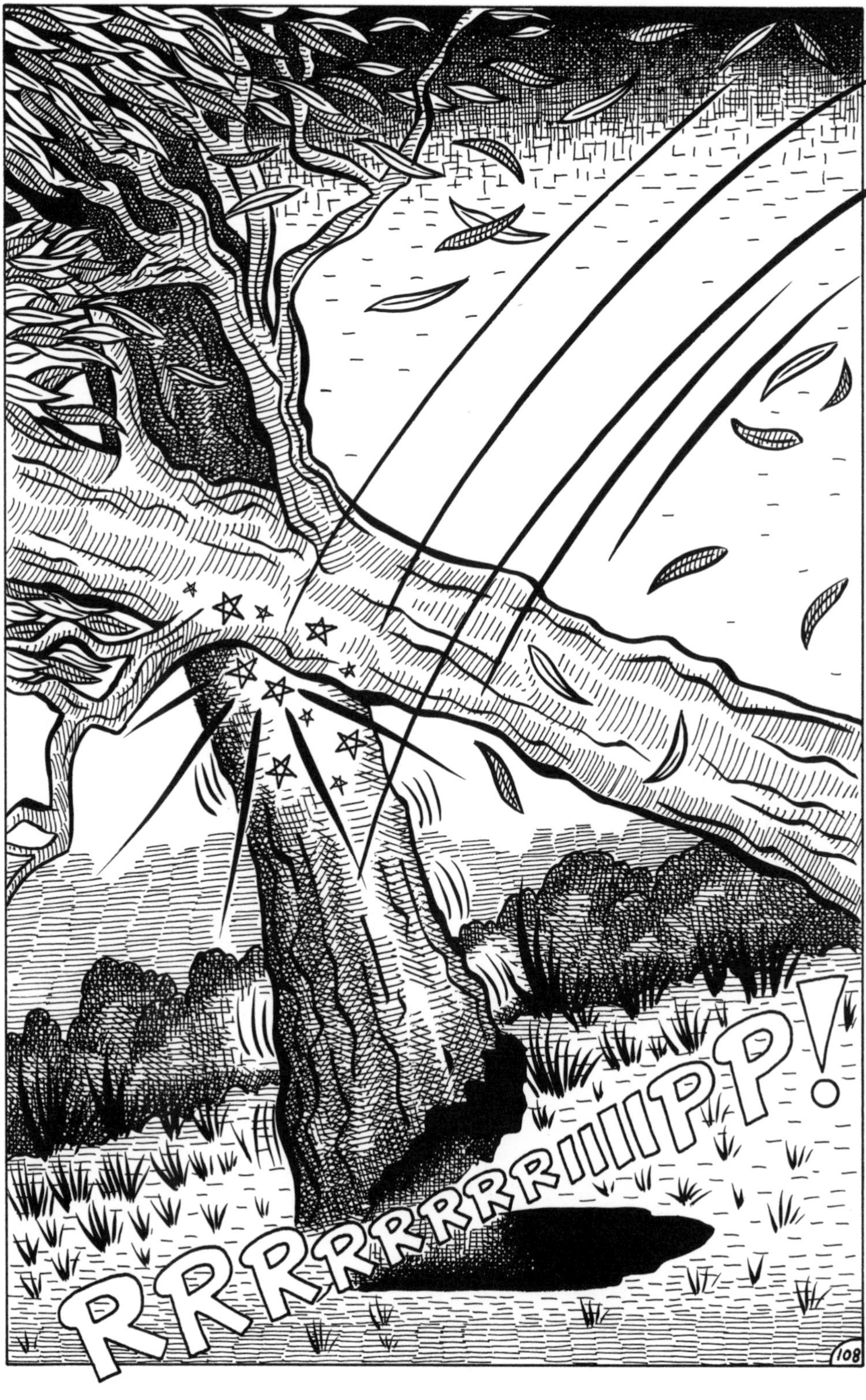
RRRRRRRRIIIIPP!

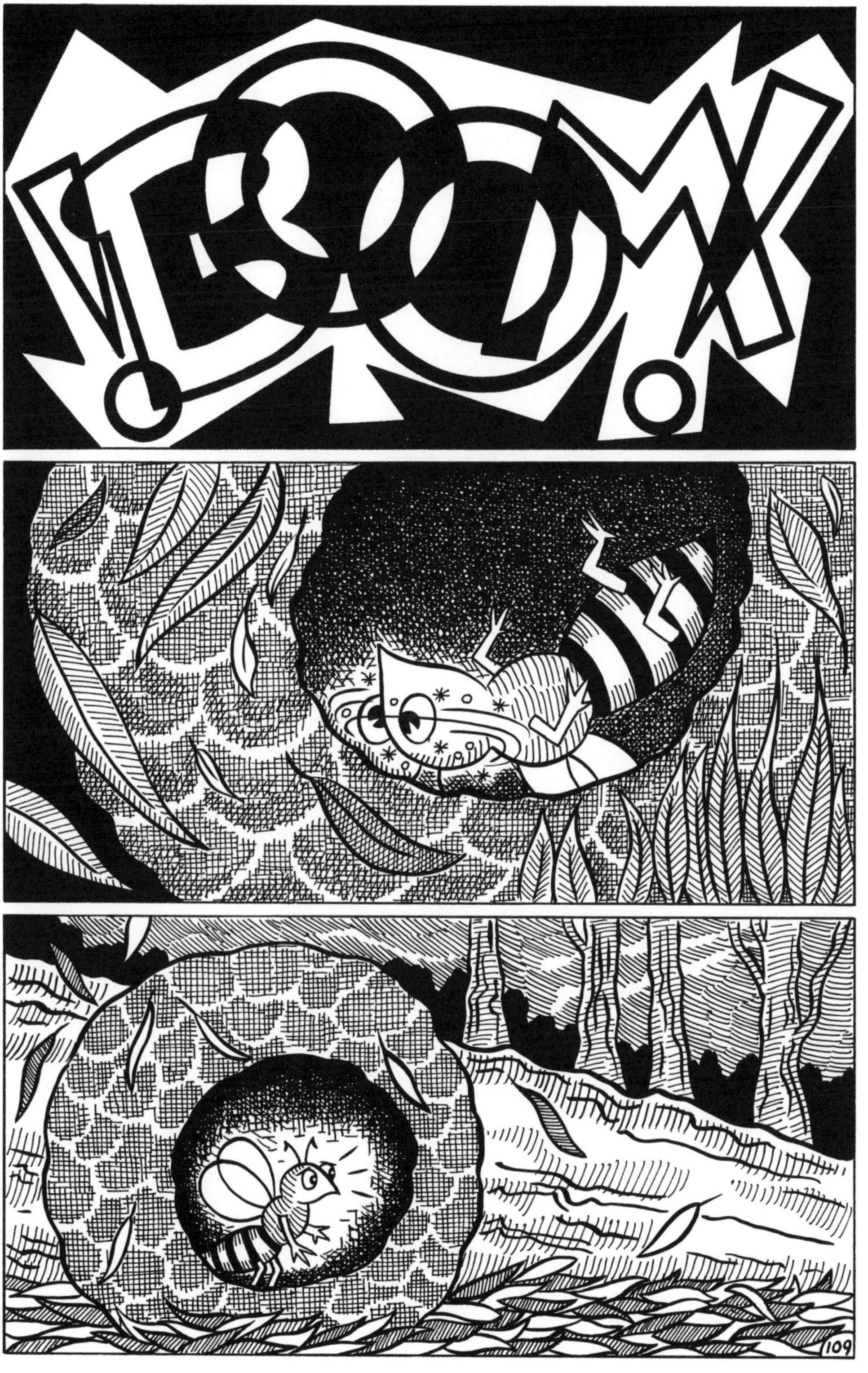
!BOOM!

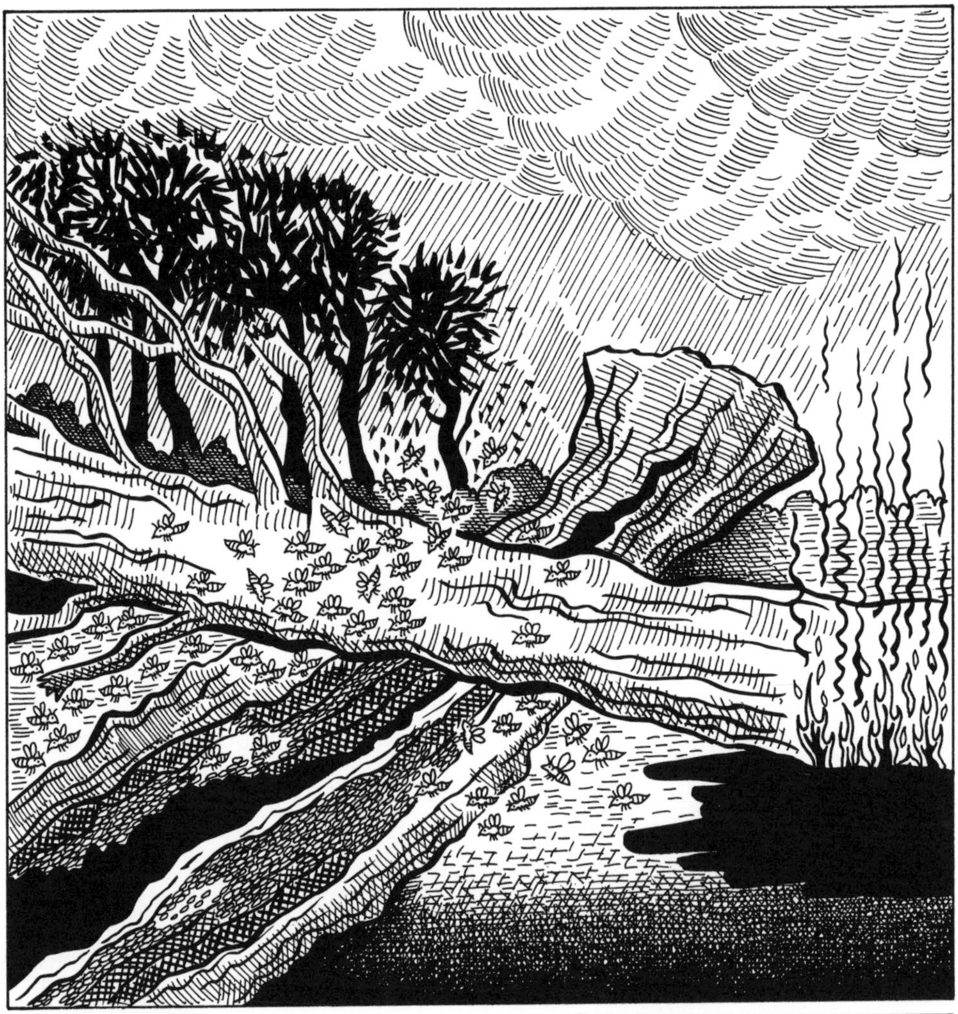

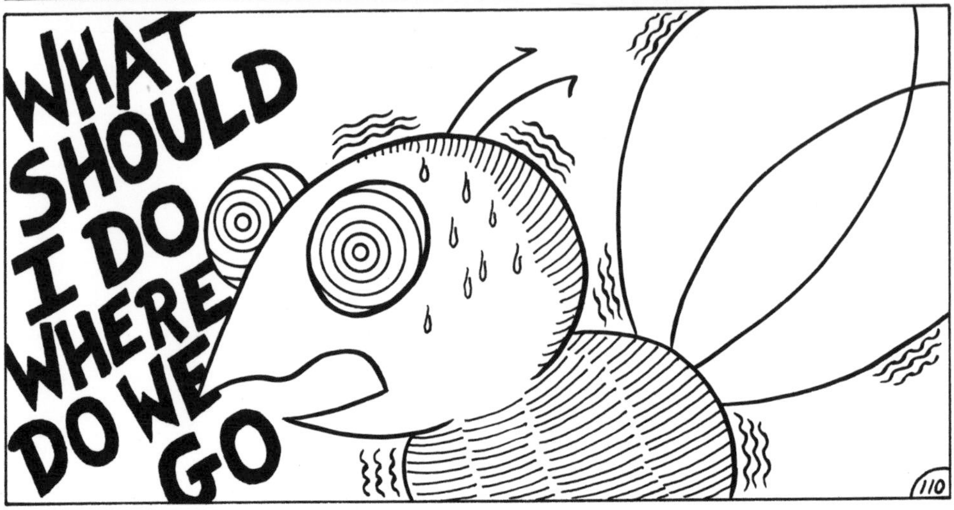
WHAT SHOULD I DO WHERE DO WE GO

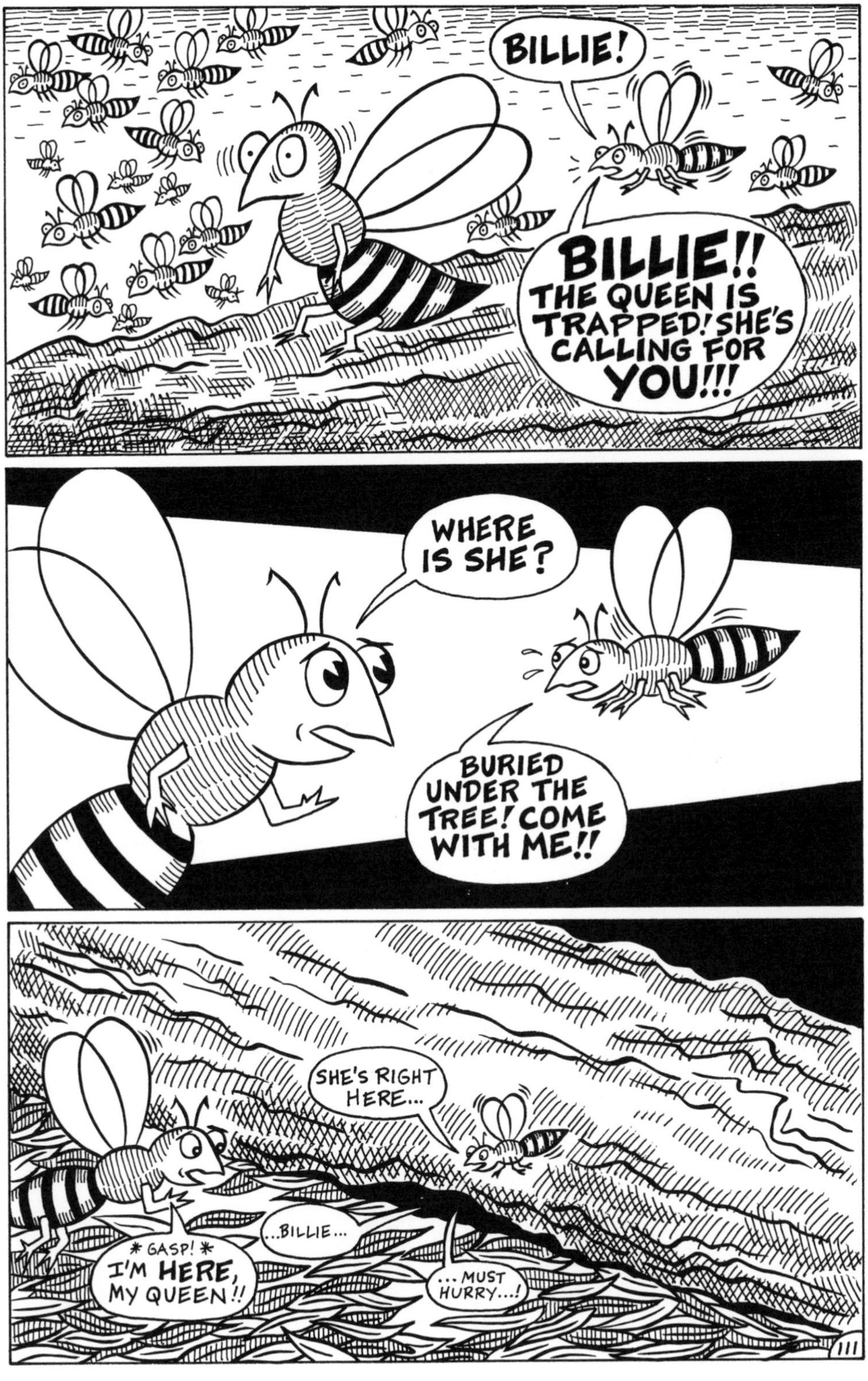
BILLIE!
BILLIE!! THE QUEEN IS TRAPPED! SHE'S CALLING FOR YOU!!!
WHERE IS SHE?
BURIED UNDER THE TREE! COME WITH ME!!
SHE'S RIGHT HERE...
GASP! I'M HERE, MY QUEEN!!
...BILLIE...
...MUST HURRY...!

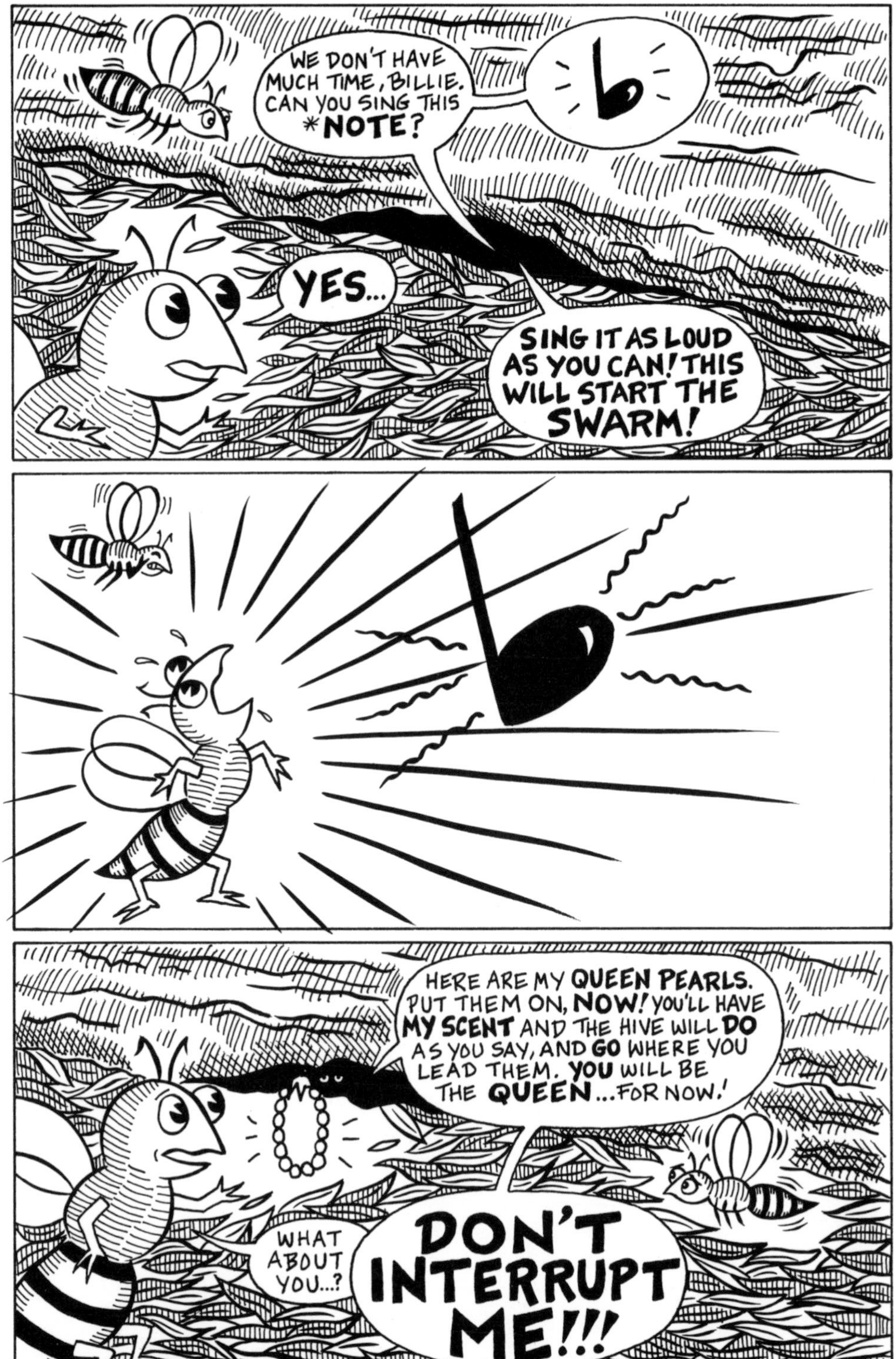
WE DON'T HAVE MUCH TIME, BILLIE. CAN YOU SING THIS *NOTE?
YES...
SING IT AS LOUD AS YOU CAN! THIS WILL START THE SWARM!
HERE ARE MY QUEEN PEARLS. PUT THEM ON, NOW! YOU'LL HAVE MY SCENT AND THE HIVE WILL DO AS YOU SAY, AND GO WHERE YOU LEAD THEM. YOU WILL BE THE QUEEN...FOR NOW.'
WHAT ABOUT YOU...?
DON'T INTERRUPT ME!!!
112

*QUEEN BEES MAKE A SOUND, CALLED "**PIPING**," TO COMMUNICATE WITH THE HIVE. THE **NOTE** IS A **G#** (AKA **A**♭).

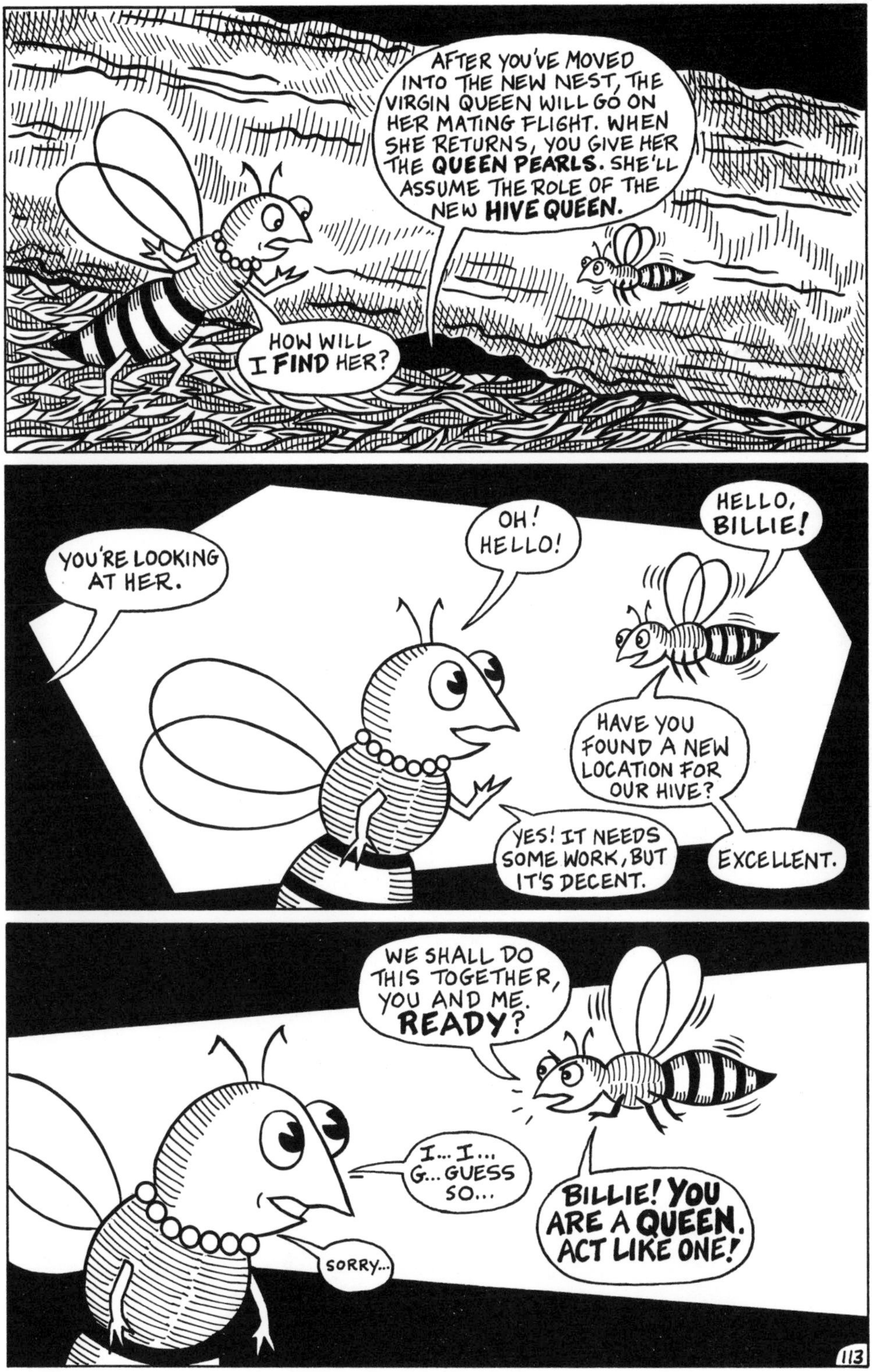
AFTER YOU'VE MOVED INTO THE NEW NEST, THE VIRGIN QUEEN WILL GO ON HER MATING FLIGHT. WHEN SHE RETURNS, YOU GIVE HER THE QUEEN PEARLS. SHE'LL ASSUME THE ROLE OF THE NEW HIVE QUEEN.
HOW WILL I FIND HER?
YOU'RE LOOKING AT HER.
OH! HELLO!
HELLO, BILLIE!
HAVE YOU FOUND A NEW LOCATION FOR OUR HIVE?
YES! IT NEEDS SOME WORK, BUT IT'S DECENT.
EXCELLENT.
WE SHALL DO THIS TOGETHER, YOU AND ME. READY?
I... I... G... GUESS SO...
SORRY...
BILLIE! YOU ARE A QUEEN. ACT LIKE ONE!

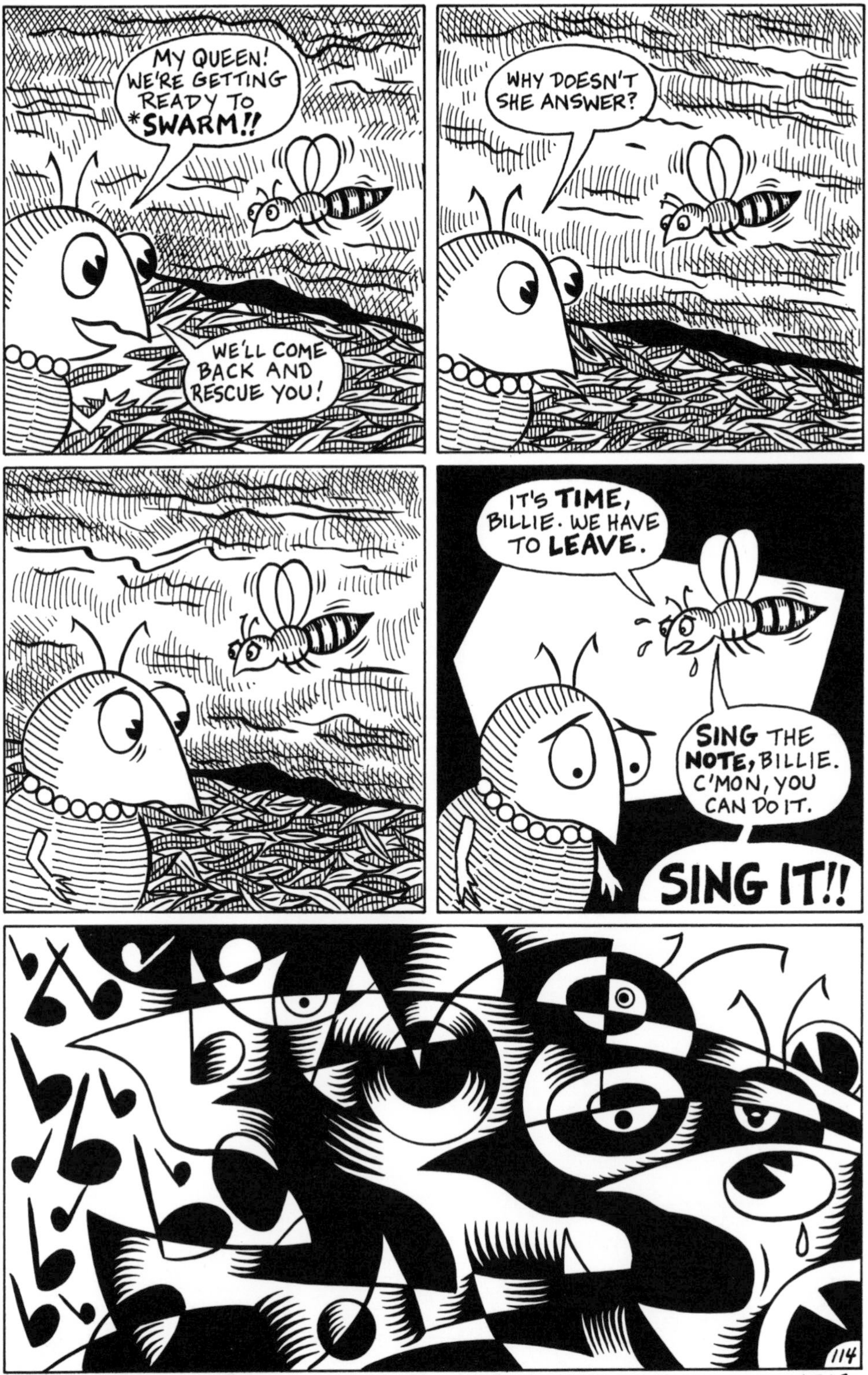
MY QUEEN! WE'RE GETTING READY TO *SWARM!!
WE'LL COME BACK AND RESCUE YOU!
WHY DOESN'T SHE ANSWER?
IT'S TIME, BILLIE. WE HAVE TO LEAVE.
SING THE NOTE, BILLIE. C'MON, YOU CAN DO IT.
SING IT!!

* WHEN A COLONY OF BEES LEAVES ITS HOME IN SEARCH OF ANOTHER, IT IS CALLED **ABSCONDING**. EITHER **TERM** IS OK, IN THIS CASE OF EMERGENCY!

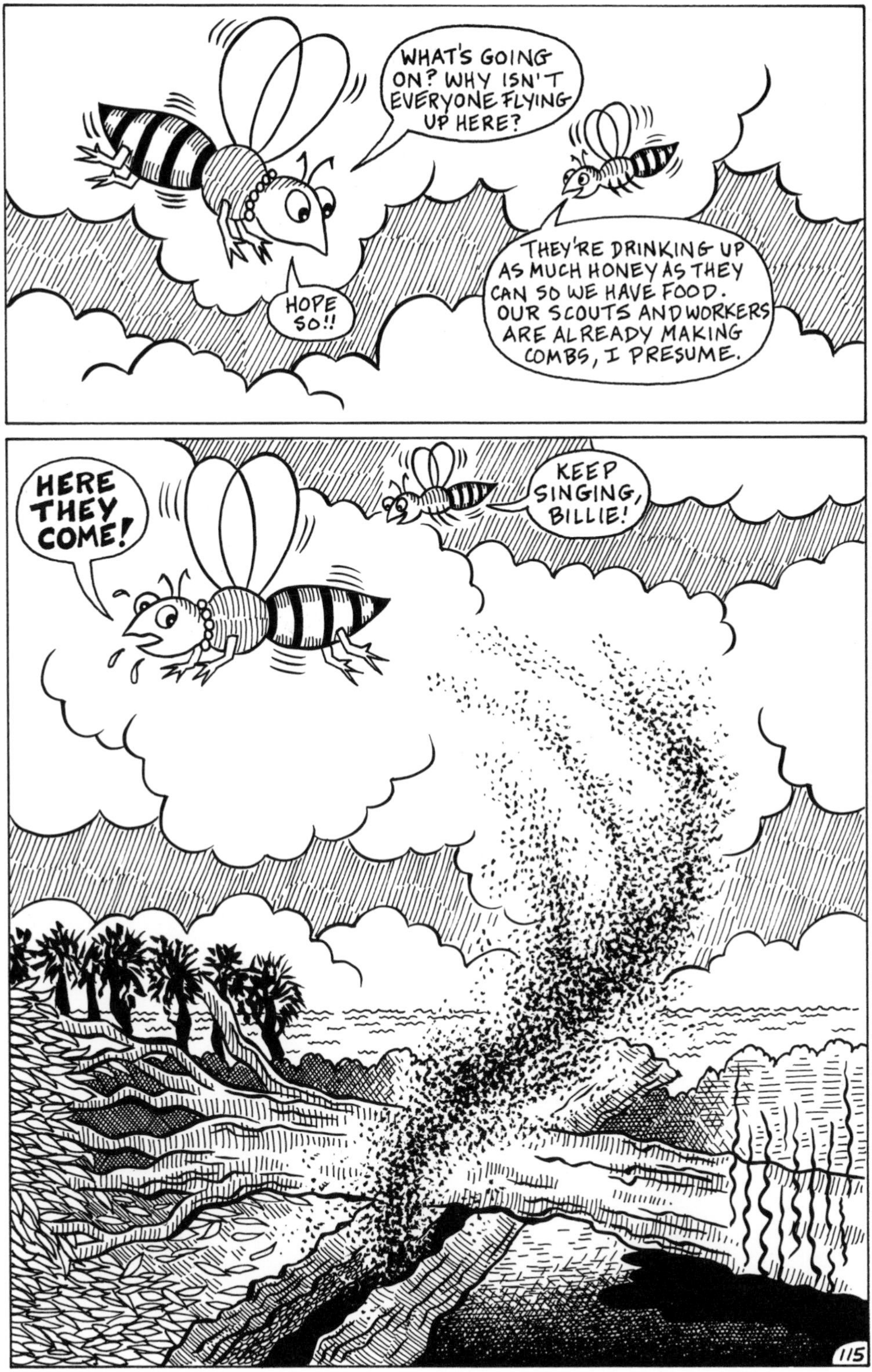
WHAT'S GOING ON? WHY ISN'T EVERYONE FLYING UP HERE?
THEY'RE DRINKING UP AS MUCH HONEY AS THEY CAN SO WE HAVE FOOD. OUR SCOUTS AND WORKERS ARE ALREADY MAKING COMBS, I PRESUME.
HOPE SO!!
HERE THEY COME!
KEEP SINGING, BILLIE!

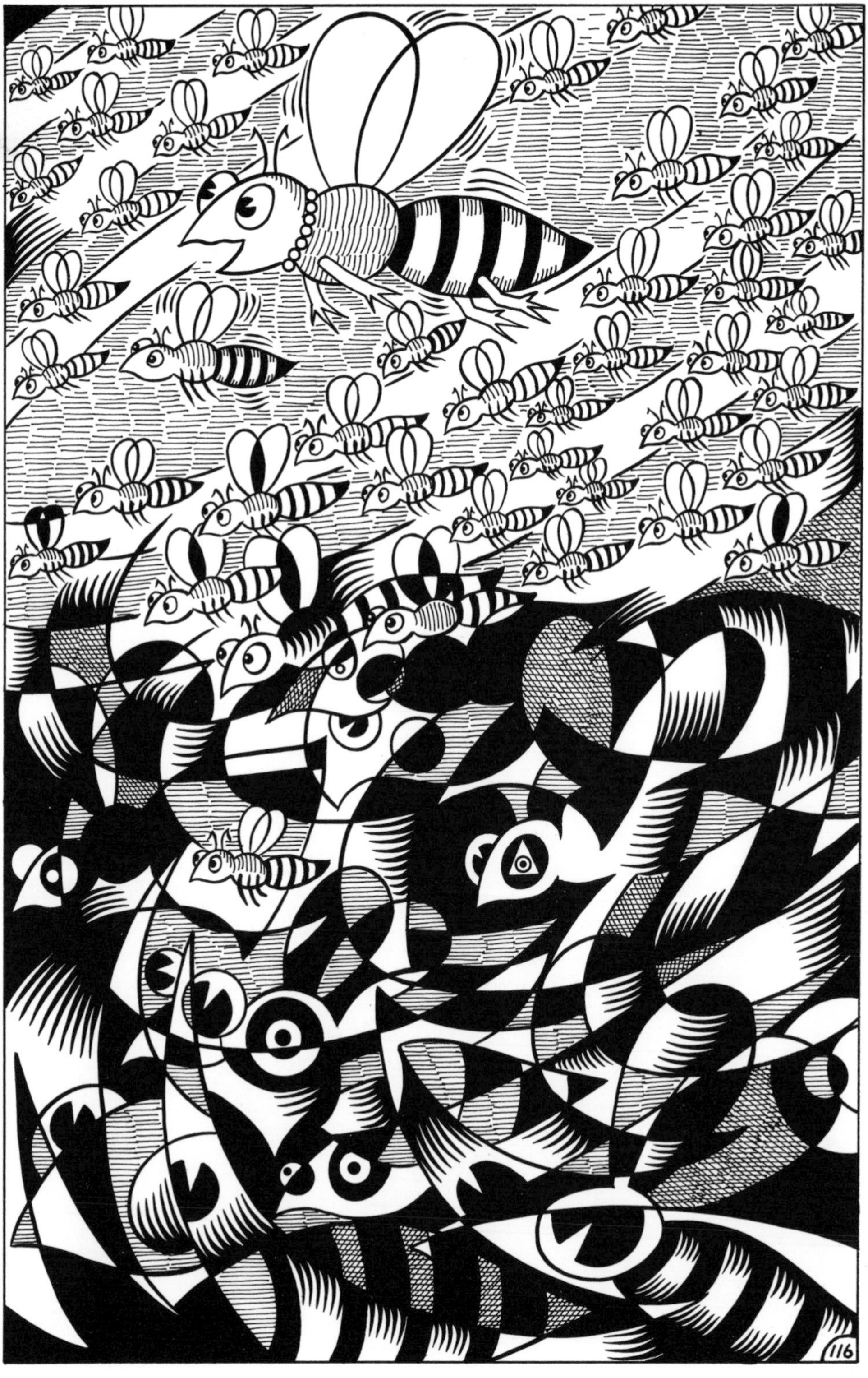

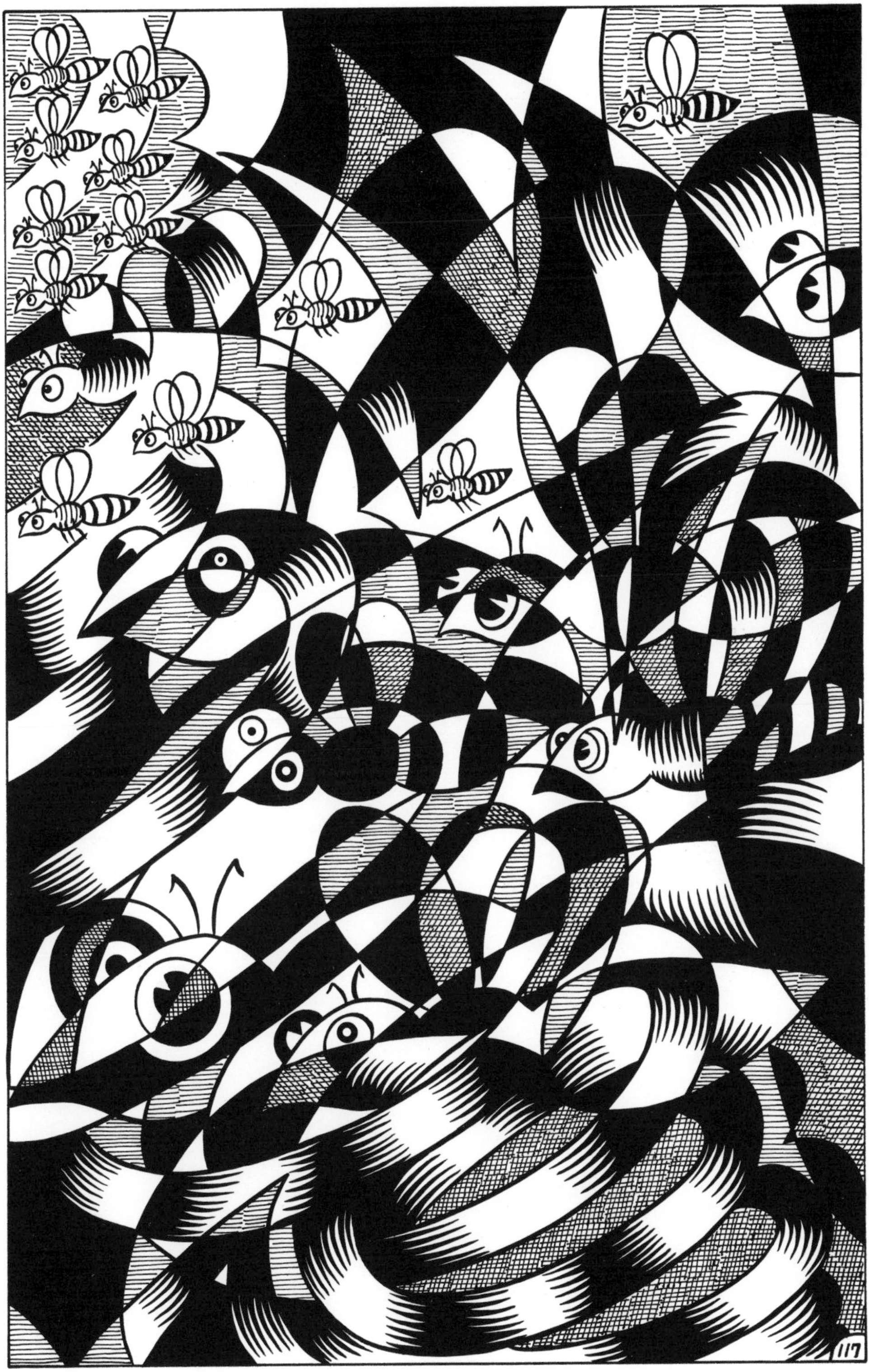

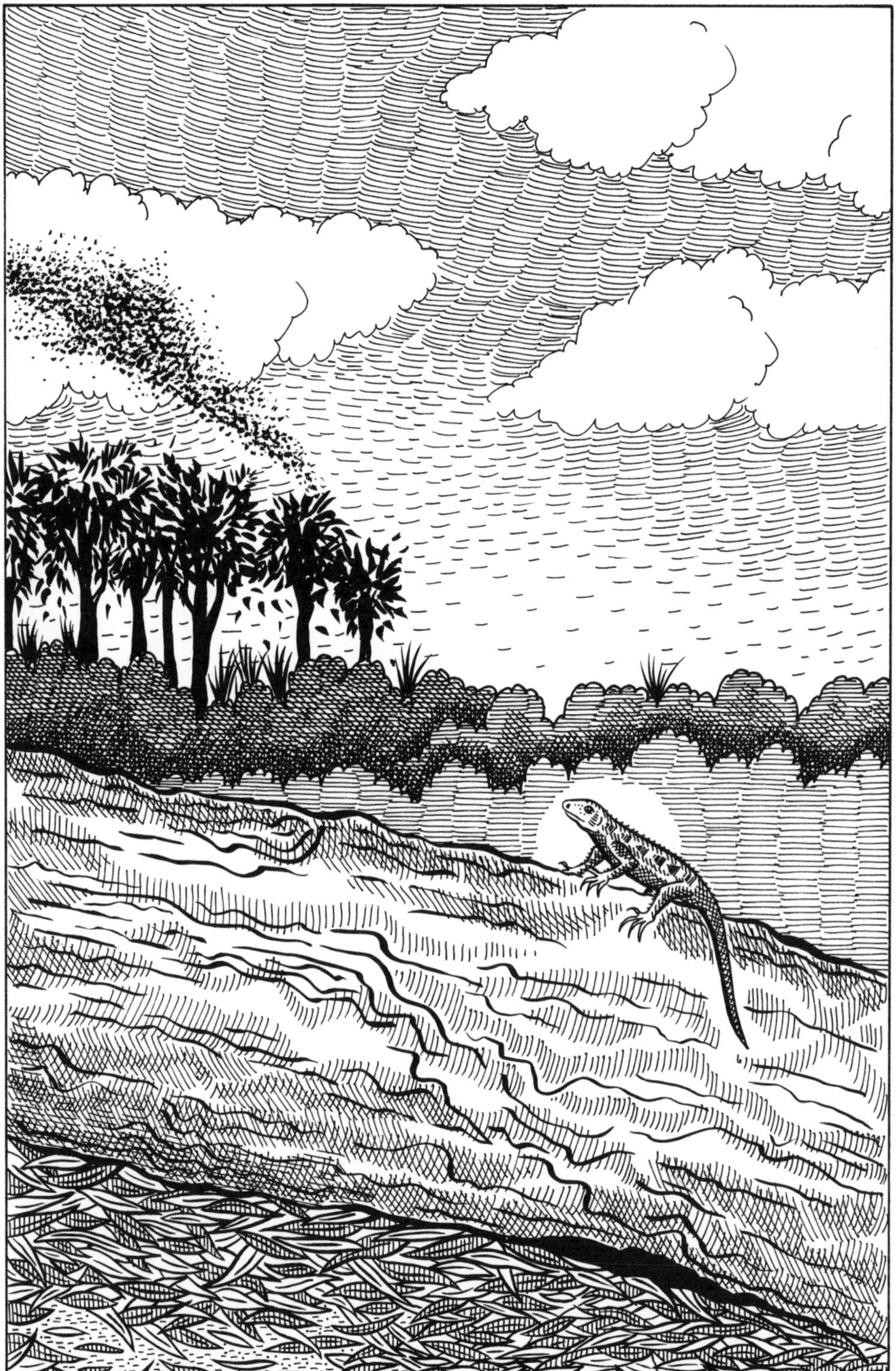

CODA

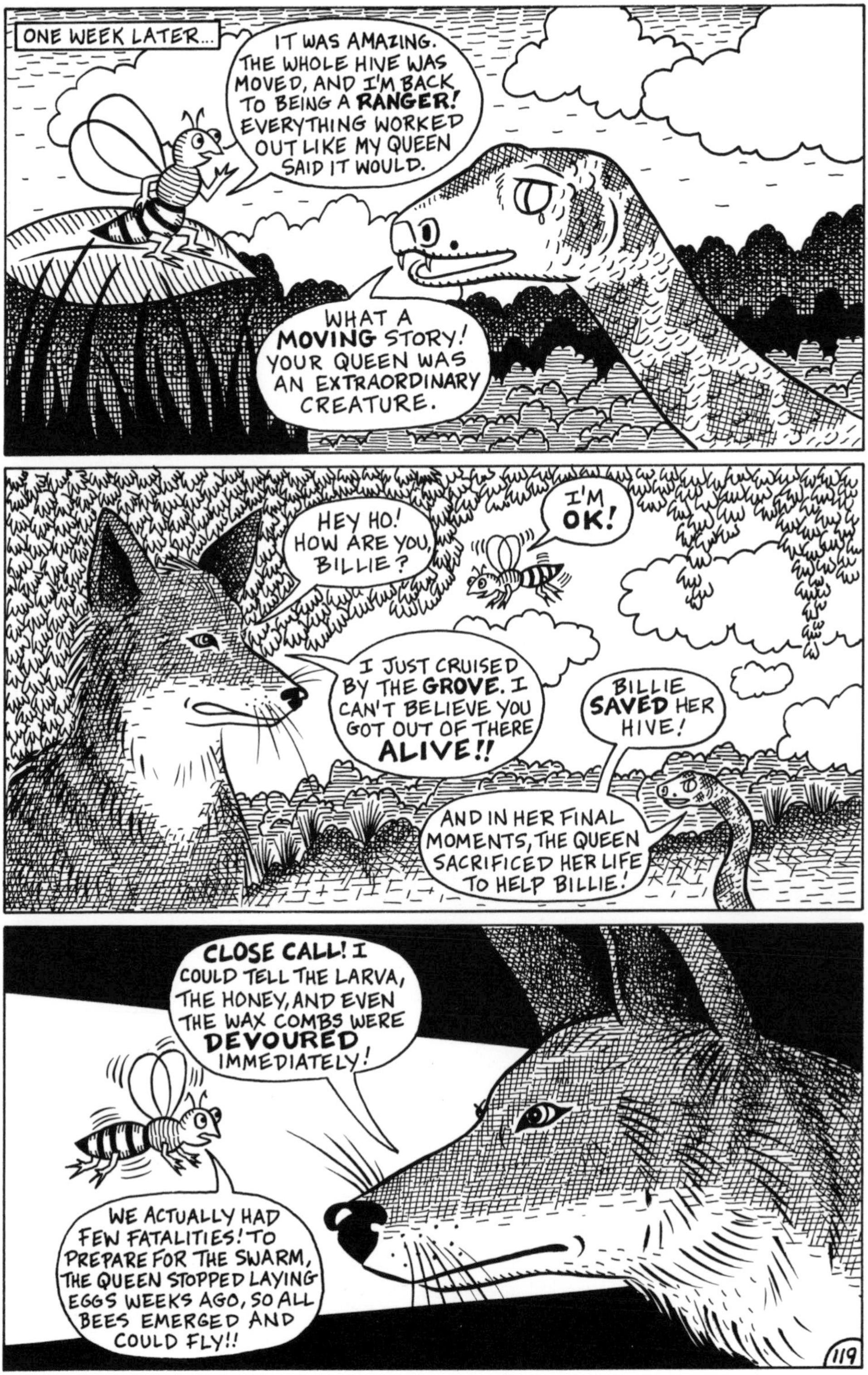
ONE WEEK LATER...
IT WAS AMAZING. THE WHOLE HIVE WAS MOVED, AND I'M BACK TO BEING A **RANGER!** EVERYTHING WORKED OUT LIKE MY QUEEN SAID IT WOULD.
WHAT A **MOVING** STORY! YOUR QUEEN WAS AN EXTRAORDINARY CREATURE.
HEY HO! HOW ARE YOU, BILLIE?
I'M **OK!**
I JUST CRUISED BY THE **GROVE**. I CAN'T BELIEVE YOU GOT OUT OF THERE **ALIVE!!**
BILLIE **SAVED** HER HIVE!
AND IN HER FINAL MOMENTS, THE QUEEN SACRIFICED HER LIFE TO HELP BILLIE!
CLOSE CALL! I COULD TELL THE LARVA, THE HONEY, AND EVEN THE WAX COMBS WERE **DEVOURED** IMMEDIATELY!
WE ACTUALLY HAD FEW FATALITIES! TO PREPARE FOR THE SWARM, THE QUEEN STOPPED LAYING EGGS WEEKS AGO, SO ALL BEES EMERGED AND COULD FLY!!
119

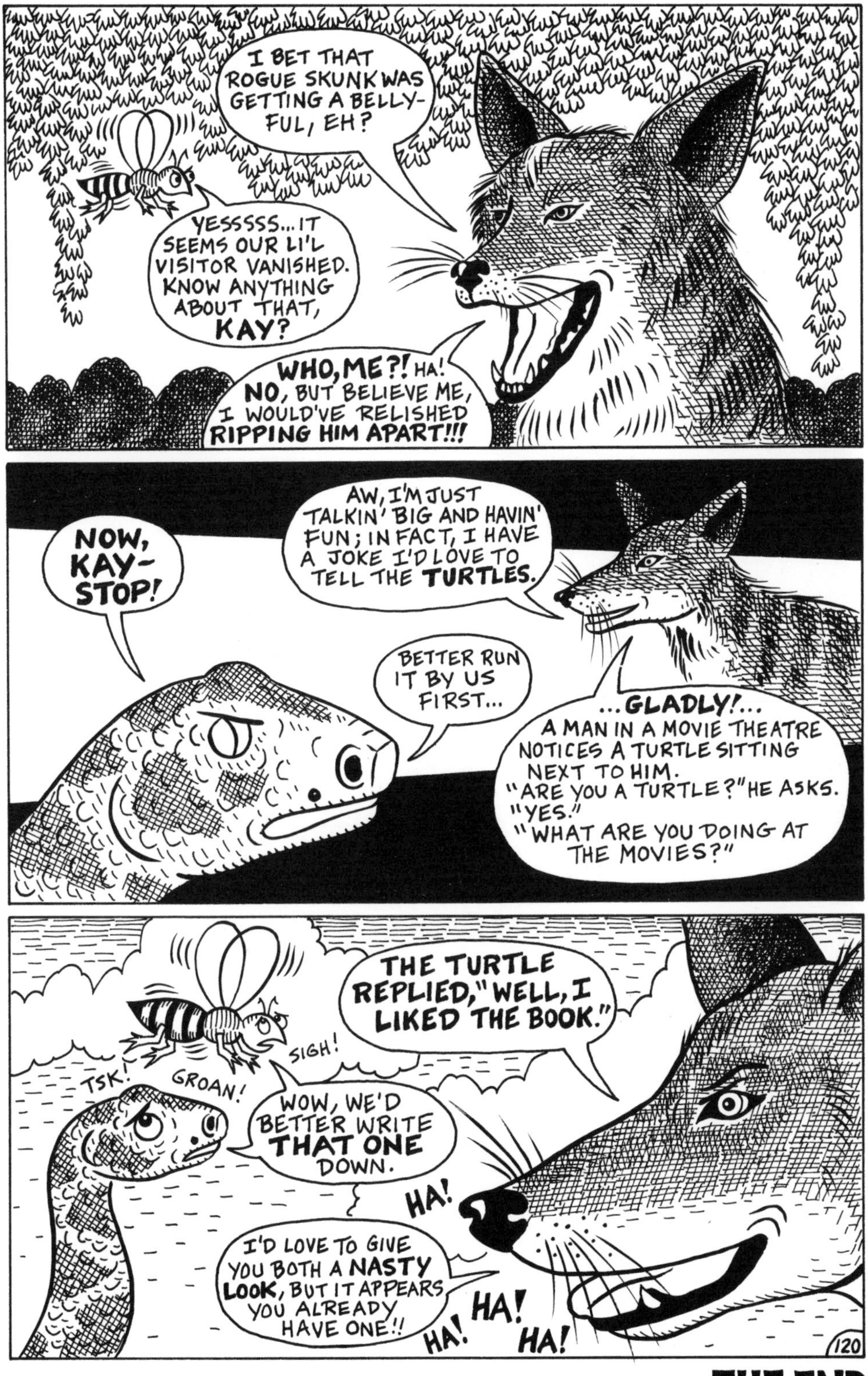
I BET THAT ROGUE SKUNK WAS GETTING A BELLY-FUL, EH?
YESSSSS...IT SEEMS OUR LI'L VISITOR VANISHED. KNOW ANYTHING ABOUT THAT, KAY?
WHO, ME?! HA! NO, BUT BELIEVE ME, I WOULD'VE RELISHED RIPPING HIM APART!!!
NOW, KAY-STOP!
AW, I'M JUST TALKIN' BIG AND HAVIN' FUN; IN FACT, I HAVE A JOKE I'D LOVE TO TELL THE TURTLES.
BETTER RUN IT BY US FIRST...
...GLADLY!... A MAN IN A MOVIE THEATRE NOTICES A TURTLE SITTING NEXT TO HIM. "ARE YOU A TURTLE?" HE ASKS. "YES." "WHAT ARE YOU DOING AT THE MOVIES?"
THE TURTLE REPLIED, "WELL, I LIKED THE BOOK."
SIGH!
TSK!
GROAN!
WOW, WE'D BETTER WRITE THAT ONE DOWN.
HA!
I'D LOVE TO GIVE YOU BOTH A NASTY LOOK, BUT IT APPEARS YOU ALREADY HAVE ONE!!
HA! HA! HA! HA!

THE END

Editor: Gary Groth
Editorial Assistance: Conrad Groth
Designer: Keeli McCarthy
Production: Paul Baresh
Proofreader: Rocco Versaci
Associate Publisher: Eric Reynolds
Publisher: Gary Groth

Fantagraphics Books, Inc.
7563 Lake City Way NE
Seattle, WA 98115

www.fantagraphics.com
Facebook.com/Fantagraphics
@fantagraphics.com

ISBN: 978-1-68396-173-4
Library of Congress Control Number: 2018949685
First Fantagraphics Books edition: February 2019
Printed in China

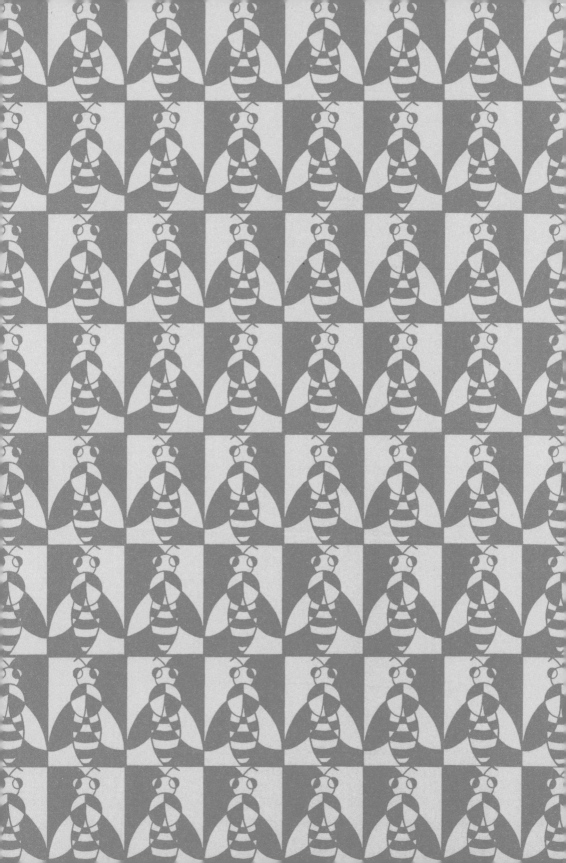